LUNCHING THE GIRLS

LUNCHING
THE GIRLS

Martin O'Brien

Just how well do you know your friends...?

MOBUK
PRESS

The Daniel Jacquot Series

The Waterman
"Well-drawn, and strongly flavoured. Rich, spicy, and served up with unmistakeable relish."
The Literary Review

The Master
"Martin O'Brien creates a sexually charged atmosphere that is as chilling as it is engaging."
The Sydney Morning Herald

The Fifteen
"Well written and compelling. Tight plotting, lyrical descriptions and excellent characterisation mean Jacquot is here to stay."
The Daily Mail

The Angel
"French country life has never been so fraught with sinister atmosphere."
The Rough Guide to Crime Fiction

Confession
"O'Brien's evocation of the hot, vibrant and seedy port in which everyone seems to be either a cop or a criminal, and sometimes both, is as masterly as Ian Rankin's depiction of Edinburgh."
The Daily Mail

Blood Counts
"Daniel Jacquot of the Marseilles Police is fast becoming one of my favourite fictional cops."
The Daily Mirror

The Dying Minutes
"A wonderfully inventive and involving detective series with vivid French locales creating the perfect backdrop. Jacquot is top of le cops."
The Daily Express

Knife Gun Poison Bomb
"An absolutely brilliant novel which had me hooked from the first page in."
Eurocrime

Also by Martin O'Brien

All The Girls
(Non-Fiction)
"A classic among travel books."
Auberon Waugh, Books & Bookmen

Lunching The Girls

Writing as Jack Drummond

Avalanche
"Big, high-pitched disaster novels don't come much more thrilling than this."
The Daily Mirror

Storm
"A classy old-school thriller."
The Daily Sport

For the three girls in my life,
Fiona, Katie, and Polly

*"Let us have wine and women, mirth and laughter,
Sermons and soda water the day after."*

English Bards and Scotch Reviewers
Lord Byron

Contents

Murphy's Landing

Murphy's Landing

Murphy's Landing

The storm passed us in the night. It's the first one to come our way since I moved down here, and we'd been waiting for it, preparing. It came from behind us, from the land side out back, like we'd been told it would, like the first storm of the season always does, so we didn't have any high seas racing up the beach which was maybe a good thing.

But that doesn't mean it wasn't a powerful blow.

We knew for sure it was headed our way round lunchtime yesterday when the local radio station hereabouts started putting out bulletins tracking its course. It got to be the main story as the afternoon passed. Some huge depression rolling down the Allegheny slopes bound for Richmond and the Chesapeake.

And us.

By tea-time the sky was a low, mean scud of racing grey, screwed down tight as a lid, great smacks of rain slapping against the windows and squally gusts chasing through the tall grass out on the flats.

Which was how it stayed the next few hours, supper through bedtime.

Which was when it hit for real, round midnight, rattling all the loose window panes, playing the roof shingles like warped piano keys, and shouldering hard and determined up against the clinker boards of the house. I listened from my bed as it raged around outside, cussing, moaning, pushing here and there, searching for a way in.

But the old place stood firm.

I never heard it move on, but by first light the waders were back. Out front the tide was low, the sea a steely grey, and the sky far out a shade darker where the storm still lurched about, a drunken brawler casting about for something to punch. Maybe by lunch it'll think to swing round, come back for another try. Maybe not. It doesn't matter now. It's done what I didn't expect it to do.

Watching its sullen seaward progress from my sail-loft study, I feel kind of recharged, revived, somehow lightened. Like the storm snatched something away and left me the better for it, that dead weight of loss I've hauled around all this time just scraps of paper in the wind.

I hadn't expected it to do that, hadn't been prepared to feel the way

I do.

It's a Thursday, of all days, just past nine-thirty in the morning, and for the first time in months I'm sitting at my desk again, like I used to, ready to begin. Only this time there's no deadline, which will make a change, just a sense that I need to get it all down, to start writing.

Which, I guess, is what I knew would happen.

Sooner or later.

The first storm's passed, and the old house still stands.

Pretty much as good a time to begin as any.

So start I will, as I mean to go on – honest, straight.

The way it was.

≈

The name, which many of you may recall, is Cully Mortimer. Late of New York City. Long-time resident of Manhattan. One-time lessee of a small but (so they always said) exquisite apartment on Central Park. On the Upper West Side. In an old-fashioned but still sought-after co-operative, mid-wall, that overlooked, so I liked to say, the biggest window box in the city. I wouldn't want to live there now, I can tell you, but that doesn't mean it wasn't a fine apartment. It was. Snug, compact. Home. And for a long while I loved it dearly.

There. Already a lie, and only a handful of sentences. Recently I've learned to spot them. I can almost taste them. Cold, hard, and heavy on the tongue.

Well, not so much lie as omission.

Cully Mortimer Sykes, to be honest.

Culver Mortimer Sykes, to be precise.

Like a great many things the 'Sykes' got left where it belonged, back in Wilmington, Delaware, more than thirty years ago now, not so far from here, where I first began my working life as a junior copy-sub on The Fort Christina Courier.

The 'Sykes' made my first by-line, but never saw another. It just didn't work. The typeface howled. 'By Culver Sykes'. No, no, no, that would never do. Even I could see that. All that time I'd wanted my name in print, and when it finally got there it screamed. Sounded like some hick country boy down from the farm, and taking in the big city. If you could call Wilmington a big city back then.

So I made a few adjustments and came up with Cully Mortimer which, the next time the editor had me write something for the

Butterball column, looked and sounded a whole lot better. Leaner, more authoritative, if you know what I mean. A 'been-around' sort of name. Even if I was just a scratch past twenty.

And that's how it was from then on: Cully Mortimer. Followed, down the years, by Cully's Cuisine, Cully On Food, Cully's Diner, The Cully Mortimer Column. Dozens more along those lines, syndicated near enough every place people eat and love food. And lately, for the Times, just Cully. That's all they needed to write. Section lead. Above the fold. Boxed, top of page, white letters on a black ground. Caps. CULLY. With a head and shoulder shot taking two square inches off the first two columns. Thinning auburn hair, lush black moustache (the injustice of it), and that rather pleased, self-satisfied look I had back then.

Not quite a year ago. Seems like a century.

Like I said, I live by the sea now.

A long way from the city. Any city.

Of course I've been back there, to New York, but already it's a different place; not somewhere I care to be any more. Nowadays it just plain discomforts me, which it never did before. Whatever it is I've got to do there, I can't wait to get out, to get back here where no one knows me.

Which I hope you'll come to understand when you hear my story.

The story of Cully Mortimer.

Or rather, the last part of it. The part where it gets messy, and the wheels really left the tracks.

≈

She fell. Forty-seven floors. Five hundred and sixty-eight feet.

At her weight it took just a little under eight seconds to cover the distance. Also, there was a breeze that morning, blustering down the street, snapping at flags and ruffling awnings, so she didn't fall true, hitting the sidewalk near thirty feet off the perpendicular.

Facts. Just that.

Plain and simple. The way it was.

Like the Medical Examiner at the County Coroner's hearing, I can say it all just pat, like I'm reeling off ingredients for some warming winter stew: broken legs and splintered pelvis, smashed wrists and arms, ruptured spleen and liver, snapped ribs and punctured lungs, shattered spine and massive cranial displacement – his kindly euphemism for brains spilled on the sidewalk.

I remember him in the witness box. Check sports coat and suede elbow patches, thin blond hair combed across a shiny pate, pale blue eyes magnified by the lenses of his tortoiseshell spectacles. An earnest young man who looked like he sold insurance, who might ring at your door and ask if you loved Jesus. There he sat, smug and sure, leaning forward to the microphone to answer every question, so no one would miss what it was he was saying, his hollow, amplified words rolling around in the dead space above the courtroom.

What he found when he examined her body.

The injuries sustained.

So that no one could be mistaken.

There was never any chance of that.

You could hear the silence swell, and then a sigh slide through the panelled stalls as, slowly, methodically, he itemised the injuries that ended her life and changed mine forever. I could actually feel a stirring in the rows around me.

They heard alright.

They heard.

Apparently, too, she screamed on the way down. A tenant, eight floors below, another real estate broker it turned out, testified to that – said it scared hell out of him.

Scared him enough to call the cops.

It wouldn't have taken them long to figure it out.

Another death on 56th and Third.

≈

Afterwards, when I first got here, I didn't do much of anything. Mooched along the shoreline, collected driftwood, learned to lay a fire in the old McKinley wood burner, unpacked my things and set them out: books on shelves, pictures hung, hi-fi wired up, CDs stacked, clothes put away, rugs laid out on sandy, warped floorboards. Everything ordered, like I like it.

The only difference you'd notice is my refrigerator, and the sea-green plywood cupboards set around it. I filled them with supplies. Enough to last weeks, not just a night or two. So there'd be no call to go anywhere, see anyone. It was the first time for as long as I could remember that I had any real food in my home.

Back then, being out here, alone, by the sea, was all about time and space, I guess. Having room to breathe. No longer the center of attention, stared at, whispered over, a suitable subject for table-side speculations. No longer betrayed, set adrift.

An anonymous life. That's what I wanted, and that's what I got. Which helps provide a certain perspective when I think about what happened to me. And when I think about her. What might have been...

At first she was everywhere – curling up beside me on the sofa, looking over my shoulder as I tried my hand at the stove, taking walks with me along the beach like we'd done out on the island. The sweet scent of her, the sound of her voice, her chuckling laughter, the soft, gentle touch of her, her warm breath on my skin, her closeness.

Which was a new experience for me. The weeks and months after her death there'd been no real time to grieve, no real place for her in my heart. The survival instinct just kicked in, and I sort of skimmed over the surface of any sorrow.

Me against the world, that's how it was. And though she was a part of that world, indeed the very focus of it, there was always a sense of distance between us. Which was good, of course. Back then I couldn't afford to have her get too close.

But when it was all over, out here on the shore, I suddenly had the chance to wallow in it. And I did. I grieved. I missed her so bad. Some days worse than others – the way it is.

But after a time the pain starts to fade, all that sorrow softens and our hearts mend.

Mine has, I guess.

≈

So then, here it is. Here's my story, the story of Cully Mortimer, starting a few months before that terrible, liberating fall.

Here's the pitch. Here's the puzzle. Let me share it with you.

Someone I know killed someone I know.

And put me in the frame.

Cully Mortimer
Murphy's Landing
Assateague Shoreline
Maryland
October 1999

Part One
Tables for Two

Toucan

"Tell me again. I've forgotten. Tell me, Cully. Tell me."

"*Les joyaux*. The jewels."

"That's it! That's it!" And she pealed with laughter, covering her mouth with her hands, smothering the sound, the way she did the first time I told her what a Frenchman calls the testicles of a ram when they're gently poached and served in a white wine *jus*.

We were sitting at our favorite table in Toucan, lunch long over, waiting for more coffee – decaf for her, espresso with a twist for me. It was snowing hard, getting dark. It was a Tuesday. Christmas was still a few days away, but we'd already exchanged gifts. We'd talked about it on the phone. Brought them with us. We wouldn't be seeing each other through the holiday, so this was the next best thing.

After a brief discussion, we'd decided to open them before the meal. And like naughty children we did just that, me first, then her. Paper rustled and tore, ribbon spooled onto the table. Somewhere, for me, she'd found a near perfect first edition of Cristoforo da Messisbugo's *Banchetti Composizioni di Vivande* which, when I slipped it from its wrapping, turned it, spied the faded gold lettering on its ribbed, rubbed spine, saw what it was, left me breathless.

For her I'd bought a pair of antique knotted white gold studs with a cluster of tiny emeralds nesting in the center of each which she immediately put on, elbows on the table, tilting her head, first one side then the other, finding the tiny openings with long, practiced fingers, tucking the hair behind her ears so the gold and the stones would show.

We'd had a great time. We were in no hurry to leave. We were telling stories, like we always did.

"*J-er-oh… J-wer-oh…*" she began, trying the word out for size, experimenting with it, swilling the unfamiliar syllables across her tongue. But the more she tried, the further away that strange conjunction of sounds took her. Her lips, livid red, glistened and creased and bunched as she tried to find the right shape for her mouth. She was a picture, I can tell you.

"Nearly, nearly," I told her. "But make the 'j' softer. *Zj… zj…* Like the 'sh' in 'shirt', but with a 'j'. And then add that 'woy' sound: *Zjwoy… Zjwoy…yoh*. The jewels."

"*Zjwo-oh… Zjwo-yoh…*" And then, finally, "*Zjwoy-yoh.*"

"Bravo, bravo. That's it. Zjwoy-yoh. You got it."

"*Zjwoy-yoh*! *Lay Zjwoy-yoh*!" And she clapped her hands, green eyes and emerald studs sparkling. "And you've eaten them? You really have? You've actually put them in your mouth and eaten them?"

"Of course," I laughed. "How else would I have…?"

"Oh Jesus… *Jee-zus*!" Hands covered mouth again, eyes widening in horror above fingertips. Then she leaned forward, hands held so, either side of her head, ready to clap them down on her ears if she didn't like what she was hearing. "And what do they taste like? Tell me! Tell me!"

So I teased her. "You want me to tell you what they taste like?"

"Cully!" She turned serious then, the smile wiped off her face, brows knitting, Christmas snow swirling silently behind her, the New Jersey turning deliciously ripe. "When I got balls in my mouth, I don't bite 'em, I don't chew 'em, and I don't swallow 'em. I just… push 'em around a tad with my tongue, suck 'em maybe! But I swear to God I ain't never once tasted the fuckers, you know what I'm sayin' here?"

≈

Of all my lunch companions Beatty Carew was way ahead my favorite. With a cap F. Cap everything. Twenty-four point bold. Double underline. The works. Some of the things she came out with, the things she told me, the things she did, were just so… oh, I don't know. Outrageous, I guess. The life she led, you wouldn't imagine. What she got up to. Just unbelievable.

What I did know was to enjoy her – every minute of her. Every scrap. Every morsel. Every last bit of her. If I'd been twenty, thirty years older I'd still have felt the same. Any man would. Any age. She was that kind of girl, the kind a lot of men could easily make themselves a fool over.

And I guess I came as close as you get.

Truman Capote, whom I knew slightly when I first arrived in the city (you may be surprised to learn that he cooked up a mean shrimp gumbo), would have just adored her. He'd have made her one of his swans. No doubt about it. Another Babe, another Gloria. Even if she did come from New Jersey.

In just six months she and I were tight as clams.

Of course, favorite doesn't begin to do her justice, doesn't come anywhere near the way I felt about this pesto-eyed thirty-something, this swings and roundabouts… this entrancing, maddening, delightful…

Adjectives? Believe me, with Roo they came easy. Every day a new one. And all of them fit, all of them did the job they were called in to do. But not a one of them quite got the whole of her. No single one quite comes close.

Let me tell you how we met, how it all started. So unexpected. So beguiling. So typical of what followed. I never would have believed it if it hadn't happened to me. So ridiculous really. One of those chance encounters.

I saw her first at the Metropolitan. Not the restaurant off East 40th, but the museum on Fifth. The last week in June, a summer day hot enough to stick shirts to backs and peel the heat off sidewalks in corrugated waves. I'd gone there for inspiration, for a lead, an idea. I found it. And a lot else besides.

It was a Thursday morning, easy to remember in my line of work, and the fifteen hundred words I had to get to the *Times* sometime in the next twenty-four hours were not coming easy. It happened like that sometimes. It didn't surprise or scare me. I'd been long enough in the business to know that deadlines have about them a kind of irresistible imperative, that come what may the copy gets done, on time – give or take.

The trouble was, it wasn't there yet. And the uncertainty, that devious trickling of doubt, unsettled me. Made it harder to come to grips with words and ideas. I was also getting annoyed. Which made it worse, of course. This one would cost me. This one would make me earn my money.

I'd spent pretty much most of the morning on it, pacing the apartment, sitting at my keyboard, lifting books from shelves, flipping through my notepads. All to no avail.

First off, right after breakfast, I'd started on a profile of Menon, that great French chef who first coined *La Nouvelle Cuisine* back in the eighteenth century, cutting a path through Varenne's bloated legacy to a simpler, less ornate style of cooking. I thought he'd suit this first real taste of summer, but I was wrong. Instead the summer heat just went and curdled my interest.

Then I switched to *soufflés*, sweet and savory both, light as a sea breeze, high as a chef's pleated toque. I'd tasted one the previous week at Le Cocteau in Murray Hill made from a base paste of Louisiana crayfish and hickory-smoked almonds from New Mexico, and had been just stunned by it and determined to write about it.

But as with Menon, so with *soufflés*.

What particularly frustrated, I guess, was the breadth of my choice. For I was free to write whatever culinary fancy took me, follow any gourmet whim I might choose, my beat the city's five boroughs and beyond. A simple restaurant review with the Cully slant perhaps. Or something topical – a piece about declining table manners, cranky waiters, uncomfortable seating, or unkind restaurant lighting. I could as easily fill my column with a take on Genoa's Lavagnina and Cordoba's Arbequino cold-pressed virgin olive oils as I could a dissertation on Menon or Acton, Massialot or de Croze, or any of the hundred great chefs whose lives and times and recipes filled the bookshelves that lined my study overlooking the Park. Anything I chose. And any way I wanted to write it: witty, irreverent, derisive, apoplectic, lyrical, damning, laudatory. However the spirit moved me. Wherever. Whatever.

But none of it worked that summer morning. Nothing went further than a dead-end first paragraph – each attempt wearily, worryingly, deleted. A brick wall every which way I turned.

The Met was an excuse, of course; an interlude, time out. They were holding an exhibition on food in art. I'd been invited to the opening a couple weeks earlier but had been unable to attend. Let's be honest, now. Had not wanted to attend. All those people. All that hullabaloo. All those marvelous pictures nothing more than golden punctuation amidst the cocktail chatter. Not my kind of thing at all. I'd have gotten cross in a heartbeat, and said something I shouldn't have.

But now, I decided, the time was right. I could stroll those cool corridors and airy chambers with impunity, admire the work, and then, maybe, return and write whatever idea presented itself from the experience; dash off the requisite fifteen hundred before I could think too much about it, and head off for a quiet weekend with friends in the country. The sooner I finished, the quicker I could leave the city, and my literary discomfort, behind.

Normally I'd have walked – I was restless enough for it to be a good idea – but judging it way too hot I called down to Carlo, our doorman, to find me a cab. By the time I reached the foyer I could see its chequered flank and dirty yellow bulk panting at the sidewalk, and seven springless, seat-sticking minutes later I tipped out beneath a red flag the size of a squash court that hung limp down the front of the museum. Emblazoned in white across its listless metres were the words, THE ART OF FOOD and, stamped in smaller letters beneath, 1490 – 1990.

The paintings were magnificent, some of the really great, great names: Vincenzo Campi, Louise Morillon, a fishmonger's stall heaped and slippery by the Dutchman Franz Snyders, Pieter Claeissins' po-faced family saying grace over a prime rib au jus you could just taste, a Richard Waitt leg of lamb with cauliflowers (cabbages with a college education, Mark Twain called them), Carl Vilhelm Balsgaard's segmented oranges, a basket of spilled cherries by Bimbi, a piled panier of strawberries by Chardin, some Cézanne apples glowing in a wood bowl, mangoes and papaya by Gauguin, a Matisse dining table and a host of others. Corridor after corridor, chamber by chamber, century following century, all life and color, taste and texture, frames as curled and golden as crimped pastry, five hundred years of food.

It was in front of the Snyders that I saw her first, head tilted to one side, knuckles to hips, regarding the canvas with a rapt attention. She was maybe an inch, no more than two, taller than me, with a sand-colored ponytail sprouting from the back of a trucker's cap. She wore a sleeveless t-shirt, baggy chino shorts with turn-ups, and rope-soled canvas sandals with laces that crossed and tied above her ankles. Her legs were long and pleasingly tanned, arms thin and elegant, elbows finely pointed, hands slim and tapered with perfect unpainted fingernails.

Though I was not far enough forward to see her face, shaded as it was by the tilt and bill of her cap, what I could see, with little problem, through the open arm of her t-shirt, was the exposed crease and swell of a breast. It drew the eye, believe me, heart and breath catching at such an unexpected, intimate exposure.

Maybe it was to cover any possible embarrassment, should she suddenly sense someone beside her and turn and find me there, that I spoke. I can't imagine what else could have prompted me.

"Do you like the artist? Or is it the subject?"

She turned quickly, surprised to hear a voice so close, I guess, and pinned me with eyes the color of sweet basil.

"Neither," she replied, then turned back to the canvas, tilting her head the other way now.

It was not a response I'd expected. She'd seemed so absorbed by the painting. It made me go on.

"I'm afraid I don't follow…"

"Well, see, I was hungry. I saw the sign."

For a moment there I was perplexed, not understanding, not recognising the direction she was taking. And then I remembered the red flag above the museum entrance and the word FOOD in bold white capitals.

What a strange thing to say, I thought. What an odd association. Then I wondered if the reply was a brush-off, whether she was putting me down, cutting dead any further attempt at conversation.

And then, without further prompting, she started talking again, keeping her eyes on the painting, as though she knew that I'd still be there.

"I was starving, but it was too hot to eat. I saw the sign and thought, I dunno… I thought just looking at it – food, I mean – might take the edge off. Girl's gotta watch her weight, you know?"

I nodded, still not certain how to proceed. Not certain whether there was a way to proceed. Had I picked on a mad woman? Started a conversation with a crazy? Would she suddenly babble? Would she latch herself onto me? Would she embarrass me? Would I wish in a moment I'd never said anything, never thought to come to The Met?

"Now take this one," she continued, leaning down to the small title card beside the painting. "Snyders. Franz Snyders. I mean it's a real tease, don't you think? Like one of those kids' quizzes, you know? How many different kinds of seafood can you count in the picture. I make it thirty-eight by the way."

"You don't say."

"But see, I got a problem. Do I count the seal? Or the beaver? Or the turtle? I mean, do they count as seafood? Did you ever know anyone eat seal? Or turtle? Or beaver?"

And then she paused, and turned to face me, eyes widening. And slowly, bashfully, she started to laugh, a private little gurgle of a laugh, when she realized what she'd said, and put a hand to her mouth, green eyes twinkling above her fingertips, even a blush creeping to her cheeks.

"I don't believe I just *said* that!" she wailed. "I don't be-*lieve* it. What-*ever* will you think of me?"

"I think you'll find it's an otter."

"Well, thank the Lord on high for that small mercy," she said, and clapped her hands. "And I don't even know you…"

And that was it. That's how we met. How it began. Exactly like that. In front of a picture in the Met. Can you get more corny? But it's true, I swear it. We just struck up.

"Beatty," she said. "Beatty Carew. But you can call me Roo."

She held out a hand, and I took it.

"Cully," I replied, and for the next thirty minutes or so the two of us wandered together through the galleries; pausing here and there; me wondering whether I should move off on my own, not intrude on her viewing, but never quite able to break free; Roo quite content to share the ride as though we'd come to the place together and it was only right and proper we should stay together. Sometimes I'd be ahead a few pictures, sometimes she would, but sooner or later we'd end up side by side.

No demands, no expectations, no disagreement. We liked the same pictures, made the same responses, drew the same rewards. Being with her was easy as spreading soft butter on hot muffins. It was as if, for that brief time we spent together, we'd known each other for ever, as though our friendship had started so far back that neither of us could say exactly when or where or how it had begun, that there was no need for anything beyond those glorious paintings and the pleasure and comfort of each other's company.

We left together, pausing at the security desk to retrieve a weighty buckskin tote she'd left there. Outside, beneath the red flag with FOOD printed on it, she sat on the bottom step, unlaced her sandals, and pulled a pair of roller-blades from the bag.

"The only way to travel," she said, stashing her sandals, clipping on the boots, and shouldering the tote. I helped her to her feet. She swayed a moment, then found her balance, straightened.

"You going downtown?" she asked.

"Cross town," I replied, adding: "Got work to do."

"You and me both," she shrugged, and smiled, and let go my hands.

And with a delicate twist and crouch, she spun away from me

and sped across the forecourt. Twenty yards off she turned and, blading backwards with an elegant disregard for the people around her, cupped her hands to her mouth and called back: "Remember the Beaver!!" And waved once, turned back the direction she was headed, and passed swiftly out of sight.

And that, I remember thinking, was that.

Which, of course, it wasn't.

The Dharwar Table

"*Bhuna gosht,*" said Daphne Winterson, alice band bobbing above the top of a tall, tasseled menu.

"*Bhuna gosht,*" repeated the slender, white-jacketed Indian waiter standing beside our table.

"*Kadhai kebab sarhadi,*" she continued.

"*Kadhai…* ma'am," scribbling the words onto his pad.

"*Kashmiri mirchi korma.*"

"*Mirchi…*"

"And *sag bhaji*? Cully? *Sag*?" She tipped the menu forward, tassels swinging, a questioning look over the black ledge of her spectacles.

I nodded, shrugged a 'why not', content to leave everything to her. The way she liked it.

"*Sag* then."

"*Sag,* ma'am."

"And four *pulaos*. And some *poori*. And your lovely *nan* bread. Plain and garlic."

"*Pulaos. Poori… Nan.* Plain and…"

"And, let's see. Yes, *raita.*"

"*Rai… ta.*"

"There, that's done," said Daphne, flipping the menu closed and pulling off her glasses. She folded them, slid them into her bag, and sighed contentedly.

The waiter took the menus, bowed his head and moved away.

I waited, knew there'd be no need to remind her.

"Oh," she said, leaning back and pulling at the curtain. "And two Tigers. Chilled glasses, please."

I smiled. I'd been expecting a wreck. This was the old Daphne.

It was a month since I'd seen her, the weekend of my Art of Food piece, out at her place in the country. It had been the strangest time and I'd been quite concerned for her. She'd seemed, to me at any rate, at the very end of her tether, like a weary traveller brought up short at a final, unfamiliar crossroads.

Afterwards, I'd written a note to thank her for the stay, but received no reply. I'd meant to phone, but hadn't (there were other things on my mind just then, as you'll discover) and I'd felt a pinch of guilt whenever I thought about it. But you know how it is. The longer you leave it, the less inclined you feel to call, to explain. We were old friends, after all.

Then, out of the blue, she'd phoned, said she was going to be in town, and why didn't we meet for lunch?

"No exhibitions," she'd said. "Just a nice long lunch with lots of gossip. I've something to tell you. What about it, Cully? The Dharwar? Shall I book, or shall you?"

≈

"If you do nothing else this summer," I remember saying that last time we met, "you must, Daphne, you really must go see this exhibition."

And the moment the words were out of my mouth, without particularly meaning to, I fell silent, remembering my companion at the Met, the companion I'd so successfully used in my fifteen hundred words, the companion who'd so enchanted me – wondering, in that silly, sentimental way, if we would ever meet again. If she might, by some small chance, read my piece in the *Times* and make the connection.

And then, as quickly, the moment passed.

"There's still a couple of months to run," I continued, "so there's plenty of time and you have no excuse. It really is quite magnificent, Daphne. You'll love it, I promise."

We were sitting in prettily upholstered Lloyd loom chairs on a wide stone terrace that ran the length of a large colonial house called Netherlands. According to Daphne – who owned the place and sat beside me, the pair of us watching the sun's slow descent over a blue-dusty range of distant hills – the house had stood there for a little over two hundred years, her family home for all but twenty of those years, seven generations of van Cruizen, the first of whom, a young man named Nickolas, newly arrived from Rotterdam, had won the spread in a game of cards.

It's a story I was well acquainted with, and it's worth the telling.

The original owner, the man who'd bought the land and built the house in this distant corner of the state (I believe his name was de Whyt), had bet the property in one last desperate bid to reverse a bad run of cards and, so the story goes, he'd done it with some confidence on a promising brace of sevens and aces. But a bad run is very often just that, and the first van Cruizen's cooler nerve and better hand had seen the man off for good.

The following day, after formally signing over the property in the presence of a notary, the pack of cards that had been his undoing still in his pocket, Mr. de Whyt had gone to the stables – no more than a few hundred yards from where we sat – and put a bullet in his head. That same pack of cards was now framed and hung in Netherlands' hallway, at the foot of the stairs, fanned out on a ground of yellowing white velvet. Look closely and you'll see the Jack of Hearts, the only card fully exposed, stained black across one corner where the blood seeped down the man's collar and into his jacket.

It was, I always thought, a ghoulish memento to display so prominently but one which each succeeding generation of van Cruizens had been unwilling to relegate to some less obvious location in the house. It was a part of the house's history, their family history, and it was kept as such, at once a grim testimonial to, and stern reminder of, the consequences of personal excess and selfish irresponsibility. If Daphne Winterson, or any of her forbears, had ever conceived of making a coat of arms, there is no doubt a bloodied Jack of Hearts would have featured somewhere. Either that or the straight flush that won van Cruizen the game, the pot, and the property.

Also, according to Daphne, the name of the house had never been changed, a reference not to that distant country of sweet genever and pickled herrings from which the de Whyts and van Cruizens had recently come, nor to the new city of Amsterdam not too far distant, but to the house's position in that isolated north-west corner of New York State – what they used to call the 'nether lands'. It is, as you may know if you've ever traveled thereabouts, a country of low, forested hills and misty finger lakes off to the left of route 87, reached along a single lane blacktop that cambers so sharply on either side that you have to drive pretty much in the middle of the road, its roller-coaster length hammocked by sagging telegraph lines and the splintery grey posts that support them.

The house stands alone, no other in sight, on the slopes of an otherwise wooded valley cradled between the Catskills and Adirondacks, a valley that some four miles from Netherlands feeds its stream into a puddling of lakes and reed-fringed ponds on one of which the family keeps a small shingled boathouse. Such was the extent of the original van Cruizen windfall that it is possible to make the journey from Netherlands to this isolated boathouse without ever leaving the estate, thousands of acres of rough grazing pasture cut with streams and patched with stands of maple, elm, and honey oak. Come Fall, these same trees turn spectacularly the very color of Netherlands' ancient brickwork, a burnt marmalade orange, appropriately weathered and flakey, responsible for a thin red dust that edges the house like a sprinkling of cayenne dandruff.

As I was saying, the pair of us were sitting on the terrace, the house rising up behind us, its white-framed windows flaming the very color of its brickwork in the setting sun, a wide expanse of tutored lawn, clipped tight as a toothbrush, falling away from us to a shadowy woodland that covered the hillside opposite. This was our view, that warm summer evening. A slope of lawn, a line of paddock fences casting long shadows, that menacingly-dark pelt of trees across the valley and, simmering on a range of distant hills, a great pumpkin of a sun. Only twenty miles or so from the turnpike, here at Netherlands, great cities, five-lane freeways and all the rest are something belonging to another world.

Daphne was talking: "You know I hate exhibitions, Cully! When I get to the city I simply don't have the time or the inclination for visiting galleries, museums or what-have-you. Opera, in the evening, fine. The ballet, at a pinch. Otherwise, I'd much rather have a nice, long lunch with you, thank you all the same." She took a deep, final pull on her cigarette and then plunged it into an ashtray on the table between us. "Now where the hell is Elliot?" she said, all of a sudden short and peppery. "Didn't he say he'd join us?"

"Organising the barbecue with Shelley and the boys last time I saw him."

"Playing with fire, whatever you call it," she replied with a shortening breath, discharging a last stream of smoke through kissing lips into the softening evening sky.

The remark, or rather its delivery, surprised me. At our feet the family labrador, Lutyens, who'd been sleeping peacefully until that moment, raised his head and eyed his mistress. With a lick of his chops and a half-hearted attempt at a hind-leg scratch, like a cyclist feeling for the pedal, he laid his nose back on his paws but kept his big brown eyes fixed on her. I remember thinking that, like me, her tone had caught him unawares.

≈

It was Elliot, Daphne's third husband, who had driven me up from the city that Saturday morning. Normally we made the journey mid-afternoon Fridays to avoid the rush and make the most of the weekend, but some meeting or other had delayed him.

Exactly on time he'd squealed to a halt outside my apartment building in yet another new car. Every time I saw Elliot, a senior editor with Florez Delisle who looked after the publication of my books, he seemed to have a new model. Of course, there was no way his salary from Florez could account for these regular acquisitions and, though it was rumoured he had money of his own, I suspected Daphne had some hand in these purchases. As well as winning the house and land seven generations earlier, Daphne's forbear had gone on to make a considerable fortune from textiles and carpet weaving, a fortune sizeably increased and diversified by succeeding generations. Leaving Daphne, when her parents died a few years back, very, very wealthy indeed.

The last time Elliot and I had made the journey we'd done so in a sleek and shiny BMW, a surprisingly spacious coupé that propelled us both in tight teutonic comfort. It had a shark's snout and fat wheels that seemed to suck the tarmac whenever we took a corner on the country road that winds up to Netherlands ("downforce," Elliot had explained to me when I remarked on the car's superior road-holding after one bowel-clenching corner a few miles off the turnpike). But this time, instead of the BMW, a scarved and goggled Elliot greeted me from the driver's seat of an open-top Morgan, its long tunnelled hood cinched with buckled leather belts and slashed with ominous-looking grills, its flaming red coachwork color-coordinated, it appeared, with Elliot's wide, red suspenders. He looked even more a part of the machine than he normally did, his steely grey hair already swept back by the wind on the short drive over from his office, his arms braced against the wooden wheel, fingers twined around its buffed metal spokes.

"Toss your bag in the back," he'd said, showing me where to stow my weekender, helping to push it down between the seats with much squeaking of leather on leather. "There, that's it. Perfect." And then, seeing my frown – there appeared to be no door handle – he leaned over to open a passenger door no larger than a table napkin.

"Where's the windshield, Elliot?" I asked, finally settling and strapping myself into the ribbed leather cavity that called itself a passenger seat, nodding at the two small semi-circles of glass that sat above the dash.

"Too much drag, Cully. Too much drag. You'll find a hat and goggles in the glove." And as I leaned forward to get them – a far from flattering woolen ski bonnet and yellow-lensed Vuarnets that turned my world a watery mustard – the new car surged forward with a roar, fishtailed into a gap in the traffic and sped north out of the city.

As I've said, Elliot was Daphne's third husband, six years younger than the both of us, tall, athletic, with twinkling, toffee-brown eyes that wrinkle to cobwebbed slits whenever he smiles (which is often). He's a man of lively spirit, everyone who knows him will tell you, with an easy manner and many enthusiasms: good cars, good manuscripts, good food; the frequent and varied pleasures he gains from life. And, for a publisher, his unlikely skills. When some pipes at Netherlands burst one bitter, isolated winter, he fixed the problem himself; when a TV aerial was swept off the roof in a gale, he'd done the same, shinning up a ladder and re-attaching it much to the children's delight; and when the Riva engine failed in the middle of the lake where the family keep their boathouse he had, according to Daphne who treasured these displays of manhood, burrowed into the engine compartment and, with only a rolled headscarf and bent hairpin, fixed the damned thing. The kind of man, Daphne once proudly declared, who could light a fire in a flood.

Looking back, it's easy to see why she fell for him, though when I introduced them I failed to notice the effect he had on her ("My legs just went from under me, Cully," she told me later. "If I hadn't been sitting down I'd have fallen over, so help me."). What was maybe not so clear was how Elliot had come to fall for her. Pale as a beansprout – no matter how much sun she takes her skin never colors – with thin blonde hair held in place by a horseshoe band of velvet that tucks in behind her ears and slightly pushes them forward, a nose just the right side of prominent, and a chubby frame that billowing dresses go some way to disguising and only heavy smoking holds at bay, it was what you might call an unlikely attraction.

"She's kind, Cully, that's all there is to it, and I love her for it," Elliot told me once, unbidden, as though suspecting I doubted his good intentions (which, to be honest, I did), in a tone of voice that meant *kind* in the manner of caring and loving, rather than generous.

Which, as I've said, I'm sure she was, too.

And so the most unlikely couple I ever knew had gotten married, to the muted astonishment of all their friends. The ceremony had taken place on this very terrace, with a judge of Daphne's acquaintance officiating, and Daphne's four children (Shelley, the eldest, from her first marriage, and Will and Ty and Jimmy from her second, who all, not surprisingly, adored Elliot) attending their mother and new stepfather in their Sunday best as maid of honor and ushers. And six, seven years later, all the doubters and the doom-sayers and all their whispered misgivings had been roundly knocked on the head.

"So what did you think of the new car, Cully?" asked Daphne, lighting up another cigarette.

"I can still feel it," I replied, recalling our teeth-rattling, bone-shaking drive in a car that appeared to have no suspension, the howling blast of the wind slip-streaming over my head as I sank lower and lower into the seat. "Now I know what it's like to be a windshield."

Daphne chuckled. "Lucky you didn't get hit by any bugs. First time out, doing about eighty, Elliot gets a hornet on the cheekbone. Car swerved all over the place, and he ends up with a real shiner." And then, after a gentle laugh as though at a memory of happier times, she asked: "Did you talk on the way up?"

"As far as I remember, he talked most of the way. But I couldn't hear a damn word. I could see his mouth moving but that was it. Come to think of it, maybe it was just the slipstream, or the G-force…"

"Cully, you're teasing," laughed Daphne, the laugh disintegrating into a fruity smoker's cough. She mashed out her cigarette not half-way smoked, and got to her feet with a loud sigh that turned into another short cough and a serious clearing of the throat she did nothing to disguise. It sounded like she had an octopus trapped in there. I felt like saying it was maybe time she quit, but I knew better. Daphne isn't the kind of woman who listens much to good advice if it doesn't suit her; always makes up her own mind, thank you all the same.

She reached for my glass. "Time for a refresh, whaddya say?"

≈

Until Elliot, Daphne had not been well served by men.

She'd married first in her teens, more out of juvenile rebellion, she'd once told me, than any sense of emotional commitment to the man she lit upon, a mill worker's son of questionable talents whom she met on a garage forecourt and dated for a month at most. Despite her parents' displeasure, and over their protests, the two of them had finally gotten hitched in a courthouse in the next county, the same week that Richard Nixon moved into the White House. It was also the week when Daphne discovered that her new husband was incapable of marital sexual congress without an appetising *hors d'oeuvre* of fisticuffs, preferring a punch-bag approach to foreplay and sex. Even now, when Daphne smiles, you can see three thin arches of grey where the top front caps fit to her gum.

But Daphne, even a young, headstrong Daphne, was no martyr to first love nor, after the plenty of Netherlands, to the unfamilar experience of a taut and troubled existence on a small, uncertain income. Pretty soon the dubious pleasures of an independent life-style, an advancing pregnancy, and increasingly frequent beatings drove her back home where a divorce and pay-off were promptly arranged. It was during her subsequent confinement at Netherlands that her husband (I think his name was Donny) passed on weaving looms in favor of petty crime, only to end up shot dead in a liquor store hold-up a month before his daughter's birth.

Donny's daughter, Shelley, was eight when Daphne found her second husband, a quite delightful Englishman called Sinclair (none of that superior frostiness the English are so fond of affecting in the presence of us colonials) whom she'd met in Switzerland on a trip to Europe.

Daphne and her mother were staying at some resort in the Alps (Shelley had been left at Netherlands with her grandfather and the housekeeper, Dottie) when Sinclair, an Oxford post-graduate on a summer climbing expedition, had, in short order, won Daphne's heart and, most improbable of all, scaled the lofty heights of her mother's disapproval. He was tall and suntanned, fit and healthy, well-read and cultured in that easy European manner (not unlike Elliot, come to think of it) and in no time at all he'd thoroughly breached the old lady's reserve. According to Daphne, the casual mention of a Dutch grandmother, shipyard interests in Scotland, and a titled cousin had had not a little to do with the softening of her mother's heart.

Whatever, the two ladies were immediately taken – one way and the other – and, when their stay came to an end and it was time to move on, Sinclair was invited to come visit Netherlands that Christmas, had accepted and, after only ten days' stay, was formally engaged to Daphne on New Year's Eve.

It was through Sinclair that I first met Daphne, a year or two after their marriage, at Oxford in England where he'd been offered and promptly taken up a college fellowship (Merton? Corpus? I forget which college now). I was in London at the time, on vacation, and had been invited by a colleague, the restaurant critic on the *Daily Telegraph*, to accompany him to an Oxford High Table where the food, the conversation, and traditions, he assured me, were certain to make good copy for my readers back home.

And so it had been, the college suitably dark and gothic the evening we arrived, the mullioned windows of its pokey little quadrangle all warm and gold, and the Dining Hall where we gathered hammer-beamed, panelled, glittering with candlelit silver and hung with the blackened canvasses of past Principals. Everything, in short, that I'd imagined an Oxford college to be. Medieval, mysterious, magnificent.

It was there, at High Table, over a saddle of the tenderest, tastiest lamb I think I've ever eaten (better even than a Breton *pré salé*), and something they called Scorched College Cream but which I knew as *crème brûlée*, that I was introduced to Dr Sinclair MacLeod, fellow in something or other, (how is it I forget some things and not others?) who sat across the table from me swaddled in a scarlet collared gown.

We hit it off immediately, he and I, talking of food and restaurants we'd been to on our travels (I always warm to people who like their food), and in no time at all he'd told me about his new American wife who would be so pleased to see a friendly face from home, and, well, if I hadn't planned anything why didn't I stay on for the weekend as their guest? He would show me the college cellars, he offered, keen then to persuade me once the invitation was out, doing so in a most gracious and winning way, and would personally accompany me around the city's famous Covered Market where the food for High Table was got from suppliers who counted their relationship with the college kitchens in centuries. And, of course, introduce me to his wife. From upstate New York, he told me over a tub of Stilton scarved in a damask cloth. Near Amsterdam. Did I know it? A beautiful colonial house called Netherlands? And so on.

So I stayed in Oxford, with apologies to an understanding *Telegraph* man who returned alone to London, transferring from a college guest room where I spent the night of the dinner to the MacLeod's tall Victorian house in the north of the town the following day.

Even back then Daphne wore alice bands and favored the loose, kaftan-like smocks she still wears today. She was also, despite a second pregnancy and Sinclair's brooding disapproval, an enthusiastic smoker. I remember reaching the top of the steps that led to their front door and seeing through its colored panels this shape come looming down the hall, filling the glass the closer she came, remember her flinging open the door before Sinclair had a chance to find his keys, cigarette firmly in hand, smoke sucked into her slipstream, welcoming me with that warm and deep American burr of hers that, in an instant, made me feel, in that ancient British town, both a long way from home and yet, somehow, at home.

It was on those same front steps, one icy Oxford winter, a few years after we first met and three children later, that Sinclair MacLeod – a scholar, a traveler, a good and honorable man – slipped on a crust of ice, missed his footing and fell, scattering his books, breaking a wrist, and fatally fracturing his skull.

"A sorry end for a mountaineer, wouldn't you say?" said Daphne, tears pooling in her eyes, making poignant light of her loss when, a few months later, we met up again Stateside where she'd returned with her brood. "All those glaciers and ice-fields and crevasses and what-have-you, and what does the blighter do? Just slips on an icy step and cracks his head open. I ask you!"

And so, close on twenty years later, Elliot.

≈

"I'll say one thing for him," said Daphne, pushing open the French doors with a foot and coming out onto the terrace, an ice-clinking glass in each hand. "That man sure knows how to build a barbecue."

Passing me my drink, slippery and cold from the ice, she sat herself down in the Lloyd loom, its stiffened weave creaking in protest, lit herself yet another cigarette and made herself comfortable.

"You should see them back there. Like a bunch of kids whooping it up. And Elliot, well he's the biggest kid of them all!" She blew out a stream of smoke, flicking the filter with her thumbnail, dismissively, almost angrily it seemed to me. At our feet, Lutyens wagged his tail, sweeping it idly over the stone flags, glad to have his mistress back, but clearly misreading what I, by now, was beginning to see as the sub-text of a woman not happy.

For, despite that marvelous setting, despite my pleasure at being out of the city, I knew then with an absolute certainty that my weekend at Netherlands was not going to be like other weekends. This one was different. There was a ghost at the party, a shadow of discontent that kept to the corners but still chilled. It was the first and only time I can remember when the house was not a sanctuary, somewhere filled with laughter, affection, and warmth. And it was clear to me, that Saturday evening, as the sun finally slipped beneath wooded ridges, as the sky turned a parade of darkening fairground colors amidst a line of low shifting cloud, with the smell of burning hickory and grilled meat drifting around the house to settle unmistakably on the terrace, that something was up.

And I was right.

"To the sun," I said, raising my glass, wondering if maybe I should say something, whether Daphne, usually so confiding, would allow one of my gentle intrusions.

"To a setting sun," she replied, and tipped back her glass with an ominous finality that quietly warned me off.

Of course, things might have been different if Daphne and I had been meeting for one of our lunches. Then we were alone. On neutral ground. Somewhere the confidences, the sharing of secrets, the laying bare came more easily. But that evening, idling away the sunset on the terrace at Netherlands, I read the signs and elected not to pry.

Instead, easily redirecting the conversation, I spoke to her again of the exhibition at the Met, of Moillon and Morillon, of Campi and Agasse, Henendez, Merrett, Guttuso, Hicks, and O'Keefe. Of course, I knew she'd never go, but my chatter filled whatever it was between us until Shelley came to fetch us for the barbecue.

≈

A Netherlands' barbecue.

Make no mistake, it's a wonder.

The Tillotsons of Boston, Maude and Jeff MacAuley in Totnes Bay, the BeeJay Wilsons out on the Cape, the Withnells of Copping County, my good friends the Dusens and Donnellys, even Bill and Junior Watson, all are renowned for their tables. And rightly so. But the truth is you never eat half so well with any of them as you do when you stay at Netherlands.

Which really is all down to Daphne's housekeeper, Dottie. She's been with the family since before the days of Donny, a battleship of a black lady with a Guinness topping of tight grey curls who makes the wide floorboards of Netherlands creak and wince at her passing. In my opinion, out of all my friends, there is simply no one to compare with her in the kitchen; and even some chefs of my acquaintance would be hard pressed to match this formidable lady.

And formidable's the word. I once tried to wheedle out of her the recipe for her Amsterdam Slow-Pot for a story I was doing on country-house cuisine. But when I suggested it the hip-heavy, ham-armed, and widely-aproned Dottie had zipped her aubergine lips as tightly as a steamer lid. Even bustled me out of the kitchen. When I strayed there now, I knew to keep my counsel. As far as Dottie was concerned, it was my job to eat her food, not talk about it, and certainly not write about it for some 'noose-pepper', though I had, on occasions, used her skills for copy without her knowing.

In most other homes, the barbecue that Saturday night would have been just that. A barbecue. A pedestrian, predictable affair of over-cooked meats, paper plates that bent, and plastic cups that cracked. But with Dottie, anything to do with food consumed her entire attention. That night she'd prepared a sticky stack of baby back pork ribs, guinea-fowl drumsticks coated in a Cajun-spice crust, and salt-and-pepper prawns, all of which Elliot had worked on the griddle, all of it served up with a bird's eye chili dip, a Caesar salad, napkin-covered herb and garlic rolls, and fluffy-as-a-cloud Rosevals baked, buttered, and bedded in foil, the feast laid out on a garden table just a few paces from the kitchen door. The table had been set with crisp pink linen, horn-handled cutlery, and heavy white china, the whole shebang lit with hurricane lamps hung from an overhead trellis thick with jasmine and night-flowering stock. By the time Daphne and I came through from the terrace, the rest of the family had taken their places and Elliot, brandishing his silvery cooking tongs, was passing out ribs, drumsticks, and prawns to the soft accompaniment of some Schubert, playing, incongruously, on the kids' ghetto blaster.

Looking back now, there's not a doubt in my mind that if Daphne hadn't eaten anything she'd certainly have gotten badly drunk. Which, as you'll hear, was what Elliot thought was the case. But she did eat, with a kind of gleeful gusto it seemed to me, dipping and smearing dabs of bread across her plate to mop up the drops and juices of drumstick, prawn, and rib, forking up a goodly portion of the salad, and digging out the best part of two jacket potatoes, as though the food, at least, could be relied upon. She even managed two helpings of home-made vanilla ice-cream coated with Dottie's famous butterscotch sauce, and a wedge or two of the old lady's delicate petticoat tail shortcake. Whatever it was that was bothering her, it hadn't killed her appetite.

Alerted by her odd mood on the terrace I watched carefully during the meal, looking to pin down the cause of Daphne's discontent. It was clear the problem was Elliot, and sitting there, the seven of us teeth-stripping the meat from the ribs and drumsticks, and crunching our way through the thin, flame-charred shells of the prawns, I could almost feel her resentment building up, creaking ominously, like a field of pack ice wedged between the pair of them and bearing too much weight.

I was also in no doubt that had it not been for Dottie and I and the boisterous company of the kids (Shelley, twenty-eight, chubby-faced like her mother but tall enough to carry it off, Will, Ty, and Jimmy, all with the rangey good looks of their father) Daphne would have started in on Elliot. As it was, she just froze him out, talking with the kids between mouthfuls, asking me about new places I'd been to, complimenting Dottie on the petticoat tails, but never once addressing Elliot directly. And whenever he spoke to her, I noticed, she always managed to have something in her mouth, and would either nod or shake her head in answer, with hardly a glance in his direction.

As for Elliot, he behaved as though nothing was wrong, nothing off-beam or out of kilter, as though the chill breeze off Daphne's iciness had somehow not reached him. Sitting there at the head of the table, he chatted away about the boathouse where the kids were headed the following day (all the how-to's and where-to's and what-not-to's that made them nod and groan and grin amongst themselves), suggesting they take rifles for the rabbits, which they all agreed was a fine idea, and acting throughout the contented man about the house, surrounded by family and friends.

I remember, when it happened, I was talking to Shelley about her work in Germany (she's an Air Force nurse at some base outside Frankfurt, and was home on furlough). Daphne had complained of the cold and gone inside for a sweater, Dottie was setting out platters of fruit and cheese, and Elliot was reminding the boys (all three at Bard in Dutchess County) to please remember to idle the Riva before they opened up the throttle: "She's an old lady now and she needs gentle handling. You can't just…"

And then, it seemed, the sky just exploded above us and we all ducked our heads and the kitchen garden where we sat was flooded with wavering, flashing lights. Great blossoms of color filled the sky, showering snowflakes of red and green and white that sparkled and winked and died as they fell towards us, accompanied by screaming whines, fizzing rocket trails, and thunderous detonations which echoed across the valley.

Pop-pop, pop-pop-pop, wheeeeeeee, crump-crump-crump!

The noise was extraordinary, not least because it was so unexpected, the night sky crowded with starbursts of color that flickered through the trellis onto our upturned faces, the trees around the house, invisible until now, thrown into shadowy, strobe-like life.

For a second no one spoke, just looked up in open-mouthed astonishment.

And then: "Fireworks!" shouted Jimmy, the youngest, and he leapt to his feet, rocking the table. "It's fireworks! Yeah! We got ourselves a firework show!"

And so it was.

When we reached the terrace, there was Daphne, backlit against a stand of cascading Roman candles, a table lighter in one hand and a cigarette and glass in the other, lighting the blue touch-papers of rocket after rocket set up across the flagstones in empty wine bottles.

Fizzzzz, whoooooosh, they went, hurtling skywards, bathing everything in their bright, incandescent light, sending shadows fleeting round the house, illuminating the drifting puffs of smoke from earlier explosions.

"Jesus Christ," said Elliot quietly, standing with me by the French doors while the kids joined Daphne, reaching into the box of fireworks she'd dragged out onto the terrace and setting up fresh supplies. "The bloody woman's gone and got drunk."

He sounded stern and cross, as if, at last, he had no option but to acknowledge what he'd so assiduously refused to notice earlier. But before I could properly see the expression on his face, he turned and went inside.

Out on the terrace, unaware of Elliot's exit, Daphne finally surrendered the table lighter to the boys and retired with Shelley to the Lloyd loom chairs we'd occupied earlier. I can see her now, pitching into hers with feet stretched out and head thrown back to watch the last of the rockets as they whistled away into the darkness.

"What fun," I can hear her saying, as the last blooms lit up the sky and the delayed crack-crack echo of their explosions rolled away across the hills. "What absolute, marvelous, terrific fun."

Yet somehow she didn't sound as if it had been.

No, I thought, as I made my way to bed a little later. Not drunk. Not Daphne. Out of sorts maybe, a mite stewed, rebellious, determined to make some kind of scene. But not drunk. Sure she'd put them away, but I've known Daphne long enough and well enough to know she possesses a powerful constitution. It takes more than a few icy Beefeaters and goblets of Merlot to get the better of her on a full stomach, thank you all the same.

And though she may not have appeared until lunchtime the following day, it wasn't a hangover that kept her in her room.

No, it was something else entirely.

As I was to discover the very next evening.

≈

Sunday began, for me, with the kids leaving for the boathouse, loading Will's rust-freckled Volkswagen with their various bags and Dottie's creaking wicker hampers. I heard them from my room, woken by their shouts and the crunch of their feet on the gravel drive below my window, arguing about which case or hamper should go where, and if it went there, stupid, how where they all going to fit in the car? And so on, and so forth.

By the time I'd showered and dressed and made my way downstairs the VW was packed and ready. Elliot, in a greasy bib overall with a rag in one hand and a wrench in the other (he would spend the rest of the morning under the bonnet of his beloved Morgan), stood on the front step, reminded them again about the Riva, told them to call their mother the moment they arrived, and wished them a good holiday.

"And don't forget to bring some rabbit back for Dottie," he called after them as the Beetle, its windows sprouting with waving arms, disappeared with a tinny beep of farewell into the wood that edged this side of the house.

"Those kids…" he said, turning to me and, with a rueful smile, shaking his head. "Believe me, Cully, that Riva's in for a hammering." And then, brightly, as though nothing had happened the night before: "How d'you sleep, by the way? Good night?"

Fine, I replied, wondering whether he would say anything about the fireworks. He didn't.

"Picked up the papers earlier," he continued. "I left them in the morning room. Liked the piece on the Met. Sounds like you had fun." There was a conspiratorial twinkle in his eyes. "Anyways, can't stand here jawing. Must get on. I'll be in the garage if you need me. Damned transmission's acting up. See you later, Cully."

And with that, he headed off for the stable block and I went back inside, to the kitchen for breakfast, taking a cup of coffee from Dottie and sharing my toast crusts with Lutyens who sat beneath the table, his warm snout resting in my lap.

There were guests that Sunday lunch: Bill and Tiny Edgars, a New York couple who kept a weekend house some twenty miles from Netherlands and had known Daphne an age, and the Dwyers whom I'd never met. According to Dottie, as she sliced and shaved and peeled a selection of vegetables from the kitchen garden, these Dwyers had recently returned from a trip to India and apparently now preferred not to eat meat. They'd told Daphne when she called to invite them, and Daphne had passed on the news to Dottie. I could tell it upset the old girl that two of their lunch guests would be forgoing her famous goose that even now filled Netherlands' kitchen with its rich, unctuous aromas.

"They're Vegans?" I asked.

"Nope," said Dottie, dismissively. "Noo Yuckers."

I knew better than to say anything, finished my toast and coffee, and retreated to the morning room where Elliot had left the papers.

The room is set on a corner of the house and well-named, the predominant color a soft, watery yellow, its various shades carefully matched and coordinated through furnishings and fabrics, even to the flowers and the fire irons that glint brassily beside the grate. Sinking back into a sofa, the sun streaming through the windows, I skimmed the *Times*, found my piece on the Met, and read it through with that rising glow of satisfaction a writer feels when he sees his work hasn't been too much tampered with. The copy boys had even kept the bit about the Snyders; the kiddies' quiz – how many fish can you see?

And all the while, apart from Dottie coming in with fresh coffee and some left-over petticoat tails, Lutyens snoring gently, the rustle of my newspapers and the occasional, distant, angry revving of a car engine, the house was silent now the kids had gone, could have been deserted. Yet still no sound from the floor above where Daphne kept to her room.

At a little after twelve, Elliot put his head round the door to say he was going for a swim and did I want to join him?

I thanked him but said no, and idled my way through the last of the sections. Which was when I heard, as I knew I would, a door open upstairs and the creak of stairs as Daphne finally came down from her room, sailing brightly across the hall and into the morning room at exactly the moment that a car drew up outside, followed within seconds by a second car. There were voices, pitched high and low, the clunk and slam of car doors, the crunch of gravel, and then cries of greeting as Elliot appeared from his swim and led the Dwyers and the Edgars chattering into the drawing room. There was the muted pop of a champagne cork.

"Back to the battlefield, into the breach," said Daphne with a glint in her eye, and taking my arm in hers, with Lutyens at our heels, we crossed the hall to join our lunch companions.

The lunch was a long one. I'd met the Edgars at Netherlands before, but had forgotten how slowly the wife, Tiny, ate, no forkful larger than a pellet. It was past four when we finally adjourned to the terrace for coffee and brandies. As for the Dwyers, Pam and Bud, they were companionable enough but otherwise unremarkable, he a successful broker in Amsterdam, she a professional wife, thin as a chopstick, with a forehead still red from their Indian vacation.

"Quite astonishing," said Pam Dwyer, taking a second brandy from Elliot, "just how many vegetables there are. I mean there are just hundreds of different kinds of squashes and pulses for instance, and simply thousands of marvelously interesting ways to cook them. *So* fascinating. *So* unusual. And all *so* different. You just don't realize until you become vegetarian. But I expect you know all about that, Mr. Mortimer?"

Wickedly, I suppose, for I wasn't much taken by this rather self-absorbed lady, I told her the story about undigested red meat – how most of us carry at least a couple of pounds somewhere in our gut, rotting, probably fermenting, with no place to go. "We only ever pass a small amount of the meat we take in, you know."

Tiny paled at the thought, and Pam beamed, triumphant. Daphne laughed out loud and leaned across to slap my arm.

"Cully, really! What a thing to say!"

"There, what did I tell you?" continued Pam, turning to her husband who, I'd noticed during lunch, had eyed Dottie's goose with genuine longing as he made do with the creamed Vidolia onions, a wedge of chestnut stuffing, and a selection of steamed and roasted vegetables. He nodded and agreed. I decided he probably did a deal of that. It was for his sake, poor man, that I'd said nothing when they both helped themselves to generous slabs of Dottie's famous steamed pudding. Speckled with currants and figs and apricots, served with ice-cold creamy custard, it is an irresistible dish. It was also a vegetarian nightmare. Though neither Dwyer seemed to know this, the pudding's main constituent was suet, a substance shredded from the white boney crusts of fat that encase beef kidneys. I tried to catch Dottie's eye, give her a wink as she held the pudding tray between them and they scooped out generous platefuls, but she never once looked in my direction.

As for our hostess, Daphne was in altogether excellent spirits, making everyone feel comfortable, at ease, at home, as though the night before had never happened. It's a talent she has, you see, a talent for making everything around her seem warm and wonderful. If she wants to, that is. It had been the same all those years ago when we first met, that extraordinary coziness wrapping around me like a big, bosomy hug. Really, a marvelous woman. Willful, sometimes, headstrong, too, but still marvelous.

That Sunday afternoon at Netherlands, I can't tell you how much it pleased me to see this change in her, back to her old self after the oddly disturbing company she'd provided the evening before. It was as if that frisson I'd sensed had been nothing more than my imagination. Or so insignificant that she and Elliot had already made up, sorted out whatever little spat it was. It was with some relief, I can tell you, that I watched her maneuver things on the terrace so that she took the Lloyd loom next to his, and saw him respond with that crinkling smile of his. And when, finally, with thanks and kisses and the comradely slapping of backs and shaking of hands, the contented Edgars and hungry Dwyers left, I watched with real pleasure as Elliot took Daphne's arm on the front steps to wave their lunch guests goodbye, and kept it there as we strolled back to the terrace. Despite my earlier misgivings, just a perfect, perfect Netherlands day.

When it came, only minutes later, it was nothing more than one of those functional, unremarkable phone conversations. The phone had rung as Daphne and I settled once again in our chairs. Elliot was still on his feet and took the call in the morning room, his voice easily overheard through the open windows.

"Yes… yes, I understand. No, that's fine. Of course. Yes, I quite agree. No, it's no trouble at all. That's okay. 'Bye now." Something along those lines.

Beside me Daphne took a deep breath and let it out, somewhere between resignation and annoyance; the kind of sigh you might make in bed before falling asleep. Without even waiting to hear what the call had been about, she leaned over and touched my arm.

"If he's got to go back to town, why don't you stay on? I can drive you into Amsterdam tomorrow or Tuesday, and you could take the train? Do say yes, Cully."

Before I could reply Elliot was back on the terrace. Not bothering to sit, he rested a hand on both our chairbacks and explained that he had to leave right away. Documents needed signing, or some such, and that tomorrow would be too late. He was sorry, but there it was. One of their legal boys was flying off to Europe on the last flight and they'd arranged to meet at Kennedy. There wasn't a thing he could do. Daphne looked up at him, stretched across and patted his hand.

"I was just saying I could drive Cully into Amsterdam and he could take the train back tomorrow. Much more comfortable than rattling along in that Morgan of yours." And then, archly: "No need for Cully to suffer because you've got business to attend to."

Elliot turned to me: "Well, if that's okay with you, Cully…?"

And so it was. Within fifteen minutes, Elliot was sliding into the front seat of the Morgan, gunning the engine and spitting gravel as he drove from the house, the low red body of the sports car slicing between the trees.

It was then, back on the terrace, that Daphne began to weep, a quiet, heart-wrenching flow that dripped over her cheeks, punctuated by hiccoughing snuffles that made her shake. It was as though she had been holding back all weekend but could no longer contain herself.

"Daphne? What on earth...? Are you alright?"

"No, I'm damn well not alright. Do... do I... do I look as if I am?" She sat forward and snatched at her cigarettes.

"But what's wrong? What's the matter?"

And then: "It's her. I'm certain," she snivelled, tugging a cigarette from the pack with trembling fingers and snapping her lighter till it caught. At her side, Lutyens tried to nose affectionately at her arm.

"Her? Her who?"

Daphne inhaled deeply, sat back and wiped away the tears with the back of her hand. And then she said, quietly, letting the smoke chase after her words: "There's someone else, Cully."

"Someone else? Elliot? You're kidding me?"

"Believe it, I'm not kidding," she replied mournfully. "It's true. Elliot's having an affair. Fucking someone." The profanity seem to give her strength. She sniffed loudly and her voice hardened. "I know it. Just know it."

And so that Sunday night at Netherlands we stayed up late, moving from the terrace to the study when a shower of rain rattled across the flagstones, talking the whole thing through.

Her suspicions had been aroused slowly, she told me. First it was their lovemaking – more fierce and frequent than normal.

"But surely..." I began. I was going on to say that that sounded encouraging, but she cut me short.

"Cully, there's no point me explaining. You've never been married, so you wouldn't know."

"I see," I replied, not a little put out.

"Sometimes it was like sleeping with someone else," she continued, "someone I didn't know. It puzzled me, but I didn't say anything. For a while I thought it might be some kind of mid-life crisis, you know? Elliot feeling his age and wanting to make the most of things."

But then, she went on, there were the changes of plan: arrangements they'd made, dinners and weekends and such-like, suddenly rescheduled or cancelled. "He's become unreliable. We'll make a date – I don't know, Friday night dinner, an evening up in town for the theater or some such – and he'll call saying he's been held up, can't make it. At first I didn't mind, then it made me cross because it was so inconsiderate; such short notice, so disappointing.

"And then, Cully, I just got plain suspicious. I mean he's a goddammed publisher, for heaven's sake, not some Wall Street hotshot. There was something going on he didn't want me to know about. And there was only one thing it could be. Another woman. Simple as that. He was seeing someone else. Sleeping with someone else. Christ almighty, how could he?"

I asked how long this had been going on.

"The summer. Maybe April, May. Two, three months," she replied, sitting forward on the study sofa, smoking for all she was worth, playing with her lighter, picking at her wedding ring, the very picture of despair.

"And you're certain?"

"Certain," she said, stubbornly, no room for doubt.

And that's when everything focused for me, when I understood what had been going on that weekend at Netherlands. And instinctively, in every bit of me, I knew she was right. There really was no doubt. If Daphne believed it, and she clearly did, it had to be true. I mean, that phone call? Quite extraordinary. Papers to sign on a Sunday night? A publisher? What was so important that it couldn't wait for Monday morning? Or, if it was so important, why hadn't it been dealt with at his Friday meeting, the one that delayed us? It all seemed suddenly so unlikely. And Kennedy? On a Sunday? Out on the island? Even in the Morgan and the way he drove, it would take him hours.

"He's very careful, you know. Doesn't give a thing away. But I know! I know it! He thinks he can fool me, but he can't. I'm too smart for him."

"Do you know who?"

"Does it matter who?" she snapped.

"I… I guess not."

"But that doesn't mean to say I'm not going to damn well find out."

≈

And so, at Daphne's bidding, The Dharwar Table, a south Indian restaurant on 3rd and 27th, the two of us sitting at our usual table, hidden away in a curtained alcove. I could tell at once she'd been looking forward to our meeting. The last time I'd seen her, as we waited for my train at Amsterdam station the morning after Elliot left for the city, she'd been shakily vulnerable, deeply unhappy, almost clinging to me as we hugged goodbye. Now, a month later, she was brimming with excitement.

"So what is it you have to tell me?" I began. "What have you been up to?"

"Action, Cully. Action. I'm on the offensive. I'm up and I'm running." She pulled a pack of cigarettes from her bag, tapped one out and, heedless of the law, lit it with a flourish. "And it makes me feel... oooh, so good."

"And what exactly...?"

But she gave me no time to finish, leaning forward in her chair, elbows on the table, a curl of smoke and smile of conspiracy rippling across her lips.

"You'll be shocked, I know. You'll think I've gone crazy. You'll maybe even think less of me because of it."

"Because of what?"

A waiter arrived with a stack of *popadums* and laid it between us, then returned a moment later with our Tigers. Daphne cracked a piece off the top *popadum* and started nibbling at its edge, watching me with gimlet eyes as the beers were poured, taking a deep final drag of her cigarette before squashing it out to appease our quietly disapproving waiter.

"Well...?"

The curtain swirled and another waiter appeared bearing a trestle and tray. In a single movement – one I've always admired – he opened the trestle's legs, set it down and slipped the tray onto it. Lids were lifted, steam billowed. He pointed to the various dishes, identifying each one: a coriander-speckled *bhuna gosht*, the skewered charred-orange nuggets of the *kadhai*, a creamy yellow *korma*, a bowl of *sag*, the *poori*, the *raita*, a mountain of saffron rice and the *nan* bread, its blistered length overflowing the plate like a doll's duvet.

"Would you like me to serve, sir?"

"No, that's fine..." I began.

"Oh, would you? How kind," said Daphne, catching my eye and smiling mischievously. She was playing me, that's what she was doing. I knew it, and she knew I knew it. She never normally let the waiter serve. Far too impatient for that. She liked to heap her plate herself and tuck in. This time she made do with another *popadum*.

What *had* she been up to, I wondered?

Finally, the food served, our waiter retreated behind the curtain.

"Well?" I began again.

"I'm doing something about it," she replied. "About Elliot. I've decided I'm not going to take it, Cully." She stirred the *bhuna gosht* with her fork and started removing the chilies, just as she always does.

"You're seeing a lawyer."

She looked at me as if I was mad. "A lawyer? Of course I'm not seeing a lawyer. Not yet, at any rate."

"Then you're having an affair yourself? You've taken a lover!" If Daphne could tease me, then so could I tease her. But I kept a straight face.

"I certainly am not having an… affair," she replied, whispering the last word, realising where she was, and then, the next moment, saw the trap. "Oh Cully… you brute. Here, take these chilies, damn you!" and dumped the forkful she'd gathered onto my plate.

"So. Tell me. Why am I going to hate you…?"

"…think less of me is what I said, Cully."

"Anyway…" I picked up a wedge of lime and squeezed it over the *bhuna gosht* to douse the extra heat from Daphne's chilies.

"I've hired a detective."

"A private eye kind of detective?"

"Is there another kind?"

I put down the lime and wiped my fingers. "Well, I don't know what to say. I'm astonished. I just…"

"There you are! I said you'd be shocked."

"I'm not shocked. I'm… I guess I'm… It's just I've never really known anyone who hired a private eye before." I laughed. "I guess that's what it is. It's like the movies. So tell me, what's he like?"

"Well, he's young. Late thirties, early forties, that kind of thing. And kinda cute," she began. "Neat little office downtown. Quite like a lawyer's actually – all veneer panelling and fitted carpet and air-conditioning and rainforest-friendly furniture. That kind of thing. Really upbeat, you know? And *nothing* like the movies. I even felt uncomfortable when I lit up. Like he might not like it. But anyway, what the hell…"

"So where d'you find him? Who told you about him? Tell me."

"Where d'you think I found him? Yellow Pages. It was like phoning a plumber. I mean, I could hardly call up a chum and say, 'Hey, you don't happen to know a good private detective I could hire, do you?'"

I'd started helping myself to some rice and had fallen silent. Daphne tore off some *nan* and began rolling it in her fingers. I knew she was looking at me.

"You don't approve, do you? I can see it," she said, popping the bullet of bread into her mouth.

"No, of course I don't. I mean, yes… I mean, it's not like that at all. It's not for me to say, one way or the other. It's just a surprise, that's all. Rather exciting actually."

"Makes it real, too, doesn't it?"

"Yes, I guess. And sad. If Elliot's really…"

We sat in silence for a beat or two.

Daphne broke it: "I just had to do something, Cully. I have to know."

"I understand. Of course I do. So what happens now? What's he going to do, this private eye?"

"Well, I gave him all the particulars. A photo of Elliot, our address in town, where he works, his car registration – the lot."

"And when does he start?"

"Right away, I guess. He's on the case. As of this morning. It's the reason I'm here in town. Told me he'd have an initial report with me in a couple of weeks, and every week from then on until he has something. Or I instruct him otherwise. Simple as that."

"And what are you going to do if he does find something to report?"

"Lord, Cully, maybe there's nothing to tell. Nothing to find out. Maybe it's all in my head."

"And if it isn't? You sounded pretty certain at Netherlands."

"Oh, Cully, I don't know. I mean, if there is something… If he is… I don't know, I'd just be so… hurt."

And then she seemed to harden for a moment, went nickel-eyed. Looked past me as though she were imagining the scene.

"And angry, I guess. Real, real angry," she whispered, bitterly.

"And? What would you do about it?"

She took a deep breath, sighed. And I could see the eyes mist and the hardness pass.

"Oh, Cully, don't ask," she said, softly, stabbing a nugget of *khadai*. "I don't know… I really don't."

Zdenka's Kitchen

That Monday, late afternoon, having spent longer at Netherlands than I'd intended, I arrived back in the city. Almost the moment I slipped the deadbolt on my door, the phone began to ring. As I struggled to pull my key from the lock I was in two minds – hurry to catch the call before the fourth ring, or leave the Ansaphone to do its job. I decided to take it, failed by a split second and heard the click as I lifted the phone from its cradle.

"Hello, Cully Mortimer here…"

"*Hello, this is Cully Mortimer…*", the message tape began to roll.

"Hi Cully, you got an echo or…?" It was Sanchez at the *Times*, sounding a long way off. Sanchez was the paper's chief copy-sub who handled my fifteen hundred. We weren't exactly friends, but we'd known each other a good long time, got along in a work kind of way, if you know what I mean.

"*I'm afraid there's no one here to take your call right now…*"

"It's the damn machine…" I replied, stabbing one button after another in an attempt to override the message. "And I never know which button…"

"Okay, okay…"

"*…But if you leave your name and number, I'll get straight back…*"

"Yeah, yeah, yeah…" said Sanchez on the other end of the line.

Finally, as the message ended, I pressed the right button. "Sanchez? You still there?"

"Where else?" His voice was clearer now.

"So how's Copy? Any problems?" I couldn't see that there should be. My piece on Food in Art was out. Published. Done. Lining litter trays by now. After getting back from the Met the previous Thursday I'd sat down at my keyboard and the fingers had flown over the keys. Wrote itself. Wrapped and tight by tea-time. E-mailed over before my dinner at Small Potatoes, the new Capaldi joint on West 17th. I'd read it through at Netherlands and Sanchez hadn't cut a word, even though it was a hundred over.

"No problems, Cully. Just calling to say you have yourself a fan. Same caller. Jammed the switchboard since first thing. Finally they put her through to me. Sounds a honey. You old guys sure know how to turn it on when you want," and he started to chuckle at the end of the line.

"Any names, Sanchez, or you want me to guess? And let's have less of the old, kiddo." Sanchez is all of three years younger than me. And if you're thinking Hispanic, think again. Sanchez is an Inuit. A damned Eskimo, as I like to remind him, albeit with a Masters from NYU.

"Just one word, you old coot you."

"Which was?"

"Well, I sure don't know what she had in mind, but she said just to tell you 'Beaver'," which was followed by another of his rolling, chesty chuckles.

I dialed the number Sanchez gave me the moment he hung up. A New Jersey code. My apartment door was still open, the key in the lock, and my weekend case in the hallway where I'd dropped it. They could wait. Somewhere across the Hudson the line connected and another answering machine took up the refrain. A woman's voice this time. Didn't anyone pick up a phone these days?

"Hi there. We can't answer just now, so please leave a message…"

It was short and precise, gave nothing away. But so far as I could recall, it wasn't the voice I remembered. Close, but not hers. Older, no doubt about it, a little raggedy at the edges. Had I dialed the right number?

"Hello, ah, this is… this is Cully Mortimer calling," I began, suddenly unsure of myself. "This is a message for…" Who? Beaver? I couldn't even remember her name. I was starting to stumble: "Ah, you may remember we met at… we met at the Met." The repetition sounded odd, and I was now getting badly flustered. "I… I got your message, from the paper and…"

Mercifully, there was a click and a crackle and the line came alive.

"You wrote about me!" Somewhere in New Jersey a voice squealed with delight. It was her. No question this time. She'd heard my name and snatched up the phone. "You wrote about me. In the newspaper! The *Times*. You're Cully Mortimer. The Cully Mortimer Column. Cully. I should have known. I knew I knew the name from someplace. It just never connected, you know? Jesus, I couldn't believe it when I read it!"

All at once I was grinning like a poor, lost lunatic. "You inspired me," I managed.

"But you didn't say. I had no idea. You didn't tell me who you were. What you did!"

"And neither did you."

There was a moment's pause. "Well, hey, I guess not. We just…"

"So who *am* I talking to? It seems unfair you should know my name, and all I have is…"

"Roo," she replied. "I told you, remember? Short for Carew. Beatty Carew."

"Of course, of course. So, Beatty… Roo, did you like the piece?"

"Like it? Like it? I thought it was great. Great! Just… great. God, I mean, I know you won't believe it, but I read you absolutely every week. You're like my favorite piece. You know a lot of things. I couldn't believe it when I saw it. I mean, I know there were no names or anything, but it was me, right?"

"It was you." Like I said, I'd written about a companion, noted her comments. But there were no names, just the artists, the food, texture and taste.

"Yeah, yeah. I thought so. I just knew it. Wow!"

"You sound…" I couldn't help myself; I began to laugh.

"Hey, no one's ever written about me before. I kinda feel… I don't know… special, I guess. Does that make sense?"

"Of course, it does. Of course. But, you know, don't get too excited. If I'd been writing for an English newspaper, you'd be wrapped around fish and chips by now."

"Yuk," she said with distaste, though something in that single sound made me suspect she didn't get the reference.

"We must…" I began, sensing we had reached the end of something. "We should maybe do it again some time?" I was casting about for the right words. For the chance to see her again. But gently, needing to know how she might feel about it. A man my age. I needn't have worried.

"Gee, you mean it? I'd like that."

Instant gratification. A great, blood-pummelling cascade of pleasure.

"Well let's see, now," I continued, as though leafing through a packed diary. Which I wasn't. "Why don't I take you to lunch?"

"That would be… well, hey, that would be a real treat. Do it properly this time."

"So what do you like to eat?" And then I added, daringly for me: "Apart from…"

There was a moment's silence and then a burst of laughter in my ear as she remembered the Snyders, as I'd meant her to.

"Don't say that, don't you dare remind me… I was *sooooo* embarrassed! Thank the Lord you didn't write about *that*."

"Well?"

For a moment or two there was silence from her end of the line, and then, "Tell you what. Why don't I take you somewhere? Some place you've never been before. I want to inspire you again."

"Oh…kay," I replied slowly, uncertain again, pushed off-balance. I wasn't altogether sure I liked the idea of someone I hardly knew taking control. It wasn't how these things worked. After all, I was the expert. I was Cully Mortimer. And it was me had done the asking out, not the other way round. But even then, back in those first days, there was no denying her. Even though I didn't know it then. "Okay," I said again, "Tell me where and when."

"You'll never find it. I'll pick you up. Where do you live?"

Another intrusion. Was she always so direct? I began to feel distinctly uncomfortable, unwilling to provide someone I'd only just met with such personal information. But, of course, I told her.

"Wednesday? Round twelve? Is that too soon? I should be back by then."

"Back?"

"I'm at home. It's my Mom's birthday." Which explained the out-of-town number, and the strange but somehow familiar voice on the answering machine.

"We can always make it another time if you'd prefer? No need to come rushing back on my account."

"No, no. Wednesday's good. Really."

"Okay then."

"Alright. Wednesday. Twelve."

"That sounds… just dandy!"

≈

That Wednesday my new lunch companion was late. It was something I would become, if not altogether used to, then certainly resigned to. When Roo said twelve, there was usually no point saving my copy and switching off the word processor much before 12.30, with another fifteen minutes to clean my teeth, slip on a jacket and loafers, turn on the Ansaphone, and arrange the various locks and bolts that secured my apartment.

By the time I reached the lobby, or the restaurant, or the street corner, or the subway stop – wherever it was we'd arranged to meet – I was usually ahead of her by five or ten minutes, a span of time I could adequately fill without becoming agitated.

But I wasn't to know that the first time we lunched.

I guess you could say I'm a fastidious sort of fellow. I feel comfortable with order and routine. I dress conservatively but comfortably. I eat and drink moderately, though often and usually well, and I rarely step outside the set perimeters of my life. It's always been the same. No surprises for me. And it's the same when it comes to time. There is always a schedule, a plan; call it simply habit. A comforting instinct.

Take my day, for example. I rise at the same time each morning without need for alarm calls, and follow the same ritual of daily preparation with unerring though never particularly deliberate exactness. It just seems to work that way. Between seven and seven-forty-five, I wake, I bath or shower depending on my mood, I clean my teeth, I shave, I trim my moustache if it needs it, I dress, and then I drink a single cup of English Breakfast tea. At eight-thirty or thereabouts, I leave my building, walk to the store at the corner for my papers, return, read for an hour, then start work.

My work. There's even a comforting order to that too. Each week, like I said, I produce my standard fifteen hundred for the Times, begun on a Thursday morning, completed by Friday afternoon latest, and published in the 'Metro' section Sundays. In addition, I can reckon on a further seven-fifty to twelve hundred words every other week whenever the boys at the daily decide they need a filler – a book or restaurant review maybe, or an op-ed piece, or something general for their 'Living' section. If I'm writing a book myself – never more than sixty thousand words – I usually start in Spring and finish by late August when I take a month's vacation, alternating each year between the Caribbean and Europe. Last year, for reasons I'll come to later, it was South Africa.

Back home, between Monday and Friday, on 'Metro' section expenses, I average five lunches and four dinners out. With always enough spare for a companion. And always, whenever possible, a woman. So much more fun than men, I always think. So subtle, so layered, so... piercing. So much more rewarding, too. They suit a table, you see; they understand it. They... recognize it. Like me, it stirs something in them and they respond. If you don't believe me, next time you see a woman take her seat at a restaurant table listen out for that barely audible sigh of anticipated pleasure, that soft catch of breath as she draws her chair in, looks around, settles. Watch how she smooths the linen, touches her glass, minutely adjusts the cutlery. Recognition. Expectation. Contentment. And it's not just the prospect of good food, or the fact that she hasn't had to cook it, and won't have to clear up afterwards. For a woman there's so much more to a table than what appears on the plate. In my experience, men consume but women savor. That's the difference, I guess. And that's what I like.

It's because I go out so much weekdays and because I hate to cook that I rarely eat at home. Consequently, there's never much food in my kitchen: the tin of English Breakfast Tea from Fortnum & Mason in London, a tall Kilner jar of Muesli specially prepared for me by a Swiss chef of my acquaintance, and the daily pint of milk bought with my morning papers. (Full-cream – if I wanted semi-skimmed I'd expect to pay less). There'll also be a pack or two of Cream Milanos in the refrigerator, and always a jar of Déchine's *foie gras d'oie*, some Melba toasts, and a couple of half bottles of Meursault for when I feel like spoiling myself. And that's about it, save the small bottle of magnesium tricylicate I keep in the rack beside the Meursault for settling acid (an essential in my line of work) and, in another small compartment, my Floris Seringa Spray – so invigorating taken direct from the refrigerator. And with every weekend – sometimes long, sometimes short – usually spent out of the city, on business or visiting with friends, there's really never much call to stock up. A real Mother Hubbard, me.

As for my homes, the handful of single-bedroom apartments I've occupied since my arrival in New York City, they, too, follow a pattern. The only thing that changes is the address. If I was blind I could find my way round without stumbling or knocking anything over. The lay-out is always the same: my desk by a window, my books neatly shelved along one wall, two club armchairs picked up from the bar of the old Pierrepoint on Lexington and 68th before they knocked it down, a low coffee table, a squashy old sofa, houseplants by my desk, fresh-cut flowers strategically placed, a portable TV I can carry into the bedroom, and a matt black midi hi-fi amongst the books, with my collection of classic CDs and tapes close by. On the walls where there's no bookcase or window, I hang the half-dozen Arcimboldo prints I secured for a song on a trip to Florence one time, and on the floor there's a scattering of fringed Kilim rugs, and my marvelous silk Zeigler I bought for myself on my fiftieth birthday the last time I was in Paris. Wherever I moved, the contents of my home and their positioning remained the same.

Anyhow. Back to Roo. Back to Miss Carew. A single girl certainly. For I'd seen no ring at the Met.

Like I said, that first date of ours I was nervously ready by eleven-forty-five, and at noon expected Carlo to call up any moment announcing her arrival in the lobby.

But the call didn't come.

Twenty minutes later, I decided to wait downstairs, stopping by the desk to pass the time with Carlo. He's a museum piece, Carlo, one of those old 'dese-dem-dose' kinda guys from out on the Heights who sound like they wear ear-plugs in their nostrils. It's like another language. That Wednesday he'd just returned from a weekend trip to Atlantic City, which he'd won on a Lotto scratch card, and he was full of the place.

"So dis hooker gets inner da elevator, see, and who should be standin' der but da same guy who hit on her earlier near da craps table. Only dis time he's tuh-gedder widder wife. Da moment he sees her he just freezes, you know? But dis hooker, she dudden say nuttin' 'til dey're hitting da mezzanine, when she turns to him, nods to da wife and says, 'See what you gets for a twenny'."

And that was the moment Roo finally arrived, closer to one than twelve, while Carlo and I laughed together at his wearying tale, pulling into the sidewalk, her long legs straddling a massive black motorbike, tiptoes on the tarmac balancing the weighty machine, gloved hands twisting the throttle to make the engine roar. Then, just as she was about to switch off and dismount, she spotted me in the lobby and waved me out.

When he realized this was my lunch date I remember Carlo giving me a look that seemed to say, 'Hey, Mr. Mortimer, not bad, not bad…', as I cut short our chat and headed for the doors. I remember it made me feel good. Come to think of it, it always made me feel good when people saw us together. Roo and I. Just the two of us. It always felt… good.

"Am I late? You been waiting long?" she asked gaily over the throttling of the engine between her legs, her face lightly tanned and country-fresh, loose wisps of hair from her ponytail playing around her cheek.

"No, no, just…"

"So what are you waiting for? Here," she said, squirming forward on the saddle, "hop on. Let's go."

"Shouldn't I have a helmet or something?" I asked cautiously, still standing on the sidewalk.

"Not unless you're wearing a rug! Which, by the look of you, you're not." And she laughed. "No offence intended."

"And none taken," I replied.

But still I held back. From where I stood the bike looked enormous. Also, in all my life, I'd never ridden on a motorcycle. It looked the size of a horse, and I'd never ridden one of those either. Maybe we could leave it and take a cab, I thought.

"Maybe we should leave the bike here and take…"

"Traffic's lousy. The whole East Side. We'd never make it. Come on. Get your butt up here, Mr. Cully Mortimer."

I looked at the bike and tried to work out how best to get on. I knew if I stepped down off the sidewalk, I'd never manage it, but it was too far away from the kerb to reach it from where I stood.

"You ever been on a bike?" she asked, cocking her head to one side and putting on a knowing smile.

"Of course, it's just… it's just bigger than I'm used to, I guess."

"The biggest," she replied, twisting the throttle to make the point, then steered it closer to the sidewalk. "So get yourself up here. We're late."

I don't know how, but with the bike closer I somehow managed to swing my leg over and scramble up onto the saddle, tipping the bike dangerously as I did so. Immediately, I could feel the throb of the engine in my buttocks and down my thighs, its heat and the smell of oil and gas rising around me. It was like sitting on an oven in an earthquake. I was terrified I'd touch something hot and get burnt, or smear grease on my clothes. I was also acutely aware that Carlo was sure to be watching, so I tried to look comfortable, practiced. Which was why I put out a foot to help her keep balance as she backed the bike away from the kerb.

"No, no, put it there," she said, pointing somewhere below and behind me.

Without thinking, I tried to look where she was pointing, and felt the bike sway even more.

"Whoah, there… easy, easy," she warned, countering the sway. "There, you got it. And now just wrap your arms round me. There, that's it. Okay, hold tight…" And with a seismic snort of power that seemed to start in my anus and play my spine like a xylophone, the bike leapt forward with an incredible energy, weaved past a parked car like a current of water streaming past a boulder and shot off downtown.

It was the most terrifying, and the most exhilarating experience I can ever remember my entire life.

When the bike finally slowed and I opened my eyes, one cheek stinging sweetly from the slipstream lash of her ponytail, the other abraded by the leather jacket she was wearing, the first thing I saw was a pair of Hassidim in black homburgs, curling payots and long frock coats, watching with doleful, disapproving eyes as Roo negotiated the bike across the sidewalk and into an alleyway lined with overflowing bins and dirty, wired windows. Half way down, gently gunning the engine and rolling the bike forward, she turned into a small courtyard of worn cobbles where she killed the engine and held the bike steady for me to clamber off. Legs trembling from the journey, face smarting, senses still warmed by the close and intimate spoon-like locking of our bodies on the bike, I looked around me while Roo rocked the big black machine onto its stand.

"Here we are, safe and sound," she said, pulling off her gloves. "Told you the bike would be quicker than a cab," and taking my arm she led me across the courtyard to an open door set between two steamy windows. On one of these, painted in an arc of peeled gold lettering and black shadowing, was the word 'Zdenka's', and on the other window, similarly arched, the word 'Kitchen'.

With the benefit of hindsight I might have known Roo would surprise me. She always did, always caught me unawares. And that first date was no exception. Though I never believed it, doubted it from the moment I put down the phone and wondered at a girl imagining she could take me, Cully Mortimer, somewhere in this city where I hadn't already been, or didn't know about… well, she went and did just that. She really had brought me somewhere I'd never heard of. Zdenka's Kitchen? It rang about as many bells as… as a dead battery. Maybe if I'd kept my eyes open on the journey I might have had some clearer idea of where my new acquaintance had brought me. But I hadn't, and I didn't.

Despite my familiarity with a city I have lived and worked in for nearly twenty years, not only had I never heard of Zdenka's Kitchen, I never would have found it either, way down on the East Side judging by the frock-coated, ringleted orthodoxy of the pedestrians, somewhere off the bottom end of Second Avenue in some half-forgotten, brick-cobbled corner of Little Ukraine.

Stepping through the door, my sense of dislocation, of separation from the world I knew, the city I lived in, was even greater. Zdenka's, I decided, was well-named – no more nor less than the kind of ghetto-style soup kitchen I'd expect to find in the back streets of Prague or Kraków, or any big city in the old eastern bloc. The interior was dark and shadowy, four rooms so far as I could make out, each of them packed with formica-top tables spread with paper squares, and crowded with hunched backs. There didn't look to be a free seat in the house. Either the food was cheap, or it was very good. Maybe both.

Pushing ahead between tables and chairs, the room filled with a kettledrum scrape of cutlery on china and the vibrato hum of muffled talk, Roo led me to a glass display counter running the length of the far wall. Squeezed wherever space allowed behind its sweating panels of glass were jars of fat, knobbled gherkins in watery green brine, tubs of liver paté, glistening cakes of *pacha*, baskets of rye bread, bowls of tangled coleslaw and creamy horseradish, slabs of plump pink salmon, cuts of peppered pastrami, fat-marbled corned beef, salted beef, cold roasts and glistening breasts of turkey – each container, each tray, each board appropriately equipped with ice-cream scoops, spoons, ladles, or knives depending on the consistency and requirements of the food to be served. From a purely professional view, it looked like every Health Department nightmare rolled into one.

Here, wedged between counter and wall and working with a

concentrated energy and practiced efficiency, was a large, white-aproned woman in her late fifties, hair caught up and bound in a scarf, chubby round face red with effort, hands and arms as pink and beefy as a butcher's. For someone her size she managed uncannily well in the limited space available. With what looked like an octave span of fingers she hefted a pile of dirty plates off the glass counter, deposited them with a clatter on the top shelf of a dumb waiter, removed a tray of fresh orders from the bottom shelf, shouted new orders into a small intercom, tugged on the rope (the darned thing wasn't even electric), then turned to supervise the distribution of the steaming food to a line of hovering waiters – old, thin men in stained white jackets who snatched up the plates with unlikely speed, balanced them skillfully on scrawny arms, and scurried away with them. And all this in the time it took us to reach the counter.

In the general clamor that filled the place it was difficult to tell what she was saying, or asking for, or even if she was speaking English. But when she saw us, or rather Roo, she stopped what she was doing, lunged across the counter and clasped Roo's face in her strong red hands, too far away to kiss but close enough for cheek-squeezing contact.

"You, you," she cried, eyes sparkling like little black berries. "Where you been? What you been doing? It's so long you been here."

"Babush, Babush. I'm fine. I'm fine. It's good to see you, too. You're looking good as ever, you look so well."

Roo, her mouth badly pushed out of shape by Babush's clasping hands, had trouble getting the words out, but finally the older lady's grip loosened enough for her to turn and introduce me.

"Here, Babush, meet my friend, Cully. Mr. Cully Mortimer. He wrote about me. He is a famous writer in the newspapers. He writes about food, so I brought him to the very best place for food in the whole of New York City. He will write about you, too. About Zdenka's." And then, wagging her finger at the old lady: "But only if the food is good."

At which Babush gave a short hoot of a laugh, as though there should be any question about it, as if she cared a *knoedel* whether I wrote something or not. And why should she? Zdenka's, as I was to discover from Roo, had been going strong since before the Depression – started by this lady's grandmother, continued by her mother, and now supervised by her. And it had never, so far as I could recall, received any mention whatsoever in the Press, yet still it packed them in.

Turning to me, Babush smiled politely and reached across the counter to give the tips of my fingers a brief, damp shake, before fixing her eyes firmly back on Roo.

It felt strange to me, this unfamiliar reversal. Normally I would be the one greeted, the object of effusion, but here I was being sidelined, not sure what to do with myself, testing my weight from one still trembling leg to the other, unrecognized, not knowing what to do with my hands, waiting to be seated. It made me feel a little awkward.

And then the dumb waiter re-appeared, clattering to a halt and stacked with steaming plates. There was a squawk from the intercom, and with an answering shout of impatience over her shoulder the lady, Babush, waved over one of the waiters and instructed him in what sounded like Yiddish to show us to a table. And then, for our benefit, in English: "The best," she added, nodding to us, "find them the best. In the back room. Quick, before it go." And with a reluctant smile, she shooed us away from the counter.

≈

It was there, at Zdenka's Kitchen, a Wednesday lunchtime, first week in July, away from the steam and the heat and the hubbub of the main room, that Roo and I first really got to know one another. At the Met we'd talked of the paintings, the artists, the food – when we talked at all. And on the phone we had done little more than arrange this meeting. But at our corner table in Zdenka's windowless back room, we set about establishing our credentials, delivering our *resumés* over a diamond of dimpled paper tablecloth, a wedge of napkins, and a bowl of dwarf gherkins as warty as a toad's back.

First off, I guess, we fenced, the two of us, initially unsure of ourselves in this hastily arranged, impromptu coming together. Where to begin exactly, how to continue? I seem to remember, as we got ourselves comfortable at the table, that I was the one who started things off.

How was the weekend in the country, I asked?

Great, she replied. It had been her mother's birthday and they'd driven down the coast to some quayside restaurant on Raritan Bay where they'd eaten a whole bucketful of steamers.

"They always look so rude," I said, "those slimy tongues sticking out of the shells."

"I thought they were tails," she said.

And we laughed, and gradually began to settle into each other.

"So tell me about yourself, Miss Beatty Carew," I continued. "Tell me about my friend at the Met."

And that was what she did. As the same waiter who had shown us to our table served the first of many dishes that would come unordered, my companion introduced herself, filled in the background, told me how she was from somewhere called Bertram, forty miles south of New Brunswick, how her father had died seven years earlier – a heart attack in his office; he'd been the town's only accountant – and how her mother, a licensed book-keeper, lived on alone in the family home, keeping the accounts of a dozen small businesses that had refused to move to other firms when her father died. She made it sound warm and homely and comfortingly average.

"She can count a column of figures faster than I can work it on a calculator," said Roo with a proud delight. "You wouldn't believe how fast she does it. She puts her finger on the first line, and then moves it down the page like an express train, just her lips counting. It's amazing. Cents and all. You should see it."

"And she's never remarried?"

Roo shook her head. "Dad was a hard act to follow, I guess." And then, sadly: "They were real tight."

"Brothers? Sisters?"

Again Roo shook her head. Like me, she was an only child.

"Wouldn't I have loved an elder brother though; wouldn't I just have loved it! But there's just the two of us. And it's great, you know. We get on real well. She's like my best friend. Sometimes she'll come into town, but most of the time I go see her."

"So what brought you to the city?"

"Good grades mostly. And ambition. After college I got a place at grad school. Wharton."

"Wharton? *The* Wharton?"

"The same," she replied evenly, giving me a kind of challenging *Yeah? So?* look. But it came with a smile attached. "*The* Wharton. That's right. To study Economics."

Economics! She had to be kidding. Economics? Roo? Even knowing about her parents, her background, I couldn't for the life of me think of anything more extraordinary, nor more unlikely. Fine Art maybe, Literature, a fashion course, modeling or acting – anything along those lines. But never Economics. It couldn't be, surely? And it must have shown on my face.

"I knew you wouldn't believe me, no one ever does," she laughed, biting delicately through one of the gherkins, leaving, I noticed, the marks of her teeth in its green, translucent flesh. "But it's true. Swear to God." And then: "Just because He gave me a great body, you know, doesn't mean I got short-changed in the brains department."

I remember clear as day how that directness, the reference to her body, flustered me.

"No, of course not. I'm sorry, I didn't mean…"

"Go on. I'll prove it. Ask me anything. How about Keynsian monetary reform? Or maybe the theory of issue? Or the monopoly of credit? Or placement calculus? Or maybe you'd like to hear about Thorstein Veblen's Scarcity Theory Of Value? Name it! Ask me. I did it all. And," she added, lowering her voice, leaning forward, "it's not so boring as people think. In fact, it's about the best thing I ever did. Because if you've got a shred of imagination it doesn't take long to learn how to work the figures any way you want. Which is what an accountant will tell you, if he's honest. Deception. That's what it's all about. Sleight of hand."

"So you're an accountant? A dealer on Wall Street."

"Well, maybe I would have been," she replied, "if I hadn't flunked out. Four years seemed an awful long time back then, and the truth is… well, I guess I got… bored."

"So what is it you do now?" I asked, thinking of the monstrous Italian motorbike parked in the courtyard outside, seeing the gold Ebel hang loose and heavy from her wrist, noting the casual but expensive clothes, and remembering that midweek afternoon at the Met, and weekdays in the country. Clearly this was a woman not bound by the normal hours of business. Or if she was, she badly abused them.

"I find people apartments," said Roo, after a brief pause, "and office space when I can." Direct, out of the blue, as though she had just lighted on the idea, the pleasant, professional, independent sound of it, and she licked her lips, took another bite of the gherkin. "So I guess you'd call me a realtor. Residential mainly, but the big bucks are commercial, whenever I can get it. And I work for myself. I don't do agency."

And then, as though suddenly keen to hear my story: "But what about you? Cully Mortimer. The man with the very best job in the whole wide world. Tell me about you. Go on. Make me real jealous."

And so it came to be my turn, telling her about growing up in Wilmington, starting work as an office junior at the *Courier*; how I began by writing the Butterball column whenever the resident columnist was too drunk to complete his copy; how I'd gotten my first byline and how, in time, I'd moved to the *Globe* in Boston, before finangling my way onto the *Times*.

And as I told her my story, I was aware that she listened. I mean, really listened, intently, as though what I had to say about my life was the most fascinating, the most spellbinding story she'd ever heard. Which made me chatter like a sparrow, made me want to never stop talking, wanting her to know every detail as though somehow it would draw us closer, this intimate sharing of the past.

And made me brave, too.

I remember at some point, with a certain flirting bravado, asking her to undo the ponytail she played through her fingers while she listened to my stories. And, with a coy smile, she did just that, slipping the band onto her wrist and shaking out the hair with a *there, how's that?* sort of look, as though only too happy to do whatever I wanted.

I tell you, it was… the whole thing was… intoxicating. You had to be there, I guess. Just the best lunch ever. Eating some of the finest Kosher food I'd ever tasted – plate after glorious plate of it – in the very best of company. And there wasn't even wine to loosen my tongue, just a jug of water cold as crushed icicles and the wide-eyed attention of my lunch companion.

"So how d'you get to know all this stuff about food anyway?" asked Roo. "What's good, what's bad? The mechanics?"

"I guess you could say it was greed started me off," I told her. "When I was a kid I was, well, I was fat. No other word for it, I guess. I see fat kids today and I think back to me when I was their age. The fat one. Had a real big appetite. But I didn't eat just anything. I was always real picky."

"Your Mom a good cook?"

"She wasn't bad, but my Aunt Jem was better."

"Aunt Jem?"

"Well, not a real aunt. Not in the true sense. She was a widow, lived on the same street, two doors up. I guess today you'd call her a child-care provider, but what she really did was cook. She ran a small catering business from home, supplying local stores with preserves and cookies, cakes, pastries, pies – that sort of thing. She cooked the best blueberry tart I ever tasted. And that's a professional opinion – no bias. She was a natural, and had a real good reputation round town. Nothing fancy, nothing big deal. Nothing she couldn't handle from home, by herself. Just regular orders, that kind of thing. And when school was out, I'd go to her place until my mother picked me up after work. Or during vacation I'd maybe spend the day there. She never had children of her own and I guess I filled a gap. I think my parents paid her, I don't know."

"What did your Mom do?"

"She was a nurse at the local hospital. Used to write poetry."

"And your Dad?"

"Du Pont. Traveling salesman; drove one of those big old Buicks with what I always called 'stagecoach' sides…"

"A 'woody'? He drove a 'woody'?"

"The same."

"Hey, my Dad too. Small world."

"So anyway, every day, I'd get back from school and you could smell Aunt Jem's cooking from the sidewalk, down the street. I'd sit there on a high stool in her kitchen, watch her bustle to and fro, tell her how my day had been, and she'd tell me all the things she'd been doing, whatever it was she was making that day: canapés for some country club do, birthday cakes or wedding cakes for some family in the neighborhood, and all these pasta sauces for the Deli downtown. Let me taste, too, but only on condition I told her what I thought. Too sweet? Too spicy? Too much salt? Too little? Which I guess is how I got to learn about food, what went well together and what didn't. All by dipping here and there, that kind of thing. I'd finger-lick something from a bowl and she'd want me to tell her what was in it. How she'd made it. Was that sugar I could taste, or was it vanilla? Nutmeg or cinnamon? And if I got a whiff of oranges, well probably that was just the ground coriander she'd used. For instance, did you know that…"

Across the table Roo sat back and clapped her hands. "Cully," she laughed, "I do believe you're writing yourself another story. In fact, I know you are. You got like this at the Met, remember? And then, like you were talking, that's how you wrote it, standing in front of that painting and counting the fish. I know I'm going to read this. I just know it."

"Heck, I think you may be right. I'm babbling, getting carried away. Could have been at my keyboard. How rude. I'm so sorry."

And laughing again, my new friend Beatty Carew leaned across the table and squeezed my hand. "What rude? I love it. Love it. Don't stop. Jeez, I could sit here all day listening to you."

And so it went, that first real date of ours at Zdenka's. Distant memories, fond reminiscences, a catalogue of life's little twists and turns. On and on, I chattered. And all the while she listened. If only she'd looked away, looked bored, I'd have been able to stop, draw breath. But she didn't. She just looked, I don't know... entranced. No other word for it. Spellbound. Concentrating on me, my story. Never took those wide green eyes off of me. And so I just rattled on, back there in Wilmington, Boston, wherever, all those years reduced to the span of a single lunch.

And then: "How come you're not married? I'm right, aren't I? You're not married?"

"Right."

"So, why d'you never marry, good-looking guy like you? Here, you got cream on your moustache."

"There were times..." I said, as she reached forward with a napkin and brushed away whatever it was.

"I bet. So tell me..."

And so I began again.

And though I didn't know it then, didn't recognize it, would have laughed at the very idea, I know now, looking back, that right then, at Zdenka's, at that corner table in the back room, its cream painted walls coated in a silvery skin of condensation, that was the moment I began to lose my way, began to fall under her spell.

Like a stone dropped into a deep, deep pool.

≈

It was afterwards – after our lunch was over, after a tearful farewell from Babush and her shocked refusal to take any money – while I waited in the doorway for Roo to start and turn the bike in the narrow courtyard, that I felt a hand grasp my arm, and a face come close to my ear.

It was the old lady again. I was expecting her to say something about Roo. To take care of her, or some such. Some final message to pass on. But I was wrong.

"Don' write," she whispered. "Plis not to write."

The bike was turned, roared once and settled to a hum. Roo, with her back to me, her hair in a ponytail again, was pulling on gloves.

"Of course not," I replied, astonished by the entreaty. "I would love to, but not if you don't want me to."

And she nodded, thanked me, pushed me gently towards Roo, and, wiping her hands on her apron, watched us leave her cobbled yard.

Bonnebouche

"I love you, Cully, that's all. Have done right from the start."

"Oh, Casey…"

"No, I know, I know. You don't have to say anything. It's alright. Just trying to get it all straight in my head is all." She sniffed, caught her breath, looked at me bravely. "Least, I think I am. Trying to."

We were sitting at a table in Bonnebouche, Casey's own restaurant, a semi-basement bistro on a corner of West 50th. It was a Tuesday afternoon, late July, a few weeks before my vacation.

At least she'd stopped crying.

With long pale fingers, scored along their sides with deep dark wrinkles that looked like old knife cuts, and topped with short clipped nails, she wiped at her reddened eyes. She wore no make-up (come to think of it, she never wears make-up), and her hair, always cut short, a shiny mix of mace and nutmeg, stood up off her head as though blown that way by the heat rising from the kitchen stoves. In fact, it was Casey herself who did this, always pushing her fingers through her hair whenever she was stressed or busy or rattled. Or, in this case, close to despairing.

That afternoon Bonnebouche was quiet, just the two of us there. The kitchen behind the swing doors was empty, the scarlet undercloths and white crochet tops that covered each table had long since been snatched away by the busboys, and sidling about with the cooling lunchtime aromas of grilled meat, garlic and *fines herbes* was the slight but still sharp scent of disinfectant. In another hour the kitchen staff would return from wherever it was they sloped off to in the two hours between shifts, pans would rattle, voices would be raised, knives would chop on boards, fresh tablecloths would be snapped out like flags over the thirty or so tables that filled the room, and – showtime again.

"It's someone else, isn't it?"

"Casey, I…"

"Okay, okay. I shouldn't ask. It's just… It's just I thought…"

"I know, sweetheart. I know. I'm so very sorry."

She sniffed, wiped her nose with the sleeve of her smeared whites, and laughed miserably.

"Me, too!" she said. "Me, too," tipping the ash from her cigarette into a bakelite ashtray, the single word 'Byrrh' repeated around its rim. "And how!"

It was the first time I'd ever seen Casey smoke.

And the first time I'd ever seen her cry.

≈

Casey Webster and I had been lovers for all of four months, pretty much the lifespan of Bonnebouche. We'd been introduced at the opening by the PR lady Casey had retained to pull in the editorial she needed, editorial which I subsequently provided, in spades – the full fifteen hundred.

It had been an easy piece to write. For Bonnebouche is a minor masterpiece, and I'm not just saying that because of how I treated Casey. It really is. A small, rare jewel reached down a canopied outside stairway and along a passageway no wider than a spread of arms, its brick sides whitewashed up to the sidewalk railings, its glass doors and net-curtain casements allowing at least some sun to splash over the floors and tables a couple hours a day.

Inside, Bonnebouche is painted the traditional tobacco-toned *faux marbre*, its walls hung with sepia prints of old Paris, and fixed with those boldly colorful enamelled advertising plaques all chipped and spotted with rust (Gitanes, Pernod, Michelin – that sort of thing). It's a surprisingly large, high-ceilinged room for a basement, lit with brass *torchères* like smaller versions of Liberty's lamp, and solidly paved in honey-colored herringbone parquet. Maroon leather banquettes with tables for four line three of its walls, and a double set of tables for two – what the French call *coude à coude*, elbow to elbow – run down the center of the room, back to the zinc-topped bar with its tall Bentwood stools, and the portholed swing doors that lead to the kitchen.

You might think it sounds like just about every bistro you've ever been to in this town. Almost a cliché. But unlike all the others there is something very real about Bonnebouche, something authentic, something unmistakably genuine, as though the whole place, name and all, had been lifted lock, stock and barrel from some Parisian *quartier*. Which, of course, it had. But I'll get to that later.

You get some idea of this authenticity the moment you sit at the bar – a real old *comptoir* with a hammered zinc top which the original Parisian owners plastered with mortar and painted brown when the Nazis came looking for spare metal (if you look carefully you can actually see tiny spots of paint in the dimples). You get it, too, when you look at the list of house specials, the *plats du jour*, hand-painted on a long gilt-framed mirror that hangs behind the bar, the original chalky white lettering turned a creamy yellow from years of tobacco smoke.

It's classic stuff, that menu – the real McCoy – the thing that makes Bonnebouche the find it is. Take, for instance, Casey's *omelettes*, always neatly tubed, lightly browned, as piping hot inside as out but never overcooked (a difficult trick with *omelettes*), with a layered interior that is soft and golden, flavored with flakes of smoked cheese, or slivers of blood-red *lardons*, or shavings of black Perigord truffle, or simply sprinkled with *fines herbes*. Or her *boudins* which, of course, she prepares herself, always perfectly spiced with that lingering pepperiness on the tongue that is elsewhere either too sharp or not there at all. Or her *gigot à la crème d'ail*, or *petit salé aux lentilles*, her *quenelles*, her *pots au feu* and *choux farcis*, her home-preserved *confits*, *patés*, *gallantines*, *rillettes*, the *tartes* and *crèmes* and *mousses au chocolat* – all of them fabulously, unforgettably good.

And unadorned. There is never any artifice in her style, no reliance on design, presentation, or modish choice of ingredient. Just the goods, pure and straightforward, served on thick white china plates, with maybe a curl of green *frissée* to one side, her carafe wines (only French, that is all she carries) poured in to chunky Duralex tumblers – no fuss, no pettiness, and no sorry surprise with *l'addition*. No wonder Bonnebouche caught on so. It deserved to. A taste of real France at a price that made its competitors appear criminally exorbitant.

Which was what the two of us talked about our first meeting, Bonnebouche's opening night, our fondness for France and for Paris, for the simplicity and genius of the food, the Frenchman's love of the kitchen and his natural, instinctive understanding of texture and flavor and method. But it was a brief exchange, cocktail talk. Casey had other guests, other journalists like me, to meet and greet, other fish to fry. But before we parted we arranged to meet again. I promised I'd come have lunch sometime. She smiled a huge beaming smile, tipped her head to one side as though intrigued by the idea, told me that would be nice, and shook my hand. And that was that.

Two days later I was back. Alone. I'd not made a reservation, and was surprised to see Bonnebouche so full so soon (my piece had yet to be written). There were no tables free, the young *maître d'* explained and, failing to recognize me, showed me, with apologies, to a stool at the corner of the bar, the last remaining seat in the house. Without consulting a menu I ordered a *soupe à l'oignon,* the *steack frites*, and a *pichet* of Chiroubles. Chilled, light, and fruity, it's what the French call *ça se laisse boire* – a wine to be quaffed – and just the perfect chaperone for Casey's steak.

By the time I'd finished my lunch – the soup, the steak, a *crème caramel*, a simple but perfect *plateau de fromages* – I'd pretty well written the piece in my head, watching the other diners tuck in to their *daubes* and *omelettes* and *magrets*, the black-waistcoated and white-aproned staff – sharp-eyed and diligent – busying themselves amongst the tables like something out of a Dégas or a Renoir. There was a gratifying hum of well-fed chatter, and a satisfying procession of scraped-clean plates toted back to the kitchen where, I assumed, Casey was hard at work.

I left without seeing her, deliberately, but called later to congratulate her. She sounded pleased to hear from me, but pretended outrage that I'd sat at her bar, eaten the steak she'd cooked me, and not let her know I was there.

Which was when I suggested we meet for lunch, just the two of us, to make up for my bad behaviour.

And she agreed that lunch, on me, would be suitable penance, but explained that Mondays were the only day she could manage, the single day in the week when Bonnebouche opened only at night.

Would a Monday be okay?

A Monday would be fine.

≈

And that was how it began.

Those Mondays.

Spring into summer.

I'd pick her up at Bonnebouche where she spent the morning on her stock-take, maybe have a *café filtre* or sip a *crème de mûre* while she finished her chores, and then, together, we'd go off for lunch. Sometimes I'd tell her to dress smart and we'd whoop it up somewhere French and grand – Le Cercle, Domain, Phantôme, Reboux, Aux Biches Vertes; or take pot luck, experimenting with new places, searching out old favorites; upmarket, downmarket, wherever there was fine food to be found.

It was at the second of these lunches, less than a month after our first meeting, that she persuaded me to return with her to Bonnebouche for a final *café-calva*. Which was when friendship became affair, the mistake I made – for that is what it was – confusing admiration for attraction, companionship for longing. Feebly protesting, I joined in the physical roustabout, shrugging off clothes, grappling for a hold on a slippery banquette, knocking the table with my elbow and leg, rattling the green, gold-rimmed chunky coffee cups, spilling the pale young Calvados, and thinking all the time not so much of the sturdy, demanding young body that lay gradually revealed beneath me, but the likelihood of her staff returning before we had gathered ourselves together.

For Casey, such discovery would have meant nothing, a laugh perhaps, a jape. For me, it would have been oh… where to begin? Humiliation, embarrassment, a dreadful compromise. But the deed was done, that second Monday afternoon, thankfully without interruption, its subsequent repetition somewhat mitigated by the continuing pleasure of her company at the table. Because Casey was never anything less than a marvelous lunch companion, a knowledgeable and gifted chef who knew her ingredients and knew how to cook them honestly – in my opinion the hardest way of all. Indeed, that was the meat of the fifteen hundred words I wrote on Bonnebouche – the wonder of simple cooking, the satisfaction of it, its disingenuous difficulty to achieve.

Our first lunch together, at Phantôme, I got the lowdown, how Casey had learned to cook at home, wherever that home happened to be. For Casey's father, now retired and living somewhere in the Virginia countryside, had been a career diplomat, serving at various embassies and consulates in Europe. Madrid first, when Casey was ten, then Rome, Frankfurt, Zurich and finally, in her teens, Paris, where her father was first secretary.

It was here, in these various postings, that Casey learned to love, like me, the workings of a kitchen – its heat, its aromas, its stolen, fingered flavors. And learned, too, the secrets of each country's specialties – *esqueixada* and *cocido madrileno* in Spain; *stracotto* and *coniglio* in Italy; *klosse* and *knodl* in Germany; *rosti* and *Geschnetzeltes* in Switzerland. By the time a teenage Casey reached Paris she knew how to pickle salted cod and bone and stuff a pig's trotter, how to rescue curdled sauces and knead the necessary lightness into spicy dumplings, how to glaze fruit, burn cream and how, always, to cool her hands in iced water before working with pastry.

It was in Paris, she told me, that first Monday lunch of ours, the day after my piece on Bonnebouche appeared in the *Times*, that her interest in food really took off. Every day after school, she'd make for the embassy kitchens where a young *sous-chef*, who'd taken a shine to her, disguised her in whites and smuggled her in.

"He was the first man who ever kissed me," she confided, recalling with shy smiles the gentle progress of that first *affaire du coeur*. But it was a liaison destined not to last, neither in the steamy embassy kitchen nor beneath the shadowy plane trees of the Luxembourg gardens where the two of them sometimes strolled. Six days after her seventeenth birthday, her father suffered a minor stroke which badly affected his speech. Within a week the family was back in Washington.

"What really pissed me off," she told me, "I was about to learn how to make *quenelles* – Michel had promised to show me. I was just so cross."

"And Michel? What of Michel?" I asked, teasingly.

"You can always find a man to kiss if you look hard enough," she replied, with a grin. "But there aren't many men who can teach you how to cook perfect *quenelles*! By the way," she said, working a forkful of Phantôme's *Côtelettes de saumon Pojarski* over her tongue, "you ask me, they've used skimmed milk here when they should have soaked the breadcrumbs in a single cream. I'd have thought a place like Phantôme would be above such small economies."

According to Casey, the next few years were the usual teenage doldrums. Which in her case meant no embassy kitchens and no attentive *sous-chefs*, just the dulling drudgery of school and college. Added to which, she missed Paris like an eel misses mud.

"It was always there, you know? I'd wake up mornings and think, I'm in Paris, and the next minute I'd realize I wasn't, and it was all a long, long way away."

A waiter slid between us, and white gloves whisked away our plates. Casey wiped some crumbs from the table, licking the tip of her finger to lift the last from the cloth.

"So?" I prompted.

"So, college," she continued. "I didn't want to go. I really didn't. What I wanted to do was get back to Paris as fast as I could. But Mom and Dad were determined. Said I'd always regret it, that kinda thing. And when I finished, well, I could make my own decisions then. But not before. So I went to college and hated it. All the kids seemed so young. So… so…"

"So provincial?"

"I guess. And modern languages, you know? I could speak French, Italian, Spanish better than any of them. I mean I was way ahead. *So-oooo* boring! So… numbing. If it hadn't been for my godfather Bobby, I'd probably have ended up doing just what Dad wanted. Working for Uncle Sam, pushing paper in some consulate somewhere."

"Godfather Bobby?"

"Fairy godfather. Literally. Gay and rich. Well, not loaded, you know, but real comfortable. Old Boston stuff. He and my Dad were at Exeter together and been friends just ages. He used to joke he only made godfather because he was rich and didn't have kids, and Mom and Dad always agreed with him. So anyway, my last year at college, he goes and dies and leaves me like a real big pile. Like big enough to be sensible about, big enough to set up a trust. That big."

"And?"

"The day I graduated I booked a flight to Paris. Told my parents I was going back to France. Told them I wanted to learn to be a cook."

"And they were disappointed?"

"You could say. Dad kinda shook his head like, at long last, he really couldn't find the words. He and Mom looked so let down. I tell you it was harder than I'd imagined. But then, when they saw I was serious, saw I'd already got the ticket, had the money to do it whether they liked it or not, they tried a different tack, started talking about Lausanne and hotel schools and all that."

A pair of waiters appeared at the table and served the *Poires Belle-Helènes* I'd ordered, ladling the fruit with a smooth chocolate sauce.

"In their way of thinking," continued Casey, dipping a finger into the chocolate and licking it – not really the done thing at Phantôme – "everything had to be respectable. There had to be qualifications. Paper. *Resumé*. If I wanted to cook, then it had to be done right, something they could say to their friends, show off. You know the kind of thing. But I held out," she said. "Told them I wanted to do it my way, start at the bottom and work my way up. No favors. No strings pulled." Her eyes gleamed at the memory of it. "And thanks to Bobby, I had the means to do just that. There wasn't much they could do to stop me."

And so, a week later, Casey arrived in Paris, found herself a small studio near Montparnasse and a job in the kitchens of a family bistro called Chez Des Frères Normands.

"Des Frères? Off Avenue Mouffetard?"

"You know it?"

"If I didn't know Des Frères," I told her, "I'd be a pretty poor food writer."

"Well, that's where I started."

"How long before *Monsieur le Patron* let you cook anything?"

Casey smiled, sliced a corner of her *poire*, speared it with her fork, dipped it in the pooling chocolate and chewed it slowly.

"Six months, give or take," she replied. "To begin with, my job was, well… I guess you'd call it scullery maid."

"The French say *'plongeur'*. Or in your case, *'plongeuse'*."

"That's the baby. That's what I was. Lunch and dinner, every day, all I did was wash plates and scour pots. And the end of every shift it was me cleaned the kitchen floor."

"And then one day, he handed you a small toque."

Casey laughed, pushed back her hair: "How d'you guess? Only it was a knife not a toque. Pointed me to a small work surface in the corner of the kitchen where they prepped the vegetables and I was on my way. I think it must have been the first time I held a knife in that place that I wasn't about to wash, polish, or eat with." She laughed.

"And then?"

"And then, one afternoon, before evening service, he comes over to my station and tells me to cook his supper."

"Don't tell me – *omelette*?"

Casey looked stunned. "How the heck…?"

"I interviewed him one time for the paper. I remember he told me that, in his humble opinion…"

"Humble? *Le Patron*? You gotta be kidding me."

"…that in his humble opinion an omelette was the hardest thing to cook properly."

"Well, you're right about that. And that's what he wanted for supper. *Omelette aux fines herbes*. So I cook it for him. I mean *really* cook it. I cooked the best damn omelette any woman – any man – ever cooked. Three eggs, a teaspoon of chilled water, whisked with the point of a knife, just a few crumbs of hard cheese, *au coeur* like I knew he liked it, a pinch of *fines herbes*, more salt than pepper, and a buttered skillet hot to molten, on and off the heat. I tell you it was perfect. Perfect! But when I go to his office with the tray, he just looks up from his pastis, pushes at the omelette with his finger, and tells me to do it again – it wasn't right. I just felt… I don't know. I couldn't even cook an *omelette*? I was devastated."

"How many times did he make you do it?"

"The third time he slit it down the middle with his penknife and just looked inside. Like I'd got the outside right, but what about the guts. The fourth time he risked a bite."

"And then?" I asked, knowing the answer, for *Monsieur le Patron* had once joked with me about his treatment of apprentices, how he liked to make them angry so they'd try harder – or just give it up, leave, go someplace else to work. Some other job, some other life.

"Every day for a week, he ordered the *omelette.* And I swear he couldn't have eaten more than two mouthfuls total."

I nodded and smiled. "And then life became a little easier?"

"Easier? Easier! Hey! It got tougher."

"I mean, he began to give you responsibility. He began to say, in his way, '*ça va* – you'll do'."

"I guess. I started doing the house *patés, terrines, gallantines…*"

"Stocks and sauces…" I continued.

"Meat first, then fish. Then the house specials – the Bresse pigeon in salted pastry…"

"…the *Boeuf Bourguignon*, the *magret*, the *gigot* with *sarriette…*" I chimed in, Casey nodding along with me. "And then pastries and desserts – the *Mousse au chocolat*, the *Crème caramel*, the *Baba au rhum*, the *Fraisier…*"

"…the *Soufflé glacé au framboise*, the *Île flottante*. The whole nine yards, I'm telling you."

"If it makes it any easier, it was just how he started back before the war, under his father, one of the original brothers. And he always said it was the best way for anyone to begin. The story he told me was just like yours. His father made him cook *oeuf en cocotte* – I forget how many times. But I think he's right. It's important for a young chef. There must be discipline – and disappointment – along with the talent. And it shows. Des Frères may not be the best restaurant in the city, but the food is good and honest, real *cuisine des mères*, and you know that for the same price you will not find better."

"And he would never use skimmed milk."

"And he would never use skimmed milk."

Despite the rigors of her initiation, Casey had persevered. It was clear to me early on that this young lady was not one to walk away from a fight, throw in the towel, because someone was giving her a hard time. Not Casey. No chance. Indeed, she stayed on at Des Frères another two years, even taking over the kitchen when Monsieur and Madame and their big black poodle, Pom'frite, took their annual *vacance* in Normandy.

"It was the first time they stayed open in August. I was so frightened. So terrified. And so excited. Me, *chef de cuisine*, you just can't imagine."

"Oh, yes I can."

"I'm sure if the customers had known an American was in the kitchen, the place would have emptied. I just know it."

"Not if the food was good. They wouldn't have minded who was doing the cooking. You know the French. Even if it was just to find fault."

"I wish you had been there to tell me that."

For a moment then, I was aware of a certain look across the table as she spoke these words, and I remember not so much changing the subject, as redirecting it.

"So how was the pear?"

She licked her lips. "I think… no, I am sure. They've used a Spanish *Blanquilla*. Packed in a cooler and sent across out of season. Which is a pity because a Bartlett, a good American Red Bartlett, would have done the job better. All that early, sweet, summery taste. That's what was needed. *Blanquillas* are just too ripe, don't you think, too autumny for this time of year?"

And so it went, that lunch at Phantôme, our first together, a friendly meeting that lasted longer than either of us had anticipated, a fact which brought the meal to an abrupt end when Casey pulled my wrist across the table to look at my watch and saw the time. Minutes later, standing on the sidewalk, she seemed to hop from one foot to the other in her impatience to be gone, jumping into the first cab that came along with only the briefest of farewells, but turning to wave through the rear windscreen as she sped off downtown.

≈

We met again sooner than I'd imagined, only a couple of weeks later and, once more, at my invitation.

Following Casey's lead on seasonal tastes at Phantôme, I'd decided to write something on the new summer menus that would soon start appearing, the foods to choose and the places to go, restaurants with gardens or terraces, that sort of thing. These I'd carefully selected, and matched with appropriate companions.

Despite being the source for the story, I admit that Casey was not my first choice for Lemarchelier, one of the restaurants I'd decided to feature. Nor, to be shamefully honest, was she scheduled for any of them. But, at the last minute, I was let down by one of my regulars and I needed a replacement. I could, I suppose, have eaten by myself, just as I did that lunch at Bonnebouche, but it wouldn't have worked at Lemarchelier. There they would know who I was, would make all kinds of fuss. And fuss was something I didn't want. Having a companion would make things a great deal easier.

And so, Casey. I don't know why I thought of her particularly, when there were so many others I could have called. I guess it was the short notice – she wasn't the kind to mind that – and being a Monday she would more than likely be free. She was, and I told her I'd pick her up within the hour.

It was only when I put down the phone and began to get myself ready that it occurred to me my choice might not have been the wisest I could have made, that I'd be well advised to take care. The reason for this was a suspicion that, while I might be flattered by this young girl's clear interest in me, she might now justifiably be expecting a little more from this new friendship than I was prepared to give. Two lunches in as many weeks, and a very fulsome fifteen hundred word editorial, could easily be misinterpreted. And I wished there to be no such misunderstanding. As far as I was concerned, Casey had been great company at Phantôme – opinionated, discriminating, knowledgeable, with a sense of taste (the skimmed milk, for instance, and the choice of pear) that quite astonished me. And that was it, that's all that really mattered for me. The company of a kindred spirit. Someone who liked and knew their food, someone good to talk to, fun to be with. Also, I guess I was intrigued to know more about her, hear the next installment if you like. That, at any rate, was what I had in mind when we were shown to our table an hour or so later, perfectly set for the purposes of my story in a corner of Lemarchelier's hushed conservatory, overlooking a narrow strip of well-tended lawn and clipped shrubbery.

The meal began well. A brace of seared scallops for me with smoked chipotle lentils and wild greens, which I insisted she try. And a seared *foie gras d'oie* with sweetcorn blinis for her which she absolutely refused to share and seemed to gobble up in seconds. Both dishes seemed eminently light and summery, accompanied by a white Burgundy as cold as frost and dry as onionskin. These were followed in due course with a *sucerelle* of mussels crowned with caramelised sea bass in a red wine reduction which Casey pronounced a tad vinegary, and for me a paper-thin *paillard* of veal "you could put a stamp on and send through the mail", as she so aptly described it, its surface neatly franked with scorch marks – a description, incidentally, which I subsequently used in my copy.

"If I had a dollar for every escalope I hammered at Des Frères, I wouldn't have needed a fairy godfather," said Casey, of the man whose timely bequest not only got her to France, but, as she now admitted, helped secure her future enterprise. Bonnebouche.

"I'd been working at Des Frères long enough," she continued, flaking the sea bass and scooping it up with the mussels. "It was time to move on. But where to, and to do what? I'd had offers, sure, plenty of them. Even though I was American," she smiled. "But it was always the same thing, you know? Swap one kitchen for another. Negotiate a few francs more. No. I wanted something for myself. And after nearly three years in Paris, I realized all of a sudden that the other thing I really wanted to do was come home. I'd done what I'd set out to do. I could cook an *omelette* that even *Monsieur le Patron* would eat. It just seemed like the time had come to start out on a new track."

And once again, it was her godfather made it all possible.

According to Casey, it all came together with an old café called Bar Bonnebouche, a regular haunt of hers where she'd stop for coffee on her way to work, or a late-night cognac going home.

"One morning I come by and the place is closed, all dark inside so you have to put your hands to the glass to see in, all the chairs stacked on the tables. At first I think they're maybe on vacation, but later, at Des Frères, I hear the property's been sold to the gallery next door. Apparently, too, the couple who ran it were still living upstairs, waiting for the notaries to complete the paperwork.

"That afternoon, soon as lunch was finished, I was round there hammering on the door. It was like something was driving me, Cully, pushing me along. Even then I don't think I really knew what I had in mind. It was just, I don't know... some kind of urge... a compulsion to go there, see them, talk to them. Anyhow, eventually, down comes Madame, she recognizes me, invites me in, and upstairs, in their front room, over coffee and a plate of *madeleines*, I tell them I want to buy the contents of their café. The lot."

A waiter arrived at just that moment to clear away the dishes and Casey sat back, blowing out her cheeks as though to say *well, I'm done*. For someone her size, she has a remarkable appetite, accommodating not only every scrap of her own *foie gras*, mussels and sea bass, but weighty forkfuls of my scallops and *paillard* to boot. When the table had been cleared and without need of the menu, I ordered Lemarchelier's signature *Beignets soufflés fourrés aux cerises* with kirsch cream for the both of us. I was certain Casey would put up her hands in surrender, and I remember being surprised when she nodded approvingly. The order taken, I waited to hear what came next in that first-floor parlor above Bar Bonnebouche.

"Well, I tell you. You should have seen it. The two of them, dear old things, they look at each other like I'm truly out of my silo. Which I guess I was. Then they whisper a bit, and the old man asks how much I'm prepared to pay.

"Well, you know, I had no idea. About the money. How much and all. I hadn't stopped to think. I just knew I had to do it, buy all that stuff. But an actual figure? I hadn't got that far, hadn't even worked out what I was going to do with it all. I mean, Cully, this was just impulse, you know? Like I was driven. Absolutely nothing I could do about it. Something else in control."

I nodded, smiled, caught up by her enthusiasm.

"So anyway, sitting in their parlor, I try to work out what the hell was down there, like a mental inventory, you know? Well, there's the mirror of course, I wanted that, the old one behind the bar with the set specials painted on like chalk and the prices in francs. I could cook every one of them with my eyes shut. The tables I probably didn't need, but the chairs and barstools were kinda neat; and the old napkin drawer with the white china handles and enameled numbers – well, I mean, you just can't find something like that any more.

"Then, of course, there were the bracket lights with those cute little glass shades. And the bar stuff – original beer pumps, Art Nouveau water spigots, that sort of thing. And the pastis jugs they hung from the beams – Ricard, Pernod, Quarante et Un, St Raphael, Suze. And the cutlery and china, all good solid stuff; the crochet tablecloths; the lace curtains; the pots and pans – those old copper-bottomed *sauciers*, you know the ones; even the little round chrome stand they kept on the bar to hold the hard-boiled eggs. And let's not forget the bar – the *zinc*. I had to have that. It was fabulous – well, you've seen it so you know. Twenty feet long with that little bend at one end, all dimpled and hammered. And worn. I mean it was old, old. Twenties, Thirties. It was antique. Survived the war and all."

At this point the hot battered cherries arrived, and Casey fell silent once more. With due reverence the twin silver domes were lifted (such a dreadful pretension and so damaging to the food beneath), steam rose in a billow, and with a white-gloved flourish spoonfuls of kirsch cream were ladled onto the summit of each small mountain of cherries. A magnificent spectacle. Just magnificent.

"Well?" I asked, when the waiters withdrew. "So what did you say?"

"Well, I couldn't think. I just couldn't think, Cully. So I just up and asked how much they wanted."

"And?" I said, picking up a spoon and chipping away at the snowy slope of crusted cherries.

"Well, I think it took them by surprise. Madame looks at Monsieur. Monsieur pushes out a bottom lip you could use for a shelf. Shrugs, you know, the way they do. *Boufs* and *bahs*. A few *alors*. Looks at his wife again, scratches his head. And then, like he doesn't want me to hear, he mutters what sounds like two hundred thousand francs.

"So without thinking, without even working it out, but knowing it seemed about right, I say a hundred thousand. At which point he gets up and walks around the room, and Madame's like following him with her eyes. She looks so anxious, you know? I'll never forget it. And then, finally, he comes back with a hundred and sixty in that take it or leave it tone, as if he doesn't give a damn one way or the other."

At this point, seeing me at work on my cherries, Casey started in as well, savoring the first spoonful with a '*mmmmmhhh*' good enough to frame, and then attacked the rest as she though she hadn't eaten for a week.

"Anyway," she continued between mouthfuls, "trying to be grown-up as possible, I tell him yeah, sure, but I want all the wines and spirits. I'd suddenly remembered the stock behind the bar and what was probably down in the cellar. I didn't reckon the gallery would need it and maybe, I thought, I could off-load it somewhere. Des Frères would give me a price. Which they did, as it turned out. And that was that. A done deal. Monsieur nods, shakes my hand, Madame gives me a kiss, and we seal it with a cognac. Everything under my feet – all the fittings and fixures – belonged to me. For a little over forty thousand bucks. I'd never spent so much money in my life. If it hadn't been for the cognac, I'd have fallen over."

And so the contents of Bar Bonnebouche, on the corner of Avenue Girolles and rue de Persille in the fourth *arrondissement*, were relocated to a semi-basement on 50th and Ninth which Casey promptly found and leased on her return to New York.

"You know what? I even got the original parquet flooring. Did a deal with the gallery who wanted polished concrete," said Casey triumphantly, pushing away her plate and stretching out in her chair, hands clasped over her stomach. All that was missing was a mighty '*oooufff*' of over-indulgent satisfaction.

I felt like some kindly old uncle taking his niece out of school for a slap-up lunch. For that was how she looked. Like a gangly schoolgirl in a neatly pressed blouse and plaid skirt, laid out in her chair, stuffed to the gills. If I'd dared, I might even have done the same myself – stretched myself out like her. I certainly felt like it. Instead, I leaned forward and heard her say, more wistfully now: "Looking back, it all seems like it never really happened. Just a story."

But what a story, I thought, and wished I'd known the whole of it when I'd sat down to write my fifteen hundred words. Casey, I remember thinking, deserved all the success she could get. She was honest, hard-working and grittily determined; she was young, ambitious, energetic, with a sharp, pixie prettiness that grew on you; but most of all she possessed this feeling for food, this respect for it – and clearly an appetite for it, too – that was simply entrancing. She was as much a find as her marvelous little restaurant.

And there was my error. There, at that table at Lemarchelier, seduced by a post-lunch sense of well-being, by the agreeable warmth of the conservatory, by the scent of freshly-mown grass drifting through the windows, there, just as I'd feared, just as I told you, I allowed my guard to slip.

When I called to order coffee and suggest a small *digestif*, Casey shook her head, said she mustn't be late this time and that, if I liked, why not go back with her to Bonnebouche for a quick *café-calva*? And I agreed without a thought to consequences, paid the check and followed her out to the street. Well, maybe there was one thought, as we stood there on the sidewalk and looked about for a cab – that beguiling, irresistible sense of *well, if it happens, why not? Just this once, it can do no harm*. That tiny, fatal whispering voice that lures us to our ruin.

And that, my friends, was that.

For despite my certainty, as I left Bonnebouche an hour or so later, straightening my hair and settling my collar, that what had just been acted out on Casey's maroon banquette was just something that had happened on the spur of the moment, a pleasant enough experience but not one that would likely be repeated, our meetings, with their increasingly regular ending, continued into the summer. We would meet on a Monday, go someplace for lunch and then adjourn to Bonnebouche for what remained of the afternoon, there to indulge, always at Casey's instigation, in semi-drunk love-making wherever the spirit moved us. Or rather, wherever it moved Casey. For she was a hungry, demanding little lover, taking me first on that maroon banquette and later, seeming to delight in my initial unwillingness, on one of the restaurant tables, over a rocking bar stool, in the kitchen, even luring me up onto the zinc itself, that chill bed of hammered metal that left its dimpled pattern imprinted on my knees and in the palms of my hands. Sometimes I could respond to these endeavors, sometimes I felt foolish – too old to properly enjoy or feel comfortable with her youthful exuberance. But with Casey, never able to do much about it.

I'll be honest. I am not a young man. My body is not... what it once was. My eagerness for sex, I find, is not as finely tuned as it might once have been. I guess you could say I've lost my appetite, or rather, am not now as hungry as I once was. But that never stopped Casey. It didn't seem to bother her that I was... well, not in my prime, not the kind of lover she might reasonably expect given her youth and prettiness. She even seemed to like me the more for it. Enjoyed coaxing me on, teasing me for my occasional middle-aged vulnerability.

Sometimes, too, those Mondays, we would go nowhere, stay put, and she would do the cooking. I'd arrive at the appointed time, let myself in, and there she'd be, sleeves rolled to her elbows, a tennis-player's sweat band on her wrist, rattling one of her long-handled, copper-bottomed *sauciers* over the flame. Her hair would be ruffled, her face sheened and reddened, and, as I learned to expect, her body, beneath stiffly starched whites, invariably naked.

I would open and pour the wine I brought for these occasions, draw up a chair and talk as she worked – rolling out the thinnest sheets of *millefeuille* pastry for a *Truffe entière au chausson doré*, or whisking up a sauce Nantua for the crinkled *goujons* of Maine lobster that spat and wriggled in the pan like fattened pink worms protesting their fate, or tossing, in a heavy black skillet that needed both hands, her special *sarladaise* mixture of *ceps*, garlic and potato that she would serve with her very own *confit de canard*.

The moment the food was ready, the flames turned down, the oven door slammed shut, Casey would send me from the kitchen to lay up a table while she put the finishing touches to her work. Then she would push through the swing doors with her backside, follow me out with whatever it was she'd prepared, and place the dish before me. Strangely, at Bonnebouche, she rarely ate herself, beyond maybe sharing my fork to try this or that from my plate, always more interested in my response to her food than in any satisfaction she might derive from it herself. She would watch me take a bite and then ask me to describe the taste, guess at the ingredients, or challenge me to explain some reference, some association the food suggested. It was like a session with Aunt Jem.

Let me try to remember for you how these conversations would go.

"How's the polenta?" she asked one time, as I tasted her version of it, cut like a golden wedge of flan and served with a *fricassée* of rabbit and red cabbage.

"Quite delicious. Good color, bold flavor. But light. Dry. Almost biscuity. Cooked, cooled and then brushed with butter and grilled – the best way. And you've used the long-grained maize from Verona, I'd hazard, though I can't imagine where you manage to get a hold of such a thing in this city. Altogether an unlikely, but inspired companion to the cabbage and rabbit. Yes," I replied, taking another bite as though to confirm my opinion, drawing the moment out, and enjoying her eyes trained expectantly on me. "Yes, it really is very good. Very good indeed."

"So how come Byron loved it so much?"

"Byron? Er, because…"

"Don't you go guessing now. No guessing."

"I don't need to guess."

"But you don't know, do you? Go on, Cully, admit it. Just say you don't know."

"But I do know, as a matter of fact." And I did. On that occasion I'm pleased to say I did know. And told her. "Because, let me see, Byron had a mistress, in Venice I think, who kept pellets of polenta in her… between her breasts, to keep them warm, and she would feed them to him in their gondola."

And success again with a calf's liver, tattooed from the grill, pink as a new day and dripping with *jus*.

"So tell me, Cully. Why do they call it *fegato*?"

"An easy one that," I replied.

"Oh yeah?"

"Oh yeah?" I mimicked, slicing a corner off the meat and sliding it into my mouth.

"So?"

"So," I continued, biting into its smooth flesh. "*Fegato* comes from the latin word *ficatum*. It means stuffed with figs. It's how Romans fattened up the livers of their calves, their geese. No one does it now, of course. But if they did, I like to think it would be possible, just, to actually taste the sweetness of the fruit. There, told you I knew."

But then, other times, she would stump me: "Why, do you suppose Cully, the tip of your knife is rounded?"

"So I don't lean across the table and stab you to death with it?"

"You don't know?" she asked, taking my knife from me and

rasping her thumb against its blade.

"I remember someone once telling me…"

"But you've forgotten. You don't know?"

"Something to do with…"

"'Something to do with…' just ain't gonna make the cut, Cully."

"Okay. So I don't know. You can't expect me to know everything."

"Well," she began, savoring the triumph, "it's because Cardinal Richelieu once had a guest for dinner who picked his teeth with the point of his knife. And the Cardinal was so appalled that he ordered his knife-makers to grind away the tips. There. Now you *do* know."

And then, flushed with pleasure at catching me out, or delighted by my congratulations, she would come to me as I took my last bite of whatever marvel she'd concocted, push away the plate and sit herself astride me. As though the next course was now in front of me, there beneath her buttoned Bragard chef whites – by now somehow unbuttoned – in the shiny valley between her breasts, and beyond.

Always, this was how it began, her hot little body pressed against mine, my hand taken and led to some secret, shadowy place, her breath in my ear, her arms cradling my head, until simply the nearness of a woman's body, rather than the fact that it belonged to Casey, would begin to arouse me. It was physical response in its purest form, like the involuntary pang of hunger you feel when some wonderful dish is laid before you. Even if you're not hungry, you'll try it just because it's there for you to take, to taste.

And so it was with Casey those Monday afternoons at Bonnebouche, the same concentration, the same grim absorption she showed in her work brought to her love-making, a tautness to the body, a frowning intent, that focused look in her eyes.

Which was what unsettled me the most about Casey. The depth of her commitment and the urgency of her passion – all those too-long, insistent, Chablis-breath kisses; the way she pushed her sturdy little breasts and pebble-hard nipples at me to be kneaded, pinched, licked and bitten; her rough-skinned hands reaching and gripping and pulling. It was a passion and commitment I knew I could never match.

For mine, I knew, was a selfish connivance, a guilty complaisance, simply taking advantage of all that was offered with little intention to pay the forfeit, if, indeed, there was any forfeit to pay. And given the limits of the time available to us, the few hours between lunch and the arrival of her staff for the evening's opening, there was never any real risk of getting caught up in any post-coital examination of motives or intentions. By the time I'd provided Casey with what she expected, the imminent return of her staff was always a reliable get-out, allowing me to disengage without suspicion.

On occasions, as I straightened myself, there might be a certain silence from Casey as she cleared away the dishes, that expedient womanly silence that begs to be questioned. But I was adroit at filling such silences with a steady flow of careless, inconsequential chatter, failing deliberately to recognize the fact that she might want me to ask if she was okay, if she was feeling well, and thus give her the lead to open up with whatever it was she wanted to say.

And what I quickly came to know she wanted to say.

In short, that she loved me.

She might gasp it breathily in our love-making, in the rocking, rutting, cup-and-saucer-rattling heat of passion. But afterwards she would hold back from its declaration, hoping that somehow I would provide an opportunity for it to be brought into the open and properly discussed. Which, as I've said, I took great care never to do.

What's more, at no time in the few months we spent together, did I ever allow our arrangement to change, by suggesting, or agreeing to, a meeting outside Bonnebouche or the other places we ate – at my apartment, say, or at hers, despite her enthusiasm that I should visit, stay over. It would give us more privacy, she would say, give us longer together. But I countered this move whenever I saw it coming, playing the light notes to Casey's deeper, more insistent rhythms. I can't remember now what on earth I said to put her off – pressing deadlines, prior engagements – but it was always managed without too much difficulty.

Like I said, and I really am ashamed to admit it, I knew from the beginning that the affair would go nowhere. It was like patronising the same restaurant week after week; sooner or later, you simply tire of the repetition. Of course, I should have done something about it, to soften the eventual blow. But somehow the time never seemed right, the opportunity for harsh words never presented itself, and I succumbed to delaying tactics, unwilling to face the cruel consequences of my casual involvement, early on identifying my approaching vacation as the perfect moment to bring matters to a close. A month apart and she would soon learn to do without me, maybe even find someone else to take my place.

In the meantime… well, it was a satisfactory way to pass a few hours, a pleasant enough start to the week.

And that was how I planned it, and how I would have gone through with it, callously and comfortably, but for one unforeseen event – that dog-day hot trip to the Met, and my chance encounter with a woman who changed everything.

Roo.

Imagine, if you will, an immaculately-laid table, the various dishes, cutlery, glasses all neatly and properly arranged. And then imagine the cloth snatched away and all those well-ordered pieces sent spinning into disarray. Well, that was what happened the day I met Roo. Where before my life had been firmly anchored, suddenly I was adrift. And Casey, I'm afraid to say, suffered for it. As I, in my way, have done since. Though I didn't know it then.

For it was impossible not to compare the two women. Whenever I was with Casey, I could think only of Roo. Whenever I was with Roo, I thought of no one else. The more I got to know Roo, the more I began, wherever possible, to hold back from Casey, even though it brought the likelihood of confrontation and cruel words – which all that time I'd tried so diligently to avoid – uncomfortably closer.

Week after week, as that long hot summer progressed, as Roo came to occupy more and more of my time and my thoughts, I planned ways to stay away from Bonnebouche. Or, if that was not possible, to get through our time together with the minimum of difficulty. Until, finally, there was no way to sustain the pretence any longer, no way to hold off until my departure for Europe, the escape route I'd devised to get me off the hook.

≈

And so it was we sat, the two of us, Casey and I, in an empty Bonnebouche, the desolate silence between us filled with the distant hum and toot of traffic, the wail of sirens and, closer, the creak of our chairs and the occasional hiccoughing snuffle.

"Who is she?" she asked.

"It's not important. Just someone I met. By chance. No one you know…"

"Is she pretty?" she sniffed, the smoke from her cigarette coiling upwards into a thin slice of afternoon sunshine. "Do you love her, Cully? Does she love you?"

"It's too early…" I began. I shook my head. "I can't answer that. I don't know." Which was true, in its way.

And then, after a tick or two of silence, when I felt at last that maybe now was the time to take my leave, her plaintive voice began again:

"What can I do, Cully? What is it you want? I thought…" Tears had begun to well and shine in her imploring eyes once more.

"There's nothing Casey. Nothing you can do. It's just… That's the way it is…"

"I'll do anything, Cully. Anything. I do love you so, so much. You know that, don't you? Just tell me, and I'll do it. Anything…"

And the sobbing and the tears spilled out together, building with the words, until she bowed her head and hid her face in her hands, weeping and snuffling, her shoulders shaking.

And quietly, thinking it best, I left her there, let myself out through the French doors, and climbed the steps to the street.

Which was when, moments later, all hell broke loose.

I'd reached the sidewalk by the time I heard the first crash of china, the vicious cascade of splintering glass. Which was followed a moment later by a bitter, snarling voice that seemed to rise up out of the ground, spiralling up after me from the basement.

"Cully – FUCKING – Mortimer. Fucking, *fucking* BASTARD."

Casey.

For a terrifying moment I thought she might come chasing after me, continue the tirade in the street, and I quickened my pace.

Then more sounds of smashing china.

Heads turning on the sidewalk.

"You bastard. Bastard. Bastard. Fucking BASTARD."

And without looking back, I hurried on, heart thumping, praying for a cab.

Twelve Sutton Row

Of course I wrote about Zdenka's Kitchen. That same day. E-mailed my copy through to the paper not two hours after Roo dropped me back at my apartment, with a kiss on the cheek and a promise to meet up soon.

Not that there was any rush for the story. That weekend the *Times* was running my piece '*New Chefs on the Block*' (Vincent Capaldi, whom I'd met the previous week at his Small Potatoes opening, Steve Witherspoon at Capers, Cliff O'Neill who'd just taken over from Barney Woo at Dundee Corner, and Mimi Switzer at Salt Makes The Juices Run, all featuring among the main contenders). Then there was my story on '*Food in the Movies*' for the weekend following. And, for the last Sunday in July, my take on '*The Ten Best Pizza Joints In Town*'. According to Sanchez, Zdenka's Kitchen was slated for the second weekend in August.

I was good and pleased with the story for obvious reasons. It is not often, in this city, you get to find a place like Zdenka's, three generations of great kosher cooking, and never a word written about it. Never. Not a single word. I had Sanchez check while I worked on the story. No records on file. No references in our library. Not even a telephone listing. It was irresistible.

And everyone loved it.

When I stopped by the paper the Tuesday following publication, after a long working weekend out of the city (more of which later), Sanchez, sipping a hot chocolate and unwrapping a mid-morning Danish from the deli on the corner, was the first to spot me stepping out of the elevator.

"Great copy, Cully," said Sanchez, taking his first mouthful of sweet pastry and leaving a rim of sugar around his lips. "You sure punched the button on that one. How d'you find 'em, that's what I gotta know?"

I tapped my nose as I passed him and smiled conspiracy. Between Sanchez and my desk (rarely used for writing but useful as a mail-drop and listening post whenever I want to know what was cooking on the paper) there were similar responses from Jimmy McNaughten on the Diary, Lizzie Kovacks who does Style & Living – "gotta take my Dad, he'll just love it" – and Doug 'Last Minute' McKintyre, the paper's chief Sports writer.

A giant of a man who once played running-back for the Philadelphia Eagles, McKintyre earned his nickname making vital touchdowns in the very last seconds of those either-way games that had the crowds squeezing the ketchup out of their hot-dogs. When he left the Leagues and joined the *Times* the nickname stuck, thanks to his habit of delaying his copy until – you guessed it – the very last minute. The only reason he keeps his job is the quality of that copy. Quite simply, and I guess surprisingly, the man writes like an angel – a chatty, breezy, informed style that even I, not the least interested in sport of any kind, find utterly compelling. He's a likeable enough fellow, too, always telling me that if he wasn't such a darned good sports writer, he'd probably be doing my job – patting a stomach swollen by a million jugs of beer in the commentary boxes of a million out-of-town stadia as if that were all the qualification he needed.

I'd just reached my desk and settled myself down when he lumbered over and perched himself on its edge, drawing a dangerous creak from the woodwork. As always his big hands played compulsively with the stitched and autographed Yankees' baseball he uses as both comforter and paperweight. He's the only man I know who regularly sees an analyst, and about the most unlikely. When I asked him why one time, his reply was suitably sporty. "When you're three divorces down, Cully, you gotta reckon it's time to talk tactics!"

Anyway, he was sitting there, in the middle of telling me, not to be outdone, about some place in Philadelphia he'd been to one time which sounded just like Zdenka's, when Larry Daley, the 'Metro' editor, clapped me on the back, dug his thumbs into my shoulders in a friendly if painful pretence at a massage and bent down to whisper conspiratorially, "Zdenka's. They loved it…", meaning the powers that be, the paper's managing editors, the boys on the tenth floor.

"How come they saw it?" I asked, nodding to McKintyre as he slipped out of Larry's line of sight. Late with his copy again, I suspected.

"They didn't," replied Larry, taking McKintyre's perch without, I noticed, the accompanying creak. Larry's a tall, thin man with impossibly long legs and arms that, at rest, seem to fold and cross like an albatross wing, more times than they should; when they start unraveling you know the meeting's finished, the attention gone. "That is," he continued breezily, "not until the *Post* called up yesterday crowing about how there was no such place. Said they never heard of it. Sent some guy to check it out first thing, and it wasn't where we said it was. Said they were gonna splash it big how we sailed kites when we didn't have anything better to do. Said all sorts, which sent the boys upstairs into some spin, I can tell ya. Had a call out for you, but you couldn't be found…"

"The Rôtisseurs. Chicago…"

"Yeah, yeah, I remember now. How was it by the way?"

"It was…" I waved my hand vaguely, not really knowing what to say, and not wanting to stop him mid-flow.

"Good, good. So, anyway. Got a couple of our boys to go down, check it out from our end. You missed some party, I can tell ya – upstairs was humming according to Rita." Rita had once been Larry's assistant before being poached by James Rowlands, the paper's Managing Executive Editor. "Anyhow, the bottom line is, our boys do find it. But before they get to call in, the editor of the *Post* is on the phone saying there seems to be some misunderstanding. Of course, Zdenka's Kitchen, great place. Know it well. Can't think what the *Post* Weekend editor was thinking about… blah, blah, blah. Great piece. Great copy. Cully on top of it again. How does he find them? And all that kind of shit." Larry's arms began to unwind. "And suddenly the boys upstairs are just loving it. Stepped on the *Post* but good. Even wrote a small para for today's first edition. '*Post* Boast Toast', or some such strap Sanchez came up with. Take a look: Stop Press, back page. Major point scoring. They love you upstairs, I'm tellin ya. Keep it up, Cully, and they'll probably give you my job."

And with that Larry got to his feet, scanned the room, spotted whoever it was he was looking for – McKintyre probably, skulking over by the vending machines – squeezed my shoulder one final time, and loped off like he was walking on stilts.

After that, I didn't stay long at the paper, just time enough to open some mail, then leaf through the Sunday edition and check out the copy on Zdenka's. It was wedged into the fifth page of the Weekend Section next to a large three-quarter page ad for fitted kitchens. Thanks to Sanchez, the four-column piece had been left pretty much intact. I skimmed through it, spotted one or two well-judged cuts amounting to no more than a sentence or two, re-read a couple of lines that sounded sweet, nodded at the neat little illustration of meats on a cutting board that accompanied the story and then left, pausing only to thank Sanchez for his care and slip him a wad of dinner vouchers I'd received in the mail from some PR company.

Outside, after the cool of the air-conditioned office, the street felt as hot and close as a basement bakery. But I didn't even notice, just turned uptown and walked a half-dozen blocks without feeling a footstep. I can still remember that sense of warmth and contentment at a job well done; even after all that time it still felt good to punch the button as Sanchez had so aptly put it. At 58th I jumped a cab that pulled up ahead of me, and didn't feel a rattle or a bump the rest of the way home.

The fact is, I was so damned pleased with my piece on Zdenka's Kitchen and the ruckus it had caused vis-à-vis the *Post*, so exhilarated by Larry's inside story from the tenth floor, that I just up and forgot the one thing that had bugged me all weekend.

And bugged's the word, alright.

For the last three days, up in Chicago, I might as well have been on the moon. I just couldn't get to grips with it at all. The Grand Order of Rôtisseurs of America must have thought they'd invited the wrong man. Held at the Ritz Carlton, where I'd been generously accommodated by my hosts, the Rôtisseurs' do began with a 'Welcome Delegates' banquet Saturday night, followed by a Rib-Fest Sunday Brunch out at Soldier's Field, an Awards ceremony Sunday evening where I was presented with a suitably hefty gold medallion in recognition of my services to the American Meat Industry, and ended with Monday's uncomfortably bloated leave-taking.

But right the way through – Saturday to Monday – I was a man with his mind elsewhere. All I can remember with any kind of clarity that Welcome banquet Saturday night was a suffocating press of large, overly familiar and predominantly balding men, all of them broad and beefy in a meaty sort of way, more comfortable, I suspected, in aprons, rolled sleeves and white paper homburgs than in their shiny Sears' suits and knuckle-knotted ties, all of them glad-handing and back-slapping and beaming as if a century had passed, rather than just a single year, since they'd last seen each other.

That first evening I can't remember who I met or what I said, or if it made any sense whatever I did say. All I do remember, as they pumped my hand and filled my glass and hemmed me in like a calf fit for branding, was thinking that if a fire broke out in the Ritz Carlton's banqueting hall I'd never make it to the door. With these barrel-chested, stocky-faced, red-meat types stampeding for the exits like the very cattle they bred, butchered, and barbecued, I'd be trampled underfoot.

It was the same at the rib-fest Sunday where lounge suits surrendered to loud checks and sporty open-necks, a sense of separation from my surroundings, an inability to concentrate on what the hell I was doing there, walking back and forth from the roasting pits to the drinks tent with a glass in each hand so I didn't get waylaid: "Back in a minute," I'd say, "just got to…", flourishing the two glasses like I was fetching someone a drink, that kind of thing. Anything to keep on the move, anything to avoid being trapped in butcherish bonhomie.

And at the awards ceremony that same evening, as I leaned into the microphone, it was like someone else was speaking. Amplified, delayed, echoing round the great banqueting hall of the Ritz Carlton, my few words of thanks either whistled with feedback somewhere up among the dimmed chandeliers or swooped down over the upturned red faces of my fellow black-tied banqueteers whenever I tried to correct. When their applause finally came, it swept up towards me from a vast acreage of candlelit darkness and thankfully carried me back to my seat where I nodded and smiled and held up my 'King Cut' gold medallion.

But for all the world, it was as if the hoopla was for someone else.

And that was it, bar the leave-taking and the flight home. That was Chicago. I can't even remember what the food tasted like. And all because of that last Friday night in New York.

When I tell you what it was that happened, what I saw, you'll understand.

And how!

≈

I'd booked a flight out of La Guardia for Chicago's O'Hare early Saturday morning and had arranged to spend the Friday night with two old friends, Evelyn and Lydia Langhorn. It was an easy date. I knew Evelyn liked to eat early, so I could reckon on being back in my apartment, after seeing them home, and still have time to get my hour before midnight. You know what they say. An hour's sleep before midnight is as good as two after.

They make unlikely sisters, Evelyn and Lydia. Or rather half-sisters. Evelyn, the elder of the two from their wandering father's first marriage, is a fifty-something divorcée who, in her middle thirties, married an older man intent on fatherhood, bore him no children and subsequently lost out to a woman half her age who promptly complied in the hatching department. Not that Evelyn ever expressed any kind of regret at the loss. Indeed in Evelyn's case, 'lost out' and 'loss' are maybe not an accurate description of her condition, suggesting an aching impoverishment of purse and heart with which Evelyn is, take my word for it, absolutely not familiar, though she'll sometimes try to make a good fist of it.

In the years since her divorce Evelyn has filled her time with Caribbean cruises (the two of us met on a lecture cruise in the Antilles), European tours and a string of worthwhile causes, all of which eased her into the kinds of social circles she had earmarked for herself as 'appropriate' (present company included), without at any time making too many serious inroads on either her generous divorce settlement or the Langhorn family trust which both sisters enjoy. She is, in short, what I suppose you would call a rather selfish woman, overbearing, over-sure of herself, blind to her own many slight imperfections, and untroubled by any serious doubts as to the validity of her convictions or intentions. In small measures Evelyn makes for good company, if only for the unwitting entertainment she provides.

Her sister Lydia, on the other hand, is altogether a different model of the Langhorn name (a name, incidentally, which Evelyn swiftly reverted to in the interests of advancement after her separation from Mr. Brendan O'Leary – she might keep his money, but not his name; that's the kind of woman Evelyn Langhorn is). But back to Lydia. Thin as lemon grass, contentedly single at thirty-eight, Lydia is a waif, a twig to Evelyn's branch, trailing after her elder half-sister like a yacht's tender bobbing along in the larger vessel's wake. A sweet, sensitive woman with a frissée-d tangle of blondish hair and sad, soulful eyes, I've always felt a stir of attraction for her, and though I've never done anything about it, I've always been gently aroused by the whisper of possibility.

She's extremely artistic, Lydia, in a flaky sort of way, always taking up some course or other – painting, sculpting, pottery – and has an unlikely fondness for marijuana which, she once admitted to me, she took up at college and has never quite let go of. Though I've never seen her indulge, the sweet smell of it, underscored by a gentle application of patchouli, seems to drift off her in clouds. It gives her a certain drowsy wistfulness as though her train of thought operates at a different speed to the rest of us, propelled by some other fuel – which I suppose, in her case, is true.

She can also, without her realising it, often discomfort people with the honesty and directness of her observations. She once picked up my hand across a table (this was soon after we first met), spread the fingers and pointed to my bitten nails, telling me it looked awful and I should stop it at once, and how it showed a deep-seated insecurity I should have grown out of long ago.

Which, I'm sure I don't need to tell you, embarrassed hell out of me and made me cross. I was forty-four years old, I told her, pulling my hand from hers, and had been biting my nails since forever, so it was hardly likely I was going to stop just because she had drawn attention to it. And then felt foolish that I'd so over-reacted. She'd looked at me sagely and nodded, as though my petulance somehow proved her point.

And then, other times, she'd just delight me with… oh hell, I can't think now… Oh, yes. Yes, I can. In fact, I don't think I'll ever forget it. It was one Christmas and the three of us were talking about presents, the one thing we each hoped we'd receive.

"One of those pretty Pirelli bracelets," said Evelyn.

"Peretti," Lydia corrected her. "Not Pirelli. They're calendars. And tyres. Elsa Peretti's the name. They sell her in Tiffany. Very beautiful."

"So… Pirelli, Peretti, whatever," replied Evelyn, pretending not to be put out.

"And you?" I turned to Lydia, who gazed up at the ceiling as though seeking inspiration.

She pursed her lips, umm-ed and ahh-ed, and I remember thinking she was giving the question altogether more consideration than it deserved, or I'd intended, when she finally said: "I think what I'd really like are the taste buds of a child."

And I remember, in that instant, being completely taken by surprise at her response and quite enchanted by it. The taste buds of a child. Imagine.

"The taste buds of a child?" said Evelyn. "What on earth are you talking about, Lydia?" and she'd looked to me as though to someone who would confirm her bewilderment.

Which, of course, I did not, so taken was I by the notion, an idea, incidentally, that I subsequently used in one of my columns, much to Lydia's easy delight and Evelyn's lemon-lipped irritation.

"Wasn't it Keats," continued Lydia, "who said that only children and birds know what strawberries really taste like?"

"And maybe prisoners released from lonely stone cells," I added, recalling the passage.

"Fresh-picked *gariguettes* served in a chilled glass bowl," said Lydia, wistfully.

At which point Evelyn, even more perplexed, managed to steer the conversation back to more familiar ground.

Anyway, that Friday night before leaving for Chicago, around eight, I duly pitched up at Evelyn's duplex apartment, in a portered and canopied block on West 72nd which she'd bought with the sale proceeds of the much larger O'Leary marital home in Brooklyn. Apparently you can see the shadowy gables of the Dakota if you lean far enough out of the kitchen window and know which direction to look in. I've never tried it, or wanted to, so I can't really say, but Evelyn is inordinately proud of the fact, that closeness.

"I still see her every now and then," says Evelyn. She means Yoko Ono. I've heard her say it a hundred times, studiedly casual as though the fact is hardly worth mentioning, but still… As if the two of them enjoyed a neighborly nodding acqaintance, maybe more. Which, of course, they don't. Yoko and Evelyn! Really. There was even implicit the suggestion she'd enjoyed the same easy familiarity with John Lennon. Which, of course, she couldn't have. She'd have heard the news of his shooting in the Brooklyn parlor she shared with her husband, Brendan. But to Evelyn, dear deluded Evelyn, five blocks in whatever direction is close enough to claim kinship if it suits her. Sometimes I try to imagine what the Lennons and Evelyn would have made of each other. Impossible. But entertaining nonetheless.

And so, that Friday night.

"Evelyn, lovely to see you," I said, as she drew me into her hallway and pushed the door closed behind me, tipping a splash of Scotch on her braceleted wrist as she brushed against me. Evelyn does love her Malts and, judging by the way she fills her glass, could teach the boffins at MIT a thing or two on the subject of surface tension.

"Cully, how simply marvelous. So pleased you could make it. I know you're going to love it. Lydia. Lydia, darling. It's Cully…"

And so the evening began.

We had a drink or two, carried on our established brand of easy chatter, and less than an hour later were on our way downtown, the two half-sisters spread out on the back seat of the hired limo, Evelyn with her sequined clasp, Lydia in her trainers with the crumpled backpack she never seems to go anywhere without, and me occupying the plush little jump seat set in back of the driver. We were headed for a restaurant called La Gave, Evelyn told me excitedly, that had recently opened somewhere around 9th Avenue and 37th Street.

When I said that I'd read about the place, but never been there, Evelyn became instantly proprietorial.

"Oh, you'll just love it, Cully. It's so… I don't know, so… well, anyway, I just know you'll want to write about it." It was clear she was still out to level the score with Lydia, who smiled gently at her sister's determination to impress. When we arrived at La Gave, Evelyn issued instructions to the driver (as I'd guessed, it was to be an early night) and the three of us trooped inside.

The restaurant, reached in one of those wood-slat service elevators they have in gangster movies, occupied an open third-floor space in what looked like an old sweat-shop. Its ceiling was still cobwebbed with pipes and power ducts, the floorboards dark, pitted, and patterned with metal squares where machinery had once stood, and its windows dusty and dirty. Some of the panes were even broken. I remember a colleague on the *Times* had called it 'industrial minimalist' in a profile on the two architects. Two architects, I wondered as we were shown to our table? One seemed extravagance enough.

It is a habit of mine, for obvious reasons, to always take a seat facing the room. On this occasion, though, Evelyn and Lydia slid between table and wall where places were laid for two, leaving me with the single chair, a single table setting, and my back to the action. Fortunately, some kind of antique clocking-in contraption had been hung above their heads. Interestingly, and for no apparent reason, a strip of mirror was incorporated into this *objet* and I discovered that by tipping my head forward I was able to see behind me satisfactorily enough.

I forget what we spoke of as we settled there at our table, fluffing out napkins, rearranging cutlery for elbows, choosing from the wine list and menu. But when the complimentary *amuse-bouche* arrived, I do recall saying that La Gave was hardly well-named.

"Why so?" asked Evelyn, trying to decide how best to deal with the minute and fluffy *Croustade d'oeufs de caille* we'd each been given, whether to eat it in one go or err on the side of gentility by attempting to bite it in two.

"Yeah, Cully, how come?" echoed Lydia who, with no such thought for propriety, simply picked up the flakey *millefeuille* boat and popped it into her mouth.

A *gave*, I began, was the funnel-like utensil employed by French farmers to ram maize down the throats of ducks and geese in order to fatten the livers. After a couple weeks' force-feeding the fowls were killed, the swollen livers extracted and, hey presto, the finest, plumpest *foie d'oie* and *foie de canard* you could hope to find. Lifting my own boat-shaped *croustade* and following Lydia's example, I explained that these first servings would hardly constitute a threat to the liver.

For a moment the two sisters looked perplexed, not certain whether they believed this quaint Gallic custom, and, if they did, whether or not they entirely approved of it. Then Lydia chuckled, and Evelyn smiled with a *well, well* kind of expression, still not altogether sure she understood what it was we were talking about, and lifted the *croustade* to her mouth. But instead of slipping it in whole like Lydia and I, she decided to bite it in half, a misplaced attempt at delicacy that showered her with flakey pastry, littering the front of her dress and the table with what looked like gold confetti.

It was at that exact moment, leaning forward to offer my napkin, that my eye was caught by a reflection in the mirror above their heads.

A reflection that stopped me dead.

"Cully?" asked Evelyn, seeing me freeze.

"Are you alright, Cully?" said Lydia, reaching out a hand.

I didn't reply. Couldn't. Because, in that band of silvery, foxed glass above their heads, I'd seen, across that crowded third-floor room, a man and a woman, leaning towards each other. A tall, well-dressed man who reached out a hand to rest lightly on the woman's wrist, an elegantly curved brunette in a sleeveless, scarlet dress, long legs crossed beside the table, who slid that hand into her own and held it to her cheek. Sitting at an angle, she was half-turned away from us, her profile concealed by a light sweep of hair and their clasped hands.

But the man. The man I could see clearly.

The wiry, windswept hair. The easy smile. The man who climbed ladders to mend aerials. The man who talked about downforce and drove like a whirlwind. The man who could light a fire in the rain.

Of all people!

Elliot!

With a woman. Staring into her eyes. Whispering to her. And not just any woman. But the woman! I was certain of it. Just knew it must be her.

So Daphne had been right. Elliot was having an affair.

Wide-eyed now, I watched him take her hand and move it to his lips.

"Cully?" This from Lydia.

"Cully? Is something the matter?" From Evelyn.

"No. No," I told them, tearing my eyes away from the strip of mirror. "No. Goodness. Where was I?"

"The name of the restaurant. The *gave* thing. You were telling us what those dreadful French do to their poultry," said Evelyn, still picking flakes of *millefeuille* from her bosom. "And I always thought they were so chic. In fact, I don't think I want to hear any more."

"It was like you were suddenly in a dream." This from Lydia, looking at me strangely. The half-sisters had clearly not realized there was a mirror behind them. "It was like, just for a moment, it was like you were looking into another world," continued Lydia. "You know? Like you were… I don't know… transcending."

That was the word she used – 'transcending'. But then Lydia would. And I guess in a way I was. If staring wide-eyed and speechless were signs of transcending, then that's what I was doing alright.

"No, no," I said. "Just… what's that expression? Devil over my grave. The shivers."

"Spooky," said Lydia.

"Mmmmmh," said Evelyn doubtfully, sweeping away the last of the pastry flakes with an expression close to disappointment. If I'd been paying attention, I'd have guessed what she was thinking: *Eighty bucks a head and most of it in my bust? They gotta be kidding me!*

But I wasn't paying attention. I wasn't taking in a word they said, let alone trying to guess what they were thinking. More carefully now, I stole another look in the mirror.

Across the room, Elliot was shifting his chair round the table, drawing closer to his companion, making her turn towards me as she followed his eyes. Now I could see the two of them in profile. I watched him slide his hand onto her knee, her legs seeming almost to reach up to the touch, her fingers playing with his tie.

I just couldn't believe my eyes.

Elliot.

And then he whispered something.

Which made the woman tip her head back and laugh.

And made me go cold.

The woman. I knew her too.

Even with the dark hair.

It was Roo.

So now you know. Now you know why Chicago was shot to hell.

Roo with Elliot.

Elliot with Roo.

Even now, the memory of it makes me turn kind of cold and hot all in one go.

≈

Since Zdenkas, Roo and I had seen a lot of each other. In a little less than a month we'd become firm friends. She was my new and favorite lunch companion, my latest swan, and we fit into each other's schedule as snugly as an egg in a cup.

I always knew, if the phone rang, when it was Roo on the end of the line. Without ever being told, she understood my ways. She never called before eleven in the morning, always seemed to know exactly the moment I would be happy to turn away from my keyboard for a chat, and sensed instinctively when the moment was right to say, "Let's meet…", "What're you up to?", "Why don't we…?"

And me? Well, sometimes I had to hold myself back from phoning her all the time, inviting her to every restaurant I visited, every do, every opening I'd scheduled. And whenever I did give in and call with an invitation, she was always there, always agreeable, always available. And always at home.

The card she'd given me when she dropped me back after our

lunch at Zdenka's had an office number on the front and, scribbled on the back, her home number. The first few times, diplomatically, I called her at work, where one of two friendly ladies always answered promptly.

"Relocate. How may we help you?" they would say in a clipped and practiced manner, and then, when I gave them my name, would admit that Miss Carew wasn't there at the moment, but I could always try her at home, and I had the number didn't I? As if they knew I did. As though Roo had told them I did. After calling the office a few times, I soon learned to call her at home first. For that was where she was most likely to be, always, in the mornings, sounding warm and drowsy as though she were still wrapped cosily in her bed.

The last time we'd spoken, the day of the dinner with Evelyn and Lydia, I'd let slip it was my birthday the following week and, when she'd ferretted out of me that I had nothing particular planned, she insisted we get together to celebrate. Where should we go, she asked? What was my favorite place? Her treat, she said. It would be her birthday present. And so we arranged to meet the following Friday at my favorite restaurant in town, Twelve Sutton Row.

I've never known a day take so long to come. Which will maybe come as no surprise. Seeing Roo and Elliot together at La Gave had shocked me to the core. No other way to describe it. I never saw them arrive and I never saw them leave – one minute they were all but entwined at their table, the next time I looked they had gone. But their reflected image in that foxed, letterbox length of ancient mirror stayed with me, sharp as a blade, while the closeness that I'd seen between them just punched the breath from my body.

Because the woman Elliot was having his affair with – for that was surely what it was – was a woman who, in the last few weeks, had woven her way so successfully into the fabric of my life and affections that I was just devastated by what I'd seen, overcome with a numbing sense of loss, a sense that something that belonged to me, something pure and new and exciting, had been snatched away. Could never be the same again.

All weekend in my suite at the Ritz Carlton I thought to call her, confront her, have her explain things to me – tell me what was going on. Twenty years ago I'd have picked up that phone and made the call. But somehow I held back. It was too soon. I needed time to work the whole thing out, to become familiar with it, to understand its intricacies, and somehow try to come to terms with it.

As well as the shock, there were other responses I came to feel too, added one by one like ingredients in some poisonous brew. First there was anger – three different kinds. Anger at Elliot's infidelity, anger at my consequent loss, and an additional anger that I'd unwittingly become party to Elliot's deception. I was furious with him for putting me in such a difficult position – even though he hadn't done it deliberately; even though I knew, of course, that his secret was safe with me, that I would never tell Daphne.

And then, after anger, disbelief.

Did Elliot have any idea what he was doing, I wondered? How much hurt it would cause? Apart, even, from me? How Daphne would take it when she was presented with the facts, as her private detective, of whom Elliot clearly knew nothing, was sure to do sooner or later? Sooner if he and Roo maintained such a high-profile dalliance. And how would the kids, who so adored Elliot, respond? They'd never understand. None of them would.

But I did. I understood. I knew what it was that drove Elliot. I knew what it was that seduced him away from that comfortable life he played so contentedly at Netherlands. Roo. I knew first hand that tantalising effect she had. Because, and this was when I think I began to realize it for the first time… because I was just as besotted as he was.

Which accounted for the last and most unsettling ingredient of all. The thing which really bothered me. Because I wasn't just angry or disbelieving. I was jealous. Curdled with it. For close on a week I slept hardly at all, was unable to concentrate on anything, even lost my appetite. It had taken every shred of resolve and discipline to finish my fifteen hundred words that Friday morning – thank God, nothing more taxing than a puff piece on the Rôtisseurs – and even then I knew the story was well below par. I just hoped Sanchez would be able to knock it into shape.

As the cab drove me cross town for my birthday lunch at Sutton Row, I alternately worried about my lacklustre copy and drove myself crazy with thoughts of Elliot and Roo. What was she doing with Elliot? How long had they known each other? How long had this affair been going on? And, most unsettling, where was it headed?

And then… and then those dreadful doubts, that churning uncertainty.

Did I really imagine I stood a chance with someone like Roo? A fifty-two-year-old man a shade below a respectable height, a shade or more above a respectable weight, a confirmed bachelor, with bitten nails and thinning hair, getting together with a woman near half his age? A woman like Roo? It was ridiculous, I knew, but still…

Elliot, on the other hand, though it galled me to admit it, was altogether a more likely candidate for her affections. Younger, fitter, taller, handsome. Everything I wasn't. And that contact between them, the way they looked at each other, the way they touched, the way her body seemed to respond to him, her knee rising so very slightly to his hand. There could be no mistaking it. They were in love. Lovers.

And that's how I arrived at Sutton Row, jangling with nerves, a badly executed nail bite from the night before that had left a spear of hardened quick catching on everything, to celebrate my birthday with a woman who had come to occupy every part of my waking life. And was now, more than likely, about to leave it in the space of a single lunchtime.

At last the moment had come, the moment I'd been thinking about for the best part of a week, running late because of that goddamned copy. And I still had no clear idea how I was going to get through the next few hours, how I was going to behave, what I was going to say. Indeed, whether I'd say anything at all. Even the prospect of lunch at my favorite place in town failed to raise my spirits or calm my heart.

Maybe, I thought, as the cab turned into the mews, I'd manage to get myself in order over a stiff drink in the bar before Roo made her appearance.

Which, on this day of all days, was not to be.

≈

Like Zdenka's, Twelve Sutton Row occupies a small cobbled courtyard, hidden behind a line of muted brownstones on Sutton Mews, and, like Zdenka's, provides some of the most remarkable, most memorable cooking in the city. But there all similarity ends. Where Zdenka's is cramped and faded and down-at-heel, Twelve Sutton Row is grand and imposing, a double-fronted merchant's mansion on the National Register that was built with ballast stone in the 1870s, furnished with exquisite taste, and lived in as a family home until a few years after the last war.

For close on half a century, Twelve Sutton Row has been one of the city's most sought-after rendezvous, not so much a restaurant as a home in the city, a refuge for like-minded souls. There is no name here, no awning, no framed menu, nothing to give the game away, simply the number, painted in white letters on a lacquered black door in a sloping copperplate. As you climb the steps and reach for the brass bell-pull, the overriding impression is of a private residence rather than commercial premises, or an exclusive club maybe. Indeed, you could easily be forgiven for thinking that only family ties or the stiffest, most rigorous membership conditions could gain you admission.

And in a way there is a membership of sorts – a restriction of custom imposed by cost. For it is, quite frankly, comprehensively pricey, though in my opinion worth every last nickel and dime, its clientele limited to those who can afford a check for lunch or dinner that can easily run to the cost of a first-class flight to Los Angeles. And back.

Once past the black door, opened by a tail-suited butler almost the moment your hand touches the bell-pull, you step into a graceful hallway hung with covetable oils of merchant ships, lit with creamy chandeliers, and carpeted in a thick scarlet weave that ends a foot short of each wall, the space between taken up by wide boards of mahogany burnished with a century's worth of wear and wax.

Either side of this hallway you'll find two beautifully and identically proportioned rooms, the Library and the Bar. Each has high ceilings, lavish mouldings and generous bay windows, each room warmed in winter with crackling log fires, each cooled in summer with genuine ante-bellum paddle fans and a whisper of air-conditioning. In both these rooms, indeed throughout the whole house, you'll also find a comforting and cultured hospitality; a private, peaceful retreat where you cannot help but feel pampered, aware that your worth is recognized, your credentials gratifyingly assumed. I guess it could also be just as easy to feel out of place here, an outsider – the house's character and cost a tad intimidating for some.

While the Library, on the left as you enter, all darkly red and snug, lined with bookshelves that reach to the ceiling, furnished with deep leather chairs and buttoned chesterfields, is the place where coffee and *digestifs* are served, the room to the right is the Bar, though no bar in the real sense of the word is evident. Instead, in the far corner of the room, ranged along the top of a glorious black Bechstein grand piano, stands a double line of bottles and decanters, rows of crystal glass and the gleaming chrome of cocktail paraphernalia, all set out on starched white linen, supervised for as long as I can remember by a white-jacketed, black-faced steward called Joseph who, without question, mixes the best damn cocktails in town. As soon as you take your seat at any of the small plumply-cushioned sofas or armchairs that crowd this room, all of them squared off around low club tables, Joseph will be there to take your order, nodding deferentially as you make your choice, bearing back a perfectly-mixed Martini or Gibson or Highball on his scalloped silver salver. It is, without question, the most civilized place in town to meet friends and enjoy a drink before moving upstairs to an equally exceptional dining room.

Or, in my case, to catch one's breath.

But that Friday, perversely, there was no time for catching breath or ordering thoughts.

For there was Roo, unaccountably on time, early even, sitting on the club fender by the fireplace, legs crossed, chatting away to Joseph as though they were the oldest of old friends, nothing less than a vision, more beautiful, more radiant than I'd ever seen her, ever imagined she could be. For the first few moments she didn't see me, and I stood in the doorway scrabbling nervously at my hair and collar, looking across the room at her.

She was dressed impeccably – perfectly for Sutton Row – in a black linen frockcoat, gauntlet-cuffed and silver-buttoned, over a cream silk blouse, with a tightly-contoured yellow linen skirt creased with pleats across her lap. Her legs were bare and brown, and her shoes shiny black and high-heeled, a sharply-pointed toe tipping lazily to and fro, the heel falling loose with every tip.

I'd been concerned, when we agreed the lunch, that Roo might feel uncomfortable at Sutton Row, or bored by its stuffy, old world European grandness which I have always found, along with the food, so gratifying. But I should have known better. Not only did she seem entirely at home, as though she came here regularly, was known, she seemed to shine in these surroundings, looked so bright, so immediate, so central to the room, as though some wonderful light shone out from her. Her hair was loose, straight and darkly blonde (another wig, or had she just come from the hairdresser?), its corners tilting forward either side from a central parting, swinging back over her shoulders as she looked up at Joseph who was smiling widely.

I don't think I have ever seen Joseph smile. Certainly never as wide, as deep, as warmly as he did that day. But old though he was, a veteran bar steward, probably poorly paid, with little but pride in his skills to relieve the daily grind, he was also a man. And he was entranced by her. I knew it at once. Could see it clear as day. Understood immediately the pleasure she was giving him, that he was feeling as he stood there before her. He had stepped into her circle, felt the warmth of her, and was held there, like a cat by the fire, reluctant to let it go, to give the moment up.

For she filled the room. Everyone there, I could tell, was acutely aware of her. Men and women both. And as they sat in their sofas and armchairs, or stood together in the bay window, it was as if every word they were saying to each other was about her, every glance, every look, turned in her direction, a low and urgent hum of whispers, all around the room, suddenly cut clean by the splashing lightness of her laugh, as though Joseph had just told her the funniest story she had ever heard.

And I, like the rest them, watched, almost enviously, as he spread his hands modestly, one of them clutching his silver salver as though that was the only way he could keep his balance in such precarious company, moving back and away from her as though the closeness, the heat, was almost too much to bear, yet still sadly sacrificed. And she tossed back her hair, gave him one last high-voltage beam, and then turned and caught sight of me, standing in the doorway, mesmerised like everyone else in the room. And smiled with delight at what she saw, electrifying every nerve and cell in my body.

How I walked across that room towards her, straining every resource to appear calm and collected and in control, past guests who I'm certain watched every step I took, I shall never know. I had all the willpower of a pin being drawn to a magnet. That day she was… she was just luminous.

"Cully," she said, patting the fender for me to sit beside her, the invitation drawing every eye in the room, her face wreathed in brightness, leaning forward to kiss me (disconcertingly close to the mouth), whispering "Happy Birthday", secretly, privately, so near that I could feel her breath in the words. And then, reaching for my hand to hold in her lap, the valleyed warmth and shape of her thighs pressing against my knuckles, "I do believe you're late," she continued. "And you haven't called. Not once. A whole week. I thought for a while there you were going to stand me up. Thought I was going to be left here all alone, that you'd forgotten all about me."

I have no idea now what I said by way of reply ("No, of course not"; "How could I possibly?", "You're looking quite lovely"; something along those lines). But what I do remember, as I sipped the drink that Joseph brought me, is that all my misgivings, uncertainties, anxieties seemed to ebb away as I allowed myself to bask in her spell – just as Joseph had done; in the pure headiness of her closeness, the marvelousness of the moment, aware of every eye in the room taking us in.

That day, my birthday, she was nothing short of radiant, entrancing, brimming with delight. And she was there for me, as sweet as Chantilly cream, as intoxicating as the finest *cru*, as precious then as the last caviar. I knew, oh yes, I knew, somewhere in the back of my mind, what I had to say to her, knew there were things I needed to know, but I simply couldn't bring myself to dull that moment, darken that light. Couldn't bring myself to look her in the eye and ask what I had to ask. I was disarmed, distracted, as though some powerful narcotic had stolen into my blood to dim my senses, blunt my edge, dilute my resolve.

It wasn't until later, in the first-floor dining room, after chilled mint and sorrel vichysoisse and a shared Châteaubriand that Roo declared was absolutely the best thing she had ever tasted, waiting for Sutton Row's legendary *Tarte tatin*, that I finally summoned the nerve to broach the subject which for a week had entirely preoccupied me, but which, for the last two hours, had been banished to the sidelines. My heart began to beat like a big bass drum.

"I quite forgot," I began lightly, tasting an ice-chilled Lafaurie-Peyraguey that Henri, the *sommelier,* had suggested would prove a fitting accompaniment to the *Tarte tatin* which even now, I could see, was approaching the table. "It seems… it seems we have mutual friends."

There. It was said. Now there was no going back.

She cocked her head to one side, frowned.

"Oh, yes? Who? You're kidding me?"

"No indeed. In fact, a very old friend of mine…"

The wine was poured, the darkly caramelised *tarte* presented, sliced and served, and we were left alone. "I've known his wife for years. And known him almost as long. He's my publisher – foreign rights, that sort of thing. They live here in town, and have a place upstate. Elliot Winterson."

I expected her to blanch, to blink, to swallow. Maybe start at the knowledge, deliberately included, that she was seeing a married man. She did none of these things.

She shook her head. "Elliot? Elliot who-did-you-say?"

"Winterson."

She thought for a moment, frowned. "Nope. Doesn't mean a thing."

"Roo," I said, disbelieving. Which I was. I'd seen them sitting at the same table. I'd seen them touch each other. I'd seen them look into each other's eyes. Only the week before. I knew it as certainly as I knew that the main constituent of the *Tarte tatin* was apple. I couldn't have been mistaken.

"No. It's true," she continued. "I don't know any Elliot. I mean, I'd know a name like that now, wouldn't I?"

It was a good try. But not good enough.

"I saw you together."

Now she did look startled.

"You saw us together? Where on earth…?"

"You must have been wearing a wig, but I'd have known you anywhere. It was you."

She flushed slightly, suddenly seemed uncertain, looked down. She picked up her fork and cut through the point of the *tarte*, spearing the tip and lifting it from the plate.

"I think, Cully, you're mistaken. It couldn't possibly…" She placed the *tarte* in her mouth, and began to eat.

And in that instant I knew I was right. She was lying, playing for time. I could almost see her mind racing ahead, looking for a way out. But there wasn't one.

"La Gave. Last Friday night."

She blinked and swallowed. The detail threw her. It was clear she was feeling uncomfortable, cornered.

I let the silence last a little longer. And then, "Are you having an affair with him?"

At which, astonishingly, she did look surprised. "An affair?" For the first time she looked me straight in the eye – and smiled. The idea seemed to amuse her.

Which, frankly, was disconcerting. Things were not turning out quite as I'd imagined. Here was I rapidly losing my way. And she was finding hers. Now it was my turn to feel unsure. Doubts began to creep in. Maybe they were old friends? Old lovers? Any number of possibilities I hadn't thought to consider. But surely I couldn't be mistaken? They must be having an affair. This was the woman Daphne had hired some detective to search out. And quite by chance I'd found her. I was sure of it.

"Isn't that what it's called?"

She sighed. "Not in my part of town, Cully."

"I don't follow."

"He's a client."

"Elliot? A client? You mean he's buying an apartment from you?" I couldn't believe it. Could it be that simple? But of course it couldn't. Realtors and clients didn't carry on like these two had carried on. I'd seen them. I knew.

She smiled, but sadly now. Then she seemed to come to a decision. She put down her fork and reached across for my hand which, unwillingly, I allowed her to take. She stroked the fingers, turned the hand over and gazed down as though she were reading my palm: "Oh Cully, you are a dear, you are really. I was going to tell you. I promise. It was just the time never seemed right. I didn't want to spoil things."

Of all her many voices this was her quietest, her most confiding.

"Tell me what?"

She looked around the room, then turned her eyes back to me. "I'm not a realtor, Cully. Well, let's be accurate. I am, but I'm not. Sure, I find people apartments, homes. I even relocate businesses when their premises get too small. I even have an office and two girls who work for me. You know that, you've spoken to them. But it's not how I make my money, Cully. My real money. It's not how I live. It's… I guess you could call it a good cover."

"Cover? Dear me, what on earth are you talking about?"

"I knew if I didn't tell you that somehow, some day, you'd find out.

Sooner or later. I just knew it. I mean, this is some small town. But I kept postponing it. Next time, I'd say to myself. I'll tell him next time. But I just didn't want to spoil it, you know? Spoil what we had going. I wanted to, I wanted to tell you. It just... it just got harder to do."

"What, for goodness sake? What got harder? What is all this?" I laughed then, but my heart was hammering fit to bust.

She took a deep breath, caught and held my eyes, then smiled, almost mischievously, as though her amusement at what she was about to tell me might somehow transfer to me. A secret shared.

"I'm a hooker, Cully. A call-girl. Very expensive. Very exclusive. And very, very discreet."

Hocho

Whenever and wherever we lunched – irregularly, hurriedly, fashionably, and usually expensively – Susan Tellinger, probably the city's most celebrated magazine editor, would slip off her ear clips and lay them on the table between us. It was just as well she didn't take off all her jewelry – the extravagant rings, the bangles, the necklaces, brooches, and clips that clung to her like leaves on a tree; there'd have been no room for the food.

When we first knew each other, this removal of ear clips always seemed to me an oddly intimate gesture which I rather liked. It spoke of a lowering of her guard, a comfort and confidence in my company. What it really was, I soon learned, was Susan's version of rolling up the sleeves, her way of saying, "time's short, so let's get down to business", "let's tell it how it is", "let's cut the crap". And while we talked she would play with these ear clips, arrange them, maneuver them like counters around the table, or use them to hammer home some point.

I asked her once how many ear clips she lost, forgot to pick up at the end of a meal?

None, she replied. It would be like leaving the restaurant without putting her shoes back on, she said.

Which is the other thing Susan Tellinger always did. Slipped off her shoes. Mostly she could tip them off toe to heel (she's tall for a woman and favors flats that come off easily), but sometimes she'd reach down, fumble for a moment, then sigh dramatically as her feet "breathed fresh air" – her description.

This time the two of us were late-lunching at Hocho, a newish sushi joint off Madison Avenue. Named after the long-bladed knife used by its chefs to prepare the fish, the place was packed and noisy with a post-lunch, ad-world crowd blithely *saké*-ing its way into a stifling Tuesday afternoon, a clientele high enough up the salary scale not to bother too much about the time, or the cost of the tiny splinters of fish, pellets of rice, and nests of shredded *daikon* that passed for a meal here.

Our reservation had been made for twelve-thirty, but the previous afternoon Susan's assistant had called from the magazine to re-schedule. Miss Tellinger would be held up. Could I make one-forty-five? Which was fine by me. I'd turned up five minutes early, was shown to a corner window table, and fiddled with my chopsticks until I caught sight of her playing chicken with the traffic, stop-starting her way across the road, ladened with the bags and wraps and shawls and folders that she found it impossible to go anywhere without. Within moments of being shown to my table she'd piled everything onto the floor, tipped off her shoes, ruffled her crop of terracotta-colored hair, re-arranged her bobbing accordion Miyake sleeves, and released her ear clips, both together, pushing them forward like gambling chips with those wrapped and varnished nails of hers that must have cost a hundred dollars a hand.

"What *am* I going to do, Cully? I'm near frantic. You have *no* idea…" she whispered dramatically, as though about to pass on some state secret. "The January issue should be all signed off and I've still got nothing firm. Kevin said 'maybe' he could do something on Cruise and Kubrick – but of course he's away till the end of the month. Grace has got Mario shooting an Eddie Bauer outback story in Oregon – hey-ho – for *Vogue*, which means he's off the map until well past our color dates. Matt wouldn't leave Graydon if I paid him in stock options, and Gail's somewhere in central Africa tracking down some hot-shit general called Kaliba or Kabila or some such, who runs an army made up of kids – 'kadogos', if you please – and is going to be big, *real* big, like next week.

"And to make life just that little bit more complicated," her ear clips tapping the table with every word, "there's not a damned Brit to be found anywhere. Time was you fell over them. Now they've all gotten five-bedroom cottages on the island, their phones off the hook, and hundred-thousand-dollar advances for writing captions and strap-lines. I mean, what's this town coming to when you can't even get hold of some *Brit* to write you a lead piece? By the way, you're still coming out to the island this weekend, aren't you? I'll pick you up Friday, right? I can't wait for you to see the new place."

Susan is not a pretty woman. Never was, never will be. For all the wrapped nails and elaborate make-up, the extravagant hair crops and colors, the Bliss facials, the airily denied implants and improbable cuts and tucks ("I'd only ever do it if Donna did the stitching", she once told me), none of it has ever quite worked. Her teeth are too small and her gums too exposed for her pumped collagen lips, her nose too pert for her oddly slanting eyes, and her cheeks way too rounded for the wire-framed Chekhov spectacles that she's favored since her earliest days.

But the energy and the talent! Make no mistake, Susan is *the* editor to get a call from – a photographer's dream, an art director's nightmare, and a writer's passport to those Long Island acres.

I've known Susan since she worked the fashion pages of the *Times*, and though we're as different as can be – she's always teasing me about my bow ties and horn rim spectacles and my "daring use of the polo-neck" – for some reason or other we've never lost touch. She's somewhere in her mid forties, I'd guess, single most of the time, but always, scandalously, on the look out. Oh yes, and gay.

Susan has never actually concealed her preference, but she's always been very discreet. About the only thing she ever is discreet about, come to think of it. When she first arrived at the *Times* after a graduate course at the New York College of Fashion and Design, the job was set up, so some on the paper whispered, by the woman she was then having an affair with, a designer of some considerable standing who just happened to control a substantial advertising budget.

But when that same designer's affections strayed elsewhere and the advertising budget was no longer an issue, it was Susan's talent kept her on. It wasn't just the way she set up the shoots she was assigned, the models she used, the photographers she found, the pictures she produced, it was the bulletins that accompanied them that never failed to surprise.

Like McKintyre, Susan's a born journalist, the writing easy and effortless, a sharp, stabbing style that has every word work for its place in the sentence; honest, incisive, and always right on the ball. And when, eventually, her *Times'* boss moved on, Susan moved up not out. Back then, between trips to Milan and Paris and London for the Collections, we'd make a date, have a bite to eat someplace, gossip, laugh and fifteen years on nothing has really changed. The same old Susan.

That lunch at Hocho, after fretting over her January issue, catching up on *Times'* scuttlebutt, and telling me all the hot Hollywood stories, generously larded with extravagant-sounding homosexuals and unbelievable excesses (the feature section of her magazine, *Rituals*, is required reading for anyone wanting the scandalous inside track on

Hollywood's high and mighty), she was dipping a last ruby wedge of *magoro* into a dish of soy and *wasabi* when she spotted someone over my shoulder, and waved whoever it was over with much jangling of bracelets.

"Haydn! Haydn! Here." And then, when the late-arrival reached our table: "Cully, meet my new assistant, Haydn Rossetto. Haydn, this is Cully Mortimer. The best goddamned food writer in the city, and he won't damn well give me a word!"

And as she made the introduction, I saw Susan's hand drop ever so slightly, tenderly, to the small of Haydn's back, and rest there possessively. I stood and shook Haydn's hand, said how pleased I was to meet her and, sharp as the blades they use at Hocho, Haydn said how much she enjoyed and admired my writing. She was a pretty little thing, preppy and fresh, with a young boy's floppy cap of black hair and a breathless enthusiasm.

As I sat back down, gently warmed by her compliments, I caught Susan's eye and smiled.

And she smiled back. Yes, indeed. The same old Susan!

"So. What news?" she asked.

"I thought you should know right away," said Haydn, her hand to her throat. "We got an e-mail from Gail. From the Congo. Says do you want a Kabila profile?"

"Yes!!" cried Susan, loud enough for the tables around us to turn in our direction, even in Hocho's hubbub. "God*dammit*, yes, yes, yes. Mail her back and give her the go-ahead. Six thousand, no eight thousand words. And, let me see… Yes, see if you can get Guido for the pix. He's still in Rome and has all the jabs from that Abyssinian shoot."

And then, turning to me, her husky voice gentling, imploring, her free hand swooping with a manic jangle across the table onto mine: "Are you sure you won't do something for me? Please, Cully? Anything you like. Anything."

I shook my head. "You know I can't. I'm contract. Staff."

"Maybe something ethnic…?"

"Susan, I keep telling you…"

"…Something European? Whatever you want… How was Europe, by the way?"

≈

Ah, Europe. Europe was... a dream. It was only two years but it seemed an age since I'd last set foot there. The summer before I'd spent my vacation in South Africa, ten days with friends in Cape Town followed by a week-long guest-lecturer accompanied tour of the Garden Route in which I was said guest lecturer. The whole thing had been set up by some whizz in the *Times*' promotion department and an ambitious mid-town travel agent, and had featured as a *Times* Weekend Supplement competition, the lucky winners of which, ten in all, got to travel and dine with yours truly. Tedious, but convenient.

Once again I'd done a handy deal with the paper. Rather than have my Sunday space rented out, avoiding that *Cully on holiday* tag at the end of someone else's, usually inferior, fill-in piece, I'd agreed to send stories from each of the three countries I intended visiting – kind of from-the-front-line sort of thing. Which was fine by me, given the first-class round-trip ticket which the management boys were persuaded to throw in as a sweetener.

I got into London late August. Or rather I got into London's Heathrow airport, before promptly taking a train south to the cathedral city of Salisbury. Not that I don't love London; I do, and couldn't wait to visit. But first I was seeing an old chum, Sara, an artist friend from Boston days who'd left the *Globe* the same time as me to work as an illustrator in London. Back then Sara lived in a basement apartment in Fulham, long before it became fashionable, where I stayed once or twice, put up on a ruinously uncomfortable sofa bed that smelled of cat pee and white spirit. Just when Sara was thinking it was maybe time to come back home, she met a City banker called Jamie, fell in love, and the rest is history.

At their home a few miles outside Salisbury I was given my usual room with its slanting floor and blackened beams, and every morning was left to my own devices while Jamie traveled up to his office in London and Sara hid herself away in her garden studio. At around midday, the two of us would meet for a glass of wine, a plate of assorted charcuterie, and a basket of the crusty bread I picked up each morning at the village baker. Real rural. Just great.

As a concession to my being there Sara took the afternoons off, and the moment lunch was finished we'd jump in her car and head for the coast in search of treasures, pouncing on the scallops and mussels and crabs and lobsters brought in each morning from the English Channel.

By the time Jamie returned from the City, dinner would be well-advanced and we would sit in their garden with gins and tonics until the time came to eat – long, langorous dinners taken under the stars when the weather was warm enough, or in the cottage's stone-flagged dining room when it wasn't. Which was pretty much always.

On the fourth morning I went up to town on the train with Jamie, parted company at the station and took a cab across town to Soho, my favorite London district. After buying some ruinously expensive Blue Mountain beans for Sara from the Algerian Coffee Store on Old Compton Street, I lunched at the new Conran restaurant, Mezzo, interviewed the head chef in his glass-walled kitchen office, and then called on the owner, Sir Terence Conran, for tea at his riverside home. At five-fifty-five I met Jamie, as arranged, beneath the clock at Waterloo Station, and together we caught the six-ten for the journey home.

Sir Terence, as usual, had been a delight. We've met once or twice in New York and have always gotten on well, probably because we like and admire the same things. He is a large, enthusiastic fellow, with a wide ruddy face, ready smile, and a voice you could coddle eggs with. By the time our train drew into Salisbury station I'd decided (and wrote as much) that if Sir Terence had been thin and quiet he would never have achieved half of what he has. Back at the cottage, while Jamie showered and Sara prepared dinner, I began my profile, finished it early the next morning, and e-mailed it back to the *Times* by the usual time.

A piece of cake.

≈

A few days later I packed my bag, said my farewells, and flew on to Paris where I checked in at my favorite hotel, the Logis des Gourmets Véritables on the Left Bank's rue de Sèvre which not a single American tourist has ever heard of (until now). August is not the best time to be in Paris if you have serious eating in mind; many of the city's great restaurants like Jean-Pierre Vigato's Apicius, Le Grand Véfour, and Faugeron shut up shop for the month. But Guy Larenne and his delightful wife, Danielle, entertained me royally when I called in to see them on rue Salette.

I'd always believed that it was Danielle who once told me that only Paris could have a street called rue de la Fidelité running into another street called rue du Paradis, but when I mentioned it to her over dinner my last night in Paris she looked perplexed, could not remember whether she had or had not told me such a thing, though of course, she added, it was certainly true. Guy, dressed in his whites with his name embroidered in gold on his breast, was not so certain. Scratching his stubbly chin, he declared that as far as he knew only a rue de la Table, an avenue de la Cuisine, or possibly a boulevard du Marché could ever lead to a rue du Paradis which, unsurprisingly, merited an indignant slap on the arm and some fruity French invective from Danielle.

But I hadn't come to Paris to work on a story, though Guy and Danielle brought me up to date on all the gossip which would, undoubtedly, come in handy in the months ahead. Instead, the third morning, I cabbed to the Gare du Lyon and caught a train for that city on the Rhône and Saône to research the second of my three pieces, putting up, thanks to the *Times*' Travel Editor, at the marvelously decadent Château de Bagnols.

In a city justly famed for its cuisine, with names like Bocuse, Chavent, Orsi, and Lacombe sharing a constellation of well-deserved Michelin stars, the humble Café des Fédérations might seem an unlikely choice for my first lunch in Lyon. But, hidden away in the old silk-weaving *quartier*, des Fédérations is as well-known among local gastronomes as the city's more illustrious names, one of a dozen or so *bouchons* which have fed the citizens of Lyon since the days when Rabelais was a medical student here. Very much the kind of restaurants that Simenon's Inspector Maigret would have loved (I said as much in my piece, mentioning *en passant* Casey's Bonnebouche for a local reference), Lyon's *bouchons* are what most Parisian bistros used to be – authentic, family-run establishments serving locally-based dishes in surroundings that have changed little since the turn of the century.

Here are tiled and wood floors scattered with sawdust, marble-topped tables spread with gingham cloths, Bentwood chairs, ancient cash registers, gaslight fittings, dimpled 'zincs', wall-mounted railway-carriage racks for briefcases, marvelous wood-panelled fridges with curved metal handles that have long since lost their shine, and weighty wrought-iron radiators that heat to scalding come winter and chill to ice in summer.

The menus I tried in the days that followed varied little from *bouchon* to *bouchon*, but were no less memorable for that: a feast of kidneys, hearts, brains, tongues, bone marrow, and sweetbreads prepared in dozens of different ways, not to mention Lyonnais specialties like the notoriously 'perfumed' offal sausages known as *andouillettes*, and *tablier de sapeur*, a weighty width of honeycombed tripe marinaded in milk, coated in breadcrumbs, and grilled.

Despite the emphasis on offal, I could as easily have chosen a delicate *quenelle* of pike caught in the nearby Dombes lakeland (and did), with a texture soft as shaving mousse; or a *Poulet au vinaigre* that puckered the cheeks; or a *Côte de porc rôti* served with prunes and puréed carrot; or a simple *pavé* steak, thick as a doorstep and pink and tender as a broken heart, each dish accompanied by a slab of steaming *Pommes Lyonnais* gratinéed the color of old ivory. Served on thick china plates you'd need a sledgehammer to chip or break, this was the kind of food you'd order after digging up the road or ploughing a field: gutsy, wholesome and always served in such challenging portions that I sometimes found it an effort of will to order the *dessert du jour* – an almond *Pithiviers* or *Tarte aux pralines* – or the local cheeses like St-Marcellin, and the ochre-colored Condrieu.

But, of course, I managed.

≈

To be honest, I'd made no plans for my third story. All I knew was that Seville must have something to offer and that my good friend Felix Doñano, head of a Madrid publishing house and son and heir to a family sherry business, would know better than anyone where to find it.

I'd met Felix through Elliot during negotiations over rights to one of my books (a collection of *Times'* articles on my favorite tables around the world, if I remember correctly). We'd gone out to dinner in New York and Felix and I had hit it off from the start. He is the very picture of a Spanish nobleman, tall, urbane with a deep, honied English accent and a taste for elegant English suiting.

By the time my plane touched down in Seville there he was, customary cigar in hand, waiting for me at passport control to waft me through formalities as though I were some visiting dignitary, before driving me at breakneck speed into the center of town.

"Tonight you will eat like a *Sevillano*," he told me, as he carelessly maneuvered his large German saloon through the hot and perilously narrow streets of the city, its fat tyres screeching against the kerbstones. "Tonight," he assured me, casually flicking cigar ash through his open window, "you will eat the finest food in Sevilla, in all of Spain."

And, of course, he was right. After an hour's siesta, a shower and change of clothes, Felix came to collect me at my hotel and the two of us set off on foot in search of a feast, Felix releasing my arm only to relight his cheroot or usher me into yet another of his favorite haunts.

According to the story I subsequently wrote (mercifully I took the precaution of making notes), we visited more than a dozen establishments that night, dark shadowy bars where the locals gather for flutes of chilled *fino* sherry and the tiny dishes called *tapas* that accompany them, the two of us sampling what Felix considered to be each house's speciality: a plate of oily Jabugo ham taken with the dry biscuits they call *picos* at Casa Roman; spit-grilled sardines at Kiosko de las Flores; vinegared anchovies called *boquerones* at El Bacalao; *Calamares in su tinta* at the Bar Estrella; juicy balls of meat called *albondigas* at La Giralda; a *Ternera de salsa* at El Rinconcillo; *Pimenton picante* at Sol y Sombra; an onion and chicken blood stew called *Sangre encebollada* at Ostrato; fanned slices of purple-skinned octopus at Gallego del Pulpo; spikey-shelled *canaillas* at La Trastienda that you tap on the bar to dislodge the flesh inside; slivers of cod stewed in Rioja wine at Modesto; and at Alta Mira a sweet, cinnamon flavored *Arroz con leche* that was simply delectable.

It was in this last bar, spooning up the last of the rice, that Felix, without any warning and in that coaxing, teasing Latin manner, asked after my love life.

And I, clearly intoxicated by the fine food and *finos* and grateful for his hospitality, proceeded to tell him about Roo.

Of course, not a day had gone by since our last meeting at Sutton Row that I hadn't thought of her. That day, my birthday, I guess I crossed some kind of Rubicon and made it to the other side, and did so with no sense of loss or sadness or disillusion. To be honest, finding out about Roo and Elliot, what she did, was more relief than anything. It meant, as she assured me it did, that he was just a client. Nothing more, nothing less. But for her I was something different. Someone she genuinely liked, someone she trusted, someone she felt safe with. I was a friend. Maybe more one day... who could say?

And she'd smiled at me like she smiled at Joseph and I felt, as we sat there in the library of Sutton Row, as seduced by her magic as he had been, listening to her explanations, the rest of the story left untold at Zdenka's.

"We have a strange relationship, you and I," I told her, reaching for her hand.

"We have the best relationship," she replied, not missing a beat. "Since I met you, you've never pushed, you've never intimidated, you've never... overwhelmed me. No, that's not the word. Never... bludgeoned me. You let me be, you let me breathe. Like now, when you find out what I really do, you don't make any kind of judgement call. You just accept." She took a deep breath. "And you listen. God! That's the most important thing. I can talk to you – and I know you're taking it in, not waiting for a chance to interrupt and talk about YOU! I listen to that 'me' talk all the time."

For a moment in that library, lulled by her voice, warmed by her feelings for me, and the brandies we nursed in our nest-like sofa, I'd been tempted to ask Roo to join me for the trip to Europe, to be my companion if nothing else. But, of course, I didn't. We hadn't known each other long enough, I decided, to spend three weeks together. Instead I sent her postcards from every place I went, and bought her tiny gifts I hoped would amuse her: a stick of pink candy from Bournemouth, a jar of violet *pastilles* from Fauchon in Paris, a fan and castanets from Seville. That sort of thing. Nothing expensive, nothing significant – not then.

"You have slept with her, of course," said Felix, pushing away his empty plate and leaning back in his chair. A cigar was slipped from its leather case, snipped and lit. Tipping back his head and letting the smoke stream through his lips to the ham-strung ceiling, he glanced across at me. "Of course, I don't mean to intrude," he said with a grin. "If you'd rather not..."

"No, no. Please." And then: "To tell the truth, Felix, I haven't. In fact, I'm not even sure that I shall."

Felix thought about that for a moment. "Of course you will," he said. "And the way to do it is to cherish her. Women love to be cherished."

"It's not as straightforward as you think."

"Cully. It is never straightforward. That is what is so good about it."

"No, you don't understand."

"So what's to understand, Cully? She's a woman, my friend. A woman. There to be loved."

"She's also…" I took a breath. "She's a hooker, Felix. A call-girl."

I cannot now imagine what prompted me to confide like this in Felix. For all our closeness, I'd said nothing to my old friends Sara and the Larennes of my new companion, and had felt pleased and strong-willed at my restraint. Yet here I was with Felix, in this pokey, smoky bar in Seville, spilling the beans like a lovelorn teenager.

"You should have brought her with you," said Felix later, walking me back to my hotel. "I think I would like very much to know this young lady," and he turned to me with a sly, mischievous look, then punched me lightly on the arm to let me know he was joking.

Maybe it was the drink but I felt a great affection for him then. The way he hadn't been shocked, the things he'd said, the questions he'd asked. He'd taken it seriously, and had been only occasionally flippant which was, of course, a part of his character, his charm, and easily forgivable.

It was only later, as I prepared for bed that first night in Seville, that I began to feel a certain discomfort at just how much I'd confided. And as I lay my head on the pillow, I resolved never, ever again, to tell anyone what Roo did for a living.

≈

I'd been back only a few days when I met up with Susan for lunch at Hocho. Of course, I'd called Roo the moment I returned, and for the next three days, but there was only her Ansaphone to speak to. I also tried Relocate but the two ladies were unable to help; as far as they knew Miss Carew was still in town.

But she wasn't, I just knew it, or she'd certainly have returned my calls. She had to be away somewhere. I wondered where, wondered what she was doing. Was she with someone? Was she working? The least she could have done was let me know – a note, a phone message. After all, she knew when I was coming back. I admit I was a little put out, impatient to see her again, to give her the presents I'd brought back for her. But then I decided not to call any more, nor to leave any further messages. I knew she'd get in touch eventually, so I would wait.

As things turned out, I didn't wait long.

The new house that Susan wanted me to see the weekend after our Hocho lunch was out on Long Island, a few miles from Sagaponack and an odd choice for someone who hated the water, couldn't swim, and never much liked the sun on her. And this was the second place she'd gone and bought by the sea, finally selling off her first weekend hideaway when she found herself with the money to trade up.

"Four hundred and seventy-five thousand dollars," she told me that last weekend in September, as we drove past the turning to her old house on our way to the new. She'd been waiting for me on the platform at Bridgehampton, wrapped in a tightly-belted Bogart macintosh, sheltering from the sun under a waxed oriental parasol. Driving between low potato fields on one side and dunes on the other, along a road windswept with sand, she glanced across at me. "Can you believe it? That's what I got. Four hundred and seventy-five. For a hut."

"So how much was this one?" I asked, as we turned off the road and slithered down a sandy track leading to what looked like a substantial two-floor property built on stilts at the edge of the beach. Its wood-boarding was a light salty grey against the evening's blue ocean sky, its twin decks trimmed with peeling gingerbread.

"Don't ask, Cully. I won't tell you." And as we pulled to a stop and got out of the car: "I wouldn't dare. Absolutely not. And, anyway you wouldn't believe me."

And there, suddenly, dancing down the front steps and running towards us, was someone I recognized, but at first couldn't place, so out of context.

Of all people.

Roo.

"Oh yes," said Susan, with a curling smile of satisfaction at my dumbfounded expression. "I forgot to mention. Apparently we have more friends in common than we thought." And then, as she handed me my bag from the trunk: "And you didn't even tell me."

"Cully, Cully, Cully. It's you. Oh…" Roo, warm and fresh and smelling of the sea, flung her arms around me and hugged me tightly. "It's so wonderful to see you again." And then stepping back, holding my shoulders like a mother inspecting a son after his first term away at school. "Look at you. You look great. Doesn't he, Susan? Doesn't he look just great? And you're tanned. Have you ever seen him so brown?" And then to me again: "I've missed you. I really have. I couldn't believe it when Susan said she had you coming to stay." And chattering on, she linked her arms in ours and led us to the house, twisting in front of us as we started up the steps to pull at the apron she was wearing: "And guess who's cooking dinner?"

There were five of us for dinner that evening. Susan, Roo and I, and Susan's other house-guests: a grubby-looking, goatee-ed Norwegian fashion photographer called Niels, dressed in leather jacket, too-big surfer shorts and trekkers' boots, and a willowy, waif-like model with breadstick arms and kohl-rimmed eyes called, of all things, Tubby, both of whom Susan had flown over from Paris for a fashion shoot. The rest of the crew – Niels's assistant Hez, Kuto the make-up man, Kerry the hair stylist, and Susan's assistant, Haydn – were staying at a motel in nearby Wainscott and would join us the following morning.

As Susan explained as she showed me up to my room – bare plank walls under the eaves, sandy floorboards and a squeaky brass bed – this was going to be a working weekend. She still had five color spreads to fill for the January issue. Ten pages. "And what better location than a Long Island beach and a new house?" she said. "My house. Do you have any idea how much the magazine has to pay for spots like this? I'll get a new kitchen out of it, no problem."

Dinner that night was *al fresco*, on the lower deck overlooking the beach, candles hardly stirred by the still night air, knives, forks, plates, and glasses shimmering on a white linen bed sheet that served as a table cloth and bunched in our laps. Beyond, in the darkness, the sound of the ocean was nothing more than a soft, regular thump and sometimes audible hiss as a high tide approached.

Roo had clearly been working hard. Though Tubby contented herself with a single bowl of cereal, the rest of us tucked into a warm scallop salad with a soy and lemongrass vinaigrette, and a very creditable Lasagne (Roo was delighted when I asked for a second helping), followed by a wedge of the Manchego cheese and quince jelly which I'd bought at Seville airport's Duty-Free for Susan's weekend gift.

It was over dinner that I discovered how Susan and Roo had met. It was the simplest of connections. Susan had gotten Relocate to sell her 'hut' and Roo had found a buyer ("some second-year kid at Lehman

Brothers," said Susan, "with more dollars than sense"). Roo had also found her this new house, helped arrange the finance, and Susan had moved in only the weekend before. Firm friends by this time, and knowing that Roo was freelance, Susan had asked her to stay on and help organise things – she was too busy to do it herself and didn't want to have everything drag on. While Susan and I were having lunch at Hocho, and I was fretting about why I couldn't reach her, Roo was out here on the island all the time, getting the place ready, on hand for the utility services and the movers.

"If it hadn't been for you, my darling," said Susan, reaching across the table and squeezing Roo's arm, "why we'd be sleeping in tents on the beach right now."

"Tents – how romantic," said Tubby wistfully. "Like a sleep-over. Wow. Let's do it anyway."

"If it was tents for the sleeping I stay in hotel," said Niels, playing with the candle wax, rolling it into balls with his grubby fingers. It was about the only thing he said all evening.

"Isn't he just the pits?" said Roo, as we cleared up after Susan had pleaded an early rise and shooed her team off to bed. Like the rest of the house the kitchen was still a few days from being finished. A step-ladder stood by the windows with a set of wood blinds resting against it, knotted electrical wires stuck out from beneath the wall cupboards and, tantalisingly, the corner of a dishwasher peeped from a half-opened box only a few feet from an electric point and the empty space in the work surface where it would stand. "Just before you came down," she continued, "I went out onto the deck to ask if he wanted a drink and he was just sitting there, picking his nose. And he didn't stop when he saw me. Just kept on... you know..."

"Picking."

"Really. Gross."

Ten minutes later, the kitchen as tidy as we could get it, we were back on the lower deck, the candles guttering a little now, the Montauk light sweeping out its distant signal as Roo pulled a tobacco tin from her bag and began rolling herself a marijuana cigarette.

"I didn't know you smoked that stuff?"

"You never asked." And then: "Does it bother you? If it does, I can always..."

"Good gracious, no. Each to their own," I said, thinking of Lydia.

"You ever try it?"

"To be honest…"

"You'd like it."

"You think so?"

"You don't have to, you know."

"I'll take your word for it. Live dangerously."

And so, the cigarette rolled and lit, we made our way down the steps and walked barefoot along the beach.

"It'd be easier if you smoked," said Roo, handing it to me. "Just don't try to inhale the first go," she said, clapping my back when I did just that and coughed and spluttered, trying to find my breath. "Just a little, just a little. That's the way. Easy does it."

…That's the way. Easy does it… Easy does it…

I don't remember how far we walked and I don't remember one iota of what we talked about, nor can I explain what we found so funny, out there by the shoreline, the sea racing up the beach and sluicing past our ankles. All I do remember is a warm night sky and silent, glittering stars, sand sinking beneath our feet, and Roo guiding me giggling back to the house, shush-shushing me as we climbed the stairs, helping me up to my room. Nothing but that, nothing but darkness and cool air and the scent and the sound of the ocean until, some time later, a great bright light and the gentlest shake on my shoulder brought me awake. Roo, with a cup of tea, some buttered toast, and a glass of orange juice.

"Hey there, party animal. I let you lie in long enough. Now it's time to get up and get out. Everyone's arrived. It's really fun. Come on, lazy bones. Shake a leg there, soldier."

≈

If Niels had remained silent most of the previous evening he made up for it that morning and for the rest of my stay, spurred on by Susan in the various locations the two of them chose for the shoot. As I came down the stairs I could hear his voice out on the beach, lilting, brusque, pleading, sharp. While Roo moved and unpacked the various boxes that still littered the living room, I sat out on the deck with a second cup of tea and watched them at work on the beach.

Fashion shoots. Extraordinary things. For the January issue Susan was doing fur coats which, the night before, had hung around the house in zip-lock plastic cocoons – a half-million dollars worth of fake fur

("Doncha just love it," Susan had remarked). Now, in eighty-degree heat, clearly naked beneath a long Dalmation-spotted fur of unknown provenance, Tubby was rolling her way down a nearby dune – all flailing, furred arms and white boyish body – with the team watching from the bottom of the slope: Susan, under her parasol; Niels, behind his camera; his assistant, Hez, a tall, lanky youth in similar uniform, flashing forward every minute with his light meter; Haydn, in chinos and knotted check shirt, who waved her clipboard at me when she saw me on the deck; the make-up man, Kuto, standing amongst his various bags; and the harrassed hair-stylist, Kerry, who seemed most put out that his carefully constructed creation was being so thoughtlessly ruined in the sand.

Between two reflector boards, Niels knelt and leapt, shouted and screamed in what sounded like three different languages while Tubby rolled down the dune, stood up, trudged back up the slope, with Kerry and Kuto doing what damage control they could, and rolled down "just one more time".

A few yards away, a handful of joggers, dog-walkers, and surfers gathered to watch proceedings. Each time Tubby did the roll, they applauded loudly.

"Way to go, baby."

"Just one more roll, lady," followed by enthusiastic wolf-whistles.

Tubby loved it, of course. Having an audience clearly pleased her. At the top of the dune, for another of Neils' one-more-time rolls, she wrapped herself up in the coat, bowed briefly to her fans, and flung herself down the slope.

"She won't be able to walk straight for a week," said Roo, refilling my cup and pulling up a chair beside me.

"I doubt it worries her. She's probably earning more than you and I put together."

"I wouldn't bank on it," said Roo, with a wink.

Lunch was eaten on the beach. Haydn and Roo had set out blankets by the steps to the house and unpacked one of the weekend hampers ordered in for the shoot. Out of the wicker basket came a wedge of smoked Virginia ham, devilled chicken wings, a dozen cold lobster claws, a potato salad with chives and gherkins, hot-buttered *ciabatta* rolls, and a tomato, basil and mozzarella salad that Roo had put together that morning.

One by one the team plumped themselves down around the food and cool-bags. Roo and I drank a very chilled Chablis, the rest an assortment of beers, spritzers and exotic-sounding mineral waters. Kuto was the last to join us but he didn't sit down. He was gripping his wrist and looked distraught.

"Has anyone seen my watch?"

"You've lost your watch?" This from Kerry.

"I had it this morning, on the beach. I'm certain."

"Maybe you left it someplace? Have you checked the bathrooms?" suggested Susan.

"No. Yes. I have searched absolutely everywhere."

"Good watch?" asked Niels, tipping back a bottle of beer.

"Only a Breitling Chronoliner. Gianni gave it me the first time I worked with him. As a thank-you. Gianni!"

"Bet you dropped it in the sand," said Tubby, still wrapped in her Dalmation coat.

"Maybe one of the crowd...?" said Hez.

"But I'm sure I had it when we finished and came back in. I'm certain of it."

"You insured?" From Niels.

"Of course, but..."

"I bet Tubby's right," said Roo. "It's probably over there on the dune someplace. Come on, let's go look," and up she jumped, took his hand, and led him away to the dune.

In the end, of course, we all went to look, leaving our picnic lunch to scrabble about in the sand. Trying to remember where Kuto had been standing, where he'd gone. Kerry volunteered to look through his bag in case the watch had somehow gotten in there, and Hez did the same with all the film and camera cases.

But we never found the watch, and by the time we got back to our lunch the lobster was gritty with sand and the ham a tad dry.

And so the three days I spent at the beach flew by: early morning starts, picnic lunches, frantic evening shoots to catch the light while it lasted, and long, lazy dinners taken on the deck. Twice, Roo and I took Susan's car to go off in search of supplies, shopping happily along the main streets of Bridgehampton and East Hampton, taking too long over iced teas at Angelo's and then having to hurry back to the house to prep the next meal. She even bought me a swimsuit when I admitted I didn't have one with me – I don't have one at all, but I didn't tell her that – and then, horror of horrors, she insisted I go swimming with her.

With a towel over my shoulders and hers trailing in the sand, we made our way to the water where I dove in fast as I could. She thought me terribly brave and told me so (she seemed not to think I might be embarrassed by my body, and want it covered whatever the chilling cost), and I remember thinking how lean and graceful she looked in her navy blue one-piece, high-stepping through the waves, and how Susan should use her for a swimsuit shoot, even said as much.

"Only if you'll do it with me," she called back over the waves, as though my sucked-in stomach and nascent breasts, which she appeared not to notice, would prove no obstacle to a modeling career.

That weekend, out on the island, I tell you, it was as if I'd never been away from her, but Monday morning, sadly, I returned to Manhattan alone. I'd hoped Roo would join me, but Susan wanted her to stay on.

"Please say 'yes', please, please…" begged Susan over breakfast. "There's still so much to do. Come back with us Thursday. We'll be finished by then. We can go back together. You don't mind, do you Cully?"

There was a moment's hesitation from Roo, which I interpreted as her preferring to return with me. But it was only a moment. In the end, she elected to stay with a reluctant "oh, okay then" to Susan, and an *I'm-sorry* shrug to me.

And who, I suppose, could blame her? Three more days on the beach. If I hadn't had a story to write and a whole book-full of appointments to keep, I'd have stayed on myself. Even gone swimming again.

≈

The next time I saw Susan there was snow dusting the sidewalks and she looked, appropriately I suppose, like death. It was a grim, brittle November afternoon out on Riverside Drive. She'd recently gotten back from a Collections' marathon through London, Paris and Milan and we met on the steps of Riverside Baptist Church for a colleague's memorial service. A month earlier, the *Times* fashion-page editor who'd moved on to make way for Susan had choked on a fish bone. By the time they removed it, she'd died of a heart attack. Which, if you didn't know, is often how it happens. Apparently the heart gives out in panic as you struggle for breath.

Anyhow, the great and the good had turned up for the service. Writers, photographers, editors, some well-known designers. Susan and I arrived in separate cabs but stepped out onto the sidewalk the same moment, kissed, linked arms and went in together. It wasn't until we were sitting in our pew, listening to an *a cappella* litany from the Harlem Boys Choir, that I realized that what at first, when we met on the church steps, I'd taken for a deathly shade of mourning make-up and artfully sorrow-darkened eyes, was actually the real thing. And she'd lost weight as well – lots.

After the service we stood on the church steps as the first of the city's snow gave up the effort and turned into a chilly drizzle.

"Bite to eat?" was all I could think to say.

"Why not," she said, burrowing her hands into the pockets of a camel hair poncho. "But a quickie. You know somewhere? You ought to."

And it just so happened I did.

Spoonlickers had opened a couple of months earlier. It had started out as a kind of theme restaurant for kids ('from cradle to college' ran the promotional bumpf), but the grown-ups had quickly hi-jacked it. The place served every kind of comforting suck and swallow nursery food you can imagine, from Boston beans to Welsh Rarebit, from bangers 'n' mash to admiral's pie. But the real pull was Spoonlickers' 'Stickies' – a mouthwatering roster of fools and fritters, *clafoutis* and *croquignoles*, pavlovas, pancakes, melbas and meringues, syllabubs, *brûlées*, *mousses*, jellies, cheesecakes, trifles, tarts and flans, sponges, *roules* and pastries, everything dusted with sugar, filled with fruits, draped with warm caramel, ladled with pooling chocolate, drizzled with honeys and syrups, or served with any of a hundred assorted ice creams, *granitas* and sorbets. And not a single dish over six hundred calories. How could they fail? We waved down a cab, and I gave the driver instructions.

At this early hour Susan and I had no trouble finding a table, and with a sigh she pulled off her ear clips and leaned down to release her shoes.

"I'm gonna have me some words with that Manolo, don't you worry," she said, as the waitress came to the table. Without bothering to consult the menu, I ordered the Praline Cracnel with hot butterscotch sauce and hazelnut sorbet for the two of us. Susan waved a hand –

'whatever'.

"I ought to say you look great," I began, when the waitress left us. I tried to make it sound light-hearted but didn't quite pull it off. Which, I guess, was understandable. In the bright lights of Spoonlickers, after the gloom of the church, Susan looked even worse, pale as uncooked veal.

"You noticed."

I shrugged – how could I not?

"Are you sick? Did you catch something?"

"You could say."

She looked around her – at the clown pictures on the walls, at the plastic tables in bright primary colors, and up at the tented 'big-top' ceiling – as though hoping, it seemed to me, to find something else apart from her appearance to talk about, maybe wishing she'd not accepted my invitation, suddenly vulnerable and tense in the unforgiving light. She nodded to herself a few times, then said it would make a great location for a shoot, asking, in a not-that-much-interested voice, how long the place had been going?

I told her I'd come to the opening a few weeks back. "With Roo, as a matter of fact."

Susan gave a start – as though I'd said something I shouldn't have.

"Do you two still see each other?" I asked. Suddenly that summer weekend at Susan's new house out on the island seemed a very long way away.

For a moment or two she said nothing, playing with her ear clips. Then she looked me straight in the eye. "In a manner of speaking."

"I don't follow…"

Susan looked away again, clearly trying to decide whether she should continue. And then, taking a deep breath: "I don't know if I should be saying this. You knowing Beatty and all."

"Saying what? You're sounding very mysterious, Susan."

"Beatty, Roo, Beatty, Roo," she said, tapping her ear clips on the table in time to the names. "Christ alive," she sighed. And then she seemed to make up her mind about something. "You realize, I suppose, that this property thing of hers, Relocate, it's just a sideline?"

"Sideline?" I asked, cautiously.

"Lucrative, of course, but a sideline," Susan continued. "Look, I don't know how much you know and, like I say, I don't even know if

I should be telling you anyway… But that's how Beatty finds them, the big spenders. Through the properties. And in her case the real deal, the real money, is what happens after. You see, Beatty… well, I guess you could say she's not all she seems to be."

And that's when I knew what Susan was trying to say. I decided to help her out.

"You mean, she's a hooker."

Susan looked taken aback. "She tell you that, or you found out for yourself?"

"I saw her once, with someone I know. I asked her about him and she told me."

Susan smiled, wearily: "And?"

"We're just friends."

"Take my advice. Keep it that way. Me, I'm in big time."

"You?" It was my turn to be taken aback. "How so? I thought you and Haydn…"

Susan smiled. "Haydn's a sweet girl, but she's a child. Beatty's a whole different specimen. You remember that weekend at the beach? The shoot? Well, that's when it all started."

Our order arrived, and we waited while the waitress poured the hot butterscotch sauce around the cracnel and sorbet. I was reeling.

"You really want to hear all this? You're sure?" asked Susan, when the waitress had gone.

"If you want to tell me." If she hadn't, I'd have pulled out her lacquered and wrapped fingernails one by one until she did.

"Well now, I do and I don't," she said, picking up her spoon and incising a pattern around the lumps of praline. "But let's be brave, right. Old friends and all." She put down her spoon without tasting anything and gathered up her ear clips, rattling them in cupped hands like a pair of dice. "Where to start, Cully, where to start? The day you left, I guess. That Monday night. I suppose that's as good a place as any. It was late, we'd all turned in, and Beatty comes to my room. A little tap on the door, and there she is. I'm in bed reading, got the bedside light on, and in she comes. Wrapped in a towel from the shower. Doesn't say a word, just comes right over and sits on the edge of my bed. And puts her hand under the sheet. Just like that. And with the other she takes away my book, switches off the light and then gets in to bed with me. Oh God, Cully, what on earth am I saying to you?

What will you think?"

"What's to think?" I managed to say. "You're a grown-up."

"It doesn't bother you?"

"Should it?"

"I don't know. I guess not," she said, putting down the ear clips and picking up her spoon again, dipping into the butterscotch sauce this time but still not eating anything. "You're still sitting there, so I guess you're up for it. Anyway. That night. It was… unbelievable. It was… I mean the sex was… whoa!! That girl was indecently dee-fucking-*licious*. Knew every turn, every which way. And the strangest thing was, you know, I hadn't seen it the whole time we were out on the island. Fancied her, sure. Who wouldn't? Great-looking girl. Even made a couple of half-hearted passes. But there were no vibes coming back, nothing. And then, that night after you'd gone, she just came at me right out of left field. *Totally* unexpected."

I nodded, beginning to feel a little guilty now. "Maybe I should have told you. Said something. I didn't think."

"Who would, for God's sake, I mean… hookers are for men, right? Not for women. That's how it's supposed to be, isn't it?" Susan finally scooped up a curl of the sorbet and slid it into her mouth. "Except, of course, I didn't know she was a hooker back then."

"You didn't know?"

"That came later, Cully. Right then, that Monday night, Tuesday, Wednesday, we were lovers. Believe you me. Soon as the lights were out, in she would come, slide into my bed. And I just… I just couldn't resist her. And she seemed to feel the same."

"And then?"

"And then… well, let's just say the honeymoon didn't last. Or rather it did, but the rules of engagement changed."

"How changed?"

For a while Susan said nothing, just played with her pudding, then took up the story once more, quieter now. "We'd been back in town a few weeks, seeing each other, you know how it is. And then, suddenly, she doesn't call. I don't know where she is. A week passes. Two. And I'm going *mental*. I even call the hospitals. Maybe she's been mugged, run over, a brain tumor, whatever. Nothing. And then one evening I call on the off-chance and, hey presto, she picks up the phone. She sounds fine, says she's been away someplace. Had been meaning to ring, sorry and all.

"So we agree to meet up, that very evening, a bar she knows over on Lexington. Well, I get there, dressed to kill and ready to roll. So hot for it it hurts. And that's where she spells it out. In a booth, in a bar, on a stretch of Lexington I didn't even know existed. It's been great but it's over, she tells me. Or rather, she says, it's over if I want it to be. Which I don't, and I tell her so. So then she says, leaning closer, maybe we can come to some arrangement. Which is, I ask? And then she comes out with it, tells me she's on the game, and that if I want her I'm gonna have to pay. How do you like that?"

"I'm astonished." And I was.

"You and me both. Didn't know what to think. Except I still wanted her. Despite what she'd told me. And she just sat there in the booth and watched me, as if she knew what was going on in my head, what I was thinking. So finally I ask how much? What would it cost? Anything to keep it going, you know? I don't know what got into me. I should have just left. Walked out. But I couldn't, Cully, I just couldn't tear myself away."

"So what happened?"

"She said it would cost a thousand bucks. Just like that. A thousand, cash. Otherwise, well, it had been fun, nice knowing you sort of thing. She said she quite understood if I didn't want to go that route. Not for everyone… No hard feelings. But she had me on the hook, and we both knew it." Susan took a deep breath. "So I paid. We went back to my place, and I had to pay her. Before she even took her coat off."

"And?"

"And it was great," Susan laughed, a brittle little laugh, snappy as the cracnel. "I mean as good, if not better. A whole different thing. Rougher, too, as though she knew that was how I liked it. Before, I'd kept that down a bit – the heavy stuff. I didn't want to frighten her off. But she seemed to know it was what I wanted, and she… you know, she gave it to me…" Susan paused, rolled her eyes to the ceiling, brought them down onto me. "Cully, I don't believe I'm *saying* all this to you."

"Nor do I, to tell the truth."

"And yet, you know, it makes it better, telling someone. Sharing it." She reached out a hand to cover mine. And then, like me with Felix, as though she realized she'd said more than she'd intended:

"But promise me, Cully, faithfully, you'll never tell a soul. And specially not Beatty."

"Of course not. Of course, I won't." I put my hand to my mouth and coughed, an icy sliver of the hazelnut sorbet going down the wrong way, pricking tears into my eyes as it went. "So, how long has all this been going on?"

"It was like that for a month or so. End of September. October, save a break for the Collections. Once a week, maybe twice. Okay, so it wasn't going to be the great love affair I'd planned, not on her side anyway. But at least we were still seeing each other, getting it together, you know. And maybe, just maybe I thought, I could get through to her. Maybe I could get it back to what it had started out as. What I'd imagined it had started out as."

"And did you?"

"Some chance."

"And now?"

"Now it's not so often."

"How so?"

"One night," Susan paused, pushed her plate away. "One night she tells me it's going to cost a little more. A thousand isn't enough. Now it's going to be two."

"Jesus H." I was flabbergasted. "I can't believe this is the same girl we're talking about."

"It's the same girl, okay. And I couldn't believe it either. I just felt, you know, shattered. Suddenly, I realize there's *no* chance... no chance *at all* of getting away from the... from the business aspect. To her, I'm commerce. Plain and simple. And it hurts, I can't tell you. But I *can* still afford it – just. Certainly not as often but, you know, now and again. A treat. Because you know the funny thing? I still want her. She's just... magic. Magic."

"I know what she does, but I never knew the details, how she sets things up. She tells me stories now and then, but that's all. Just kidding round really. I guess it intrigues me. The journalist in me."

"And she's never said anything about me?"

"Never. Not a word."

"I guess I should be grateful. At least she's discreet. I'll tell you something, though. She's got a temper. I mean, that girl can be... hostile."

"Roo?"

"Well, maybe you never see it. No reason why you should. She thinks the world of you, you know that? Always Cully this, and Cully that. You ought to hear her. If I didn't like you so much, I'd hate you for it."

Despite everything Susan had told me, I felt a warm curl of pleasure at this. "So tell me, where does the temper come in?" I asked.

"It's very quick. There's no warning. But believe me it's… it's swift and it's savage."

"Come on, not Roo. Now you really are kidding."

"Let me tell you," said Susan, suddenly earnest, leaning across the table and lowering her voice. "You don't believe me? Just listen to this. One time we arranged to meet, had dinner, went back to my place, and I was a couple of hundred short. Cabs, tips, that sort of thing. So she takes the money, counts it, as though she can't believe I haven't got enough, and then tells me she's in a hurry and has to leave. With my money in her hand, *ex-cuse* me. A little over seventeen hundred dollars. I tell her, 'hey, I'm sorry and all, I'll get you the rest next time'. And then, without the slightest warning, she just hits me with the money, slaps me across the face with this wad of notes. And tells me, in no uncertain terms I might say, that I had just better mind that I do. And her eyes are real narrow, you know, with… with, like, malice. You wouldn't believe it."

"And she stayed?"

"She stayed." Susan paused, sighed. She'd started playing with her ear clips again. "And how. To tell the truth, sometimes I don't know if she's really losing her temper or just playing the part she thinks I'm after; what I want. Whatever, it works. It *really* works. And that, Cully, is the problem. What's happened is, I just can't do without her, money or not. In fact, in some ways, the money makes it even wilder. The more I pay, the more I see her. And the more I see her the better the sex. And every time I see her the deeper and deeper and deeper I'm getting into her. To put it bluntly she's driving me nuts.

"So you see, Cully," Susan said with the saddest smile, "I'm getting fucked every which way. And you know what? Sooner or later I'm going to start hating it more than I love it. And then… well, then I don't know what I'm going to do."

Spoonlickers

"So anyway, like I say, this guy is big, I mean *big*, in the fashion world. You'd know the name, believe me. Straight off. Once a month I go to his apartment and there he is, just beautifully turned out, you know? The best hand-tailored suit, wonderfully shined black Oxfords, whiter than white Sulka shirt, silk tie. I mean, the business.

"So, the deal is we have a drink, a chat. Maybe half an hour. Lights are down, a little opera in the background. And then he leads me into his study, goes to his desk, and finds me a pair of those big cloth-cutting scissors – the really big ones you almost need two hands to hold – and all I do is very carefully, very slowly, very quietly, so you can hear the sound of the scissors working through the material, cut the clothes off of him. Everything. I start with the jacket sleeves, right up into his armpit, then up the back from vent to collar, like I'm skinning some animal, then the buttons off his shirt, one... two... three... Then the pants, the shorts..."

"I get the picture."

"...And for that small exertion he pays me five thousand bucks."

"A month?"

"Sometimes more. Cash. Not bad, huh?"

"Do you take off your clothes?"

Roo shook her head.

"Do you ever, you know, make love?"

"Never. Not a once." And then she gave me that look – patient, making allowances. "You gotta under*stand*, Cully; that's not what it's all about. There's a lot more to it than just getting naked, doing it, you know? There are... levels. That's why there are people like me, people who aren't afraid, people who aren't going to hold back. People, I guess, who know the game and'll go that extra mile. Or two. Or three. Take care of people who have, let's say, eccentric tastes.

"Besides," she said, licking her spoon, "he'll have come by the time I finish cutting the clothes off of him."

"So you think I could do it? You think he'd mind? A hundred dollars a snip. I could really play it out, you know. And if I don't have to take my clothes off..."

We were sitting in Spoonlickers. It was tea-time, let's see... mid November, the week before Thanksgiving, a week or more since

Susan and I had talked. We were entertaining each other with lurid stories, trading professional secrets. We'd been shopping.

≈

"We're going shopping."

The phone had rung within minutes of my e-mailing that Sunday's column to Sanchez, a seasonal offering on Thanksgiving with sidebar recommendations from some chefs of my acquaintance: classic cornbread stuffing, pumpkin wedges, a southern states' tarragon and pecan bake – that sort of thing. I knew it was Roo the moment I heard the first bleat. An hour later, scarved, gloved and coated, I was down in the hall waiting for her. She'd said fifteen minutes, but I knew better now.

She arrived in a smart silver-grey Volvo estate, the ones with the rear lights high up either side of the hatch-back door. But it wasn't Roo doing the driving. Instead a bulky-looking black man spun the steering wheel with a hand the size of a serving dish and pulled up at the kerb. I could see her sitting in the back, pointing me out to him, waving and leaning over to open the passenger door at about the same time he came round to open it for me – menacingly dressed in black leather jacket, black polo-neck that seemed to fit him far better than mine ever did me (how did he keep the ribbed collar so stiff around the neck?), black moleskins, and pointed black leather boots.

I nodded my thanks and slid into a warm, perfumed interior, all snugly intimate, the hide seats soft and slippery, the door clunking shut behind me, to find Roo, wrapped in a tie-belt, high-collared cashmere coat, taking my hand to draw me to her and brushing my cheek with warm lips.

"Bruno," said Roo, as the driver sunk back into his seat, "meet Cully."

"Mr. Cully." Bruno nodded at me in the rear-view mirror, shifted into gear, then slid forward smoothly as though there was no other car on the road.

"Bruno is magic," said Roo, as we turned downtown, and she patted my hand excitedly. "Just you wait."

And so he was. For the next three hours Bruno would drop us at the front door of whatever shop Roo wanted to visit, and would then drive off to wait someplace. His talent, which you'll appreciate if you live in this town (but have to take my word for if you don't), was to reappear at the shop doorway at exactly the moment Roo and I came out. And with the hatchback open to accommodate whatever bags we happened to be carrying. How he did it was beyond me. Even if Roo had had a magic button which she pressed five minutes before leaving each shop, there was no way he could have timed his pick-ups better.

He also carried a gun.

"Why does Bruno carry a gun?" I asked, as we waited at a counter in a shop called Whisper while the assistant wrapped an exquisite silk and lace camisole and flimsy cream basque that Roo had taken a fancy to. I'd noticed the gun, with some alarm, as Bruno stooped to open Roo's door, his jacket opening above the top button to reveal a strap across his shoulder, a curve of brown leather and the snugly-nested tooled metal handgrip of a large automatic.

"He has a dangerous job," she replied, thanking the assistant as she took possession of the carrier bag. "He needs it."

"A dangerous job? A chauffeur?"

"In case there's ever trouble," she said mysteriously, as we pushed out through the shop's heavy glass doors to find Bruno pulling up at the kerb. "He doesn't just take me shopping you know."

"He sounds more like a bodyguard. Looks like one, too," I said, as the man in question pulled himself out of the driver's seat.

"Got it in one, Cully," she replied, adding: "Sometimes a girl needs some back-up," before Bruno's door-opening drill brought the conversation to a halt.

Like I said, we couldn't have shopped for more than three hours that afternoon but thanks to Bruno we must have stopped at a dozen different places all over town: Whisper, for the camisole, basque, and assorted wispies that brought me out in a hot flush just imagining how they'd look on Roo; a wig-maker called Ronny in SoHo, to pick up a parcel; Charles Jourdan and Joan & David, for shoes; the cosmetics counter at Bloomingdale, for some Chanel Body Spray and a Coco refill; Ballantynes on Sixth, for three cashmere jumpers at a little over eight hundred dollars each; to the minimalist, mirrored Antonie, for two slickly-tailored Calvin Klein suits in wool and silk; Le Tout on Fifth, for three pairs of Helmut Lang trousers and four silk and cotton blouses; Floris, for various oils and unguents; Castle & Pierpont, for close on three hundred dollars worth of exotic blooms – lilies, jonquils, paper whites – that filled the Volvo with unimaginably sensuous hothouse scents; and, finally, Cartier, where Roo invested a small fortune in a gold lighter, a slim lizard-skin wallet, and a gold and platinum roped bracelet. At the last moment (I'm certain now), she shook her head dismissively at a gold Mont Blanc roller-pen in which she'd also shown an interest.

Watching her play with the lighter, hefting its weight and flicking its milled wheel, I asked why all this shopping all of a sudden. It was as if she was kitting herself out.

"I have a new client," she said, taking her sales receipt and platinum American Express card from the courteous assistant, sliding them into her wallet. "And I like to be a new person when I start a new account."

And then, as the Cartier commissionaire ushered us from the premises with a sweeping salute and the kind of smitten smile I'd gotten used to whenever Roo and I found ourselves in the company of men of a certain age, she turned to me on the sidewalk, looked up and down the street, and said: "Aren't we close to that delicious place you took me to, the opening? You know? Why don't we stop off there? Rest up. Catch our breath. I want some more of that fig and chestnut turn-over. And what was it? Mulled cider sauce? That'll warm us up."

So we found ourselves back in Spoonlickers, sharing said turn-over at the same table where Susan and I had sat just a few days earlier. I was tempted to say as much, mention Susan, but decided against it. I had a feeling Roo would not be best pleased if she thought Susan and I had been talking about her, and that I knew more about her than she might like me to know. And after what Susan had told me about Roo's temper (though I doubted it mightily and suspected Susan was being, as usual, just a little over-dramatic) I certainly didn't want to test it. Also, I'd made Susan a promise and I intended keeping it – for her sake as well as mine. Maybe some time Roo'd bring up the subject herself. As it turned out, she never did. What really stopped me mentioning Susan, I guess, was we'd had a great afternoon and I didn't want to risk spoiling it.

Anyway, we'd been sharing stories, swapping trade secrets like we always did, though there seemed to me an odd, if rewarding, inequality to them; hers were simply much more interesting than mine, though she affected not to notice the disparity.

My most unusual meal? she asked.

Why, it had to be live baby mice in China's Guangzhou province, I told her. "They're like warm, wet pork; the trick is to tongue the little squirmers between your upper and lower molars for the *coup de grâce* before you swallow."

My favorite food?

"No question: Cream Milanos and goose *foie gras.*"

Least favorite?

"Absolutely no question: rhubarb – all that gut-wrenching oxalic acid – followed by parsnip and durian; texture, taste and smell in that order. And none of them pleasant."

And then, after her tale of the shearing scissors and apropos of blades, I told her that in my business I always watched to see how a restaurant cut its cheese – ideally with different knives for sheep, goat, and cow – and how I abhorred the fashion for roughly-grated pepper corns and flakes of salt set out in little bowls on the table. An air-tight container was what was needed, with a good grinding mechanism – a Peugeot, or the faultless Zassenhaus from Austria.

"Why on earth?" she asked, screwing up her face. "They look so cute in their little dishes. And real stylish."

"And real infectious. All those fingers," I replied. "Do you know only five per cent of American males wash their hands after they visit the Men's Room?"

"You're not going to tell me…?"

"And then they come back to the table, and reach for the salt and the pepper…"

"I don't think I want to hear this…"

"…The very same pepper and salt you'll be using when it's your turn at the table. So, minus points straight away."

And then it was her turn again, with a question from me.

"So what's the most popular place?" I asked.

"The office."

"The office?"

"I used to do it more in offices than anywhere else. There's a block just off Wall Street, twelve floors – a brokerage house, lawyers' offices, financial PRs, you know the sort of thing. Well, there are something like sixteen firms operating there, and I had clients in, let's see…" she counted off her fingers, "three, four, no, five of them. And we always did it right there. In their office. 'I'm-not-to-be-disturbed' kinda thing. On the floor, across the desk, in a chair. On the telephone.

The telephone's a real favorite. They call their friends, or their clients, or colleagues – one even used to call his wife. You look surprised?"

"Stunned more like. The office? Doesn't anyone get suspicious?"

"One of the girls in the brokerage house, she was my client's secretary – he told her I'm his sister. In another, I was the girlfriend just calling by. Or they think I'm some lawyer. It's the way I dress, the way I behave. I'm an actress, Cully. I always play the part. One time I was in the elevator with my 'brother', going to visit another john on the floor above him, and he never even recognized me. I've always been very discreet. And I'd never compromise a client."

"You said 'used to'. The offices, I mean. You don't do that now?"

"Not like that. I moved on."

"Moved on?"

She leaned across the remains of her fig and chestnut turn-over and fixed me with those basil-green eyes. "There are two types of men in this world, Cully. One'll put his hand in his pocket and come out with loose change. The other comes out with a wallet. I no longer deal with the first category."

"What about women?" I may have made Susan a promise, but I couldn't resist taking the conversation a step further.

"I don't get you?"

"Is it always men? Your clients?"

"Most times. But not always." She gave me a look. "Does it surprise you, that I have female clients?"

"With you, Roo, nothing would surprise me."

"You wanna bet?" she said, pulling a fifty dollar bill from her pocket and slipping it under her plate before I could do anything about it. "You'd lose."

Back in the car, Roo leaned forward and asked Bruno to take her home.

For a moment it didn't register.

And then… We were going to Roo's home. I couldn't believe it.

For the first time since I'd met her I was about to find out where she lived.

It was a startling departure. Sure, she'd been to my place a couple of times – on her return from Long Island (and Susan's bed, though I didn't know it then) and for some champagne before the Spoonlickers' opening – but in the five months I'd known her I'd never actually found out where she lived. 'Uptown', 'cross-town', 'not far', was all she'd ever volunteered, and for some reason I'd never pushed it. Of course, I'd looked her up in the book, but I wasn't much surprised to find she wasn't listed. Which made what followed quite an eye opener.

If you'd asked me to guess the kind of place Roo lived, I'd have plumped for somewhere arty and fun, make-do and unplanned, untidy and cluttered maybe, a place with that air of transiency that attends the young in their choice of home – frequently changed, places to move on from. Which is not to say that I didn't think it would be stylish – not at all. Which was why I'd thought SoHo or the Village as a likely neighborhood for her. But as Bruno swept us uptown that chill November evening, somehow managing to bypass a queue of red tail-lights around mid-town, I realized I was wrong on all counts. Only a handful of blocks from the Park, Bruno swung a right and minutes later pulled up outside one of the East Side's most sought-after co-ops, in a price bracket that excludes all but the seriously rich.

The building is called Blaise Heights. It's on 56th and Third, an easy walk from both Phantôme and Lemarchelier, and is one of the city's most striking residential blocks. Built by a Trump subsidiary in the early nineties, its uppermost levels are stepped with roof terraces and its steel and mirrored glass façade belted every seventh floor with wide limestone piers and columned balustrades that give it a kind of gentle neo-Palladian feel.

From the very start Blaise Heights attracted a deal of attention, not only from style and architecture publications but from the serious broadsheets, too, as an indicator of renewed confidence in the property market. '*Blaising A Trail*' ran one financial report, at a time when a heap of developers were reading the small print in Chapter Eleven. The tabloids also pitched in. '*Blaze Heights*' was another headline, when someone discovered there'd been a minor infringement of fire department regulations.

I remember it going up, had even written a piece about it myself. '*Progress and Pratfalls*', or some such title Sanchez had given it, all about a great little family *trattoria* that had been in business on that very spot since around the time Americans wrapped puttees around their legs and sailed for France. Yet in a single week it had vanished. First the boarded-up windows, then the roofless skeleton of the three-story block of which it was a part, and then, the very next thing, this monster rising up behind a ten-foot-high plywood fence fixed up around the site where once upon a time they served the best *zuppa di finocchi* and veal *Polpettine* in town. Progress maybe, but for meatball fans and constipated food writers (*finocchio*, or fennel, is a marvelous *digestif*) a massive pratfall.

So there was Bruno, reaching into the trunk and stacking Roo's bags against one of the chased chrome poles that supported the glass canopy above our heads. And there was Blaise Heights' doorman hurrying over to lend a hand when he saw it was Roo. And there was I, quietly astonished at our final destination, preparing to say my goodbyes and expecting Bruno to drive me on, when Roo turned, looked at me over the blooms in her arms and said: "You want to help me up with all this stuff?"

It wasn't how I'd expected the invitation to come, but it was invitation enough.

"Sure. Be pleased to."

Which was some understatement, I can tell you.

If I'd been curious about where Roo lived, I was positively aching to know how she lived, had been ever since our stay with Susan on the island. That was the first time we'd slept under the same roof, albeit in separate rooms, and it prompted a desire in me to see how she spent those other moments that I knew nothing of – the quiet moments when she was by herself. At home. I felt it would help me get to know her more, give me the wherewithal to place her, provide some clues to the real Roo.

With the trunk emptied Bruno was sent on his way, leaving the doorman to help us into the foyer with the bags and across to the elevator. But that was as far as he came.

"Thanks, Bill, that'll do fine," said Roo, as the elevator doors opened with a sigh and a well-dressed, middle-aged man stepped out. He seemed vaguely familiar in that frustrating *I-know-you-from-somewhere* sort of way. But try as I might, I couldn't place him. Kindly, he paused for a moment to help me stow the bags in the elevator and when we were done Roo thanked him, shyly, almost hiding behind her armful of flowers. He smiled back and, with a nod and a 'you-bet', the doors closed on him.

"Couldn't you just eat him all up?" said Roo, as we stood among the bags, watching the floor numbers blink their way upwards.

"Who?" I asked, knowing full well she meant the man in the foyer who'd helped with the bags.

"Why, Mr. Douglas. You know, Michael Douglas. *Fatal Attraction. Wall Street.* He's got a triplex at the top. Real cutie, don't you think? And always so, *so* polite."

"Didn't I read someplace that he had some kind of sex addiction?"

Roo cut me a look. "So tell me a man who doesn't?"

And then the elevator sighed to a halt on the forty-seventh floor, the doors slid open, and all thoughts of Mr. Michael Douglas disappeared as I followed Roo down a marbled vestibule wide enough for the bags I carried not to scuff the walls. After passing three sets of lettered double doors, Roo turned a corner and came to a stop in front of a single door. She fished out a card from her coat pocket, ran it through the swipe and with a quiet click the door swung open.

"So. Here we are. Home sweet home. Come on in," said Roo, reaching for the light switch.

Which is what I did, sideways because the doorway was narrower than the hall, pushing the bags ahead of me and hauling them after, fingers stinging from the cord handles, but with eyes wide, not wanting to miss a thing.

I'm not unused to top-dollar homes. Indeed I've been in quite a few, in the city and the country, here and overseas. But nothing could have prepared me for Roo's apartment. It was, well... simply sensational. No other word for it.

The room she led me into, all warm terracotta with cream and indigo detailing, was certainly not as large as some I know, but it was still pretty spacious, maybe thirty foot square, with polished parquet the color of maple syrup, a gallery level that I assumed would be her bedroom, and a high, slanted ceiling half of which was glass. I remember looking up and seeing my reflection, standing there, upside down and oddly diminished thanks to the angle, with two handfuls of carrier bags ballooning around me like oversized pasha pants.

"Just drop 'em by the table, Cully, and come on through to the kitchen," she said, bustling through a swing door with her armful of flowers. I did as I was told (a beautiful refectory dining table, by the way: English, Jacobean by the look of it, an arm and a leg), pulled off my coat, gloves and scarf, and then followed her into a kitchen so perfectly-equipped and arranged that it looked as though it had stepped out of a 'Metro' Lifestyle feature: German oven, grill and refrigerator, ceramic hob, double porcelain sink, black marble work surfaces backed with bright, primary-colored tiles, windowed cupboards and open shelves stacked with glass and china and, above our heads, a steel butcher's rack hung with copper-bottomed pots and pans. Lizzie Kovacks would be drooling. At one end of the room was a breakfast bar lined with chrome and leather stools, and at the other end a narrow picture window with a view of what looked like every high-rise on the East Side, every one of them spangled with lights. And everything was immaculate. Surfaces shining. Not a dirty cup or plate to be seen. It was as if the kitchen had never been used, though I detected a whisper of oregano in the air and the sinuous scent of garlic. The only things that looked out of place, personal things, were Roo's rollerblades lying on the breakfast bar, a tangle of receipts that looked as though they'd been tipped out of a handbag and, I was touched to see, broken up into a glass Kilner jar, the sticks of candy I'd brought her from England.

"What a gorgeous, gorgeous place. How long have you been here?"

"Coming on three years now," replied Roo, unloading the flowers into the sink and turning on the faucet. She hauled off her coat and flung it over a stool. She was wearing blue Capri pants, a black jumper and cardigan combination, and looked very Fifties. "Used to be a storeroom for the service crews and window cleaners, which maybe explains the weird shape, but they got moved on when the building went automatic." She switched off the water and pulled open the refrigerator. "Suddenly Blaise Heights had six new apartments. Four like this, one on each corner, and two higher up. The pricier ones. You want some wine?" she asked, flourishing a bottle.

"Thank you, yes. So how come you found out about them? I wouldn't have thought a place like this needed to advertise."

"You're right. They don't. Got a waiting list so long you need the Hubble telescope to see the end of it." She pulled the cork on the word 'Hubble' with a solid, satisfying plop, set down two glasses, and poured the wine. "Here," she said, passing me a glass.

"So how did you manage it?"

"The usual. Right time, right place. And knowing the right people. A Relocate contact let it drop that the developers had applied for residential permission on the conversions. Now, it just so happens…"

she swirled her wine and winked at me over the glass, "…it just so happens that I know one of the developers. Made the right noises in his direction, applied the necessary pressure and, my-oh-my, Miss Beatty Carew goes straight to the top of the class. Still had to pay the earth, mind you, but it's money in the bank, Cully. Money in the bank."

"I'd imagined you somewhere like SoHo. A loft. Something like that. This seems a little…"

"Grown-up?"

"I suppose… well, yes. It's not at all what I'd expected, but," I laughed, "in a funny sort of way it suits you."

"So you want the tour, or you want to snoop?" She looked at me archly.

"Why don't I snoop?"

"Why don't you? Go right ahead. Give me time to sort these flowers, and get myself organised. Gotta hot date tonight."

"The new client?"

"Not tonight. Tonight's familiar territory. Now go on, you," she said, waving me out of the kitchen, "go on and get outta here."

And so, a little self-consciously but as instructed, I left Roo in the kitchen and began my snooping.

Of course, it wasn't the first time I'd snooped. At some point that weekend at Susan's out on the island, Roo had sent me upstairs to fetch a hair clip – "on the dressing table, Cully, by the window" – her hands floury from pastry making. I remember it seemed like an invitation not to be missed, an opportunity to snoop, the first chance I'd had. Upstairs, alone, I'd opened her door and caught my breath as much at the view, across the dunes to the sea, as the feeling of intimacy which just going into her bedroom provided: to see and touch a crumpled sleep-shirt lying on an unmade bed, feel the pillows still creased and dented, brush my fingers against a pair of jeans folded over a chair, and breathe in that warm, private scent of her.

It was the first time I'd come so close to her, in this kind of intimate way, and it thrilled me. I don't know how long I was there – a matter of minutes only – but it felt longer, and it was with something approaching regret that I finally made for the dressing table, found the clip she wanted, and went back downstairs. It was only later, when Roo went up to change for supper, that I realized her room was above the kitchen. I could hear every footfall and the gentle accompanying creaks on the bare wood floor, just as she would have heard mine as I poked around her room rather than going straight to the dressing table for the clip.

But this time I had an invitation.

As I've said, the main room was a good size, large enough and high enough to accommodate the apartment's upper-level gallery which ran the width of the room. Thanks to this gallery, the seating area below it had a comfy, hunker-down feel, with a pair of plumply-cushioned, damask-covered sofas placed either side of an English-style fireplace and a carved wood surround.

There were alcoved bookshelves either side of this fireplace. On the left, the latest Tom Wolfe and a line of Sebastian Faulks, two McInerneys, Annie Proulx, a row of Dominick Dunnes, a Capote Reader, Gore Vidal – all hardback. And on the right, shelf after shelf of dry, dusty titles like *Understanding NASDAQ*; *Order in Chaos: Predicting the Market*; *The Science of Complexity - Theory and Practice*; *Risk and Reward - The Structure of Speculation*; and *Market Trends: Cracking the Code*, which, given her time at Wharton, I guess, didn't surprise me that much. On a low coffee table between the sofas there were yet more books, four piles of the kind of pricey coffee-table volumes you get from the Art section in Rizzoli on West 57th, a pile at each corner, neatly stacked according to size, spines showing, and all, so far as I could see, design-based: Le Corbusier, Frank Lloyd Wright, Bauhaus, Georgia O'Keefe's Santa Fé, French châteaux, Balinese pavilions, and fairy-tale German castles.

From the kitchen came the sound of cupboards opening and closing as, presumably, Roo rooted around for some flower vases, shouting out to me a "How're-you-doin'-out-there?"

"Fine," I called back. "Just reading your love letters."

I heard her laugh. "Yeah, right. Some chance."

Moving on, it was clear at once there was easily enough to keep me occupied in the main room for a month of Sundays, and everything, so far as I could tell, was very nice indeed: some really fine early American water-colors, a pair of Cornish School beachscapes, and a stack of figurative and abstract studies that I didn't recognize but which all looked like serious stuff; a set of framed native fabrics (ancient Hopi and Navajo blankets, mirrored panels from India, and Ikat squares from the Far East); some painted Santos statuettes recessed into the staircase leading to the gallery; a collection of silver cigarette cases and snuff boxes arranged on top of a finely-formed chest of drawers behind one of the sofas; a particularly pretty enameled clock standing proud and solitary on the mantelpiece; and, in the center of the refectory table, between two thick church candles, a large bronze oriental dog with lapping tongue and curling lion's mane. I picked it up, slipping my fingers between its legs, hefting it like a knuckle-duster. It was heavier than it looked.

The piece that drew the eye, however, was a simply lovely six-panel Coromandel screen (all tall grasses and stooping cranes) which stood in the corner of the room beneath the skylight. Lord knows where she'd found it, but it must have cost a fortune. Not a chip, not a scratch on its shiny black lacquer surface, the grasses and cranes a delicate mother-of-pearl. Concealed behind it was Roo's hi-fi (a top-of-the-range Neimeyer), and shelf upon shelf of CDs, tapes and albums. There was also a large black amplifier connected not to the hi-fi but to a slender, curved electric guitar that rested against one of those low-slung Charles Eames' recliners. I'd no idea Roo could play an instrument, but there was little doubt this was the perfect place to do it, lights out, lying back in the Eames, the instrument resting on your lap, and only the stars above you.

But I still hadn't found what I was looking for. Just assessing what Roo had on show, browsing my way around the room, wasn't the kind of snooping I had in mind. All it told me was that Roo had enough money – and taste – to spend it on fine and interesting things.

What I was looking for was something far more personal, and telling: family photos in silver frames, albums maybe, invitations on the mantelpiece. But there were none of these. I decided to look further. She'd told me to snoop, so I was going to do just that.

I made for the staircase leading to the gallery, which I'd assumed would be her bedroom. Half-way up, as my head passed floor level, I realized I'd made a mistake. This was no bedroom. It was an office, furnished with a glass-topped trestle desk, button-back executive chair and a serious-looking computer set-up. But how she ever managed to do any work there was beyond me. The view through the floor to ceiling picture window that faced the desk was simply spectacular: a glittering colonnade of skyscrapers running the length of the gallery.

In the middle of this window a sliding glass door led onto a narrow, south-facing terrace. I pulled it open and stepped out cautiously.

The terrace was maybe fifteen feet long, ten deep and clearly prepared for winter. Some terracotta pots had been herded into a corner and covered with a protective plastic sheet, a pair of recliners were folded up and secured against the retaining wall and only a slatted wood table and set of chairs looked as though they might still be used, when the weather was good enough. Which it wasn't right then. A thin sleet was falling; at street level it would be drizzle, but up here it still had to melt. There was also a sharp little breeze, chill enough to send me back inside. Instead, I pulled up my collar and slid the door closed behind me.

I've never been very good with heights. In my own apartment there's a piece of furniture in front of every window so I rarely get to see how high I am. And I'm only on the ninth floor. Yet here I was, forty-seven floors above the sidewalk, and I felt that odd but familiar compulsion to go to the very edge.

It was the view, as much as anything else, that drew me on. Layered with bands of sparkling light, a dozen or more towers rose around me, stacked into the night sky, all of them close enough almost to reach out and touch. On my left, across the East River, the sky was already an oily black, to my right there was still a faint mauve smudge where it showed between these steely pinnacles, and far below the parapet lay the sulphurous glow of the streets, veins of color coursing between the roots of this stone and glass forest, a faraway tooting of car horns borne on the breeze as it tugged enticingly at my sleeves.

I turned and looked above me, a dozen or more floors, tiers of light and dark, reaching like a stepladder to the stars. A shiver slid up my spine and puckered into my scalp, as much from the chill as the overwhelming sense of edge that engulfed me. Looking up, I decided, was worse than looking down. The sheer, vertiginous height of it all, a great, plummeting oblivion made careless by the slowly falling sleet. Emptiness. Just cold, black space. My head spun. From the height of it, the scale, the drop.

"Like it?"

If she'd come up and touched me without announcing her presence I'd probably have leapt out of my skin, leapt clear over the balustrade. As it was my heart just exploded, and a swirl of wine spilled from my glass.

"Jesus H, you scared me!"

She laughed. "You don't like heights?"

"You could say," I replied, trying to calm a heart pumping just about fit to bust.

"Funny how people who hate heights just have to go to the very edge." She came towards me, glass in one hand, bottle in the other. "Me, I love it. So high. So… away from it. Sometimes, I don't know, you feel you could just…" She stopped a pace away, looked around her, then held out the bottle. "Here," she said, topping up my wine. And then, wrapping her arms around her, glass and bottle tight to her sides: "I shoulda kept that coat on. Brrrrr. Let's get in, Cully, or you want us to freeze ourselves to death?"

Back inside, she slid the door closed after me. "Woof, that was sharp, wasn't it? I need some heat."

Downstairs she lit the fire, adjusted the flame, and then dropped into one of the sofas, tucking her legs up under her. There was a vase of jonquils on the coffee table that hadn't been there before, and she'd put on some music – Nina Simone – and that deep, mournful voice seemed to settle around us.

"Come on, make yourself at home," she said, patting the sofa. "So, what do you think? Neat, huh?"

"Well, to tell the truth…" I said, sitting beside her, sinking into the cushions.

"Yeah?"

"It's spectacular."

She laughed luxuriously, as though soaping herself with the words.

"Isn't it though? D'you get to see everything?"

"I'm afraid the terrace was as far as I got."

"Well, gracious me, Mr. Cully Mortimer," she said, pulling herself up from the sofa. "You're no detective. Come on, you get the tour after all."

And taking my hand, dragging me from my seat, she led me to the nearest of two doors which gave off the main room. She pushed it open and I saw at once that this was the room I'd been looking for – her bedroom. I remember a *bateau lit* covered with a quilt thick as meringue, a low chest of drawers beneath the window and a collection of the framed photos I'd been searching for, set out on its surface.

In one, a man and a woman stood beside a Christmas holly wreath hanging on a front door. Big house? Small house? Somewhere in the suburbs? The country? The city? Impossible to say. The couple looked to be in their sixties and I guessed they were Roo's parents. The man wore a bulky plaid logger's jacket and trucker's cap and had his arm round the woman's shoulder, the pair of them waving at the camera. The other photos, so far as I was able to make out, showed someone (Roo possibly) on horseback jumping a low tournament fence, Roo leaning forward on ski poles and, just glimpsed, a head and shoulders shot with her hair slicked wetly back and a diving board in the background. But there was no time to linger.

"And here's the bathroom," she said, pushing through a connecting door. This was lit with a constellation of star-bright downlighters, and furnished with a long vanity, twin sinks, backing mirrors, a shower cubicle, a frightening looking weight-training machine and, plumb bang in the center of the floor, one of those old cast-iron, roll-top tubs. It stood on rather petite claw-ball feet, its big brass taps set mid-way down one side of the bath and fed by twin copper pipes that rose up out of a floor of blackish, white-veined marble. It was quite a set-up, but not so striking that I failed to notice what looked like a half-dozen stout Maillot nudes in thick ebony frames either side of a door which I assumed lead back into the main room. I guessed they could have been copies, but somehow I doubted it.

"And this here's my dressing room," she said, pulling me through yet another connecting door and flicking on the lights. "My center of operations."

The space here was more limited, but only because of the closets that panelled the room from floor to ceiling. Also, there were no windows and the room had a dark cave-like closeness.

"Sit there," she said, waving me to a seat in the middle of the room. It was the kind you get in an art gallery when you want to rest up or look at a picture longer than a glance. "This is where you get to discover just how much of an actress I really am," she continued. "I should be in the movies, I really should."

And as she spoke, she swung open one closet door after another to reveal rows of jackets and overcoats, suits, dresses, trousers and skirts, glass-fronted drawers filled with woollens and blouses, a dozen racks of shoes (an entire rack each for red and for black), a section for hats, belts, shawls, scarves, gloves, purses and bags, and a line of wigs and hairpieces on hooks – short, long, straight, curly, blonde, brunette, and black – the contents of each closet illuminated by interior lights that triggered when the doors opened, the mirrored backs of these doors making the room grow larger and larger as we two shrank away to infinity.

"And these here... shift over." She knelt on the floor in front of me, pushed my legs aside, and pulled out a long, deep drawer divided into compartments. They were filled with underwear: panties in one, bras in another, the puckered straps and curved cups of various basques and corsets, piles of flimsy little shifts and camisole tops – all shiny satin, embroidered silk, and scalloped lace in a great rainbow of colors. "These here are the big guns," she said, "my arsenal. Which reminds me, Mr. Cully Mortimer..." She sat back on her heels and glanced at her watch. "You're outta here. Taking up my time and attention like this, when I've got business to attend to."

And leaving the drawer open, she stood, reached for my hand, pulled me to my feet, and led me back to the main room, picking up my coat and scarf and gloves and bundling them into my arms.

"You doing something Thanksgiving?" she asked, as I followed her to the door of the apartment.

"As it happens..."

"The truth now, Cully," she said, turning to face me.

"Well, no real plans as such..." Which was not altogether accurate. Every Thanksgiving, for years now, I've had a standing invitation to Netherlands. But I knew I could easily cry off.

I sensed there was something coming. There was.

"You want some? Plans, I mean?"

"Sure." And then, remembering: "So long as it's not actually Thanksgiving Eve. It's something I can't get out of. Work."

"I was thinking like the weekend. A few days off. Somewhere in the country." She opened the door and we stood there, inches apart, me buttoning my coat, Roo winding the scarf round my neck, tucking it into the collar. "Change the slush and exhaust fumes for some snow and log fires. You know what I'm sayin'? What do you think?"

"I think... yes," I said, and she swung her arms around me and hugged me.

"I knew you would. I'm so pleased. I'll call you. Now scoot." And she was back in the apartment and the door was closed before I had a chance to say another word.

I was in the elevator, had just pressed the Down button and was pulling on my gloves, when I heard the cool smack of bare feet on marble as someone came running down the hall.

"Hey, Cully, wait up."

And suddenly, there she was, a hand reaching out.

"You forgot something," she said, then waved, and laughed as the doors slid shut.

In my hand was the gold Mont Blanc roller-pen from Cartier.

Cazzuola

That Thanksgiving Week was a killer. And it began the Monday morning after my shopping expedition with Roo.

"You sure know how to get people riled up," said Sanchez, calling first thing.

I was in my dressing gown. I'd just showered. I was holding my toothbrush, a pink worm of paste balanced on its bristles.

"What now, Sanchez?"

"Remember the 'burger story you gave Daley?"

"You mean '*Last Orders*'?" I'd sent Larry the piece a fortnight earlier. It hadn't been scheduled, but I thought it would be of interest if he had some space to fill in the week. I wasn't wrong.

"That's the one. Thought you'd like to know the switchboard's been lit up since the early-morning edition. Phone calls, faxes, e-mail – you name it."

"You're kidding?"

"'Course Daley's ecstatic," continued Sanchez. "He's been on the horn to Circulation since he got in and heard about it from the Night Editor. They've decided to run an extra midday edition with, get this Mr. Mortimer, your story on the front page. They even had me move a Middle East peace talks report to make room. It's just the first two paras, down in the right-hand corner, with continuation on page five, but I got to tell you it looks good. Letters Page and Mail Room have been alerted. Daley reckons there's gonna be a ton of response on this one. Just thought you'd like to know."

I thanked Sanchez, told him I'd be in later (to soak up the glory), and put down the phone. Front page! The *Times*! Oh yes, yes, yes! And I danced my way back to the bathroom, cleaned my teeth, and got dressed in a dream.

Which was what '*Last Orders*' had been to write. A dream. One of the easy ones. An hour on the phone. and maybe three at the keyboard. A tad short of fourteen hundred words. Just beautiful.

> "*At 9pm on Friday, August 14, 1987, Billy-Ray Bradford (29) sat down to a medium-rare cheeseburger (double patty, double cheese), with side orders of French fries, crispy bacon,*

*and onion rings. He ate with a plastic knife
and fork, drank two extra-strength chocolate
shakes, and ended his feast with three slices of
Boston Cream Pie made by his Mom."*

That was paragraph one.
The second paragraph ran something like this:

"*Two hours later, prison officials at the Federal
Correctional Institution at Huntsville, Texas,
strapped 'Butcher Boy' Bradford to a gurney
in a room close by the hospital wing, and
administered a ten-millilitre dose of sodium
thiopental. This was followed a few moments
later by a sixty-millilitre combo of pavulon,
pancuronium bromide, and potassium chloride,
washed down with a saline solution to stop
the chemicals crystalising in his bloodstream.
It's still not clear whether Bradford's favorite
food, or the lethal cocktail of drugs he was
prescribed as a* digestif, *hastened his end.*"

According to Sanchez that was how the story would appear on
Page One. Section One. The first two paragraphs. With my by-line.
Yes!

I'd been toying with the idea of 'last meals' for some time: Martin
Luther King's catfish (Fried? Boiled? I'd been meaning to find out);
Bobby Kennedy's chicken chasseur; Eisenhower's scrambled eggs;
Patton's grits; and Warhol's prawn cocktail. But it was Sara, in
England, who'd galvanized everything. During my visit she'd given
me this clipping. She'd cut it out of a newspaper and kept it for me.
Thought I'd be interested. I was.

It was a short piece in one of the British broadsheets detailing the
eating habits of those unfortunates who found themselves on Death
Rows back in the States. More accurately, the last meals requested by
inmates immediately before execution. According to figures released
by the Texas Department of Criminal Justice, double cheeseburgers
were the most popular final request, followed by chili-burgers, and

hot dogs. French fries were way ahead the favorite side order, ice cream the most popular dessert and, in the absence of alcohol, Coca-Cola the most requested beverage.

Of course, I could have written it straight – a summary of the findings, a general interest piece – but I'd decided to take it in another direction altogether. When readers turned to page five for the follow-up they'd get the Cully Mortimer line: So what happened to cheese and truffle *fonduta*, or *foie gras* sliced and sautéed with artichokes *barigoule*, I'd suggested? Where was the *paupiette* of black sea bass in Barolo sauce? The *Pavé de merlu cuit sur la peau*? Or the *Pièce d'agneau de lait de Chioura rôti à l'os*? Surely there was someone on Death Row, only hours from execution, who wanted something a little more civilized than a double cheeseburger and fries for their last meal on earth? Someone who wanted, one last time, to savor what fine cooking and fresh ingredients are all about? Didn't these people have any taste or flair or imagination, I'd asked? Apparently not. The only people awaiting execution, it appeared, were those who rated double cheeseburger their favorite food. So far as I could make out the most flamboyant requests were jalapeño peppers and peach cobbler.

Which led me to the inevitable Cully conclusion, that if you eat too many double cheeseburgers you're more likely to end up on Death Row than someone who knows what a good *meunière* sauce should taste like; and that clearly, *ipso facto*, the middle and upper classes were obviously not well represented on Death Row. The obvious socio-economic ramifications I left to my readers' intelligence.

All in all, I thought the article both entertaining and provocative.

Just how provocative I was about to find out.

Prison reform groups, affronted Death Row families, civil rights activists, corporate reps from the various 'burger brands, public health officials, nutritionists, even the Surgeon General… by the end of the day it seemed pretty much anyone who had heard the word 'burger, let alone eaten one, was up in arms and wanted a slice of me. In short, there was uproar.

In the days that followed I must have appeared on a dozen prime-time radio and TV chat shows, sharing the couch with assorted experts, and trying to make myself heard above pumped-up studio audiences baying for my blood and guts, presumably for the purpose of making 'burgers. From Monday through Thursday I spent my time waiting in the wings with production assistants clasping clipboards to their chests, being whispered to by harried floor managers in head-sets, and welcomed to the show by over-the-hill hosts with peppermint blazers, Chiclet teeth, lacquered fingernails, and too much make-up. I drank foul coffee in windowless hospitality suites, had wires pushed up under my clothing, learned to navigate darkened studios without tripping over the coils of cables that snaked across the floors, and by the end of it all had even gotten to enjoy the whole shebang. Hell, I didn't even sweat in the lights any more.

By Thursday's recording for *60 Minutes*, my last TV appearance, I'd become the best-known name in television next to Letterman, Leno, and Rather. There were editorials in all the newspapers, topical 'ads in the tabs' from the big meat boys (there was little doubt in my mind that I would not be honored the following year in Chicago), and endless references to the debate on every TV current affairs show and radio phone-in in the country. I was beamed across the continent, had my picture on the front pages of more newspapers than I knew existed, and I even made it to one of the electronic billboards on Times Square, courtesy, I later found out, of the Meatpackers' Union:

> "...*Cully Mortimer don't eat 'em.*
> *But ninety-nine per cent of Americans do.*
> *And proud of it...*"

On the hour, every hour, Tuesday through Thursday, this digital red-letter message ticker-taped out in a continuous forty-second loop, a big-bun triple 'burger (according to Sanchez) in place of punctuation.

The paper, of course, was... very pleased. Circulation figures over the period soared, advertising was happily unaffected (needless to say, 'burger boys don't advertise in the *Times* which, I thought, rather proved my point), and Larry was cock-a-hoop. If he could have tortured his limbs into ever more angular configurations he would happily have done so for me, and whenever I passed through the office on the way from one TV studio to another ('Way to go, Cully' greetings whenever I was spotted) he would perch on my desk, knot his legs and arms into a complicated cat's cradle, and rattle off figures and daily percentage increments as though they were the keys to the Universe – which, in his case, is pretty much what they are. He was so full of it all, I could have written out the Manhattan telephone directory for my weekly column and he'd have gladly published it.

The problem was, with all this attention, all the personal appearances and media hoopla, that my weekly column was not yet written. Was not even started. I was badly behind schedule and the one time I needed it, I didn't have a single story in reserve to cover. Manhattan directory or not, I had fifteen hundred words to deliver by Friday afternoon and the hours were sliding through my fingers like rice from a torn sack.

That Thanksgiving Week I'd decided to write about waiters' uniforms. '*Black Waistcoats or Mao-Tse Tung Collars?*' was the title Sanchez finally settled on, a good long one to cover the paucity of words. Over the years I've seen it all – cowboy chaps, monks' robes, pyjamas, dirndl and lederhosen, boiler suits and boots, even hospital scrubs – and had decided to give the phenomenon a Cully make-over, lining up interviews with Jean-Georges Vongerichten and Keith McNally to get their take on changing trends. At Vongerichten's new place on Central Park West he'd gone for the afore-mentioned Mao-style tunics and menacing double-breasted suits, while McNally favored more casual, traditional wear. But the morning of the interviews I'd had to call them both and reschedule, and was pretty darned lucky they were able to switch times. Keith, being Keith, suggested we meet at a 'burger bar he knew, but I wasted no time knocking that one on the head.

It was around five o'clock Thanksgiving afternoon when I finally got back to the apartment armed with the quotes I needed. But two hours later I was still struggling, only half way through the story, snacking on a mixed box of Vongerichten's outrageously good marshmallows which he'd kindly given me, and half-listening to a radio phone-in I'd taped the previous day.

As with other phone-ins the abuse had been rich and raucous but, cocooned in the darkened studio, with Lydia to keep me company, I'd stayed unruffled through the whole thing.

"Wow," said Lydia, as we left the building. "How could you keep so cool? They were just so horrible to you. Doesn't anyone understand what you're saying? Don't these people realize what they're putting into their mouths?"

Dear Lydia. The usual guff. But she'd been a gem throughout, ferrying me here, there, and everywhere.

But that Thursday evening, squinting at the screen, tapping out my story, time was against me. Another couple of hours and I'd maybe have cracked it, but now it would have to wait till morning. It was closing on seven and I had a big night in front of me. Black tie, pleated cummerbund, and shiny black patents. Something I couldn't cancel, even for Roo. Work. Or rather, an evening with Mr. Player Leland, the man who happened to own the very newspaper – among many others – that carried my column.

An hour later, suitably scarved and overcoated, comfortably folded in the back of a Leland limo, I was still trying to come up with some witty one-liners and a pay-off para for the uniform story when my driver turned into Adams Square and what was left of my creative juices just went and dried up. I'd been expecting a bash, but not quite on this scale.

Every window of the Leland mansion was lit. All five floors. Compared with the houses around it, their upper levels uniformly darkened, the Leland place looked like a Christmas tree. No. More than that. Almost Disney. A kind of fairy-tale palace twinkling with honeyed squares of warm, golden light. And all those lights, take my word for it, had not been left on by accident. The place looked grand as all hell.

I'd been there only once before, an early summer supper, and it had looked pretty good then, a turn-of-the-century townhouse at the far end of the square with ivy scaling the first three floors and window boxes spilling blooms. But now, at eight pm precisely on Thanksgiving Eve, the house looked just spectacular. The lights from its twenty or so front windows winked through the leafless trees in the small park that filled the center of the square, and glittered in the rain which had started earlier that evening and now lashed down in stair-rods. As my limo approached I could see one of the staff standing at the open door with a large umbrella. By the time my driver pulled into the sidewalk, he'd sped down the front steps and snapped it open for me.

Inside, a real, well-stacked log fire blazed away in the hallway grate, the flames' reflections playing over a highly-polished travertine floor and licking between a scatter of Tabriz rugs. Even with the front door wide open the room was snug and inviting, the comforting crackle of the fire vying with the gusting spatter of rain on the front steps, and

a mass of spiky, exuberant winter blooms from the Leland hothouse
in Fauquier County, Virginia, filling the air with a scent of warmed
vanilla and tuberose. Gold frames and dark *settecento* oils (all ermined
noblemen, Lilliputian landscapes, and halo-ed annunciations) jostled
for space in gallery-like profusion on the walls, while the crystal tears
of a magnificent chandelier that had once belonged to a Venetian doge
tinkled gently in the breeze from the open door.

A maid approached, took my scarf and coat, not a raindrop to be
seen, and a liveried footman led me to the stairs. They were wide and
grand, the banister as broad as a railway sleeper, the wall stepped with
yet more gilded portraits. At the top of these stairs, another flunky
offered me a flute of champagne, and as I stepped into the first-floor
drawing room I stepped into close proximity with the very, very rich.
What Aunt Jem would have called 'tall clover'.

The first person I recognized was Avery Blanchard, and she was at
my side in an instant. She just seemed to float out of the crowd, take
my hand and welcome me, as though she'd been waiting all evening
just for me.

"Cully, darling. What can I say? Welcome to the one-per-centers."

And as I held her hand, brushed her cheeks with mine,
acknowledging her reference to the Times Square billboard message
with a sly grin, certain that in her time she'd probably eaten more
'burgers than anyone else in the room, it was almost impossible not to
reflect how very far Mrs. Avery Blanchard had come.

≈

"*Principessa!*" he would exclaim.

"*Professore!*"

Rising from nothing less than the bow of a *primo tenore* on center
stage at the Lincoln Center, unctuous as a well-executed *besciamella*,
Pietro Calvi may have been wickedly wrong on both counts – and
known it as surely as he knew the difference between Barolo and
Chianti – but Cazzuola's socially adept *maître d'*, with his cockatoo
quiff of creamed and dyed black hair, his cheeks as red and shiny as
maraschino cherries, also knew to make a meal of guests like Cully
Mortimer and Avery Blanchard.

As did Cazzuola's staff. How often had I heard the same whispered
'*che bella signora*' from passing waiters, and noted the ever so slight
flush of pleasure these endearments elicited from the '*bella signora*'

in question? It was a practiced, productive procedure (the waiters probably had it written into their contracts), and though she liked to poo-poo it with a certain cool disdain, I have more than a sneaking suspicion that my lunch companion really rather enjoyed it all.

Not that Avery Blanchard didn't deserve these whispers. In her late forties, or early fifties, (maybe even older; it's hard to be certain), she is still a remarkably good-looking woman (though I noticed early on in our acquaintance how her fingers sometimes strayed to chin and cheek, discreetly searching out those first springy curls of tough hair that, at a certain age, can appear in a second). Tall for a woman, maybe the same height as me in her Louboutins, she's a trim and curvy package, blonde and blue-eyed, always cool, crisp and elegant in her clipped little Chanel suits, her Jil Sanders, Bill Blass, and Geoffrey Beene outfits, with a measured, gently swinging step that always draws the eye.

As for the title, well, she may still be a few ranks short of actual princess-dom, but she's not far off it, the... how to put this delicately? ...the acknowledged muse and companion of said publisher and philanthropist, Player Leland. In short, both she and I, as Signor Calvi well knew, with a single word, could have cooked his goose good and proper if either of us had so chosen.

So, '*Principessa*' and '*Professore*' it was, titles which Calvi reckoned carried the appropriate weight to make us feel welcome. And on those occasions when he saw the Leland Bentley draw up outside his striped-canvas portico, that was how he greeted us, with an arm-spreading bow and this conferring of dubious titles.

"*Principessa*, indeed," observed Avery, almost regally I remember thinking, the first time she heard the title. "Wasn't I *Contessa* – or just plain *Bella*, the last time?"

"At least *Bellissima*..." I whispered.

"Cully Mortimer, I do believe you're teasing," she replied, as we followed in Calvi's footsteps, our host gliding ahead of us, arms at his side, fingers extended just so, almost on tiptoes it sometimes seemed, glancing back with a nod and a smile, to ensure we were still with him.

And so our lunches would begin. 12.15 to 2.20 precisely. And always, always at Cazzuola. At least once a month, for six months, through summer, fall, and early winter, usually, and annoyingly, midweek when I had copy to think about. On the dot of midday Avery would pick me up in the chauffeur-driven Bentley, and drop me back home by 2.40.

Cazzuola was her absolute favorite place for lunch. And as she always reminded me when she called to make the date, she had the number, Cazzuola's private number, the one that got you a table in one of the most sought-after dining rooms on the island whenever you wanted it, when everyone else in the world had to content themselves with a three month wait. She'd gotten the number from me, of course, but she seemed not to remember that. For Avery the important thing was having the number, not who gave it to her. That I might have done so would have astonished her. I can almost hear her saying: "Really, Cully? Surely not," then dismissing the subject as though not worthy of further consideration, before moving on to something else, something more relevant.

As for me, the pleasure of these repeat visits rapidly palled. It's something food writers just don't like doing – Daphne and The Dharwar aside – being seen in the same place too often. And I knew at least a dozen other restaurants which Avery would have liked just as much, if not more than Cazzuola; restaurants which would have treated her with equal, if not greater, deference. But when Avery called to say lunch, it was always Cazzuola.

"I have their number," she'd say. "I'll have Tally call and make the reservation."

And that, believe me, was that; no room for maneuver. That's where we were going, and that was all there was to it. You didn't argue with Avery Blanchard.

It was the stability of it all, I guess. That's what she liked about Cazzuola. The security of known surroundings. The exclusivity. The right table. The favored patron status. She'd been introduced to a place that made her feel comfortable, that recognized her position in the world. And Avery was the kind of woman who liked that kind of thing. Liked it very much indeed.

That's not to say that Cazzuola was a waste of time. Far from it. The kitchen, as some of you might know, is run by Stefano Ruggero who started life at the stoves of Milan's Enoteca before arriving in New York to head up brigades at Trentino, Antica, and Dal Pescatore, three of the city's finest Italian restaurants, before finally being lured away by Calvi and his backers to a cobbled street off Broadway and Broome. Amongst Stefano's signature dishes are a Risotto *Thermidori* to die for – a pyramid of glistening, creamy Carnaroli rice suffused with Iranian Sar Gol saffron and studded with bite-sized coral-spotted langouste tails – not to mention his formidable *Orecchiette cime di rapa* which comes as close to melting in the mouth as it is decently possible to get without compromising an *al dente* pasta, especially the hard durum pasta of Puglia.

But whatever pleasures I derived from Ruggero's risotto and *orecchiette*, these were easily mitigated by Signor Calvi's hand-wringing satisfaction at seeing me return so regularly. That and the table he always led us to, at the back of the restaurant, one of four on a raised dais, the two of us side by side, looking out over the throng.

Avery loved it, of course – the only thing missing was a spotlight – but I hated it. However you try to cut it, just two people sitting side by side is so ill-thought-out, so elbow-y, so pigs-at-a-trough, don't you think? All that turning to talk to one another, all those enforced and often unflattering profiles to deal with. Fine at a dinner party, on separate chairs. But in a restaurant? Quite ridiculous. The way I absolutely hate to eat. Except, maybe occasionally, for that gentle, intimate sensation of your companion's weight shifting on the same banquette, like a body beside you on a mattress.

Anyhow, once we'd slid our way in, and had the table pushed against us, trapping us like a couple of veal calves in a coop, Calvi would snap fingers for menus and, leaning stiffly from the waist, quiff tilting precariously, proceed to acquaint us with the kitchen's offerings. Spoken through spittled chili-red lips, it would go something like this:

"The risotto is e'cellent, if I may suggest. With shaving of the white truffles from Piedmont. And also the *Saltimbocca*, the… 'ow you say? 'The jump in the mouth'." Or some such little joke, and he would chuckle wetly. "Or you prefer something lighter maybe? Today we have special, the *Cavatelli al fungi* and *Maccheroncini primavera*. Or maybe the *Strozzapreti*. Or *Fagioli d'Isernia* – you know? The beans without the skins? Like soft green pearls. They are *stupende*! I say so myself. Anyway…" noting at last our absorption in his leather-bound menus (apart from the specials, I knew it almost by heart), "I shall return. *Per favore*. I am at your service…" cupping his hands as though he held a little bird, rounding his shoulders, and extending his

elbows just so. "*Principessa*," bowing to Avery. "*Professore*," bowing
to me. "Welcome to Cazzuola. So nice to see you 'gain. *Buon appetito*.
Anythin' you need…" And, still bowing, he'd finally withdraw amidst
a flurry of waiters, a chamberlain and his minions, leaving us to our
decision-making.

And as she sat there beside me, pondering the menu, taloned
fingernails tough enough to grate parmesan sliding across its
parchment pages, covertly aware of the whispered glances of other
diners when she was recognized, and the ministrations of attentive staff
bearing water, butter, bread, and the first of her four Bacardi Dry's that
frustratingly never seemed to loosen her tongue, it delighted me to
think how much I had managed to find out about this quite compelling
woman, given how few details of her past, her background, she ever
let slip.

Though she didn't know it, and though there were still some
substantial blanks to fill in, I had made myself quite the expert on
Avery Blanchard's rise to social prominence.

≈

One of the marvelous things about working for a newspaper, something
I have always loved from as far back as Wilmington, is the free and
easy accessibility of information, the opportunity to be nosy without
anyone knowing. I could, and did, with impunity, check things out.

Which is exactly what happened the first time I was invited to a
Leland/Blanchard soirée, back in early summer when the whole thing
began. Mr. Leland, no less, had phoned me, introduced himself, and
hoped I would accept an invitation that was even then being delivered
to me.

"Just a small get-together, Mr. Mortimer. Sorry about the short
notice and all, but I wasn't due back in town before the weekend, and
Avery insisted you come. She's a slave to your column, and, well,
we'd both be delighted if you could join us. Trust what we have on
offer is up to the mark… Loved your piece on the Met, by the way.
Avery and I went to the opening. Sorry to have missed you. What a
show!" And then he was gone. Apologies. Another line waiting.

I'd been surprised by the call, surprised he should imagine that one
of his employees might seriously consider not accepting an invitation
from Player Leland, even if it was prompted by someone else, and
needing a personal phone call to ensure it.

Of course, I'd replied, I looked forward to it. And the instant he rang off I went to the library, found myself a snug little corner, and called up the files from the *Times'* archive. Digitalised at enormous (and still ongoing) cost, they afforded all the relevant details of my host and his latest companion, scoured from our own records and supported with items from other publications. With a click of the mouse, everything I needed was on-screen in just a matter of seconds.

Since I knew enough of Mr. Player Leland – his well-reported buying trips to Europe, his chairmanship or membership of every board of trustees of what appeared to be every museum and gallery in town, his possession of a sumptuous Thyssen-like collection of art, and a wildly acrimonious separation from his last wife – I concentrated my research on his new companion.

Mrs. Avery Blanchard. Née Petersen. From Solvang, California, that quite hideous Scandinavian simulacrum in the Santa Inez Valley. At one time or another Mrs. Avery Harold, Mrs. Avery Russell and, most recently, Mrs. Avery Blanchard, each association lifting her rung by rung, ever upwards, as one husband replaced another. Not that the circumstances of their various departures were in any way suspicious. It just seemed the lady suffered an uncommonly sustained run of bad luck – not, I'd hazard a guess, that she would have called it that.

According to the files, said run began with Stan Harold. In an obituary that appeared in the Solvang *Daily Poster*, September 1982, Mr. Stanley Cooper Harold, middle-aged head of a local engineering company, community leader, city councillor, etcetera, etcetera, had suffered a stroke on the tennis court of his country club, never made it to hospital, and left his grieving widow, Avery, sole beneficiary of a useful annuity that promptly sped her on her way to Los Angeles. As anyone in Solvang, California, with any ambition, talent, or working synapses would be well advised to do.

The next mention came nearly eight years later, May 1990, when *Variety* carried the obit of a fifty-eight-year-old so-so successful TV producer called Jerry Russell who'd married Avery Harold the previous year and been done for by a drunk driver on the canyon road that led to their Hollywood Hills home. I'd found no notice of their wedding, indeed no mention of Avery at all for her first few years in LA, but Jerry had clearly done well enough in the twelve months following their union to merit his final notice in *Variety*.

Once again the records failed me. For seven years after her first husband's death in Solvang, not a word on Avery. And for the four years following Jerry's departure the same. It's as though she ceased to exist. At some point during this time, however, she must have decided to swap coasts and move east, because this was where she made the acquaintance of Mr. Bill Blanchard and came back on-line.

Like her other husbands, Bill Blanchard was far from the first flush of youth when he met the widow Russell. Widowed at fifty-nine, he took up with Avery two years later, and in October 1994 the *Times* itself carried a notice of their wedding at St Barnaby's Presbyterian Church in Utica, New York State. In the accompanying photo, the first I'd found of her, she stood on the church steps, arm in arm with a pleased-looking Blanchard, the two of them waving off clouds of confetti.

Her new husband was a timber man, from a family of timber men, the owner of huge saw and paper mills in western New York State who, compared with his two predecessors, was a very wealthy man indeed. For Avery, it must have seemed a magnificent haul. They had an apartment in the city, a house in Bermuda, and spent a lot of their time at the Blanchard family estate someplace up-country in Vermont or New Hampshire. It was here, one morning in the spring of 1996, that Bill Blanchard decided to go back-packing. He was never seen again. Rescue services found a torn rucksack, but they never found a body. Bears were blamed.

Avery, needless to say, was practiced at the widow stakes by this time. There may not have been too many smiles in the photos of the Blanchard memorial service, but you couldn't deny she really looked good in black – tall and blonde (all that Scandinavian blood), willowy, veiled. Which is probably when she came to the attention of Player Leland, whose east coast newspapers were printed on paper from the aforementioned Blanchard Mills.

Before anyone knew what was happening the two of them were an item, seen around together whenever Leland was in town. Which was increasingly often. At all the best parties there they were: Avery, soon out of widow's weeds, hosting theater suppers at the Waldorf; dressed exquisitely in Valentino, Versace, Norell, and Armani; in sporty white at Newport; in wide hats at Lexington and Sarasota; in trimly-tailored salopettes at Aspen and Vail; in ballrooms and deckside; at the Opera,

Broadway first nights, and thousand-dollar-a-plate charity galas. For more than a year every gossip column was full of them, until the liaison was so familiar it was no longer news.

What was needed was a wedding.

And there was the problem.

Avery Blanchard wanted to, but Player Leland didn't. And frankly who could blame him? Like Avery he'd been married three times, but there the similarities ended. Unlike Avery, marriage was the one deal that Leland had failed to profit from. All three wives still lived and, so the gossips had it, extracted a hefty portion of his fortune to support them and a half-dozen assorted offspring. At fifty-seven years of age, a large, florid-faced man as bald as an *entrée* cloche, Leland had clearly learned his lesson. Once Avery and I had each other's measure, his poor performance in the proposal stakes was a subject frequently discussed at our Cazzuola get-togethers.

For those of you not familiar with Player Leland, I should, I guess, provide at least some kind of introduction. I've mentioned his various positions of influence, interests, and possessions, but that misses out the real color of the man.

Player, as I knew without checking the files, was not a nickname. It's how he'd been christened, his mother's maiden name, the cotton-wealthy Players of Charleston, South Carolina, re-jigged into a given name (there's bold Southern style for you). And after his stern and overbearing father – scion of the Virginia coal and banking Lelands – passed away, it was a name Player wasted little time living up to.

While I was cleaning copy on *The Fort Christina Courier*, Player was partying. The gossip columns bulged at the margins, tales legion, legends in the making: the clubs, the girls, the fast cars; a very quiet suspension from New York Collegiate, followed by a very public sacking from Yale; the grand tours and escapades in Europe, the Far East, Africa; and, finally, the prodigal's return. Not, you can bet, that he came back of his own accord.

The story goes that Leland was in Africa, on a hunting safari, tracking a wounded buffalo. The beast had gone to ground in a grove of bamboo and Leland and his guides had followed. It was here, on a narrow path, that the buffalo decided to have at them. The first tracker was dismissively tossed, the next in line was swift enough to fling himself out of harm's way, leaving Leland face to face with a ton or

more of irritated beef. Apparently he'd let off a shot, then done the
same as the man in front of him, diving for cover into the bamboo. The
problem was that, though the buffalo missed him, a broken, splintered
limb of bamboo didn't, piercing his throat and coming out his cheek.

For more than an hour Leland was thus impaled until his
companions managed to unstick him. He was driven to some field
station, treated as best they could, then flown to the nearest hospital.
A week later he was back Stateside, admitted to Manhattan General
for a series of cosmetic procedures that left him with a smear of scar
tissue on neck and cheek, a certain stiffness on the left hand side of his
face, and an odd lisp which, so Avery informed me, was what had first
attracted her to him. That, I guessed, and his money.

With the reconstructive surgery behind him, and a decade's worth
of thrills and spills to his credit, those in the know duly expected
the young man to pick up his old exotic ways and hit the road. But
he didn't. The accident had clearly proved some kind of epiphany,
for it was around this time that Player Leland took a new direction
altogether. Instead of further philandering, he found himself a small
apartment and went to work for a little-known broker on Wall Street.

In an indecently short space of time Player Leland had made
himself a fortune. And then another, as well as the fortune that came
his way when his mother finally passed on. But soon the markets bored
him. It was time to change the game again. He started with computers,
of course. The coming thing. Nothing creative, the servicing side:
programme packaging, maintenance contracting, and distribution.

And then he got his hands on a few trade publications, special
interest stuff as well as some local newspaper titles – Kansas, Nebraska,
the Dakotas; places no one ever heard of, with papers no one ever
read. Buy and sell. Buy and sell was the new Leland entertainment.
The financial Press started sniffing. He was on a roll. Soon it wasn't
just the trades and local papers, it was radio stations, TV stations, then
cable, satellite. It all just snowballed until, about two years ago, he
became my boss. The major shareholder. The *Times*.

I only met Player Leland twice, but I liked him. His privileged
background and his years of traveling had given him an easy-going,
cultured charm that few Americans manage to pull off. And elegance,
of course. Oh boy, did Player Leland know elegance. Hand-tooled
brogues from London's Cork Street, lightweight double-breasted

suits from Milan, and the finest cotton shirts which he ordered by the score and wore with brightly-colored ties knotted as tightly as the bud in his buttonhole. It was a sleekly European style of dress meant, ideally-speaking, for a man of less bulk and substance than Leland – the double-breasters really did him no favors despite the via Montenapoleone tags. But he was rich, very, very rich, so, of course, the whole paraphernalia of the best worsteds, silks, cottons, and leathers somehow worked. They wouldn't dare not to. Leland was that kind of man.

And that was how Avery Blanchard came into my life. Through Player Leland, her lover and my boss, the introductions made that early summer evening on the steps leading down to their garden (possibly the largest private garden in Manhattan). I remember Leland's evening suit was a signature double-breaster, broad enough to cover a table, black as squid ink and silk-lapelled, the stiff-fronted shirt studded, the bow tie crisply tight but too narrow and level for my taste, the pumps shining and the trousers double-striped. When it was my turn to step forward, to shake his hand, I made a point of holding his eye, refusing to notice the pink puckering of skin below his ear and the shiny snarl of smoothness peeping above his collar.

"Ah, there you are. Glad you could make it, Mr. Mortimer. Or may I call you Cully?" And then, half-turning: "I don't believe you've met Mrs. Blanchard. Avery Blanchard."

And I hadn't. But I recognized her instantly from her photos. Though not a one of them came a whisker close to doing her justice. Standing beside him, dressed in a green sequin sheath that, really speaking, ought to have been worn later in the evening but somehow still seemed appropriate at a little after seven, she looked, well… just fabulous. And, something I hadn't been prepared for – very, very sexy in that arch, knowing sort of way.

A lot of very rich women, I've found, often come across cold and removed, surely incapable, I often think, of indulging in any act that might entail the willing exchange of bodily fluids. But Avery Blanchard was different. When Avery Blanchard smiled at a man, let me tell you, it was the kind of smile that gave off one big message: that she just knew every little thing there was to know about you, what you liked doing, what you liked having done and, what's more, that she would just love to do that too, happy to indulge any guilty little peccadillo. Believe me, that smile of hers was *eeee*-lectric.

"Mr. Mortimer, how lovely," she said, smiling, electrifying me, taking my hand in the two of hers, strangely rough and knuckly. "After reading your pieces so long, I feel like I'm meeting up with an old friend. I should really keep you all to myself," she continued, drawing me away from Leland, sliding her arm through mine, and guiding me down the steps into the garden, "...spend the whole evening with you. But I musn't be selfish, must I? Plenty of time for that later. In the meantime, come meet the Wyeths..."

And so it had gone. A soft, early summer evening. Seventy degrees or thereabouts. Thirty or so guests. Drinks in the garden. A string quartet in tails sitting beneath the acers on thin gold chairs. Some Mahler. Mozart. A rustle of talk. Expensive perfume. And then – a distant gong – summoned inside for dinner.

"So where should we all be going this month, Mr. Mortimer?" asked one of the ladies, all Georgetown backbone and fat fingers with rings to match, when we'd found our places, gotten ourselves comfortable, spread our napkins. It's a question I get asked a lot, and I've learned how to field it with whatever response seems appropriate in the circumstances.

"There's a new place I visited just the other day, just off Broadway and Broome," I confided. "It's called Cazzuola." A few more faces turned interestedly in my direction. "If you'd like to know my opinion..." Polite laughter. "...Well, you'll just have to read it in the *Times*." A slight pause at that, but then, when they saw the twinkle in my eye, a more relaxed response. A gentle, delighted laughter which, I like to think, broke the ice, causing a gradual rise of conversation as my *bon mots* were passed down the table for those who'd missed them, a tiny dish to savor, to talk about. Most gratifying.

And then, later, when it was time to take my leave:

"It was so good of you to join us," said Avery, clasping my hands again and drawing them to her in the hallway, a maid stepping forward with my coat. "Really. Such fun. And you must *promise* me we'll have lunch together one of these days. Just you and me. What say we try that restaurant you mentioned at dinner? Casual something, wasn't it?"

And that was it.

Two weeks later, Avery picked me up in Leland's Bentley and the two of us went to Cazzuola for the very first time.

≈

I guess now's as good a time as any to try to explain just how come the two of us got into this routine, try to explain why Avery should have taken such a shine to me. At first I couldn't work it out at all. The whole thing just seemed so extraordinary – being taken up by Avery Blanchard, our monthly *à deux*s at Cazzuola. Whatever for? How come? I mean, this was a woman walking out with Mr. Player Leland. They might not be getting married any time soon, but no one was going to call her on that. And Player Leland, as I've already pointed out, is one of the city's… hey, one of the country's major operators. This man is very powerful indeed. This man fly fishes with Ted Turner, shares a golf buggy with the President, and hangs out with the Sun Valley crowd. Like the Brits are fond of saying, Avery was treading well below stairs when she took up with me. But then, I guess, it was a *milieu* she was familiar with, even if she wasn't prepared to acknowledge it.

It was Casey who made me see what it was all about. I remember telling her about Avery on one of our Monday rendezvous, and it was Casey who, after a moment's consideration, put her finger right on it.

"She's scared of you," she told me.

Of course, I couldn't see it to begin with. But the more she went on about it, the more I began to see that Casey was maybe right. The truth is, I think I did frighten Avery. From that very first introduction, the moment she took my hand and looked into my eyes, she knew immediately that I had her measure, recognized her, sensed where she'd come from. Which was true. It was as though she'd been at my shoulder in the *Times'* library as I scrolled through her past. She wouldn't fool me, and she knew it. So the obvious, next best thing for her to do was ignore me completely, let me slip back to my ordinary little life without another thought. Or make me her friend. Neutralise any threat.

But what kind of threat I represented, what harm I could have done Avery Blanchard that needed neutralising, I could not imagine. I wasn't rich. I wasn't influential beyond my own small field, and while I enjoyed a certain celebrity there were far greater talents than mine she could more usefully, and with Leland beside her, more easily have courted. And I said as much to Casey.

"Then she probably thinks you're a faggot," she retorted, with a delighted laugh, reaching for me, "and reckons you'll make entertaining company. Ladies like her always love a fag around, some undemanding arm candy."

So, faggot or not, for whatever reason, I became an Avery Blanchard walker. A 'laughing man', as Truman used to call them. Someone to entertain her, someone who wouldn't pick her up on anything, someone she could show off to about her high-profile orbit, someone she could talk to, gossip with, try things out on, knowing I'd likely have something smart and sassy to say about it all, something she could repeat to Leland in the evening and, knowing Avery, pretend was her own.

But despite the frequency of our meetings, there was always a sense, for me at any rate, of something missing in our relationship, our conspiracy not as tight nor as confidential as I'm used to. We never really... progressed. So to that extent Avery Blanchard was never really a true lunch companion, not a real swan. Of course, knowing what I know now (you just won't believe it) it's clear that there was just too much to risk for her ever to lower her guard.

It was at Cazzuola, the beginning of November, over her final Bacardi Dry and Stefano Ruggero's definitive *Tiramisu*, that Avery saw fit to remind me of her forthcoming Thanksgiving entertainment. As if I'd forget.

"Now you haven't forgotten, have you?"

"Forgotten?" I put on a puzzled expression.

"Thanksgiving, Cully. Don't tease. You know very well. You're my guest of honor."

"Avery, you're starting to sound like Signor Calvi. Given the company you gather round your table, the term 'guest of honor' might be more appropriately directed elsewhere. So far as I remember it, you've gotten the Secretary of State..."

"...ex-Secretary of State..."

"...two Senators, most of Allen's Sun Valley Crowd, the head of the Metropolitan... " I paused. "Has it arrived by the way?"

"That, my dear Cully, is why I'm reminding you about Thanksgiving. You must promise me you'll come. It's not the easiest date, I know, but I'm relying on you. You see, it's a kind of double celebration."

"The hanging?"

"The same," she said, coyly. And then, brightening at the very thought of it. "You'll simply love it, Cully. It's different, of course, but quite brilliant. Kalloway is just a genius. Did I tell you the Met have asked Player if they can show it in their Spring 'New Portraits' Collection? Imagine."

≈

And so, that Thanksgiving Eve, after my week of media madness, I found myself being led by Avery through a throng of gowned and black-tie guests, my fellow one per-centers, with greetings and hand-shakes and gratifying glances of recognition as I followed a step behind her, heading for the portrait which Player Leland had commissioned, and everyone had come to see. A portrait of Avery. It was as close to a ring, I'd suggested at one of our lunches, as she was likely to get. But no less significant for that. The moment the words were out of my mouth I'd wished them back but, surprisingly, she'd taken them as they were meant. An honest, if hasty, assessment of the situation.

The painting had taken six months to complete, about the same length of time we'd known each other, requiring many Concorde flights to London where the portrait painter, Julius Kalloway, who'd painted a senior member of the British Royal Family to much acclaim but who refused to come to New York, sat Avery in a chilly little studio for the laborious process of committing her to canvas.

I'd been given regular up-dates at our Cazzuola get-togethers, and had seen Avery's feelings for the portrait range from anxious to uncertain to a final what-the-hell, couldn't-care-less abandon. Now, as we made our way across the room, I was about to see it for myself, desperately hoping with every step that I would think of something appropriate to say when the time came to offer an opinion.

The very next moment, it seemed, we'd stepped out of the crowd and were there, Avery and I, arm in arm, standing in front of a flower-filled fireplace where a space had opened to allow room for study and admiration, looking up at the latest addition to Leland's collection, the Kalloway, the size of a championship pool table, isolated in dark splendour and somber solitude where I remembered a magnificent Bonnard bath scene hanging my last visit.

I took a deep breath. Took another deep breath, pursed my lips, leaned forward a fraction as though to commit some minor detail to more critical scrutiny, aware every second of Avery's eyes glancing nervously from me to the canvas and back again, waiting for my reaction. Waiting, waiting… while I wondered what on earth to make of the torn and crumpled polaroids, charred scraps of newsprint, gobs of acrylic, tangles of knotted wire, shrapnel shards of metal and crockery all set in a horseshoe halo round a ragged smear of yellow exactly the shade and shape, I quickly realized, of the shoulder-looped gown that Avery was wearing that night, as though somehow it had stepped from the frame, magically free of the debris that surrounded it on canvas. So far as I could tell, without closer inspection of the blurred necklace of polaroids which might have held some clue, there was absolutely no visible sense of Avery beyond that canary smear of paint. But it was, I remembered, a Kalloway, so identification, likeness, was secondary. More important to recognize the artist than the subject.

"It's… extraordinary, Avery. Quite, quite… And he's caught you exactly!" Which I swiftly accompanied with a wink and a squeeze of her arm. She laughed and slapped my hand.

"Cully Mortimer, you are such a… But I'm so pleased. *So* pleased you like it. You do, don't you?"

"It is astonishing. Completely… astonishing."

"Isn't it, though? And everyone is raving about it. Jeffries, Player's man at the Met, called it… let me get this straight…" Avery rested scarlet lips against the scarlet tip of a fingernail in a frown of concentration. "That's it," she said, looking up. "He called it 'furiously parodic'. Which threw me a little, I can tell you. But then he redeemed himself with 'focusing, perplexing and intuitively magical'." Avery hesitated once more, looked up uncertainly at the picture. "Or did he say 'magically intuitive'?"

It was a well-practiced line. I certainly wouldn't have been the first to hear it that evening, and I probably wouldn't be the last.

"Whatever," she continued, gazing proudly at the canvas. "He likes it."

"Well, that's alright then," I said, and we giggled like school children at a shared secret. And then, telling me again she was so, *so* pleased I liked it, as though she needed my approval before she could entirely feel comfortable with the new acquisition, Avery led me back into the hubbub of eagle-faced men who ruled empires, and their boney, bare-shouldered wives who knew the oily heft of high-carat diamond necklaces.

"By the way," she whispered, before passing me on. "Player's in a black mood, so don't be put off if he seems a little abrupt."

"What on earth have you done, Avery?"

"Not me, silly. The staff. Seems someone's been helping themselves to this and that. Tiny things. Some books, some silver here and there. Player went *ba*-llistic when he found out. Still hasn't recovered."

And then she was gone, back to the staircase and some late arrivals, leaving me with a couple called Pulteney who lived near Leland in Fauquier County until, some ten minutes later, we were finally summoned to dinner.

And what a dinner. What a feast.

I'd recently reviewed Dr George Almond's riveting biography of the Empress Elisabeth of Russia for the *Times'* Books page and, as I took my seat, made those minute adjustments to the cutlery that we all do, felt the taste buds pucker and sweat in anticipation, I recalled Almond's reference to Ivan Ivanovich Schuvalov, an exiled lover of the Empress, who remarked to his chef and travelling companion, Francesco Leonardi, that the greatest privilege of a rich man is to eat well.

Whether Player Leland knew of this encomium I cannot say, but Schuvalov would undoubtedly have approved of the spread that had been prepared that Thanksgiving Eve at Player Leland's Adams Square mansion.

The burr walnut-paneled dining room was lit by candles, hundreds of them, winking from walls sconces, from a pair of mighty chandeliers, and from a line of tortured gilt and silver candelabra that ran the length of a cherry-wood table that didn't see a single elbow touch. Each of the forty place-settings was laid exquisitely with Sèvres china, each dish rimmed with a double ring of aquamarine and gold. The cut glass sparkled. The silver, dulled and heavy, looked extravagantly ancient and costly.

And the food? The food. Unforgettable. For each guest a nest of wondrous *bouchot* mussels flown in that day from Brittany and served shell-less on a single rock of ice. So tender was their flesh, so chill the ice, that on removal, there was the briefest sensation of sticking – a second's resistance – as a fingertip might to frosted metal. After the mussels, a ladled soup of salsify and creamed herbs, a fabulous half-cutlet of North Atlantic halibut lightly smoked and then pan-fried to a golden tan and, of course, the turkey, oysters only, four each... (eighty turkeys in total, I calculated, to feed forty people), in a Pernod and citrus *jus* the exact same shade of Avery's dress. A sensation.

It was only after dinner that I realized there was something more on the agenda. Quitting the table with the other guests and moving through to a balconied drawing room that overlooked the garden where Avery and I had first met, a hand caught my elbow and Player Leland drew me to one side.

"A moment, Cully? Here, let's slip away to the library..." his lisp failing to register the two 'r's, which made the word come out like 'li-bwawee'.

"Great picture," I said, as we settled into our chairs, scroll-winged leather monsters positioned just so either side of a tiled Victorian grate.

Leland's face lit up: "Isn't it, though? I'm real, real pleased. Mind you, that Kalloway wasn't the easiest fella to deal with, I can tell you. Why, Avery had to fly Concorde to London a good half-dozen times for sittings. Can you believe that?"

Not by looking at the picture, you couldn't, though I guess the artist had gotten the yellow right. And Avery wouldn't have minded the travel arrangements. But I didn't say that, of course, just nodded and said how Avery had told me so. And wondered what all this could be about, the two of us sitting there. I didn't have long to wait.

"So anyway, enough of that," said Leland, waving the subject away and gazing instead at the shelves of leather-bound volumes that rose around us, showing no sign of the 'black mood' that Avery had warned me about. "What I really wanted," continued Leland, now levelling the same gaze on me, "was a chance to talk to you privately, away from the paper." He rearranged himself in the chair, grimaced as though he couldn't quite find the right, the most comfortable, position. "See, as you may have heard, there are going to be some changes at the *Times*."

I'm sure I stiffened. For a few months now, there'd been rumours flying and long faces at the paper, doomed looks, editors resigned to the possibility that their desks might not be, for much longer, the safe bets they once had been. That contracts, arrangements, sinecures might, under Mr. Player Leland's leadership, soon be done away with. The fact he was new to national print media sharpened that anxiety. Word had it he might do something really off the ball court.

"See, we've made some studies," he continued. "Seems the service sections – Life-Style, 'Metro', that kind of thing – they're the ones our readers turn to. Consumption, that's what it's all about, Cully. Ways for them to spend their money. They can get all the hard news they want or need from CNN and the car radio and, if we're lucky and they're not stupid, they just look to us for a weekly analysis, an op-ed comment on whatever's been happening. No need to tell you that, I'm sure. Plus, of course, there's the advertising. Your kind of sections bring in a whole heap more revenue than hard news. Which is good for stock, and therefore good for stockholders. So you can understand what we need to do. And need to do swiftly."

I began to feel the tiniest worm of dread, a faint, fragile fluttering of butterfly wings. I'd been at the paper a little over seventeen years. Up till now those years had given me a certain confidence, an edge. I'd built a nest. I belonged. Now those years were beginning to look like a liability. Maybe the people who mattered – Leland, Rowlands, and the boys on the tenth floor – had come to the conclusion that I'd been there too long, grown stale. New blood. That's what they were looking for now. Something fresher, bolder, something to keep the readers satisfied and advertisers happy. Leland, in a kindly way, befitting my seniority perhaps, was softening the blow. He was probably going to tell me I would always be a part of the family (hah!), but for now I was out. It was over. Seventeen good years, Cully, but time to move on.

"Maybe I should have left this to Rowlands," said Leland, ominously, following the words with a hesitant cough, "but I wanted to talk to you myself. I… We… We'd like to change your column."

I think my heart stopped. I know my heart stopped. Life as I knew it, loved it, was suddenly, here in this book-lined room, in an instant, over. OVER. I could feel a deep, leaden slide in my innards, that first cramping twist and coil of the guts that heralds a bad case of food poisoning. The worm had turned into a hungry anaconda, the butterfly wings flapping now like a leathery pteradactyl's. My mouth was dry as sand, and my eyes started to prick. For a second I wondered if Avery knew about this. Not that she'd have said anything.

"We're looking to introduce a new section, Cully. Twenty-pager to start with. Color, of course. Life-in-the-city sort of thing. The 'Metro' section plus, plus, plus. And, well..." Leland pulled at the crease in his suit trousers, crossed his legs, settled himself again. "We'd like you to run as front lead, Cully. Half-page. Where everyone gets to see you. Thought we might box the by-line too. Give it a bit more ooomph. Something strong. Reverse it out – isn't that what you newspaper boys say? White on black. A trade-mark maybe – your glasses, pen and fork, something like that. What do you say?"

Section lead, a half page? I reeled.

The hesitation spurred Leland on.

"Fact is," he continued, "you've had some real valuable exposure the past few days, Cully. Pretty damn near a brand name yourself. And we need to capitalise on that. Have to capitalise on it. Seems y'all represent a considerable slice of readership. Hadn't realized it, to tell you the truth. Thought it was down to Business. Sport. But seems I was wrong. Which pretty much backs up what Avery's always telling me." He chuckled affectionately. "Thing is, can you handle the extra space, Cully? Sure be pleased if you could help us out on this one?"

Toucan

It was the smallest voice. But unmistakeable. Roo.

"Cully?"

Beneath the Ansaphone's clear plastic cover I could see the tape winding away. It was late Monday afternoon, and I'd just gotten back from my Christmas break with the C.C. Haddons out at Hyannis. Frankly, I'd have preferred to stay in town with Roo, but the Haddon invitation was set in stone. Their eldest, Lara, is a Christmas baby. And twenty-one. She's also my goddaughter.

"Cully, are you there? Pick it up if you are."

There was a brief pause. I could hear her breathing into the mouthpiece. And then: "Call me. I need you. Please, call me." And the line went dead.

There were other calls, too. Four or five. Much the same message. The last had been logged only fifteen minutes before my return. I picked up the phone and dialed her apartment. It rang and rang and then, finally, she picked it up.

"Oh Cully…"

"Are you okay? You sound…"

"Cully, I'm scared…"

"Shall I come over?"

"I can't stay here. Can we meet some place?"

"Tell me where."

There was another pause, a beat. "Toucan…"

…But I'm getting ahead of myself. Thirty-two days ahead. A whisper more than a month. The best time of my life. Looking back, I still can't quite get a grip on how good it was; *that* good. Starting with a sleigh ride that Thanksgiving weekend. In the middle of a snow storm. On the slopes, I learned later, of the White Mountains.

That's where I'll begin. So you know. How things were…

≈

By the time I'd finally finished my story on staff uniforms, sent it through to the *Times*, and packed my bag that Friday after Avery's bash, I felt like a plate of cold left-overs. Despite my astonishing and heartening encounter with Mr. Player Leland in the library in Adams Square, I felt completely wrung out. If it had been anyone other than Roo I'd have cried off the weekend and taken to my bed. Instead,

I was waiting in the foyer when I saw her pull up outside. She was driving Bruno's Volvo.

"Where's Bruno?" I asked, strapping myself in.

"At home with the kids, if he's got any sense." There was a cool edge to her voice.

"Night off?"

"You could say."

"Sounds ominous."

"You really want to know?"

"Not if you don't want to tell me," I replied, as we pulled away from the kerb, the Volvo's rear wheels spinning momentarily for a grip. There'd been a brief but heavy fall of snow that afternoon which the traffic had churned into a treacherous, and now icy, mush.

"I had to let him go."

"And he let you keep his car?"

There was a snort of laughter at that. "My car, Cully. My car. Bruno was just a driver. One of six. A little sideline I run through the agency." And then her mood lightened. "Big expense, of course, but very, very cost efficient."

Cars swished past us, spattering the slush, headlights and streetlamps glancing off her face and mine.

"But hey, enough about me," she continued. "What have *you* been up to? I read the piece they're all talking about. It was so funny. And sad, you know? And so true. But I guess not everyone saw it like I did."

"You could say."

"I tried calling but your line was always busy. Couldn't even get the Ansaphone."

"It ran out of tape."

"No kidding?"

She swung off 65th at Second Avenue, heading for the Roosevelt Expressway. "I even caught you on TV. Good Morning, Mr. Cully Mortimer," before adding mischievously: "I watched you in bed. Hope you don't mind?" We stopped at a red light a few blocks on. She glanced at me and her voice softened. "You look exhausted."

"I feel exhausted. It's been a long week."

"So sleep on the way," said Roo. "Go ahead. I don't mind."

"Where are we going?"

"It's a surprise. You'll find out when we get there. When you wake up. Now be a good boy and get some rest. You're going to need it."

And though I didn't want to, that's exactly what I did, dropping back my seat, lulled by the leathery, scented warmth of the Volvo's interior, the swish of its tyres on the snowy streets of the city, and the metronome hum of the wipers.

Later, much later, it was the soft, sliding crunch of the Volvo breaking through an icy crust of snow that woke me. It was pitch black save for the glow of the dashboard instruments and, as I pulled myself up in my seat, praying I hadn't snored, the twin pools of the headlights illuminated a narrow corridor between snow-laden trees.

Roo was driving slowly, five, maybe ten miles an hour, no more. She was peering ahead.

"Hey, great timing. We've arrived. Well, almost."

If Roo knew where she was, I certainly had no clue. According to the dashboard clock, we'd been driving near three hours, with me asleep for most of them. On a snow-ploughed freeway we'd be a good two hundred, two hundred and fifty miles north of the city, I estimated. If she'd been driving in the conditions we now found ourselves in we were probably no more than half that distance from Manhattan. I settled for the former and, as it turned out, I wasn't far wrong.

And then, as though recognising where she was, Roo spun the wheel to the left, then right, shifted into reverse and, twenty feet back, pulled the car to a stop. She switched off the ignition, but kept the headlights on.

She looked at her watch. "Just perfect. Any time now. How was your sleep?"

"Anytime what? Where on earth are we?" I wiped the side window and looked out. As far as I could see, the path we'd followed between the trees had opened up into a sloping square of snow fenced by a stand of still, shadowy firs. About fifty yards away I could make out a half-dozen other cars, parked side by side and lightly layered in snow. But no sign of their owners.

"You'll find out," she said. "Come on, let's go stretch our legs. Get some air."

Outside, the night crackled with cold and snow pushed up around my ankles as I stepped away from the car. I rewound my scarf to cover my ears – quickly starting to burn with the cold – and looked around.

Beyond the spill of the headlamps there were no lights to be seen, not
even an orange glow from some nearby settlement. Nothing. Just the
night sky above us, sprinkled with silent, icy-bright stars, and new-
fallen snow glittering like a froth of whipped egg whites.

In the silence the Volvo's engine ticked and creaked as it cooled.
Roo sat on the hood, leaning back, taking great gulps of freezing air.
She called me over and caught hold of my hands, rubbing them with
hers, clouds of our breath shifting across the headlights like cigarette
smoke in the beam of a cinema projector – leastways, back when you
could smoke in movie theaters.

"So? Where are we?"

"You'll love it. Dreamland. Absolutely my favorite place in the
whole, wide world."

"You're kidding? There's nothing here."

"Oh, but there is, Cully. Just you wait and see."

We didn't wait long.

Roo heard it first, knew it would come of course, had probably
been listening out for it.

"There! Hear it?"

At first I could hear nothing, maybe a gentle stirring of breeze in
the trees, the dull clump of snow falling from branches close by, but
nothing else. And then, yes, something at the far end of the clearing,
coming from the trees. Bells. A tinny, distant jingling of bells.

"Over there. See?"

And I did, two tiny points of light dancing through the firs and
then bursting into the open, turning towards us and suddenly glaring,
accompanied by the snow-softened thud of hooves, the rattle of
bridles, and the ringing of bells. Sleigh bells. Fixed in an arch over the
heads of two galloping horses.

"I don't believe it…"

"Told you, Cully. Dreamland," and she leaped off the hood, went
round to the trunk for our bags, while I watched the sleigh race across
the pitch of snow towards us. As it drew closer I could see, between
the two riding lights, a driver bundled up against the cold, whipping
the horses on. Thirty yards from the car he turned the pair, hauled on
the reins and the sleigh slid to a stop in a cloud of whirling, sparkling
snow dust not twenty feet from the Volvo's front fender, the horses'
breath, their shivering flanks, swinging manes and stamping feet

caught in the beam of the headlights like some fairy-tale illustration, conjured out of thin air.

"Hope I haven't kept you folks waiting too long," said the driver, as he clambered down from his seat, pulling off his gauntlets and stuffing them into a pocket to shake my hand, then reach over to take the cases from Roo. Marlboro Man in a Davy Crockett racoon hat. "Miss Weaver, pleasure to see you back."

"Bob, how're things? Still wearing the hat, I see."

"Wouldn't be without it, Ma'am. Best thing I ever got. What you see here is the warmest, snuggest little head in these parts, and all thanks to you. Surely appreciate it."

"Weaver?" I asked, as Bob swung our cases on to the back of the sleigh.

"Don't ask, Cully," she whispered, taking my arm. "You ought to know by now."

Bob came back to us, carrying a long pole. "You made it just in time. Snow's coming down fast from up Vermont. We've had a couple of falls already, but the big one's on its way. Looks to be here midnight latest. Soon as I get this here tag in, Ma'am, you can douse those lights and climb aboard."

Seeing the puzzled look on my face, Bob hefted the pole: "This here's just so we can find your ve-hicle if the snow sets in. Best to take precautions hereabouts," and as he spoke he plunged its spiked end into the snow, inches from the fender. He tested it and it held steady. "That oughtta do it. So let's get movin' 'fore you folks catch yourselves a chill."

And so, snugly wrapped beneath swaddling fur blankets in the back of the sleigh, with Roo gripping my arm and the horses tugging us through that dark snowy forest, we set off on our Thanksgiving adventure.

≈

And what do I remember after all this time, sitting here in my sail-loft study close on a year later? Well, pretty much everything. It's so clear I can run it past in my head almost frame by frame, like a film. Cut and jump. Whatever I want. It's so sharp I can hear her voice, smell her perfume, see the way her body moved, feel her touch even.

Give me a time that winter weekend, and I can tell you exactly what we were doing. I don't even have to shut my eyes for the images to flood back. Like everything to do with Roo it's there, right in front of me, shifting sometimes, I'll admit, but easy to get a hold of if I really want to.

Maybe the reason I remember it all so well is the number of times I've gone over it in my head. That, and the surprises. As much as anything, it was the surprises that help me remember it. Things that came out of nowhere, that lodged in my memory and won't move on.

Just one of them after another.

It began, of course, with Bruno's car. Or rather it's her car, she tells me. One of six. Another little sideline I didn't know anything about, another string to her bow.

And then there's the new name. Weaver, if you please. Weaver? Why on earth should she have another name? What did she have to hide? Which is not to say I haven't, on occasions, in a professional capacity, used other names myself to conceal my identity. But what reason did Roo have to conceal hers? Mystifying.

And it wasn't just the cars or the name either. That weekend there was a whole slew of things you wouldn't believe – the fridge, the music and… aw heck, just one thing after another.

And then there's where we ended up, where we spent that weekend, this private, very remote mountain lodge that must have cost a thousand bucks a night if it cost a cent. Beartree, it was called. Just that. That much I learned from the fancy vellum writing paper in my room and the menu cards in the dining room. And the address, of course. Redmond, Mass.

I really don't know what I'd expected vis-à-vis our accommodation that weekend. Some chintzy New England country inn, maybe? A week-end rental? A friend's place? Roo hadn't specified apart from "somewhere in the country" and "snow and log fires". These were the only clues she'd offered. I'd gotten the feeling she wanted it that way, so I hadn't pressed.

Not that it mattered one way or the other. During that mad Thanksgiving week with the 'burger story, what occupied my mind most was not so much where we were going, but what would happen when we got there. It was the first time we'd been away together, alone, the two of us, so I couldn't help but consider the possibilities. Yet nothing was certain. It was all anticipation, conjecture, anxiety. You name it. All of them. And maybe more I can't think of right now.

Of course, I remembered what Felix had told me in Seville. After hearing me out in that smoky bar he'd said, as though it was the most natural thing in the world: "Then pay her, Cully. Pay her and sleep with her. Be done with it. It's easy. And then maybe one day you don't pay. And it changes. Becomes what you sound like you want it to be. Or maybe, when you sleep with her, you learn that she is not the one for you. Either way, you win."

And I'm ashamed to admit that, although I was pretty busy that week, I did find time to withdraw some money from my bank. Five thousand dollars. For the weekend. Expenses, I persuaded myself. I was a single man, no kids, well-paid – I could easily afford it. But deep down I knew I was taking precautions. Just in case. Normally, a few dollars and a credit card would have sufficed. But this was different. If the opportunity arose, and that was the way Roo decided to play it, then at least I'd have the cash. Because I knew I wanted to sleep with her. Make love to her. Hold her in my arms. See her naked.

But despite Felix's advice, and what I'd taken precautions to lay in, I knew I didn't want money involved. That was a last resort. What I wanted was something else. In short, for her to want me. To reciprocate. Mad maybe, but it's true.

And why not? We got on so well, we were so good together. We joked around, we laughed, we told confidences, things we'd never ever tell other people. Trust, that's what we had. Affection too, you know what I mean? With Roo and I there were always looks, touches, moments, things that seemed to make it clear that this all had to be headed someplace, to something. I just felt it.

But then again, maybe our friendship had gone too far. Maybe it was already too late.

Talk about wound up.

≈

That night, somewhere miles from anywhere, it was the sleigh ride first set my senses on full alert.

The snow that Bob had warned us about began a few minutes into that ride, the first flurries washing around the lights like a cloud of white moths, settling thickly in the folds of the fur wrap that covered us. Up ahead I saw him push down his hat, lean forward and whip up the horses, making us jolt in back and fall together in our seat. And that was the moment Roo pushed herself under my arm to burrow round my waist, her body closing around me, the two of us rolling gently together in the back of that sleigh. So natural, yet so easy to misinterpret. So easy to get wrong. And that's how we stayed until, maybe ten minutes later, at the end of a snow-banked track, we reached our destination.

Roo's Dreamland seemed just that. A picture on a Christmas card. A fairy tale. With snow whipping past, we sped through a gateway set with high stone pillars, careened down a snowy tunnel of trees lit by lanterns in the branches, and pulled up in a clearing in front of two of the sweetest little log cabins you can imagine. They stood about forty yards apart, screened from each other by a stand of fir, as though their plots had been cut out of the tree line, leaving this natural fence. A single path, banked with snow, led off the clearing where the sleigh came to a halt, then forked away to each cabin. So far as I could see they were identical, though one was higher up the slope than the other, the logs used in their construction interlocked at the corners, their ends chipped and scored by axe blades, a pale mortar spread between each timber like the filling in a sandwich. Like something out of Fennimore Cooper their windows glowed warm and inviting, the cleared plank steps leading to their verandahs lit with torches that seemed to lick up the snow-flakes now falling in some considerable volume, silent, fat, and white.

Climbing down from his seat, Bob hauled off the rug that covered the two of us and helped us down.

"Fires're lit in both cabins, Miss Weaver. Just tell me which case where, and I'll leave you folks to it. Dinner'll be waiting up at the Lodge whenever you're ready."

"I'll take Spruce," said Roo, hefting her case and starting along the path, "and Mr. Mortimer'll take the higher one. If that's alright with you, Cully?"

Of course, I said, and before I could do anything Bob had hoisted my case onto his shoulder and was bounding up the path to my cabin.

"I'll come fetch you," Roo called through the snow, "and we'll go up to the Lodge together. Say twenty minutes?"

"Sounds fine," I called back and, treading cautiously, followed in Bob's footprints to the verandah steps and climbed up after him. Hung above the door was a plank of wood and branded upon it the word 'Conifer'. We passed beneath it, Bob and I, him coming out, me going in, waltzing together in the doorway.

"Put your case in the bedroom, Mr. Mortimer," he said. "You need anything, just pick up the phone and punch three. You have a good stay now," and with that he lumbered down the steps and back into the snow.

Inside, the cabin was just gorgeous, just like you'd imagine. Solid, four-square, log and stone, a pitched beamed ceiling, bare wood floors scattered with native rugs, the stone chimney breast hung with crossed muskets and a splay of horns. You almost expected to see some bonneted, crinolined settler down on her knees polishing the planks with mustard oil.

But that was about as pioneer as Conifer got. Everything else was high-end and toney: thickly-lined Liberty curtains; a pair of cozy club chairs and a sumptuous Butler & Makepeace sofa set around the fire; a Sony hi-fi and TV tucked away in an old dresser; and, in what the English call a butler's pantry, in a small hallway leading to the bedroom and bathroom in back, the Zanussi. The fridge.

It was set on a shelf at waist height so there was no need to stoop, and even though I didn't need anything from it I pulled open the door for a peek inside, as you do. Just like Bruno and Beartree, just like Roo's new name, the fridge – or rather its contents – took me by surprise. But not immediately. The first thing I noticed were the Cream Milanos in the door – my favorites; on a rare evening off, I've been known to demolish a pack of these fiends in front of Masterpiece Theater (I'm sorry). And beneath them, why Doliol's unsweetened orange juice, the brand I love. And then I spotted the melba toasts stacked on a shelf beside the sealed pots I knew so well, a pair of them, not my absolute favorite Déchine *foie gras d'oie* which is damn near impossible to find outside of France, but a very creditable Piotto from Mirepoix. And ranged above them on the top shelf four half-bottles of '92 Meursault chilled to an icy sheen. Why there was even – I couldn't believe it – a bottle of Floris Seringa Splash.

And that's when I realized what I was looking at. Everything in the fridge had been tailored to me, had been put there with me in mind, all the things that I love, that over time I'd probably told Roo about, or she had noted on her visits to my apartment. Pretty much exactly what I kept in my own fridge back home. And she had set it up. All that was missing was the bottle of magnesium tricylicate. It quite took my breath away.

And then the phone rang. I took the call by the bed, its quilt so plumped up beneath the patchwork New England spread I didn't dare sit on it.

"Cully. It's Roo."

"You've caught me raiding the refrigerator. I can't believe it," I laughed.

"Just wanted to make sure you felt at home, honey." And then: "Listen, I've got some things to get done. Shouldn't take more than an hour. Why don't you go on up to the Lodge when you're ready, and I'll join you there later?"

"Sure. Sure. How do I find it?"

And so, when I'd unpacked, showered, changed, I did what she told me, wrapped up warm and set off for the Lodge, following the trail of lanterns that led through the trees behind the cabins, a pair every twenty metres or so, gilding the snow that fell and settled around them.

If the cabin had enchanted me, the Lodge was just perfect. It, too, was set in a clearing, log-built like the cabin but raised off the ground on a six-foot skirt of stone. But it was much, much larger than Conifer, a whole two floors higher, its shuttered windows set into what looked like pretty big tree-trunks and its chalet-style roof, rising above the treetops, covered in a thick circumflex of snow. As I reached the steps leading to the verandah, a massive plank door swung open and a shaft of light spilled out onto the boards.

"Good evening, Mr. Mortimer," said a man around my age, dressed in a check sports coat and black trousers. "Please, please. Come on in," he continued, closing the door behind me, taking my scarf and helping me out of my coat. "We're delighted to have you stay here with us. My name's Jack. If there's anything you need, you just let me know."

Passing my things to a younger man in a matching check waistcoat who seemed to appear from nowhere, Jack led me down a wide hallway carpeted in tartan and hung with hunting trophies, the horned skulls, I noticed, varnished to a bony shine. There was no reception desk and no office that I could see, only a broad staircase at the far end of the hall and, on the right, where we were headed, an antlered archway that opened into a galleried drawing room. It was a vast space, plumply furnished and softly lamp-lit, its panelled walls shelved with books and set with more hunting trophies reaching up to the topmost rafters, the whole place warmed by a blazing log fire in the largest hearth I'd ever seen. I swear you could have roasted an ox in it.

"Please," said Jack, stepping to one side, "make yourself at home, and help yourself to whatever you want," the sweep of his hand indicating a long sideboard just inside the room set with all the paraphernalia for mixing drinks.

On overlapping starched white cloths were cocktail shakers, a range of liquors, mixers, beers, two decanters of red wine (judging by the empty bottles beside them a very respectable claret and Burgundy), and in a pair of glass ice buckets (in the shape of a bear's head no less) bottles of *premier cru* Chablis and Gosset *Grand Millésime* sealed with silver clasps. In the middle of the sideboard, surrounded by ranks of glasses, was a wooden carving board and a line of bone-handled kitchen devils, a vase of celery stalks, a bowl of lemons and limes, olives, cherries, a goblet of swizzle sticks, salt and pepper shakers, Tabasco and Worcestershire sauce. All that was missing, I thought to myself, was Joseph to work his magic, this place that Roo had brought me to nothing less than Sutton Row in the country. And there I'd been, worrying she'd feel uncomfortable, out of place, that birthday date of ours. As if.

Mixing myself a gin and tonic, I glanced around. Roo and I were not the only guests in residence. There were maybe three or four other couples in the room, owners of the other cars down in the clearing, the men late-forties and up, the women younger; the kind of people who, if I'd gone up to any of them, introduced myself, would have graciously accommodated me – a fellow house-guest making himself known – and accepted me into their circle.

But I didn't do any such thing. Instead, nodding a '*good evening*' when I caught an eye but keeping resolutely to myself, I wandered across the room to a pair of armchairs set in a book-lined corner by the fire. As I made myself comfortable, another young man in check waistcoat appeared with a plate of canapés which he set down on the table beside me.

I was on my second gin and tonic, and second plate of canapés – I've always loved canapés and these, frankly, were sensational, the best I'd ever tasted – when I saw Jack coming towards me.

"Miss Weaver's apologies, Mr. Mortimer. Says she'll join you at your table. May I show you through?"

And whisking my drink onto a tray, he led me down a log-lined corridor into a low, candlelit dining room, no more than a dozen boothed tables set round the room, two or three already occupied. The fire was smaller here – which was good, or we'd all have roasted to death – with a snarling bear's head above the hearth, a glass-cased salmon trophy for each booth, and faded photographs of long-past hunting parties grouped around the Lodge steps. In the center of the room, all but concealing the diners on one side of the room from the diners on the other, was one of those early hotel serving stations, all gleaming ebony with identical work space and shelves on both sides, presided over by a corps of trim-waisted waiters busy polishing glasses, cutlery – no hand idle.

I was nursing the remains of my drink and looking over the small menu card – grilled woodland funghi, seasonal leaf salads, partridge, trout, salmon, a loin of venison, the kind of food that sounded as though it had all been caught, killed, or picked within a mile or two of the Lodge – when I looked up and saw a young woman come into the room. She was about Roo's height, slender, thirty-ish, but her hair was dark as chocolate and urchin short, her dress a nightclub singer's sheath of sequined blue, the sequins snatching at the candlelight as she walked over to the *maître d*'s desk.

In short order a chair was brought for her, and a waiter appeared with a guitar. Settling herself, she took the instrument, crossed her legs and began picking at the strings, tightening the keys till she was satisfied. Someone lowered the overhead lights, and the table candles shone brighter in the gloom.

Now I've never been a fan of live music or singing in a restaurant – if that's what you want, go to Las Vegas – but any initial vexation I may have felt drifted away as the woman began to play, bending over her instrument in concentration, fingertips picking their way across those six elusive strings to conjure up a gentle, shifting prelude of classical phrases, a passage of delicately executed and deliciously clear chords that ranged across the canon of classical signatures, blending sweetly one into another and bringing the room to a rapt silence. Like everything else I'd seen at Beartree, the performance somehow seemed to fit. Classy, acceptable, a fine accompaniment to the dining.

Which was when I began to recognize the direction in which the phrasing was headed, the guitarist starting to concentrate her efforts into a line of notes that were becoming increasingly familiar. I'd heard the same haunting rhythms not three months earlier in Seville, at one of the bars Felix had taken me to, a piece by the Spanish composer Joaquín Rodrigo, he'd told me, who had died just the month before. And the guitarist, whoever she was, played it perfectly, the notes gently building and rising, a sun-splashed, fountain-tinkling melody that floated through Beartree's dining room, lingered in the air above our heads, held every one captive. You could almost smell the dust, taste the oranges in every plucked string.

And then, astonishingly, as the fingerwork became increasingly complex, moving from *adagio* to *allegro*, as the notes began to weave around themselves like the twisting branches of a vine, everything suddenly went haywire, and the strings screeched and wowed, and this familiar voice rang out: "Sorry folks, that's all I remember of that one," and there was some laughter and enthusiastic clapping for what had, until then, been a masterful performance. And this woman I'd never seen before put the guitar on the chair, gave a quick little bow, and then bounded over to my table, sliding into the seat opposite.

Roo.

"What the heck…?" I spluttered.

"Surprised?"

"Roo? It can't be." But it was. And then, absurdly: "What on earth have you done to your hair?"

"Don't worry," she laughed, pushing her fingers through it. "Just a wig. I got it the other day, remember? Ronny's, in SoHo? Thought you'd like it."

Close up it was more black than chocolate brown, cropped short around her ears and spikily fringed across her forehead. She looked fabulous, just… fabulous. I couldn't believe my eyes. Or hers. I looked again.

"And your eyes. Your eyes are blue."

"Green didn't work with the outfit." She pulled at the sleeve of the sequined dress as though the answer lay there. "So what do you think?"

"What do I think?" I laughed. "You can't imagine. But which are you, really? Blue or green?"

"Green. I promise. Like you wrote in that story when we first met. Remember? 'Pesto-eyed' you called me. Your 'pesto-eyed companion'. I loved that. Believe me, if my eyes had actually been blue, I'd have worn green contacts the rest of my life."

And only then, belatedly: "And that was you playing? I didn't know you played…" Yet the moment I said it, I remembered the guitar back in her apartment, lying on the Eames recliner.

"I've been taking classes," she replied with the sweetest giggle. "Anyhow, I remember you talking about the piece out on the island, when you got back from Europe, and saying how much you liked it, Joaquín Rodrigo, rooting through Susan's CDs to see if she had it. So I got a hold of the sheet music and a tape and started practicing. But hey, Cully," she said, blowing onto her fingertips, "you didn't say it was so difficult. It drove me nearly nuts. I mean, the chords and fretwork on that *con spirito* section are just way monstrous."

I was astonished. And genuinely touched. So much effort and all for me. I could hardly take it all in.

"But you played it beautifully."

"Don't exaggerate. I didn't get a half-way through it."

I was shaking my head. "You are unbelievable. And I never recognized you. Not for an instant."

"I thought you'd spot me at the end of the block. You did before, remember? With that friend of yours?" And she twinkled mischievously at her reference to Elliot, picked up the menu card and scanned the list.

"Well, I know what I'm having. What about you?"

≈

She played once more that evening. But not as you might imagine. We'd finished our meal (a shared parmesan and truffle oil salad, breasts of partridge grilled over sage-brush, a ripe cube of really sublime *pavé d'affinoise*), had thrown down our napkins and said 'no, thanks' to coffees, when one of our fellow diners, a man, came up to our table, said how beautifully Roo had played, and would she mind doing so again?

I'd seen him when I came in to the dining room, sharing a table on the far side of the room with a woman whose dress allowed extensive exposure of her bosom, even from thirty feet; the kind of cleavage

Daphne might have had if she'd worn the right support. It was impossible to tell how old this woman was, but I guessed maybe early forties. As for the man, he looked to be in his sixties. Chief Executive type. Not exactly good-looking, but someone who knew how to use his years and his powers, the kind of man who'd grown accustomed to people doing what he wanted. He'd planned it, too. Set the whole thing up. As he spoke, one of the waiters came up with a chair and another with the guitar. He took the guitar and offered it to her. Very gallant. He knew she wouldn't refuse.

But, goddammit, she did.

With a playful dash of her fingers across the strings, Roo slid from the booth, squeezed past him, and held out her hand to me.

"I know you'll understand," she said, turning to the disbelieving CEO. "But that's simply not possible." And then, sweet as sugar, deciding to let him down gently, she said: "You see, I only ever play for my man."

The CEO smiled uncomfortably, now looking rather awkward, holding the guitar, not quite sure what to do with it. He nodded a mite curtly, like he was cross but knew he had to hide it, caught my eye, tried another smile then stepped aside for us to pass.

"Maybe next time," he said.

"You never know," she replied, and taking my arm we walked from the room.

"I didn't know where to look," I said, as she swapped her heels for a pair of fur boots on the verandah, and we went down the steps, pulling on our coats, suddenly chilled, the snow falling thicker than before. "I couldn't believe it when you said 'no'."

"He was trying it on, that's all. He should have known better. I hate it when people try it on. I mean, he was there with someone else, for God's sake. How dare he?"

"Maybe it was their anniversary, and he wanted you to play them something."

"Anniversary? Cully, you're a sweetheart. You can't see the bad in anyone. Not even me. I wonder about you sometimes. How do you make it through the day?"

And with that she fell silent as we walked across the clearing, arm in arm, and into the wood, following the snow-haloed trail of golden lanterns until the lights from our cabins showed through the trees.

By now, of course, my heart was beating loud enough to hear. Dinner was over. A few minutes earlier she'd called me 'my man'. And now we were walking together through a silent, snowy wood, closing on our final destination. The moment was fast approaching when things I'd imagined, hoped for, might really happen. Or not. I knew the words I needed to say, had rehearsed them a thousand times, just as I'd rehearsed how I'd respond should she reject my advance – with grace, and a dignified acceptance of the inevitable. Of course, of course. I quite understand – that sort of thing. Yet all I could hear was this clamoring thump in my chest, all I could feel a tightening in the throat, and this mad desire to leap across the minutes that lay ahead, to put them behind me.

And then, when we reached the point where the path forked to our separate cabins, she slid her arm from mine and turned to face me. Which was the moment I should have said something, drawn her to me, led her to Conifer. But I didn't. Instead, as I tried to muster my nerve, she beat me to it.

It was late, she said, pulling the collar of her coat around her cheeks. She was tired. The drive up and all. Would I mind if we called it a day?

So I told her 'of course not', and she leaned forward to kiss me on the cheek. Then she wished me goodnight, wrapped the coat tighter around her and, with one arm held out to give her some balance, she swayed down the path to her cabin, opened the door onto a spill of light and disappeared inside.

Another man, braver than I, would have stood his ground, there in front of the cabins, caught a hold of Roo as she leaned forward for that peck on the cheek and tried, with sweet supplications that I had never mastered, to change her mind. It was certainly romantic enough. The lanterns swinging in the trees, the lights from the cabin windows, a thick, swirling goose down of snow settling silently around us.

But I didn't. I was not that man. Indeed, never have been. Instead, I watched her down the path to her cabin and when her door closed, turned towards my own cabin. And as I shut the door behind me, pulled off my coat and shook the snow from it, what I felt more than anything was a kind of comforting relief.

You'll know already from my earlier account of Casey that I'm not an adventurous lover. I enjoy women's company at the table, where I can orchestrate the whole event, make it memorable, guarantee good food and good company. But when it comes to the bedroom, I'm nervous, shy, about as cack-handed as a Taco waitress trying silver service. I just don't feel comfortable with my abilities. Or my body. At my age, naked, I know I'm not the prettiest sight.

Which is where the relief comes in.

There have been many times in the course of my life when I could have just kicked myself for not taking the initiative when I knew I should have. And this was certainly one of those times, letting the possibility of something good slip by. But that's the way it's always been with me, and I've grown to accept it. Also, you have to remember that I had a certain position to protect, a professional reputation for, let's say, probity, that I would have just hated to see compromised. So I'm even more careful than I might otherwise be. I have to feel safe, I have to be sure, before I'm prepared and ready to make a move. That's just the way it is with me. Which is what I mean by relief. Relief that the status quo remained unshaken, relief that nothing had been forfeited, and relief that I'd kept everything intact. Relief is a marvelous comforter. And an even greater deceiver. It is, after all said and done, far easier to imagine acquitting oneself with honor, than actually being put to the test.

But that evening, wandering around Conifer, chewing my way through the Milanos, suddenly not the least bit sleepy, I felt, beyond that familiar relief, a whole new slew of emotions: frustration that I now found myself alone when, who knows, with a bit of courage, I could have had company; annoyance at my faint-heartedness; disappointment that what I'd hoped for had not come about; embarrassment at what Roo might now think of me – my lack of resolve; and, running through it all, an increasing sense of loss. An opportunity had been missed here, and because of it the two of us would move on, and the chance to do something about it might never come again; that from that moment on Roo and I would only ever be friends. Good friends, great friends even, but nothing more.

Maybe tomorrow, I consoled myself as I prepared for bed, maybe tomorrow another chance would present itself. And as I climbed under the quilt I determined, for a change, to be more forceful, more direct, take what I wanted, make a stand, a declaration, without thought for the consequences.

But as things turned out, there was no need for making resolutions I probably wouldn't have kept to anyway.

For, at some dark, unknown hour, the woman I wanted more than anything else in the world came to my bed and coaxed me from sleep, rousing me with small sighs, breathless whispers, and cool delicate fingers. It could have been a dream, deep, soft and sinuous. But it wasn't. It was as real as the snow falling from the night sky, banking up on the window ledge, bellying the branches of the trees in the woods that surrounded us, muffling us from the rest of the world.

≈

In the end it turned out we were three days and four nights at Beartree. And if the temperature hadn't risen a few degrees through the weekend and the snow hadn't changed to sleet and then rain come Monday, there was no telling how long we would have been there.

As far as I was concerned it didn't matter how long we stayed. It could have been forever; I couldn't have cared less. It was as though... it was as if... oh hell, let's be content with clichés: it was like the whole world just stopped spinning, as though time stood still, and there were just two people alive. Roo and I. Snug as bugs, deep in the woods, sharing a log cabin miles from anywhere. And snowed in. Can you believe it? Could it have been more perfect? No.

The first day, Saturday, the snow never stopped, blanketing the paths from the cabins to the clearing where Bob dropped us Friday night, sweeping through the woods to fall in smooth white waves that banked up high against the tree trunks. Occasionally I'd wipe the fog from a window pane and look out, watch silent, fat flakes float down like tattered lace, or spin and tumble past, swirling with the breeze and cutting visibility to just beyond the porch rail. But that was it. Instead, we stayed put the whole day, me and Roo, whose every breath, every movement, every word...

The day began alone. I woke to a band of white snow-light cutting across the bed, where the curtains hadn't properly pulled together, and a folded sheet of Beartree stationery on the pillow beside me. The paper was so stiff the fold had sprung open a little and a few scribbled lines peeped out at me.

For a time I just looked at it, noting the way the paper warped around the Beartree engraving, wondering what message it contained.

'Cully, you're a doll, but let's just be friends.'

Or, 'Cully, it was great. Had to go back to town. I'll call.'

Or, absolutely worst case scenario, a bill. Maybe some bank details. Account number. Sort code. Branch. A snip at five thousand dollars.

What it did say, when I finally dared open it, was: 'Darling Cully, be an angel and order breakfast. I'll be back by the time it arrives.' At the end of the note was a small, nicely-formed 'R'.

I remember it was the first time I had seen her handwriting. A strong, solid hand, confident, clipped and mature, the words sloping left to right, comfortably separated, the letters loosely curled but consistent, a style quite without artifice – just scribbled off in a moment. If I'd been the one writing, I'd have gone through a whole ream of paper trying to get it to look and sound just right. And I was the one wrote for a living.

Like I said, it snowed all day Saturday so we stayed put. And it was glorious – every second of it. And uncanny. Whatever I was thinking, Roo seemed to know it. Whatever it was I wanted, she thought it the very best idea. And then some. Like that first morning, leaving the bed while I slept. As if she knew I'd want time to myself, a chance to rally my thoughts, to collect myself. I'm certain she thought that.

And after breakfast in front of the fire, with the pancakes gone and the last of the maple syrup licked from each other's fingers, in that first awkward silence, she judged the moment perfectly, carried it off so easily, made me feel brave, unassailable. She just got to her feet, took me by the hand and led me, shyly, back to the bedroom, as though she knew I'd never get round to suggesting it myself.

And all I had to do was follow.

"More of the same, please," she said, closing the gap in the bedroom curtains – which I would have done if she hadn't; shrugging off her gown to fall at her heels, and leading me to the bed.

And there, the quilt pushed aside, my mouth sweet from toast and honey, pancakes and syrup, her breath warm and slow, in that dim curtained light, she lay back on the bed and I saw her body for the first time. Long and tanned, the small of her back gently arching, a hand reaching up to grasp the wood headboard, stretching herself slowly, luxuriously towards me.

"Go on," she whispered, closing her eyes. "I know you want to. Go ahead. Please. I want you to."

And raising myself on an elbow, I looked down at her, put out a hand to touch her, fingers tracing down that long arm to her breasts, her ribs, over her stomach and, with breath held, parting her thighs with the gentlest pressure to burrow smoothly and warmly between her legs. She smiled, sighed, told me it was nice, and in that gentle abandon, coiling and softly mewing at my touch, gave me a kind of courage I'd never encountered before, the freedom to do whatever I pleased.

Like I said, I've never had a great appetite for sex. It's always been an occasional, enjoyable, but secondary experience. I couldn't go as long without food as I've gone without sex, which always puts it into perspective for me. Roo changed all that, sharpened my tastes, made me hungry for pleasures in a way that surprised me. She seemed to know intuitively what I was comfortable with and what I was not, though that didn't stop her drawing me on if she felt I was ready for it. Yet always, somehow, making it seem that I was the one doing the leading...

I'd always imagined Roo would be a demanding lover, and though there was nothing in the world I wanted more than to sleep with her I'd always felt anxious I'd fail to match her skills, her expectations, in short, satisfy her. But I needn't have worried. She made me feel I was making all the right moves, made it feel as though we were inventing the whole act ourselves, working out the whats and the wheres and the hows, encouraging each other to come up with embellishments. And when we made love I knew for certain I was getting her full attention, that she was giving me more than she'd ever give a client.

Don't ask me how I knew, I just knew.

We spent that day in our nightclothes. Pyjamas for me, Roo in a nightshirt, both of us belted tight in Beartree dressing gowns, shod in woolly socks that she found in a bathroom closet. We banked up the fire until it was roaring, switched up the heating, and raided the Zanussi for lunch – a whole pot of Piotto *foie gras*, a pack of toasts, and two half-bottles of the Meursault, all laid out on the rug in front of the fire. Afterwards, she found a backgammon board in the dresser and beat me hollow, game after game, until she looked at her watch and asked if I liked Bette Davis?

"Isn't she just the best?" said Roo. "And there's a double bill."

So we put more wood on the fire, opened another bottle of Meursault and curled up together on the sofa. Heaven. Until, half-way through the second movie, already dark outside, with Bette Davis and Paul Henreid stranded in Rio, I began to wonder whether Roo intended spending that night with me, or if she planned heading back to her own cabin.

"Do you mind if I stay?" she asked, at almost exactly that moment, turning in my arms to look up at me. "Only it'll be real cold and lonely back there in Spruce all by myself."

"I think that'd be great," I said, and hugged her clumsily. "I'd love you to stay."

"In which case," she replied, kissing a fingertip and placing it on my lips, "soon as the movie's over, let's roll up a spliff and have us a hot tub."

The tub was on a deck outside the bathroom. I'd seen it the night before during my Conifer recce, or rather its chrome hand-rails and canvas cover. An hour later, gazing up at the snow as it fell from the darkness to melt in a damp, woody ring around us, the water bubbling and steaming, with a soapy blue light flickering from its depths, I decided I'd never been happier. Weightless with pleasure, stoned into a near stupor, and exorbitantly proud of my latest semi-submersed performance – kneeling, with bubbles bursting at my chin, as Roo clung to the edge of the tub and maneuvered herself onto me. Now all I wanted to do was sleep.

"You're falling asleep," said Roo, her foot stroking my leg. "And you can't do that until you've finished your treatment."

"Treatment?"

"Won't take but a minute," she said, in her best Bette Davis, and climbing from the tub, her slim, glistening body steaming in the icy night air, she turned and pulled me up after her.

Naked, holding hands, we skittered across the deck and down some steps into a small clearing behind the cabin where the snow was banked in soft, mountainous drifts.

"Which one do you think?" she asked, wrapping herself around me and starting to shiver.

"Which what?"

"Are you ready?" She clutched me tighter.

"Ready?"

"Are you steady?"

And before I knew what was happening, she'd tipped my feet from under me and flung us both into a slope of snow piled high against the side of the deck.

The effect was heart-stopping. I thought I would die. I wanted to scream but could find no purchase on any sound save a panting, hissing stream of breath gasping out of me at the shock. And then, helping each other up, brushing the snow from our bodies, we hurried back inside, toweled dry, and fell into bed.

I was asleep in her arms in seconds.

≈

Sunday was a dazzler. The snow had stopped in the night, and the sky was cut into canyons of glorious blue between the snowy peaks of the firs.

"Perfect," said Roo, throwing open the curtains and letting daylight spill past her naked body and into the bedroom. "Just perfect."

Coming back to the bed she picked up the phone and called the Lodge, taking my hand and pressing it against her breast as she spoke.

"Hi. Jack? Can you send down the Arrow to Conifer. And two suits, please? Thanks." And then, hanging up, she turned to me: "I hope you brought thermals like I told you?"

As it happened I had, and twenty minutes later, struggling into them, looking as hillbilly as Jed Clampett, I heard the sound of engines approaching the cabin. They came to an idling halt in the clearing, and a moment later I heard a knock at the cabin door and voices.

"All gassed up, Miss Weaver. Ready to go. And the suits should fit just fine."

The suits were all-in-one quilted zip-ups, blue with red leather padding on shoulders, elbows, and knees. By the time we pulled on gloves, ski hoods and goggles the two of us looked like a couple of downhill racers. As for the Arrow, sitting squatly in the snow, a set of two small skis out front and a track contraption at the back, it looked more like a bullet, its low black body lined with racing red stripes, a thin blue smoke spluttering from its exhaust.

"So let's go," said Roo, zipping up the front of her suit and settling herself onto the saddle. And with me tucking in behind her – the Arrow thankfully lower to the ground than Roo's motorbike – she gunned the throttle, released the brakes, and we were off.

You know that moment when the heart hammers and the breath catches, when the blood in your body actually feels like a million

hot pulsing streams rather than a warm, sluggish job-lot, when every
sense snaps to attention and life lets you catch a glimpse of its fun
side, gives you a shot of something that makes you whoop and
whistle? Well, that ride with Roo through the snowy woodlands of
the White Mountains, beneath a sky so wide and high and blue it was
like the earth didn't figure, was a trunk-load of such moments. It was
just fabulous, a soaring, swerving, skidding roller-coaster ride, with
Roo steering the most outrageous course between snow-laden trees,
over meringue peaks of snow-drift dunes, and through banked walls
of white that exploded over the Arrow's prow, casting up bow-wave
clouds of powdery smoking snow. Miraculous. Energising. Heart-
thumping.

Somewhere miles from the Lodge, we stopped on the edge of
a steep slope above a valley of snow-cloaked firs and Roo killed
the motor. The silence was almost deafening. And then, just a high
whisper of breeze, the occasional soft, shuffling thump in the woods
behind us of snow falling from branches, and the cooling tick of the
Arrow's engine. That was all. Crisp, clean, and clear.

"My absolutely favorite place in the world," said Roo, clambering
from the saddle into knee-deep snow, pulling off hood and goggles,
and flinging her arms exultantly at the view. "Have you ever seen
anything like it?"

And truth to tell, coming up beside her, I hadn't. It was extraordinary
– a vast, still landscape of white slopes and receding peaks patched
with snowy tracts of pine and bluffs of sheer grey rock, the con trail
of a distant jet marking the sky like a faint line of chalk.

And that was when I knew for certain that something had changed.
Standing there with this snowy wonderland spread out at our feet,
as far as the eye could see, I knew things were somehow different
between us. I'd changed, we'd changed. Before I had simply wanted
her. Now, I began to realize, I was falling helplessly, precipitously in
love with her.

I wanted to tell her, tried to think how she might respond, what
she would make of the prospect. And then decided not to, bit down
the words and postponed the sentiment, persuading myself that there
would be a better time and a better place than where we were right
then, knee-deep in snow, our breath making the only clouds against a
blue sky, the cold burning into our throats and chests, with this glorious

white winter world all round us. Moses with the tablets country. You couldn't get more elemental.

And yet I said nothing.

But she did. She took a deep breath, blew it out, watched the cloud drift away and said: "I do so love this place." And then, turning to me and hugging me hard, her cheek tight against mine: "And I love you, too, Cully Mortimer. Can't think of anyone I'd rather be here with," and with a final squeeze let me go. But before I could reply, she asked: "You hungry? Me, I'm starved," and dipping down flung an armful of powdery snow at me. "Let's eat."

If Beartree had any shortcomings it certainly wasn't in the packed lunch department. Lifting the Arrow's saddle, Roo opened up a hamper and distributed 'lunch' – still warm, spit-roast poussins flavored with rosemary and sealed in insulated baggies, two small tubs of potato salad, buttered rolls, a wedge of smoked cheese and crackers, a Thermos of coffee, and two silver flasks of Chardonnay which Roo dropped into the snow – the perfect ice bucket.

Afterwards, the remains of lunch packed away, hands and faces washed in the snow, Roo handed me the ignition key.

"You drive," she said.

"Drive? This? You're kidding me."

It's easy, she said and showed me how.

"Honest, it'll be fine or I wouldn't let you. And I'm right here behind you," she said, wrapping her arms around me and laying her cheek on my back.

And she was right. It wasn't that difficult. Just like a bicycle, really – a brake on each of the handlebars, with a sliding throttle on the right. At first, feeling my way, I drove slowly, overcompensating on the steer and jerky on the speed, but after a few minutes I began to get the hang of it. And as we slalomed up and down the slopes, the trees flashing past, the snow breaking over our bow, and Roo screaming with pleasure in back, I became quite the showman.

But Sunday's fun was far from over.

Back at Beartree, we'd barely dropped the Arrow off at the motor pool behind the Lodge when Bob rode up leading two saddled horses, the breath snorting from their nostrils, the butt of a shotgun sticking out of a long leather sheath on each saddle.

"You ever ridden a horse, Mr. Mortimer? If not, you'll love this feller. Quiet as a mouse. If he wasn't a horse, he'd most likely be a librarian." He slid from his saddle and helped hoist me up. "And if you fall off," he continued, adjusting the stirrup straps, "you can bet the landing'll be good and soft."

Roo, of course, was already mounted and, with Bob and I falling in behind, she led us off into the woods surrounding the Lodge clearing.

"We got far to go?" called Roo over her shoulder.

"Twenty minutes maybe. Jack said they haven't moved much in the last week."

"What hasn't moved?" I asked.

"We're going on a Turkey Shoot," said Roo, falling back to give Bob the lead, and reining in beside me.

"I've never shot anything in my life."

"You eat the bird," she said, dismissing my alarm with a pull on her reins, "you oughta know how he gets to the table."

Which, after the extravagance of Player Leland's Thanksgiving dinner, gave me pause for thought. I was also reminded, for the first time since arriving at Beartree, of my conversation with him, the plans for the new section. And I still hadn't gotten round to telling Roo about it. But somehow that was city stuff, and here in the country there were other things on my mind. Like, right now, having to handle this horse and shoot a turkey.

The ride, wherever it was we were headed, was a good deal longer than twenty minutes. We rode in line, the three of us, Bob up ahead, picking his way through the trees, with Roo and I bringing up the rear, the horses lifting and sinking their legs into the snow with the delicacy of ballerinas on pointes.

After the howling dash of the Arrow, I decided, horses made for a lulling, easy ride, swaying there in the saddle to their slow, plodding rhythms, hearing only the gentle clink of bridles and squeak of leather, the crunch of snow as their hooves packed it down, breathing in their warm-straw smell, and the resinous scent of the trees raw, sharp, and bracing. After only a few minutes in the saddle I began to feel reassured. It didn't look like we were going to be galloping anywhere in these conditions, and if I did fall off, as Bob had said, it would be a soft landing. So I relaxed my shoulders and arms, rested my hands on the pommel, and watched the scenery sway past.

Everything was going just dandy until Bob stopped up ahead,

stood in his stirrups, and then tugged at his reins, starting up an incline on our left. Suddenly, chest high in the snow, his horse began a series of leaping bounds that soon had him at the top of the rise. Before I had time to prepare, my own horse had turned and begun the same maneuver, with me clinging on for dear life as we, too, bounded up the slope. It was a chastening moment but at least I managed to keep my seat and, being in the rear, no one noticed.

"Everything okay?" said Roo, as I pulled in beside her.

"Fine," I said. "Just fine. What's happening?"

"See them, on the slope there? Five, no six birds. By that fallen tree."

I looked but could see nothing until, finally, what I had taken to be a small brown bush raised itself up and ruffled its feathers with a distant squawk.

"Tie up your horses over there," said Bob, pointing to the nearest stand of pine. "I'll head up behind them and you get yourselves down there on the edge of the clearing, maybe a couple hundred yards ahead of them. Give me fifteen minutes. All you got to do is load up and fire."

After we secured the horses and Bob had disappeared into the trees, we slid the shotguns from their sheaths, scooped out a handful of cartridges from our saddlebags and, crouching low, headed down the slope to take up our positions.

It was tough going. In some places the snow had drifted to waist height and we had to wade through it with the guns held level with our chests. Once we reached the trees, however, the snow was not so deep, and within a few minutes we'd passed through the copse and come out the other side. The clearing lay before us, maybe two hundred yards across, much like the space where we'd left the car. According to Roo, the birds would come out of the middle of the trees along the far edge and fly right past us at maybe twenty feet.

While we waited, Roo showed me how to break the gun – a hefty over-and-under Beretta – load the cartridges, and had me practice a couple of swings. "Don't bother aiming, just follow the bird with the barrel, get ahead of it, and squeeze the trigger. Simple as that."

We didn't wait long. From the top of the ridge came a piercing Tarzan-like scream, followed by whistles and shouts and gun fire that suggested twenty men not one. It was a hell of a hullaboo, and the turkeys fell for it.

The first four birds flew unaccountably wide, cutting across the far corner of the clearing to disappear into the flanking woods, but the last two broke cover at just about the place where Roo had said. We'd already agreed that I'd shoot first, being nearer, and that Roo, three trees away, would go for what I missed. I'd told her she'd be busy then, and we'd laughed quietly.

As the birds approached, flapping wildly and squawking indignantly, I shouldered the gun, lined up the tip of the barrel until it seemed to dance around the leading bird, moved ahead of it as Roo had instructed, and then pulled the trigger. The blast astonished me, and the gun's stock slammed back into my shoulder. By the time the second bird was in range, seconds only, I was way off target but fired anyway.

Thirty feet away, Roo swung the Beretta to her shouder and into the path of the leading bird. "Close," she called, over the stock of her gun, beading down its barrel. "But no cigar."

And with that she fired once, whipped the gun back to the following bird and fired a second time.

The first turkey, an ungainly medicine ball of brindled feathers, scraggy neck and bellowing, raucous head, seemed to explode in a cloud of feathers and dropped to the ground as though it had flown into a wall of glass. But momentum carried its crippled companion into the trees, bursting through the branches and dislodging a cascade of snow before dropping to the ground with a kind of hollow, asthmatic thud.

By the time we reached the second turkey, closer to us than the first, the snowy ground was flecked with blood and feathers and the bird waggled a single, indignant wing at us. Without a moment's hesitation, Roo stepped forward and brought the stock of the gun slam down onto the bird's head, burying it into the snow. There was a thin, muffled crunch of breaking bone, a shudder through the turkey's body, a final shake of its wing, and then stillness.

"That's the bit I hate," said Roo, wiping the stock in the snow. "But then I hate the suffering worse."

It was the first time I'd seen Roo so cold-blooded, so punctilious. It was a side of her I hadn't seen before. I remember it surprising me more than maybe it should have. I certainly couldn't have done it myself. And said as much.

"Sure you could," she replied, as Bob broke cover and rode across the clearing. Dismounting, he picked up the first bird, inspected it and slung it over his shoulder, then came over to where we stood.

"Good shooting, guys. Pity about the rest of them. Reckon I came down too far to the right."

It was getting dark when we got back to Beartree. A couple of stable-hands gathered the horses and unhitched the birds, swinging head down from Bob's saddle. As they led the horses away, Bob came over and shook my hand.

"Hope you enjoyed yourself, Mr. Mortimer. Sure was a pleasure being with you." And turning to Roo, tipped his fingers to his racoon hat. "Miss Weaver," he said, then headed after the horses.

"Good day?" asked Roo, taking my arm for the walk back to the cabins.

"Incredible," I said, and meant it. "So what else have you planned for me?"

"Don't worry. That's it. Nothing more than a hot tub, a glass or two of that fancy Meursault of yours – which I gotta tell you I'm really getting a taste for – and then the pleasure of your company. In bed."

≈

Next morning every limb ached, sinew shrieked and muscle groaned. I felt like I'd been trampled by a herd of elephants. I could hardly lift my head from the pillow. For a moment I thought I must have had a stroke in my sleep. But I hadn't. What I'd done, without realising it, was push myself a little too hard. Sunday was more exercise than I'd taken in twenty years, and my body was letting me know it in no uncertain fashion. I should have known there'd be a price to pay.

Like the first morning I was alone in the bed. I'd just managed to get myself into a sitting position when Roo came bustling into the bedroom, pushing the door open with her backside. She was wearing a t-shirt and carried a breakfast tray. She plumped the tray on the bed and scrabbled in beside me. "Holy Joe, will you look at the color of that bruise?"

Hardly able to move my head, I glanced down to see a brown and yellow disc the size of a dinner plate spread across the top of my right arm and shoulder.

"Jesus H., where did that come from?"

"You didn't tuck the gun stock into your shoulder like I told you to. Couple of shots and you haven't got a snug fit, that's how you'll end up." She leaned over to examine the damage. "Poor baby. I put ointment on earlier, but it hasn't shifted any."

"You put ointment on?"

"I saw it when I got up, did it then. Maybe it needs some more attention," and she gave me a look I'd come to recognize.

The massage took place after breakfast, in front of the fire. Roo pushed aside the sofa and two armchairs to make room, spread the bed-quilt across the floor, covered it with a large fluffy towel and had me lie down on my stomach.

I did as I was told and made myself comfortable, resting the side of my face on my forearms, watching her close the curtains, switch on the Sony, select some CDs (all favorites of mine, I'd noticed) and slide them into the player. Or rather, from floor-level, I watched her bottom perform these tasks as Roo reached high for a grip on the curtains and bent over the Sony, the hem of her t-shirt rising provocatively with each movement.

When you listen to Pachelbel's *Canon* there are eight long, lugubrious, ascending and descending notes that introduce the piece. By the fourth note, Roo's knees were either side of my back and her fingers were sliding across my scalp, the sound her fingertips made and the sputtering and crackling from the logs on the fire a gentle background to the *Canon*.

I have no idea how long the massage lasted. Pachelbel, Handel, Bach, Albinoni, canons and concertos, adagios and airs, mixed with the scent of rose and rosemary, roamed through the cabin with a warm, comforting *basso continuo* as Roo's hands pummelled, stretched, eased, and cajoled my aching muscles. From my ear lobes to my fingertips, from my toes to my chins, her hands and fingers worked away at my body, turning me this way and that, bending arms and legs with professional precision, until it felt there was not a single particle of tissue that hadn't been stroked into surrender.

But, of course, there was. And that was left, despite earlier nerve-tingling approaches, until the very last when, with a low moan, she settled herself onto me.

The rest of that day we loitered around the cabin, wrapping up warm and sitting out on the porch glider to watch the sleet turn to drizzle, and the drizzle to rain, dripping off the porch roof and pockmarking the snow.

That evening we dined in the Lodge. On our way there, tucked in beneath an umbrella, I wondered whether we'd bump into the CEO Roo had snubbed the first night. But we were alone. According to Jack, who took our order, the other guests had left late afternoon. We could have done the same, but we'd decided to stay a final night.

I learned a lot about Roo that weekend. Cuddled up in front of the fire, walking arm in arm through the snow, bubbling in the hot tub, lying together in bed, she'd opened up like never before. And that last night, as we sat alone in the dining room, and afterwards, beside a blazing fire in Conifer, lingering over cognacs, Lord, we covered some ground.

Sure, she told me, she wanted to stop, when I pressed her about her work. She'd had enough of the business long ago, she said, the clients, the uncertainty, the scary things, and, "You know, the loneliness. Just try having a social life when you work my hours." But the money was hard to beat, she admitted. That's what made it difficult to quit. The more you got the more you wanted. The more you needed.

"Being a call-girl? For me, right now, it's just the gas that makes the motor run," she explained. "You got cash-flow problems? You need a few thousand to keep things straight? Short on wages, tax, keeping the contacts happy, that kind of stuff? That's why. And there's nothing easier, Cully. A pair of scissors. Snip, snip. And you've covered yourself in a shortfall month. Others go down for less."

But I'm nearly there, she continued. Just a little longer, just the time to wind everything down. She'd keep the legitimate businesses, of course – the limo service, the property portfolio, the investments – develop them, give them her undivided attention, make them work more efficiently. That's what all this was about. A few more months maybe, and then time to change gear. Maybe get out of the city. Live in the country.

"Who knows Cully, maybe even start a family."

I didn't know what to say, how to read it.

"They say there's nothing like it," was all I could manage.

≈

The following morning patches of grass showed through the snow, and I could see wood-chip on the path down to the clearing. After breakfast we packed in our separate cabins and I called the Lodge to settle the bill.

"All taken care of, Mr. Mortimer," I was told, as though it was their pleasure that I had nothing to pay, that they couldn't be more pleased for me. And when I tackled Roo about it as Bob loaded the cases in the trunk of our car, brought up from where we'd left it Friday, she told me not to be silly, it was her treat, she'd loved every minute and that if I felt real bad about it, why I could pick up the tab the next time.

Next time. Next time. Those two words rang in my ears with a piercing sense of promise as though whispered by a band of angels. So this wasn't a one-off. She intended there to be more. And as I bid Bob farewell and climbed into the passenger seat I felt like the world and everything in it was mine.

But that Thanksgiving weekend there was still one more surprise in store.

On the drive back to town.

The biggest surprise of all.

"So what did you think of your first whorehouse?" asked Roo, after leaving the country roads behind us, and heading south on the freeway. "That is, I'm assuming it's your first?"

I was thunderstruck. "Whorehouse? You mean Beartree?"

She nodded, smiling.

"You're kidding me?"

But she wasn't.

"Well, maybe not in the real sense of the word. I mean, Beartree's just what it seems – an upmarket country retreat for those who can afford it, a kind of club if you like. You can check in as a paying guest, like any other 'hotel', but it's owned by hookers and most of the time it's used by hookers. Remember the guy with the guitar? On his anniversary, Cully?" She looked across at me teasingly. "Well, Ingrid is certainly not his wife. At Beartree maybe, but not in real life. According to Ingrid, who looks after his particular tastes on a fairly regular basis, Mr. Ernest Delaford is a senior partner at Peabody Dunn, happily married, with a triplex on the Park, a place in the country on Guard Hill Road in Bedford, four kids, and scads of grandchildren." Roo paused for a moment. "He's also a breast feeder." She glanced across at me as though to check my reaction.

"A breast-feeder?"

"You know, breast feeding. Mamas and babies. That's what

Delaford likes. Diapers and breasts. And a lot of other guys too, you'd be surprised. And Ingrid obliges. She's quite the specialist. Been doing it years now."

"This is... unbelievable," I gasped, as stunned by Delaford's... requirements, as I was by the revelation that Beartree wasn't all I'd imagined it to be. And thanking God I'd found out; I'd already started toying with the idea of writing something on Beartree for the *Times*. "Just... unbelievable."

"Which is exactly how it should be. Nice and anonymous."

I turned right round in my seat, as far as my safety belt would allow, back to the door, arm up on the dashboard. "Hence the 'Miss Weaver'?"

"You're catching on, Cully. Millicent Weaver. Beartree's co-founder and major shareholder."

"You *own* Beartree?"

"Miss Weaver does. Sixty per cent all told. The place used to be a camp, you know, like one of those Adirondack lodges where the Astors and Meynards and Stuyvesants use to hang out on family holidays. Belonged to a family called Blanchard. Timber people."

It took a moment... but then the name exploded in my head.

"*Blanchard*! Bill Blanchard? Avery Blanchard?"

She looked across at me. "You know her?"

"You could say."

A light seemed to dawn in her eyes. "Of course, silly me. Of course, you'll know her. My, my. Small world. Isn't she married to that Leland Player? The guy who owns the *Times*?"

"Player Leland," I corrected. "And not married exactly, but about as close as it gets. It's where I was Thanksgiving Eve. She and I lunch together. Always the same restaurant. They call her '*Principessa*'."

"Well, hey, they would, wouldn't they? And I'll bet she loves it," chuckled Roo.

"You mean, you know her, too?"

She turned, gave me one of her sly, curling smiles.

"So how...?"

"How do I know her?" She cocked another look at me. "Well, wouldn't you like to know?"

As a matter of fact...

Roo fell silent for a moment, watching the road ahead, as though weighing the pros and cons, deciding whether to continue or call a halt right there.

And then: "Okay, why not? You want to know, I'll tell you. I first met Avery in Los Angeles. I had this boyfriend at Wharton, a couple years above me, who got a job working at one of the big studios. Something financial. Accounts, acquisitions, something like that. Anyhow, after he graduated he asked me to go with him. So I went. Just like that.

"Which was where I met Avery. She was married to this kind of B-stroke-C-list producer back then…"

"Jerry Russell."

"Could be, I don't remember. Anyhow this guy had sold some project to the studio Cal worked for – Cal's the boyfriend, right – and we all met at some studio 'do' or other. Cal took me along, introduced me to the guy and his wife and that was that. She was older than me but we hit it off. What she was doing with that guy I cannot imagine, but she looked happy enough. You could say pretty much the same thing about Cal and me. Maybe she spotted it, too."

"And then?" Sensing there was more.

Roo laughed. It was maybe a year later, she said. She and Cal had gone their separate ways – "He got very… corporate, you know?" – and Roo had discovered that she could make an easy, profitable living on the game. "So there I was, footloose and fancy-free, a small apartment couple of blocks back from the ocean. And I'm having fun – sometimes I'm charging, sometimes not, nothing formal you understand.

"Anyhow, one night the guy I'm with, some German film producer a studio has laid me on for, asks if I know a place called The Glades, out near Pepperdine. I tell him no, and he says would I like to visit? Someone at the studio's told him it's a fun place. All he has to do is make a call. So, sure, it's the studio's tab – the longer it takes the happier I am.

"So after dinner, instead of going back to his hotel, we drive to Pepperdine, leave the coast road and head up into the hills. By which time it's dark and it's late and I'm starting to get a little uncomfortable, you know what I'm saying? I don't know this guy from Adam, and I don't know where we are. I mean, he says we're going to this place called The Glades, but who knows? I never heard of it. For all I know

I'm going to end up in a storm drain with my hands tied behind my back and my throat cut. Shit happens, you know?

"Anyway, finally we turn off this itty-bitty road and pass through a set of gates and up ahead, I'm thanking God now, is this house. Like an old clapboard farm. Real, *real* cute. With maybe a half dozen cabins set out around this dinky lake. And it looks like there's a party going on. There's cars parked out front, fairy lights in the trees and music coming from the house. Not hip-hop party music, but like low classical stuff, the stuff you go for, real nice. So my date rings the doorbell and who should open it up but…"

"Avery Blanchard." Suddenly I was fitting in the pieces the *Times'* archive had no record of, the years Avery went missing after Jerry Russell's death. And maybe even the years before it.

"Well, not Blanchard yet. But Avery, all the same. And, of course, we both recognize each other. Only she's a widow now. And it turns out she owns this place, The Glades. A very high-end, discreet members-only club, where guys could go and have fun and absolutely no questions asked."

"Like Beartree?"

"Like Beartree. You'd call up, book one of the cabins round the lake, tell Avery what you wanted in the way of company, and she'd do the rest. I don't know where from, but Avery had gotten this group of girls together, real top-of-the-line material, took a cut and allowed them the use of the house."

"So she's taking from both ends?"

"Smart lady. Membership's maybe a couple of grand a year, very exclusive, invitation only. And the girls are charging top dollar, too. Little Miss Avery is making a packet.

"Now, I'm not one of her girls but maybe because she recognizes me Avery lets it go, invites us in, shows us round, tells us to make ourselves at home. But later, while Mr. German Film Producer is sleeping it off in one of the cabins, she and I get re-acquainted. She asks about Cal, I tell her. I ask about hubby, and she let's me in on the deal. And then, out of the blue: do I want to join the team?"

"Which you do."

"Which… I do. And a very neat arrangement it turns out to be. I get to meet some real big spenders, and since I'm only ever up there a couple days a week, max, I can still run my own operation in town. I mean beach-time, or what? I am having fun. Until some doozy lets the cat out of the bag and the place gets busted. Just my luck. You must have read about it. Dozens of big deal Hollywood names collecting a lot of uncomfortable lawyers' letters from outraged wives."

"And Avery?" I was still finding it difficult to think of the Avery Roo was telling me about as the same Avery I'd spent Thanksgiving Eve with. Astonishing. Incredible. Just incredible.

"No sight nor sound of her. When the cops check the land records they find Glades is owned by some holding company based in Alaska, or someplace. No names. No leads. Avery is free and clear. But she hasn't got a nickel. It's all in Glades. Her only asset now belongs to the US Treasury. Unless, of course, she wants to step forward and claim it. Which would be a pretty dumb thing to do, all things considered."

"So she comes east?"

"I guess. Like I said, we lost touch. I mean, she disappeared off the face of the earth."

"So how did you meet up here?"

"Relocate. Three, four years ago I hear about this lodge up in Vermont, Massachusetts someplace. I talk to a few people, and get the low-down. Apparently, some widow needs to off it fast. Can't wait. Her husband's died and left the whole caboodle to his kids, and only the lodge to her. So, clearly, the wife doesn't relish spending too much time in the boondocks all by herself. She wants Manhattan, and she needs to sell. For a lot. But I go and take a look anyway – Camp Beartree, the brochure calls it. 'The Sporting Estate of a Gentleman'. But I happen to know it's a guy called Blanchard. And it is just perfect. I want it. Do a Glades.

"Now, I'd been back in town a while and I'd made enough out on the coast to start up pretty nicely here. You know the Relocate story. You know about the limos. And you know about… the other. So. They all tie in and make good money. But not enough for Beartree. No way can I get close to the asking price. But I make an offer anyway. Turned down flat. So I speak to some friends of mine, in the same line of work as me – Ingrid's one, and there's a couple others – but we're still way short.

"And that, Cully, is when I discover that Mr. Blanchard's grieving widow is none other than my old Pepperdine chum. There's a picture of her in the paper. Yours, if I recall. Going to the Opera with Mr.

Player Leland no less. And the caption reads Mrs. Avery Blanchard, recently widowed, blah, blah, blah..."

"So you pay a call."

"I pay a call."

"And?"

"And the lady is not happy to see me. No, sirree. But she covers it well. I mean, give the lady her due, she is a performer. She's still at the Blanchard apartment on Fifth back then, and she invites me in. We have a drink and talk about old times – which kinda makes her uncomfortable, I can tell you. And then I tell her I'm the one who made the offer on Beartree, and I'd be *real* grateful if she could see her way to accepting it."

"Roo, that's blackmail."

"Cully, that's business."

We were silent a while. We were coming into northern New York, and the traffic was snarling up ahead around the slip for the Deegan Expressway. Roo decided the best way of dealing with the gridlock was to keep moving, weaving her way forward, changing from lane to lane, a talent she'd probably picked up from Bruno. She'd smile, wave, cut in, and no one hooted. She was through the hold-up in the time it takes to boil an egg.

"You're not saying anything. You don't approve," she said at last, making for the Park.

"To tell the truth, I don't know what I think. I'm a columnist on the *Times*, what do I know?"

She laughed. "Look at it like this, Cully. You want something, you do everything you can to get it."

"By fair means."

"I made no threats."

"You didn't need to."

"I didn't want to. I just wanted some slack. I mean, there was just so much I could raise against my apartment, the business. And we'd put in a good offer. It wasn't what she wanted, but hey! Maybe she'd overpriced the place and I was just getting her back on a level playing field. And she didn't have to worry any. I mean, she is stepping out with old whatsisname."

"You are incorrigible."

"And you are... you are my big daddy and I love you. I really do.

You're special, you know that? And you know something else, Cully Mortimer? In all the time I've had Beartree, you're the only man I've ever been there with. There, now you know."

But before I could say anything she was pulling up at my apartment block at almost exactly the spot she'd picked me up Friday. As I unbuckled my seat belt, she pulled me to her and gave me a long, tender kiss.

"Are you home tonight?" she asked, a private whisper.

"I'll be back around six. What about dinner?"

She shook her head. "Can't make dinner, but I could call round later, say eleven?"

"Eleven sounds fine to me."

≈

And so our time in the city began.

December. Low slate skies, snow that didn't know whether to settle or move on, and a sharp little wind that lay in icy wait round corners. Bundle up weather, Roo called it.

We saw each other a lot. Spoke on the phone most every day. And every time I called I never caught her at a bad time. She was always ready for a chat. Wherever she was in the city, whatever it was she was doing. Which left me with the warmest, molasses-like feeling every time I put the phone down.

Which was just so great. Because back then, despite her enthusiasm for me, I was still on the look-out, still waiting for something to alert me – a swing in temperature, an impatience, a cooling. By now, I felt, the cracks should be showing.

If Susan hadn't told me what she had, it wouldn't have been a problem. But she had, and I couldn't help but be wary. It would have been irresponsible to be otherwise. But as time passed, it became clear to me that Roo had no agenda, no 'plans', and that any fears I might have, any suspicions I might harbor that her intentions were anything other than honorable, were groundless. She may have behaved the way she did with Susan for any number of reasons, but I had no doubt our relationship was different. I mean, for starters, Roo was not gay, I can tell you that. Poor Susan never stood a chance.

And I can also tell you that I never for an instant sensed any kind of performance – the real giveaway. Even when you're charging thousands of dollars, it's got to be impossible to be faultlessly convincing the length of time we were together, to maintain that momentum, that level of response. But there was never any sense of it with Roo. Nothing mechanical. Nothing practiced. Not the slightest suspicion of her ever being disassociated from what was going on; she would initiate our love-making, and she would also respond equally warmly when I suggested it.

And the more time we spent together, the more certain I became that I loved her, as I had loved no one else my whole life (though I knew enough to keep that quiet for the time being). And I also knew, with growing certainty, that she felt the same. It may seem a ridiculous prospect – a man like me, a girl like Roo – but goddammit, it was true.

All this is not to say that love is blind. Short-sighted maybe, but not blind. I can't say that I approved of Roo's way of life, even if she did tell me she was scaling down. Nor her behavior *vis-à-vis* Avery, and the purchase of Beartree. Just as I didn't much approve of her treatment of Susan (if it was true), or, come to think of it, her gift to me of the Cartier pen which, when I remonstrated the next time we met up, she assured me she'd bought – though I can't be absolutely certain that she did.

But in the end, what of it? I doubt any court in the land would have given her a custodial sentence for her 'negotiations' with Avery or Susan, and shoplifting, if that's what it was, is hardly a capital offence. All it did was register the fact that our scruples, hers and mine, were at variance on certain points.

And that was fine. No big deal; certainly not something worth jeopardising everything else we had going for us. It's a bit like ginger; I might not be wild about the taste, but I'm not going to send back the sushi and sashimi just because they happen to share the same plate.

And being in love after... well, let's just say some considerable time, was a revelation. I felt years younger. And lighter too; a week after Beartree I was stunned to see the scales in my bathroom register nearly four kilos below my usual weight, making me feel fitter and more alive than I could remember.

And everyone noticed: Susan, when we bumped into each other at a gallery opening in TriBeCa; Avery, at our regular Cazzuola lunch (a delicious two hours knowing what I now knew); Daphne, down for a few days for the Opera and some Christmas shopping; even Sanchez at the *Times*: "You want to give me that diet you're on," he said, rubbing his chins between thumb and forefinger. And then, with a low Inuit chuckle: "Or is it single guys only?"

All of which, I can tell you, was most, most gratifying. I've tried for years to shed a few pounds – not an easy prospect in my line of work – with all the attendant pain and conscience battling. And here I was shedding the stuff like an animal in moult. And all because I was happy. Fabulously, wantonly happy.

The only person who didn't seem too thrilled was Lydia. Half-way through a lunch together at Pete Luger's Steak House in Brooklyn, set up the last time I'd seen her at the radio phone-in recording, she just stopped listening as I burbled on about the new Section, leaned across and took my hand in hers.

"Cully Mortimer, it's not just a few pounds you've lost. I do declare you've stopped biting your fingernails, too. Is it bitter almonds, or do you have yourself a girlfriend?"

I was astonished. My fingernails. I mean they weren't long or anything, but they didn't snag any more. I just hadn't noticed. Bitter almonds I told her, to spare her feelings (in a funny sort of way, and despite all her little eccentricities, I did really like Lydia). But I sensed she didn't believe me, and for just a moment a shadow seemed to drift across her features.

If Roo and I spoke on the phone most every day, we met up nearly as frequently. Lunch at least twice a week, dinner or supper maybe more. And every weekend together. Arm in arm, we'd go to the movies or the theater; or we 'bundled up' to walk in the park; or took the ferry to Staten Island (don't ask me) – all those mad, lead-up-to-Christmas, start-of-a-relationship kind of things we all do. We even went bowling, for Lord's sakes, at Bowlmor Lanes down on University Place.

And shopping of course. We 'bundled up' and went shopping. This time for me.

By then I'd told Roo about the new Section, and in the sweetest way imaginable she'd suggested a few possibilities beyond the half-dozen new polo-necks I'd been contemplating. Dressed only in ruffled hair and a loosely cinched basque, she'd gone through my wardrobe, hanger by hanger, pulling things out to hold against her, ditching anything she didn't like the look of.

"Too old, Cully. Don't you think?"

Or, "Oh, Cully, no."

Or, "Seersucker?"

Or, "Where did you pick up this delight?"

Even, "Wrong color, absolutely not you," until there was quite a pile on the floor.

The following Saturday, with a new driver at the wheel of the Volvo (a statesmanlike black sedan this time, not the silver estate), Roo and I went on an expedition to fit me out with new clothes (no shoplifting, so far as I could see).

That day I bought everything that made her smile: a very slinky two-button cashmere Kenzo sports coat; a Comme des Garçons high-collared three-piece suit that I'd never have dreamed of trying on, let alone buying, a few months before; a gorgeous double-breasted wool overcoat; a pair of Berluti loafers with just a suggestion of risers; some new ties and three shirts from Sulka; and a range of Calvin Klein shorts which she insisted on paying for herself (I saw her sign the slip). For everything else I paid cash, using the five thousand I'd kept since Beartree (save two hundred dollars I'd spent at Newby & Webb for a magnificent poinsettia arrangement sent to Roo's address as a thank-you for the Beartree weekend), the slim, crisp notes slipped from my wallet with a prickle of guilt that I'd ever doubted her, and thankful relief that she'd never find out what I had done.

≈

The new *Times'* section 'Metro Life', with Larry kept on as Section Editor and most of the old 'Metro' team still on board, debuted the second Sunday in December to catch the Christmas advertising. And it looked great. Twenty-four pages. Color, of course. And me. Front lead, full-width, above the fold, just as Leland had said. I'd been putting together a piece on celebrity dining the last few months, a who-eats-where guide to the city – Donna Karan at Sette Mezzo, Danny DeVito at Rao's, Madonna at Moomba, Gwyneth Paltrow at Verbena, Woody Allen at Primola on 2nd Avenue, and Elton John, appropriately, at Daniel – and we led with that. A good, solid, name-dropping piece with lots of interiors and matching celebrity shots.

But instead of a logo – "glasses, pen and fork, something like that", as Leland had suggested – Rowlands and the others on the tenth floor decided on a first-issue full-length photo. Of the man. Cully.

The picture was taken by Mario Testino no less, with me, ankles crossed, arms folded, leaning against the grand piano at Sutton Row, with white-jacketed Joseph and his silver salver offering me a flute of champagne. Very classy, with Sutton Row insisting no credit, just as I knew they would. In subsequent editions the full-length photo was reduced to a two-square-inch head and shoulders cropped from the original portrait, a diminution compensated for by a byline set in gratifying 24-point bold.

"Cully, it looks just great. Just great. Didn't I tell you that Comme des Garçons was irresistible? And you didn't believe me, did you?"

It was Roo, calling first thing that Sunday morning. She'd had some 'business to attend to' the night before, so I hadn't seen her since supper Friday. For all I knew she could have been having dinner with her accountant, but the likelihood was she was up to monkey business. Whatever, I knew not to enquire too deeply; on the one occasion I'd made the mistake of reminding her what we'd talked about at Beartree, she'd made it crystal clear the subject was no longer up for discussion. She'd deal with things in her own good time and not before, she said, which left me feeling like a petulant, pestering teenage.

"So what are you doing for lunch?" I asked. "Shall we celebrate?"

"Cully, I'd love to…"

For a moment I went cold. That certain tone. It would be the first time Roo had ever said no. So here it comes, I remember thinking.

Lamely, I tried: "You're not going to tell me you're leaving me high and dry when I've just gone Section lead, are you?"

"It's just… I'm really not feeling that great, Cully. Thought I might just stay home. Rest up, you know what I'm sayin'?"

A flood of relief. She wasn't making excuses. And she genuinely didn't sound that great.

And then, equally swiftly, concern. "Are you ill? Can I do anything?"

No, she said. Nothing. Snuffling a little.

Which I heard and interpreted as her way of saying that I might think she's saying no, she didn't want to see me, but that, yes, she really did.

"I'm coming right over."

"No, Cully, honest I'm fine."

"No, you're not. I'll be there in the hour."

"I look a sight," was the last thing she said.

And she did.

"Jesus, sweetheart. What on earth...?"

She'd left the door unlatched for me, and was sitting at the breakfast bar in the kitchen when I arrived. She was wearing a Beartree bath robe, sunglasses, and sported a cut and swollen lip. And what, at first, I took to be a shadow beneath the lower frame of the right hand lens of her glasses turned out to be a slim yellowing bruise the color of *foie gras* streaked across the top ridge of her cheekbone.

"Like I told you," she explained. "I'm starting to downsize. But some people just don't take kindly to the news. This one thought I was going to cash in on him and spill the beans. Took it very badly." She touched her fingers to her lip. "Ouch."

As I sat beside her at the breakfast bar, watching her slide the tip of her tongue over the offending lip, it struck me again how very precarious her line of work could be. No wonder, I thought, she had people like Bruno – or rather the new one who'd taken us shopping, Rudi something – to keep her company.

"Were you by yourself?"

"Rudi was outside waiting for me. He brought me straight home, then went back to settle the account. Formally."

I was aghast. "You're not telling me...?"

"Cully, for goodness sake! Really!"

"It just sounded..."

"Well, it wasn't. Just a little payback, a little rough house. Break something valuable – a hi-fi, a Ming vase. Maybe a finger. Nothing serious."

I shuddered at the thought, Rudi bending a finger back until the bone snapped like a pretzel.

"So go take a shower," I told her, wanting to change the subject, wanting to cheer her up. "Bundle up. I'm taking you to lunch whether you like it or not. Dumplings – that's what you need. And I know just the place."

That Sunday was the first time I took her to Toucan.

≈

Roo loved Toucan, right from that first visit, declared it her absolute favorite place in the city.

I guess I wasn't really surprised. It suited her. A real bolt-hole.

Even in the middle of the day it's dark and anonymous, each table hidden away in a tropical jungle of ferns and palms and spiky fronds you almost have to cut your way through to reach your seat. From the street, through plant-filled windows, you could easily be forgiven for thinking it a florist.

Inside, the walls and ceilings and doors are painted with toucans, sitting on branches, flying through trees, with wood and stone and plastic toucans sat on perches amongst the foliage. There's even a tape they play every now and again, the sounds of a jungle and the occasional shrieking call of what, I guess, is supposed to be a toucan. It's all very atmospheric. And fun. It's like eating in an enormous bird cage.

Toucan is way down in the rougher reaches of the West Village, the kind of neighborhood you live in en route to someplace better or, when you've moved on, where you come to retrieve your Carrera from the pound. Which was what I'd written when I featured Toucan in an ensemble piece on all-night diners.

Which should tell you something. Open twenty-four hours a day, Toucan is not A-list dining. Which is not to say it's not all bad either, especially at three in the morning when their fried and steamed dumplings are as good as the ones you'll get at Shun Lee, or Joe's Shanghai on Pell. Which is what we always ordered whenever we went there, and what I ordered when I arrived early evening that first Monday after Christmas, fresh back from the C.C. Haddons in Hyannis, waiting for Roo to show after that brief, unsettling phone call.

Which, of course, she never did.

But I didn't know that then, sitting there alone with a plate of steamed dumplings and a flask of hot *sake*, followed by three espressos with a twist, checking my watch every five minutes and expecting her to push her way through the foliage at any moment.

The week before, at this very table, we'd had Christmas lunch together, exchanged gifts, the same table where she'd once told me how to catch a man's attention.

"T.C.U.," she said. It sounded like one of those acronyms like F.H.B – Family Hold Back. But it wasn't.

"Table. Corner. Up," Roo explained.

"You've lost me," I said.

"Table – Corner – Up," she repeated. "Just watch." And then she'd dropped her eyes to the bowl of Sweet & Lows in the middle of the table, let them wander to the corner, and then raised them up under arching brows to meet mine.

I was stunned by the look, the message her eyes conveyed, the devastating effect of that subtle detouring, and the corresponding beat it set up in my heart.

"Go on," she'd said. "You try."

Which I did.

"No, no, slower, Cully, like you *mean* it. Like this."

And despite the waiting, I began to chuckle to myself, remembering those low-lidded green eyes latching on to mine, smouldering...

It was here, too, I recalled, that she'd told me that old joke about the ideal boyfriend... you know the one: great lover, then he turns into a pizza. Which cracked us both up.

Sitting there waiting for her, it was like she'd just disappeared to the ladies' room and she'd be back any moment.

But she wasn't, and the chair beside me stayed empty.

Two hours after I'd heard that tiny, scared voice of hers on the phone, she still hadn't shown up. I called her apartment a couple of times, and her mobile, but the numbers, for some reason, were unobtainable. There was nothing more I could do except wait. If I left now, went to her apartment or back to mine, I'd be sure to miss her by seconds and we'd never touch base. So on I sat at our table in Toucan's window, anxiously playing with the cutlery, and watching out for her through the palm fronds as the snow gently fell and settled on the sidewalk.

It was just unbearable sitting there, wondering where she'd gotten to, what on earth could have happened, what she could be scared about. Was someone threatening her? Had she been hurt? I tell you, my head was all over the place. And the espressos didn't help. Quite a few times I actually had to calm myself down, take deep breaths, stop my leg from jigging under the table, rein in my imagination.

And at some stage I began thinking about Susan, sitting alone in that bar on Lexington, waiting for Roo to make her appearance – and her demands. I even began to wonder whether that was what all this was about. Maybe Roo had decided it was time to move the goalposts? Maybe this was all a part of the set-up?

But I couldn't believe it. Not Roo. Not us. Yet, once in place, I somehow couldn't shift the suspicion. I didn't believe it, you understand, but the thought lingered, in the shadows, like a flavor you can't quite place.

At nine, feeling just a little put out (she could at least have called if she knew she wasn't going to make it), I gave up on waiting and called for the check. I added a ten and asked the guy at the front desk to tell anyone who asked for me that I'd gone home.

Out in the street, pulling up my collar against a raw chill from the river and looking out for a cab, I spotted one of those raggedy street people you often see in this neck of the woods, one of the homeless army tramping in my direction through the swirling snow. He carried a bulging plastic bag in each hand which stooped his shoulders, and he approached with that purposeless, shuffling walk as though he couldn't be bothered to lift his feet off the ground.

I expected him to stop and ask me for change, but he didn't. Instead he carried on, right past me, muttering to himself, his feet pushing tramlines through the snow. Then, ten paces on, he turned and looked back as though he'd just remembered a familiar face.

Mine.

Out of the corner of my eye, I could see him standing there, watching me, the snow ticker-taping around him. And then, slowly, he began to swing the carrier bags, twisting from side to side until he judged their weight sufficient to spin him like a fairground carousel.

Which he did.

And, of course, he began shouting:

"Cease fire! Cease fire!"

The next thing I knew, the spinning had stopped and he was coming back towards me, a bit more purpose to his shuffling this time.

Which was when I saw a cab and hailed it over.

By the time it slid into the sidewalk, the man with the carrier bags had come to a halt no more than six feet away from me. I glanced in his direction, knowing I was safe now as I reached for the cab door. He wore a woolen hat tucked into the collar of a thick army greatcoat, had a straggly beard matted with dreadlocks as thick as wursts, and wild blue eyes that peered out at me from a grimy, reddened face.

"Cease fire!" he bellowed at me, as I ducked down into the cab. "Tell them to cease fire!"

Then he dropped his carrier bags to the sidewalk, flung back his head, and howled at the night sky.

"Cease fire! Cease fire! Cease fire!" he cried, as the snow flakes settled on his face.

Part Two
Tables Turned

Downtown

It was the first full week of the new year. A Friday afternoon. The first time in more than twenty years I missed a deadline. I remember it as you might remember any event in your life that, in an instant, without reason and without expectation, completely reshapes your life, pays it out along lines you could never have imagined. In your worst dreams. That was what happened to me a few minutes after three o'clock that second Friday in January.

I was home in Manhattan, New York City, and I was writing quickly, carelessly maybe, anxious to be done and gone. I had a train to catch, and I was still a couple hundred words short. I had an hour more to finish the piece, and send it through to Sanchez. Then I'd be on my way. My bag was packed and waiting in the hall.

Which was when the entry buzzer rang. A short double ring. Abrupt, business-like.

The sound startled me. I wasn't expecting anyone and I was annoyed by the interruption. The piece I was working on had been the devil to write, short but demanding, and I just wanted it finished. Gritting my teeth I got up from my desk and, stepping past my bag in the hallway, switched on the new entryphone system. It had been installed throughout the building the fortnight leading up to Christmas – two weeks that cost the doorman, Carlo, his job – and I still wasn't altogether sure I liked it.

Set into the wall beside the door latch, the tiny screen blinked and settled. I could see two men in overcoats, with scarves tucked into raised collars, huddled in the doorway. Behind them, out on the sidewalk, the swirling snow looked like static on the small black and white screen. I pressed the intercom button.

"Can I help you?" I asked.

One of the men looked straight at the camera, leaned forward to the speaker grille. He was black, the taller of the two, and wore a hat.

"Mr. Mortimer? Mr. Cully Mortimer?"

"Yes," I replied.

"Lieutenant DaSilva, 19th Precinct. And my colleague, Lieutenant Monroe." He nodded briefly to his companion, then both men held up their badges to the camera; they'd had them ready. "We'd appreciate a word with you, sir?"

Without really thinking about it, I said, "Of course," and pressed the button to release the lobby door lock. I watched them push through, and was about to cut the connection when two more officers, uniformed this time, stepped into the picture from left and right. There was certainly enough room in the outer porch for all of them to shelter from the weather had they wanted to, but instead these two uniformed officers had chosen to remain out of sight until the latch was released. At that moment I thought nothing of it. The fact simply registered. But I should have. I mean, four of them? To have a word? Nine floors below, I watched them walk past the security camera headed for the elevator.

A few minutes later there was a knock at my door. I was cleaning my glasses, rubbing the lenses with a handkerchief as I went to answer it, and held both in one hand as I released the lock and opened the door. Maybe it was the pressure of a deadline looming, but I hadn't given a thought to their request for a word, had almost forgotten they were on their way up, indeed was now wishing I'd not answered the buzzer at all. Extraordinary, looking back. They could have been salesmen. I was just peeved at being interrupted.

"Mr. Cully Mortimer?" asked the man called DaSilva. He hadn't bothered to remove his hat.

Yes, I answered, looking at him, and then glancing at the stern, rosy faces of his companions gathered around him in my doorway. The snow on their coats and capes had already melted, the drops sparkling in my hallway light. It could have been raining outside.

"Mr. Mortimer," he continued. "I understand you knew a Miss Beatty Carew? Blaise Heights? 56th and Third?"

As he spoke I saw him look past me into my hallway. He must have thought he was plumb on the button when he saw my bag.

"Yes. I do. I mean… I did."

And the moment I said the words, for maybe a half-dozen pulse beats, there seemed to be a kind of freezing of time and action. Not a movement. Not a sound. And then that stillness, that silence, was gone and the horror began, rising like a wave, a terrifying acceleration of events over which I had no control, in the hallway of my apartment, on a snowy Friday afternoon, with just two hundred words still to write.

It began with the glance the two detectives gave one another, the kind of look I recognized from every cop movie I'd ever seen. They had their man. Let's do it. Already, I couldn't believe what I suddenly knew was about to happen.

Without any warning DaSilva was pushing past me into the apartment, tucking a Search and Seizure of Property order into my shirt pocket, telling me as he did so that I was under arrest for the murder of Miss Beatty Carew. His colleague, Munroe, followed, crowding me backwards into the sitting room, reeling off a mumbled Miranda like a hurried prayer while the two uniforms pressed me up against the Arcimboldos and tied on plastic hand restraints.

≈

It was Sanchez who saw it, clipped it out, kept it for me.

"Didn't you know someone name of Carew? Beatty Carew?"

It was Tuesday morning, the day after my lonely, anxious vigil waiting for Roo at Toucan. I'd called her apartment the moment I got home, but the number was still unobtainable. I'd sat in one of the club chairs I'd gotten from the old Pierrepoint on Lexington, waited twenty minutes, and called again – still with no success. And there, in that chair, deciding I'd unpack my Christmas-break case and then try her number again, like an old duffer, I'd fallen asleep.

The moment I heard Sanchez say her name I spun round.

"That's right. Why?"

But Sanchez said nothing, just handed me a fold of paper, turned away, and headed for the vending machines. He knew something I didn't, and he wanted to give me some space.

I opened the sheet of paper and began to read the cutting stapled to it, a late-news piece from the back page of the *Post*'s second edition.

The words came at me in a tumbling rush. First, the headline: '*East-Side Realtor Slain*'. And then the name: 'Beatty Carew'. I felt for a chair and sat heavily.

"You okay, Cully?" I remember someone asking.

≈

I'll say it right now, so there's no misunderstanding.

I'm not proud of what I did.

Which was nothing.

I did nothing.

Of course, my immediate impulse had been to call the police, tell them what I knew, find out more, see if I could be of any assistance.

That's what I decided to do in the cab home from the *Times*, the cab
Sanchez called for me while Lizzie Kovacks did her best to comfort
me. Looking back, Sanchez must have had Lizzie on stand-by, must
have enlisted her help just in case what he thought might happen
happened. And it had.

But when I reached my apartment, picked up the phone to call the
police, it was like this bright, piercing beam of clarity suddenly cut
through the fog of shock and confusion. I remember it as pretty much
the first rational thought I'd had since hearing the news.

Hold on a second. What on earth do you think you're doing, Cully?
Calling the cops? Are you crazy? I put down the phone with a clatter,
as though just touching the instrument might alert the police to my
involvement.

And in that instant I understood precisely what I should do.

Absolutely nothing.

I should do absolutely nothing. I shouldn't get involved. Mustn't
get involved.

Though I didn't know it then, this hesitation to contact the
authorities with whatever information I thought might be relevant to
their investigation would later count against me – if I'd had nothing
to hide sort of thing… Just as I now began to surmise, standing by the
phone, that it would undoubtedly count against me, by association,
if I stepped forward and volunteered myself. Made myself known.
I simply couldn't risk it. I could see what the police – and more
particularly the papers – would make of it. Cully Mortimer, celebrated
Times' columnist, lead writer on the new 'Metro Life' section, linked
to the gruesome killing of a hooker.

Because, sooner or later, the Press and police were certain to find
out that Beatty Carew wasn't just a realtor.

So I did nothing.

Or rather, in the days following, right through New Year, I bought
every newspaper I could find to keep abreast of the investigation, every
edition in case some new fact emerged. It was from those newspaper
reports that I learned how Roo died.

Unsurprisingly, I guess, the usually confidential 'Initial Findings'
report from the County Coroner's Office had somehow found its way
to the *Post*. Their front page lead story a couple of days later provided
the fullest account yet of the 'Blaise Heights Homicide'. They wrote

pretty much everything there was to know save the killer's name.

It went something like this: Between seven and nine pm on Monday, December 28th – almost exactly the time I spent sitting in Toucan – prominent East-Side realtor Beatty Carew was murdered in her apartment at Blaise Heights on 56th and Third. The body was discovered by a neighbor that same night. The door to her apartment was open. The neighbor knocked, called out, went inside, and found her. She was naked, tied to a chair, and had been stabbed repeatedly with what the State Pathologist described as a short, single-edged blade. The victim had also been hit on the side of the head with a heavy object. Neither weapon had yet been found. A police source confirmed – 'unofficially' – *Post* speculation that the victim had been knocked unconscious before being stripped and tied in the chair. This same source also 'unofficially' confirmed that the police believed Miss Carew knew her killer. They were currently tracing the victim's family and interviewing friends, associates and real-estate clients who'd done business with the victim in recent months (so Elliot and Susan would likely be getting a call).

It also struck me, with a chill shiver, that if Roo had me in an address book I'd probably be getting a visit too. But, as the days passed and I heard nothing, that initial anxiety began to subside.

As well as newspapers, I also watched the TV news, switching between channels. There was no lack of coverage. Shots of Blaise Heights, reporters standing in the snow with their collars up, speaking to camera on the same sidewalk where we'd unloaded Roo's shopping not two months earlier. And then, in every broadcast, the same fuzzy photo of Roo with wet, slicked-back hair. After seeing it flashed on the screen a few times, I remembered where I'd seen it before – on the dressing table in her bedroom.

But if the plain facts surrounding the manner of her death changed little in the days that followed, other facts soon began to emerge. Just as I had suspected they would. By the end of the week, *Post* investigators sensationally revealed that, according to 'well-placed sources', the murder victim was not just a wealthy East-Side realtor, but the brains behind a high-class call-girl agency supplying the most exclusive 'companions' to the city's rich and famous.

Which opened up a whole new acreage of speculation. By that first weekend in January the Press were baying. Which was when I shuddered with relief that I'd put that phone down and done nothing. So far, it seemed, there was nothing to tie me in to the murder.

It was this guilty, voyeurist attention to the media – watching the way the story grew from a back-page, breaking-news item to banner headlines in the space of a few days – that somehow sidetracked me from facing up to what had really happened, a vast overdose of information that flooded any capacity I might have had to think coherently, that somehow distanced me from the fact that Roo was dead. My friend, my lover... Gone... Out of my life.

And when I did have time to think – late at night as I lay in my bed, or in those brief moments pacing the apartment, waiting for the next edition, the next news bulletin – it wasn't so much grief that occupied me, rather an increasingly fevered plotting, setting up the scene, working it through from every angle to see if it fit the facts. Conjecture, speculation. The who and the how and the why. Because if anyone was likely to know who killed Beatty Carew, then it was probably me.

Right from the beginning, from the moment I'd gained some level of composure after the shock of reading Sanchez's clipping, had time to gather my wits, I had no doubt about what had happened, no doubt at all who had done this terrible thing.

Friends, family, business partners like Ingrid, competitors in the property world, disaffected house purchasers – all the obvious kinds of people the police were checking out back then – they just didn't do it for me.

Roo's killer had to be a client, one of her 'accounts', of that I was absolutely certain, maybe even the one who'd given her the black eye, the one whose hi-fi, or china, or finger Rudi had gone back to break; the client who didn't like the fact she was quitting the business, didn't like what she knew; a client who got scared and simply went too far. Or maybe the 'new account' she'd done all that shopping for. Or some crazy whom she couldn't control any more, like the one she used the scissors on.

What this murder wasn't, I was convinced, was domestic, in the sense of family or friends. Nor was it accidental, some chance encounter. Roo's murder didn't just happen out of the blue. There was a lead-up to it. There were reasons. She even knew she was in some kind of danger. The last thing she said to me, on the phone that

Monday, was she was frightened. If I hadn't reset my answer machine before heading out for Toucan, I'd still have the message on tape, would still be able to hear her voice, scared and tiny as it was.

Someone had frightened her, that was certain.

Someone was after her.

And she knew who it was.

So. A client. Had to be. In my book, the only possibility. And, like I say, either the guy who blacked her eye and cut her lip, or the 'new account', or some other weirdo client who'd finally flipped.

And here's how I figured he did it.

Although she wasn't listed in the phone book and never, she once told me, entertained at home, it would have been no stretch for the killer to find out where Roo lived. All he had to do was follow her home after she'd visited with him (just as I'd once thought of doing before I got my invitation) and, just to make sure she's not calling on another client, stake the place out a few days. Keep an eye on her comings and goings.

So, anyway, that Monday evening the killer phones to find out if she's home. When she picks up the phone, he doesn't have to say a word; he knows what he wants to know – she's in. A little later he arrives at Blaise Heights, hangs around until he sees the concierge busy out on the sidewalk, like he was with me and Roo when we arrived there after our shopping trip, then he slips inside and takes the elevator to the forty-seventh floor and Roo's apartment.

Which is where, the first few times I ran this particular scenario through my head, I came up against a pretty major problem. How does the killer get to find out she lives on the forty-seventh floor? And how does he know which apartment? Even if he finds out which floor (by watching the elevator numbers when he follows her?), he's still got four doors to choose from once he gets up there. And not a one of them is named, no indication which is hers. Just letters. A to D.

That stumped me for a while.

I mean, the killer's not going to knock on all four doors until she answers. If he doesn't get it right first time, the neighbor who opens up to him will be able to give the police a description. Just like he's not going to slip the concierge twenty bucks for the information, because the concierge'll do the same when the cops come calling.

And then I just remembered. Like you do. It just came to me. Her key swipe. That anonymous white rectangle of plastic with the black strip that Blaise Heights' residents use to gain entrance to the building and their apartments. Except on Roo's swipe, for whatever reason, carelessly scrawled across its face in black felt-tip pen, faded with time, someone had written 47 D. Exactly what the killer needs to know. All he has to do is check through her bag or coat pockets when she visits, the moment she isn't looking, maybe searching for a letter or a driver's license, say, and – hey presto! Her key swipe. I'd seen it; anyone could have seen it.

The rest was pretty straightforward. He knocks at her door, says he's got a delivery or something, barges his way in when she opens up, there's a struggle, (…oh God, oh God… I could see it all so clearly – the horror of it, the fear, the disbelief and desperation) and he knocks her out cold. Then, maybe thinking he might as well get some kicks while he's about it, he strips her, and ties her to a chair. And then, either while she's still unconscious (which is what I hoped), or after she wakes up, he kills her. Manically. Seventeen stab wounds to the upper body, according to Don Draper, the *Post's* senior crime reporter.

Of course, you'd never prove any of this in a court of law without the killer confessing, or having the cops establish some kind of irrefutable forensic DNA thing linking him to the crime scene. But so far as I was concerned my theory stacked up. The motive, the opportunity, the way in and the way out, without being seen, without being connected to the murder in any way. And even if the police do discover his name, he's only one of many such suspects, one of Roo's many 'accounts'. Nothing to tie him in to it. Fabricate an alibi and he's free and clear.

And that, whether or not I knew it at the time, that's how I managed to keep the shock and the numbing sorrow of her passing at some kind of arm's length – working out the hows and the whys and the wherefores; how I managed to contain my feelings.

Until, of course, the funeral.

≈

The funeral was held in Bertram, New Jersey. Roo's home town. I found this out by calling up New York City Morgue first thing the following Monday. With all the plotting, all the speculation the previous week, I'd pretty much forgotten this final, vital detail.

Roo would have to be buried.

And I wanted to be there. Couldn't have stayed away.

After keeping me on hold for something like ten minutes, the woman who'd taken my call at City Morgue came back on the line and asked who I was.

I'd been expecting this; I was prepared. My name was Mike Cole, I told her, Mr. Draper's assistant at the *Post*. I was fact-checking his copy for the following day's edition and needed confirmation about the funeral. Where and when?

Of course, they were under no obligation to give out this information but the *Post*'s influence clearly extended, just as I'd hoped, to officials at City Morgue, as well as to the Coroner's Office and police. The reference to Mr. Draper gave me all I could've wanted. The woman informed me that the body had been released over the weekend to a firm of undertakers from Bertram, New Jersey. I asked for the firm's name, but she told me she didn't have that information to hand. So I called Directory Enquiries. There was only one funeral parlor listed in Bertram, and the operator gave me the details.

There were more delays when I called the number. There seemed to be some confusion over the name.

"We don't appear to have any Carew," said the funeral parlor's director when I was finally patched through to him. He spoke in a low, slow, sepulchral tone that seemed to perfectly match his profession. "Could there be some mistake, sir? New York, you say?"

"From New York City Morgue, that's right. You picked up the... the deceased over the weekend."

There was a pause on the other end of the line. "Well, that wasn't a Carew. That would be Carmichael. Belinda Carmichael. Buffy. So sad."

Carmichael? Buffy Carmichael? That threw me for a moment. There'd been no mention of Carmichael in any Press report. And then, could they be the same? Belinda Carmichael... Beatty Carew... The same initials. Both from Bertram. They had to be, I reasoned.

Then he told me the when and the where, in the same lugubrious voice. The following day. Tuesday. As soon as that. Three pm service at St Peter's The Divine, followed by interment at the Coughlan Memorial Cemetery.

When I finally made it into Bertram station the next afternoon, I knew I'd missed the service. The train had been delayed and by the time I got to the church the place was empty, just a sense of people having been there a short while back, warm and fuggy and full of empty echoes high in the rafters, a just-missed gathering of sorrow and scent that had left a trail of damp footprints on the flagstones.

Back in the cab, I asked the driver to take me on to the cemetery.

"Which one you want?" he asked, leaning round to take a good look at me. "Got three to choose from."

But, of course, I'd forgotten the name.

"What are they called?" I asked, hoping to remember.

He reeled off some names. None of them sounded familiar.

"Take me to the closest," I said. "How far?"

"Maybe five minutes," he replied, turning out of the church forecourt. "Then 'bout six miles, the next. The furthest's pretty much closer to Belling than Bertram. Don't know why they don't just call it Belling and have done with it all. Save people like you and me a hunker of trouble."

As it turned out, the funeral was at the first cemetery. As we pulled in through the gates, I could see a line of black limos parked up ahead on the main avenue, exhausts fuming. We drew in behind them, their drivers in a huddle by the empty hearse, slapping gloves and giving off clouds of breath in the chill afternoon air.

Apart from the drivers there was no one else in sight, but there was no need to ask the way. Roo's mourners had left their tracks in the snow. Telling the cabbie to wait, I followed the trampled path up a slope and at the top of the rise saw, some forty yards away, through the trees, a group of people dressed in somber greys and black and dark navys, standing around a graveside marked out on the snow by a square lawn of Astroturf.

I approached quietly, from behind, and took up position with a nod to the two or three people who turned to check out the late-arrival. There were maybe fifty mourners in all – a dozen or so seated up front in two rows of chairs, and the rest standing in solemn, head-droop mourning behind them. Apart from the people closest to me, it was impossible to see any faces, just the backs of heads, an occasional collared profile and, between hunched shoulders, the wreath-laden casket.

Standing at its head, a priest in cassock, surplice, purple stole and scarf was holding his prayer book the way priests do, with the palm of one hand held flat to the page, not even needing to read the words, all the usual guff about the light and the life and the everlasting resurrection which provided, I'm sure, positively no comfort to any of us. Given the option, we'd all have preferred Roo, or Buffy, back with us, rather than finding ourselves out here in a snow-cloaked cemetery being asked to imagine her in some finer place.

Where she really was, I couldn't help thinking, was some thirty feet away from me, lying cold and still in her casket, pale and lacerated. The closest I'd been to her since our Christmas lunch at Toucan.

On the mid-town train to Bertram that Tuesday, with nothing to do but stare out the window, memories of Roo had flooded back – unbidden, sharp, and exquisitely painful: from roller-blader at the Met to lover at Beartree, theater-companion, bowling partner, shopping advisor and, of course, swan. She'd maybe even taken this very train when she came to visit her Mom, looked out on the same landscape I passed through – a sprawl of snow-shovelled, flag-fluttering garage forecourts, malls and trading estates, hard-scrabble streets and graffiti-walled factories, warehouses and smoke stacks, until, the further out we traveled, a kind of countryside began to assert itself.

Indeed, so vivid were some of these recollections of mine, and so hard to resist, that on a number of occasions I could feel my throat thicken and clench, had to look hard out the carriage window and concentrate on what I saw – what did they make in that factory? Who lived in that fine house across the valley? How come things closer, like telegraph poles and trees, go faster than things further away? – as a means of keeping my emotions in some kind of check. And when the train unaccountably stopped in open country for something like forty minutes, frustration at not being told what the hell was wrong with the train or the line and how long we were going to be sitting there, anxiety that I would miss everything, and irritation that I hadn't thought to catch an earlier train to make sure I was in good time, performed much the same task.

But at the graveside, her casket only a few steps away, it wasn't so easy to keep myself steady, and I had to breathe deep and hard to hold back the sobs. Roo was dead. Roo was gone. I'd never hear her voice again. Never see those green eyes flash with glee. Never touch her, never have her touch me. A week earlier she'd been alive. Now she was dead. Gone. And the dread finality of the whole thing was simply unspeakable. By the time the priest closed his book, stepped back from the graveside, I'd wrung myself into some sorry state I can tell you.

Which was when a thin whine started up the far side of the grave where an electric lift mechanism had been discreetly placed. The casket trembled slightly as the lift's gear engaged, one of the wreaths shifted, and then slowly, smoothly, it began its descent between the draped sides of Astroturf. Those mourners sitting up front now got to their feet and approached the grave, followed by the rest of us, spreading out in a crescent so everyone could see, as though all of us there were anxious to watch Roo to her absolute, final resting place, unwilling to take our eyes off of her casket.

As a late arrival, I found myself right out on the very point of that crescent, beyond the foot of the grave, close to the heap of dug earth hidden beneath further folds of Astroturf. From where I stood I could see, for the first time, the faces of the mourners – veiled, scarved, half-concealed behind dabbing handkerchiefs, shocked and solemn. But like all of them, my eyes were drawn down into the grave and I watched until Roo's casket slipped out of sight, settling finally with a scrape of wood on dirt.

Abruptly the electric motor changed pitch as the braces that had held the casket were retrieved. As they flipped over the lip of the grave, the motor was shut down and one of the undertakers stepped forward balancing a cone of earth on a small silver trowel. I knew at once who he'd give it too, the veiled woman in a dumpy black overcoat and shiny black boots, the only woman in that central part of the crescent. Roo's mother. Or rather, Buffy's mother. It had to be. And I was right. She took the trowel from the undertaker and stepped forward. A man standing beside her, a close relation I guessed, an uncle maybe, a friend of the family, somewhere in his mid-sixties, went with her, holding her arm, his head bowed, the brim of his hat snapped low over his eyes and a blue wool scarf bunched around his cheeks. At the edge of the grave the woman paused, as though not certain what to do next, then, rather than toss the earth from the trowel, she tipped it gently forward, letting the earth slide off the blade to pitter-patter onto the casket below.

And then it was over. Clasped together, Roo's mother and her companion turned back to the mourners who opened up and drew them in. There were hugs, tears, blown noses, and then they began to move off up the slope, retracing their tracks through the snow. Which was when I'd planned catching up with Roo's mother, speaking to her when we reached the cars, briefly, to express my condolences, then taking my cab back to the station and the train home to the city.

But it wasn't to be like that.

As the first group of mourners reached the top of the slope, a young man, somewhere in his thirties, detached himself, hung back to say a few words to the second group of mourners following, and then turned to me. I was a good way behind any of them, the last to leave the graveside, and it was clear that he could only be waiting for me.

As I approached, he leaned forward to shake my hand and fell in step beside me.

"It was good of you to come all this way, sir. Mr. Mortimer, isn't it? Buffy would have been so pleased."

I was quite taken aback. "You know who I am?"

"Of course. Recognized you straight away. Your picture in the paper and all."

"And you are?" I began, trying to place the strong, clean cut and oddly familiar features.

"Dominic. Dom. Buffy's older brother."

"Older brother?"

"The others – Cat, Jean, and my monster younger brother, Quinn – are up ahead with Mom and Dad. They asked if you'd care to join us at the house. It's not too far."

I know I shouldn't have been surprised. After all the time I'd known Roo, after all the things that had happened. But I was. Absolutely speechless. Stunned. Brothers and sisters? And a Dad? I didn't know whether to be cross with her that she'd spun me such a line and I'd fallen for it, or to smile at the impish twinkle which I was certain, wherever she now was, would be playing around those green eyes of hers as she saw my look of astonishment.

"I know Mom and Dad would sure appreciate it," said Dom, as we trudged up the rise, looking across at me, taking my silence for some kind of reluctance.

"I'd be very pleased," I managed. "Of course…"

We parted on the avenue as the first of the limos started off. He seemed relieved to find out that I'd kept my cab – regrettably there was no spare seat up front, he explained. But I should pay it off when I got to the house, he told me; one of the family would get me to the train station whenever I needed to leave.

Before he moved off, I reached for his arm. "Tell me," I asked. "Was the casket open at the service?"

He frowned, not as if he was trying to remember but as though I'd asked something so unexpected, so deeply intimate, that he couldn't believe or understand what he'd heard. Then the frown dissolved and he nodded. It was as I'd suspected. And I'd wanted so much to see her one last time.

Back in the cab, I told the driver to follow the limo in front of us. Eventually it drew away and at a stately speed we proceeded down the main avenue of mausoleums, turning out the cemetery gates for the slow ride to the Carmichael residence.

The house was fifteen minutes from the cemetery, through the small-town center of Bertram and out the other side, one of those large turn-of-the-century family houses in a block of similar yet not quite identical constructions. Like most of its neighbors the Carmichael residence was clad in wood, three floors, with a stone-skirted porch and stone chimney breast, and set rather grandly above a wide slope of lawn and the broad tree-lined street. A limp Stars and Stripes hung at half-mast above the porch.

The sidewalks had been shovelled clear and the snow was banked up either side of the road into icy grey hedges. These took up so much room that the cortège had to draw up pretty much in the middle of the road, one limo behind another, as the mourners got out and walked towards the house. I told the cabbie he could drop me right there, rather than wait for the limos to move off, paid him, and swayed across the icy road to the sidewalk.

Like leaving the graveside, I was pretty much the last to arrive at the Carmichael house, following an elderly couple up the gritted path to a front door I recognized from the photo on Roo's dressing table. Inside, the house was warm and, like our cabin at Beartree, brightly snow-lit from the garden, the tiled entrance slick and wet where people had missed the mat or forgotten to wipe their feet. A coat-stand just inside the door bulged, a hallway dresser was crowded with hats, and the staircase banister likewise draped with overcoats and scarves.

As I wiped my feet, the man in front helped his companion out of her coat, took off his own, and heaped them onto a hallway chair. I did the same and followed them into a traditional old parlor room that must have run one whole side of the house, divided by an archway decorated with a wood fretwork of curls and fronds still entwined with Christmas holly.

Both parts of the room, front and back, were crowded with mourners, more than I could remember seeing at the graveside. There were children too, gathered together in the bay window overlooking the front lawn, all dressed in their Sunday best, the youngest kept in order by the eldest. I could see at once it was the place to be, that bay window. Not only were the kids out of the way of the grown-ups, they were within easy striking range of a low table ladened with plates of cake, sandwiches, and other confections. They also had the largest amount of space, the rest of the room so packed with people I can't for the life of me remember anything below shoulder height: a collection of bird prints and architectural studies in the style of Piranesi set out on the walls, swagged curtains in the bay and, standing haughtily beside a garishly-decorated Christmas tree, the top half of a fine break-front bookcase.

As well as a low murmur of voices the room was also filled with the scent of oranges and spices, a scent I was quite at a loss to account for until a maid in starched bonnet and pinny came forward with a tray of mulled wine. It was served in what looked like glass teacups without the saucers, but was none the worse for that. The first sip sent a warm rush of cinnamon, cloves and mace up my nose and my cheeks puckered happily. It was just the kind of drink you needed coming in from the cold. I imagined the Carmichaels were the kind of family who always kept a pan on the simmer when winter closed in.

Before I could properly get my bearings, beyond this initial sense of a formal family room crowded with friends and family brought together in a shared grief, I saw Dom approach, leading his mother by the arm. I recognized her from the graveside. She had wavy grey blonde hair that reached to her shoulders, loose wisps of which still stood out as though she'd forgotten to pat them back into place after removing her hat, her complexion, even in winter, tanned and weather-worn as though she lived her life outdoors rather than squaring up columns of figures. If that's what she actually did.

Dom made the introductions, saying my name slowly and clearly as though his mother were hard of hearing. Her name was Ray and she looked diminished with sorrow, literally stooped beneath some great weight you couldn't see except the way it pressed her down. Maybe, too, with shame at the way her daughter's activities had been so publicly chronicled.

She shook my hand softly and, like Dom, said how pleased she was that I had come and how Buffy would have so appreciated it. She had a kind of detached wistfulness about her, as though her mind wasn't quite on it, as if she couldn't for the life of her understand why there were so many people in the house all of a sudden. She looked a hundred years older than the picture I'd seen of her in Roo's bedroom, and my heart went out to her.

"Did you know my daughter long, Mr. Mortimer?" she asked, her voice catching on 'daughter' as though she'd run out of breath, but then recovering.

"You remember, Mom," said Dom. "Last summer? Your birthday weekend? When Buffy was visiting and she was in the paper? It was Mr. Mortimer who wrote about her."

Roo's mother seemed to consider this for a moment, and then said: "That's right. That's right. She was so thrilled, wasn't she?" And a weary, long-ago smile played across her features.

Dom gave me a look that warned me I shouldn't expect this conversation to go much further. And it didn't. Ray just stood there, gazing past me, nodding her head as though recalling happier times. I remember thinking she didn't look a bit like Roo. Nothing like. Not a line, not a curve, not a gesture in common, though the few words she spoke had an eerie familiarity. Wherever Roo got her looks, it certainly wasn't from her mother.

But if there was nothing of the mother in Roo, I could easily make her out in Dom and, to a lesser extent, her other children, each of whom came up and introduced themselves after Dom had steered Ray away. Like Dom, they all took after their mother: Cat, now the eldest daughter, with her mother's sad, faraway eyes, who passed me on to her younger sister, Jean, with the same fall of blonde hair, and Quinn, who looked about eighteen, crew-cut and pimply but with his mother's sharp nose and full lips.

I told each of them how sorry I was, and all three told me versions of the story Dom had already recounted on our walk together in the cemetery. How they'd all been home the same weekend for their mother's birthday when Roo had read the Met story in the *Times*, and how she'd jumped up from the breakfast table saying she was in the paper, how she was the companion I'd written about, that she had met me there at the show, and how not a one of them had believed her.

It was after Quinn excused himself that I sought out Dom. When I found him, without his mother this time, I told him I really ought to be going.

I remember the jolt I felt when he pushed back the sleeve of his jacket and glanced at his watch.

"I'll find Dad. He said he'd run you down there himself."

"There's no need. Maybe I could just call a cab?"

"No, no. It's all arranged. Dad made a point of it."

"Well, if that's okay…?" I still hadn't met Mr. Carmichael, let alone identified him in the crowd of mourners, and was anxious to do so. "Nice watch, by the way," I said.

"Isn't it though?" replied Dom. He looked at it fondly, as though it were a most precious possession, played his fingers over its face and linked strap, resettled it on his wrist. "Buffy gave it me for my birthday. It's a…"

"…A Breitling Chronoliner. I know. A fine piece."

Which is when Roo's father stepped up beside his son.

I'd have known him anywhere.

"Dad, this is Mr. Mortimer," said Dom, making an introduction that was in no way necessary. If I'd detected little of Roo in her mother, there was no mistaking it now. Roo's father was the spitting image, the same man, I realized, who'd stepped forward with his wife at the graveside but whose features, concealed by a scarf, raised collar and homburg, I'd failed to register.

Like his wife, Robert Carmichael looked to be in his sixties, a tall, well-built man with a cap of grey hair neatly razored around ears and neck, a military type who held his shoulders back and his chin down. Like his wife, he, too, seemed worn away despite the strong handshake and soldierly bearing. But all I could see was Roo. The same eyes, green and penetrating. The same curving line to the lips that I'd bet my savings on would break into her smile. The firm set of the jaw, the slim nose, the jutting, defiant chin, all pure Roo. And when he spoke even the voice had exactly her lilt and timbre, though the strict formality of his speech was quite at odds with his daughter's.

"Always admired your writing, Mr. Mortimer. As did my daughter. As I'm sure you know. You've got a voice, sir, you surely have. A God-given talent. And you use it, too. It's important a man speaks his mind. Isn't that so, Dom?"

Dom nodded, and pursed his lips. "Yessir, it is."

"Though I guess sometimes it can't be easy," he continued, almost as if he hadn't heard Dom's reply. "I'm truly sorry we couldn't have met under pleasanter circumstances, sir, and gotten to know one another on some other, happier occasion. As it is, all we've got is the time it takes to get you to the station, I'm told. Which," he said, consulting his own watch, "we should do pretty soon if you want to get back to the city at a reasonable hour." And then, lowering his voice, "Let's find our coats, and get on out of here," he said, looking around as though he felt suddenly discomfited by the black-clad, whispered solemnity playing out in his front parlor, and would be relieved to be free of it.

Ten minutes later, suitably scarved, gloved and coated, sitting in a Cherokee Jeep he said belonged to Dom, we reversed down the drive and swung carefully into the street. Once we were on our way, heater humming and headlights glistening off the snow banks, he got right to the point.

"Is it true what they say? In the papers? You know...?" He looked straight ahead, uncertain, as though not sure what words to use.

For a moment, I didn't know how to respond. I suppose I should have expected this question, and been prepared for it. But I wasn't. Though every single person at the graveside and in the Carmichael's front parlor must have seen the TV news, read accounts of Roo's life and death in the papers, been aware of the details spelled out in hand-rubbing, scandalised prose by publications like the *Post*, it was as if there had been some collective agreement not to mention or give consideration to such... details; everyone there gathered together to mourn a death, not the mechanics of that death, nor the way of life that preceded it. That was for the privacy of their homes, out of the family's hearing. So far as I'd been able to tell, I was the only person at the funeral who had known Roo in the city, which meant, naturally, that I would know more about her life there, what she did there, than her friends and her family.

"Not the Buffy I knew," I lied smoothly.

"You can tell me the truth, Mr. Mortimer," her father replied, quite sternly. "I don't mind the truth. We're not in the parlor now. Just you and me here, the two of us."

I remembered what he'd said to me back at the house, about a man speaking his mind, and flushed to realize that he'd seen right through my clumsy attempt at subterfuge. And didn't much appreciate it.

"I'm sorry… I was…"

"I know, I know… Trying to save my feelings. I fully understand your motives, Mr. Mortimer. Even if I can't altogether say I approve of them. Well?"

I took a deep breath. "I knew your daughter as Beatty Carew," I began. "That's the name she gave me, Roo for short, as in Carew; not Belinda Carmichael, not Buffy. I only found out her real name yesterday." And in a quiet, level tone I told him everything I'd learned about his daughter, gently editing the not-so-savory facts, emphasising her legitimate businesses – the limo company, Relocate, and her various investments – rather than tarry too much on the other. Doing what she did, I tried to explain, it was simply a means to an end.

"Diligence, hard work, and straight-talking – that's the fuel makes an engine run, sir," replied Carmichael, pulling away from a set of lights in the center of Bertram, foot pressing down hard on the accelerator as if to underline the point.

I recognized the expression straight off, remembered Roo using it at Beartree. But I didn't tell him her version of it. Instead, I told him about the last time we'd spoken, how she was frightened by something, how we'd agreed to meet at a favorite restaurant, and how she'd failed to show.

"You tell all this to the police?" he asked as, finally, we pulled into the station forecourt.

"To be frank… I… No… I didn't. I guess you could say I… didn't want to get involved."

The moment the words were out of my mouth I wished them back again. Saying such a thing to Roo's father, of all people. I felt ashamed, and a little guilty. And not a little unnerved.

"I can understand that, sir. Not easy, a man in your position. But still…"

For a moment there, I thought he was going to say he'd be calling the police about me soon as he got home, have them come visit. And panicked at the possibility. But he didn't.

"Still... I appreciate your candor."

He found a space in the station parking lot, swung into it, and switched off the ignition. Then he slung an arm over the wheel and turned to face me, those hooded green eyes pinning me to my seat.

"If I sound angry with my daughter, I am, sir. She did wrong. You know it and I know it. And it don't matter a Bertram damn how we pretty it up in ribbons and black lace and pretend it's something else, like back at the house there. It isn't. What she did... well, I just can't put it into words beyond it was plain wrong. She wasn't raised to be that way, I can tell you that."

He took a deep breath, as though to hold something in.

All I could do was nod in agreement – I'm sure she wasn't, kind of thing.

"But I'll tell you something, Mr. Mortimer," he took up again, more fiercely now. "Whatever I may feel about the way my daughter chose to live her life, I loved that little girl of mine more than I loved anything my whole, entire life. More than anything else in this whole darn world."

His voice was like thin ice now, brittle and creaking, sounding like it might give at any second.

"I shouldn't say it and I shouldn't feel it, but she was always my favorite. People'll tell you all kinds of guff about how there isn't nary any difference the way you love your children. But I know they're wrong. Known it since the day she was born, the moment I held her in my arms. Buffy was... special. Something about her. The brightest. The toughest. You name it."

He took another deep breath, let it out slowly and looked away through the windscreen. But it didn't work. Tears welled in his eyes, his jaw clenched, and the words he now spoke caught in his throat. "And when they... when they find that... that goddamn son-of-a-bitch who did this terrible thing to my little girl... I hope... well, I hope they hang the bastard high and long."

And that was how we parted. Me back to the city, Roo's father turning the Jeep in the station forecourt and heading back the way we had come, to a wood-clad house in the suburbs, a parlor full of people, mulled wine, and an empty heart.

≈

I'm not unfamiliar with the way death deals with those who live on. Like everything there's a pattern to it, and I knew from experience what I was in for. My father died in a road accident when I was nineteen, my mother died of cancer six years later, thankfully fast, and old Aunt Jem faded gently away in a Wilmington nursing home shortly after I started with the *Times*.

So I knew what to expect, and I wasn't disappointed.

At the *Times*, Larry Daley couldn't have been more understanding. Or accommodating. The day after Sanchez handed me that clipping, as soon as he heard what had happened, Larry was on the phone. After passing on his condolences, his sympathy, he let me know I didn't have a thing to worry about at work. There was the *Times*' '*Chef of the Year*' interview I'd taped and sent in for transcription which they could easily Q & A for that Sunday's 'Metro Life'. Then there was an old story of mine, '*Acquired Tastes*', which he could run the Sunday following, and the Cully take on Manhattan's leading *maître d's* for the week after that. All I had to do, if I could manage it, and he'd quite understand if I couldn't, was give them something on the new Vongerichten book for the Sunday after that.

"The pictures look great," he told me. "Say five hundred words? Four hundred? Whatever you feel you can handle." And after that, he said, he didn't want to see hair nor hide of me until I was fit and ready to return.

I thanked him for his call, for his kindness, and said that sounded just fine. He'd get his copy.

Which would have given me the best part of a month away to squander. Time to grieve. Time to spoil myself with sorrow.

And so I set to work in the days following Roo's funeral, clearing the decks as fast as I could, touching base with a still tearful, sobbing Susan out on the island, cancelling lunch and dinner reservations I'd penciled in weeks before, leaving a short message with Daphne's answering service, and calling my friends Maude and Jeff MacAuley to invite myself to their home in Totnes Bay, telling Maude I'd lost a dear friend and might not be the greatest company, but just knew that they would understand.

Of course, said Maude who, before she married into the sailing MacAuleys of Groton, had been a regular lunch companion in the city. Of course. When can you come?

I told her I could train up to New London Friday evening after filing my Vongerichten story, and Maude told me she'd pick me up at the station herself.

"You just let us know what you want, and it's there. If you want time by yourself, we'll put you up in the beach cottage. If you'd prefer company, we'll have you at the main house. Why, you could even take the both," she said, "for whatever your mood. Just come see us quickly, you poor darling."

And that's where I thought I was headed that Friday afternoon, my bag packed, waiting in the hall, and only a couple hundred words left to write.

When the buzzer sounded.

Coffee & Bagels

"Sykes? Culver?"

I remember not recognising the name.

"Culver Sykes!" the Duty Sergeant repeated, louder this time, peering through the bars. "Dat's you!" he said, pointing me out with his clipboard where I sat in a corner of the crowded cell.

He was right. He might also have called me 'Double' or 'Cheeseburger', two other names I'd acquired from my cellmates in the hours that I'd spent in the holding cells of the 19th Precinct. I had no belt and no tie, my watch had been taken, and my pockets were empty. I was thirsty and hungry, tired and scared.

"That's me," I managed to croak.

"You don't say. So now we'rse gettin' somewheres." He could have been Carlo's brother. "You'se gotta visit. Lawyer. Step up here."

"Where do I go?"

≈

"This has got to be some kind of mistake."

I don't know how many times I said those words, or ones like them: "*You're making a mistake...*"; "*There must be a mistake...*"; "*You have no right...*"; "*I haven't done anything...*," the accent on this final declaration of innocence shifting between the last two words depending on my sense of outraged injustice or unadorned desperation.

I started saying them in my apartment with my face pressed up against an Arcimboldo print, the plastic ties of the hand restraints tightening around my wrists. I said them again stumbling along the hallway between the two uniformed officers, going down in the elevator, as we crossed the lobby, and in the squad car that took us downtown. But neither DaSilva, Munroe, nor the two uniforms paid the slightest attention. I guess they'd heard it all before.

I began by directing these assurances at DaSilva. He was altogether better turned out and better looking than the grubby, run-to-seed Munroe, the kind of clean-cut, well-educated man I felt would be more sympathetic to my plight, more open to an approach than his colleague. And despite their equal rank, he seemed to me to be the man in charge of this operation, the one who'd made the introductions over my entryphone, and who'd led the way into my apartment. But when he refused to be drawn, I turned my attention to Munroe.

Munroe was older than DaSilva, jowly, with bored, seen-it-all eyes, and the most appalling tie you can imagine. The color! The knot! The stains! With a finger-thick enamel clip to stop it flapping! Incredible. But all I got from Munroe was a 'Yeah, yeah', as he opened the door of the squad car, placed his hand on my head, and pushed me down into the back seat, the two of them coming in tight either side of me, my bound hands digging into the join between seat and backrest and forcing my shoulders forward.

By the time we arrived at the Precinct House I was addressing the two uniforms up front, as though DaSilva and Munroe beside me were doing something wrong, something criminal, and I needed their help, everything I said accompanied by static bursts from the radio and the muffled voice of the Dispatch caller.

The two uniforms looked a little embarrassed, I could tell, and by the time we pushed through into the Precinct's reception area, I was starting to feel the same.

Keep quiet, that was the way to play it, I told myself. Don't make a scene. Don't draw attention to yourself. All this will be sorted out soon enough.

But it wasn't.

"Name?" asked the Desk Sergeant, reaching for a pen and an admissions form. He was sitting behind a framed gap in a screen of wired glass that stretched the entire width of the room, and up to the ceiling. Through the smeared partition, I could see maybe a dozen uniformed officers going about their business, all peaked hats, shiny blue 'puffa' windcheaters, and guns and 'cuffs on their belts.

"C-Cully Mortimer," I stammered.

"That your real name?"

"I don't follow."

The Desk Sergeant sighed wearily, but didn't look up from his form. "Is that the name you were born with? The name on your birth certificate? On your tax return? Follow me now?"

"Cully Sykes. Culver... Mortimer... Sykes. With a 'y'."

"Cul-ver Mor-tim-er Sy-kes," he repeated, filling in the box at the top of the form in block capitals. "AKA Cully Mortimer. That correct?"

"Yes, I suppose," appalled at the 'aka'.

"At last," he sighed.

It was only then, as I stood there in front of the window, with my hands bound behind my back, that I realized I was shaking from head to toe.

More questions followed: address, date of birth, that sort of thing, all laboriously noted down. By now DaSilva and Monroe had disappeared, leaving the two uniformed cops to keep an eye on me and provide the Desk Sergeant with details of the offence: homicide, crime sheet number, supervising officers, and so on and so forth. And it was these two men who, when the admissions form had been completed, steered me to a corner of the room where a staircase led to the basement. One went down ahead of me, the other followed behind.

So far as I could see this basement was about half the size of the reception area and tiled throughout: green linoleum squares on the floor, cream lino tiles on the walls, and those square ceiling panels you can push up to get at the wiring and plumbing. With no obvious ventilation save the stairs to the floor above, the room gave off what I can best describe as the warm, rubbery smell of sweaty sneakers kept potent by an incubating blue-white light that flickered down from neon-tube panels set in the ceiling. Except for the steel bars – at the bottom of the stairs, over the dusty, single closed window set high on the wall at sidewalk level, and separating this first room from the holding cells beyond – the place looked like any railway station Left-Luggage office you've ever seen, right down to the long wood counter and rows of stacked shelves that led off behind it into murky depths.

Presiding over all this was a short-breathed, grey-haired Receiving Sergeant who waited for us at the foot of the stairs, relocking the barred gate once we were through. But it wasn't his wavy grey hair or short spurts of breath that drew my attention. It was his stomach. Prodigious. The biggest I'd ever seen. Its fabulous bulk stretched the material of his shirt like the skin of a balloon, curving round his waist to lie in slanting folds from his spine. Put this man on the beat and he wouldn't make the first corner, I thought to myself as he waddled ahead of us back to the counter, lifted the flap, and somehow jiggled his way through. What did he keep in there, I wondered?

But there was no time to dwell on the mystery. In short order my plastic hand restraints were cut away and I was told to empty my pockets, and remove my watch, belt, tie, and shoelaces. I did as I was told, save the shoelaces; I was wearing my Berluti loafers. As for my pockets, there wasn't much – wallet, handkerchief, small black notebook, the keys to my apartment, a handful of loose change, and my train ticket to New London.

Everything was itemised by the Sergeant, then sealed in polythene bags and boxed. He pushed over the sheet of paper he'd been filling in, and a Biro, and told me to check it and sign.

When the counter was finally clear, he reached down and pulled out an inkpad and a strip of board printed with two horizontal lines of boxes, five each line, ten in all.

"Right hand."

I had no idea what he was talking about.

"I said, right hand. Come on."

One of the uniforms reached for my hand and held it out to the Sergeant. Grasping my wrist and manipulating my fingers between his, he pressed my fingertips onto the inkpad and then rolled them side to side, one by one, onto the board strip in the appropriate boxes: 'right thumb', 'r. fore', 'r. middle', 'r. ring', 'r. little', followed by the fingers of my left hand. When he'd finished, the Sergeant handed me a piece of tissue to wipe away the ink, then took it back and tossed it in a bin.

The same Receiving Sergeant took my photo. It was a long way from my last session in front of a camera with Mario in Sutton Row. I was marched over to a wall marked out with a figured scale that reached to the ceiling and told to stand in front of it, facing a bulky tripod camera set at head height on a formica table.

One of the uniforms picked up a square plastic slate bearing the date and the legend 'New York Police Department. No: 64400132', and while the Sergeant prepared the camera, I watched him slide out the '2' and replace it with a '3', taken from a plastic vending cup filled with tiny numbered tiles.

I looked across the room at the big round wall clock above the counter. Less than two hours earlier I'd been sitting at my keyboard tapping out my story for the *Times*. It had been a fast and ruthlessly efficient process. From blameless private citizen to a tieless, beltless desperado in less time than it takes for lunch.

But there was little time to brood. I was shown how to hold the slate two inches below my chin without having my fingers obscure the details. I checked to make sure I had it the right way up and when I looked up... Flash! Then I was turned to profile, shown how to hold the slate in this new position, and the moment I looked up... Flash again!

If there was anything to be thankful for in this horror of horrors it was that there was no one there I knew to witness my humiliation. And that was my single comfort as the Sergeant declared himself satisfied, unlocked a barred gate and led me down a corridor, through yet another set of bars, into a forty-foot square room set on three sides with three separate holding cages. None was larger than my own sitting room and so far as I could tell there was only one other prisoner in residence, a rattling snore and the sweet, sinuous scent of alcohol and vomit coming from what looked like a heap of clothes on one of the three bunks that furnished the cell they directed me into.

Which was when, in as calm and measured a voice as I could muster, I asked how long I was likely to be held there? And what about a phone? I continued, as the barred entry panel to the cage slid shut between us. Wasn't I entitled to make a phone call? To my lawyer, at least?

Later, said the Sergeant, and that was that save a final grating and clang of metal gates sliding shut and the slot of locking mechanisms tripping into place, the silence that followed punctuated by the grunting, liquid snores of my cell-mate.

≈

I've never been good at judging the passage of time so I can't say for certain how long I sat there on the edge of a cot, or paced the concrete confines of my cell, or leaned against its bars chewing at my fingernails. But however long it was, I'd certainly rate it the worst time of my life, alternately outraged, isolated, scared, and anxious, all at levels beyond my experience, beyond description. And I was still shaking.

I was busily convincing myself there'd been some dreadful mistake, surely, when the Receiving Sergeant returned with a shiny metal hoop of keys and, telling me to face the wall, unlocked the cage. I was then told to step out, turn to the bars, spread my legs, and put my hands behind my back, as though I was a dangerous criminal who posed some kind of threat to this giant of a man whose considerable girth I would have been at pains to reach my arms around. Which at first struck me as lightly amusing in a wry sort of way, until I realized that as far as the Sergeant was concerned that's exactly what I was. A potential hazard. Homicidal. Which sobered me up pretty fast.

Snapping a pair of handcuffs around my wrists, he relocked the cage and, staying a step or two behind me, directed me to an elevator in the far corner of the basement, recessed into a dead-end hallway that couldn't be seen from the cages. When the elevator arrived and the doors slid open, he told me to step in ahead of him, and then positioned himself between me and the control panel until we arrived at the third floor. As if someone like me, unarmed, with hands cuffed behind my back, and a good hundred pounds lighter, stood any chance of pulling a fast one.

The room we stepped into was a lot like the offices at the *Times*, pretty much a whole floor of the building split up into islands of desks divided by shoulder-height wood panels and lit like the basement we'd come from with bright neon tubes set into a lowered ceiling. There wasn't much time to take in details but the place seemed a lot cleaner and quieter than I would have imagined – and hot, a good ten degrees warmer than the cells in the basement. I could actually feel the heat wrap around me like a warm towel as I stepped out of the elevator. Clearly Public Services didn't worry too much about heating bills.

Taking my arm, the Sergeant steered me across the squad room, following a well-worn path between work stations, past feet-up-on-desk cops, ringing telephones, glowing computer consoles, and waste-bins overflowing with crumpled paper and styrofoam coffee cups, ushering me through a door on the far side of the room labelled 'Interview 4'. Painted a light green, with a scuffed lino floor and weary atmosphere, the room had a barred window set above an ancient radiator and a simple formica-top table furnished with a thin foil ashtray, a dial-less telephone, and two chairs. Nothing else. Through the window I could see it had gotten dark. The 'cuffs were removed, and I was told to take a seat; someone would be with me shortly.

The someone was DaSilva. But he didn't come immediately. Instead, I was left alone to ponder what was happening. Strangely, I felt a kind of relief now. Everything would be sorted out. I understood that my processing had been necessary, a simple formality, like checking into a hotel. But that was all. Now I could set the record straight. And check right out.

I'd just decided I'd take an early train to New London in the morning, since I certainly wouldn't make it that evening, when the door opened and DaSilva appeared. He'd taken off his overcoat and his jacket and had loosened his neck tie. His police badge was clipped to his belt and though he was still wearing his shoulder holster, there was no gun. He carried a brown folder in one hand and a wrapped white-bread sandwich in the other.

"How you doin', Mr. Mortimer?" he asked, coming round the table and pulling out the chair. "Everything in order? Everything to your satisfaction?" He dropped the folder and sandwich (ham and cheese and pickle) onto the table, sat down wearily and sprawled back, clasping his hands behind his head and letting his eyes wander over what he could see of me, as though wanting to memorise every detail.

I made no attempt to respond or rise to his sarcastic *maître d'* tone, but I wasn't sure I liked the way this was starting out. I'd been expecting something a little more conciliatory, a little more apologetic. A mistake had been made after all.

"So what was it like?" he asked, tipping forward for the sandwich. He pulled off the wrapper, let it drop to the floor and took a bite. His black cheek bulged.

"What was what like?"

Before he could reply – not that he looked in any hurry to do so – the door opened and in came Munroe. He, too, had removed his coat and jacket, and he was rolling up his shirtsleeves as though he had something messy to attend to. His arms were matted with hair, but it was still possible to see the faded blue blur of a tattoo on his right forearm. Again, the gun was missing from his shoulder holster, and his police badge was clipped to his belt.

"How's things goin'?" asked Monroe, taking up position a little behind DaSilva and beside the barred window.

"I was just askin' Mr. Mortimer, here, what it was like."

"What what was like?" repeated Munroe. Both men had their eyes trained on me.

DaSilva swallowed his mouthful of sandwich. "You know, taking off her clothes like he did. A woman like that. Real pretty lady. I wanted to know if he enjoyed that part. Some guys do." He took another bite.

What he'd said stunned me. Such a thought. And from DaSilva. It was more the kind of crude comment I imagined the overweight Munroe coming out with.

"This is just preposterous," I exclaimed, half angrily, half dismissively. "I told you already, Detective, you've got the wrong man. Of course I knew Beatty Carew, but…"

"So why didn't you come forward day one?" asked Munroe. "Help us out with our enquiries? After you read about it in the papers." He said this with a wicked grin and questioning, raised eyebrows, as though I'd need to read about the murder in the papers.

I couldn't answer that question. Or rather I could, but I didn't want to.

"Didn't want to get your hands dirty," said Munroe for me, pulling a pack of cigarettes from his pocket and lighting up. "That it? Just didn't want to get involved."

The phrase had a familiar ring. I'd said exactly those words to Roo's father on the ride to Bertram station. There was a moment of clarity. So that was what all this was about. Just as I'd feared, Carmichael had gone home and called the police. He'd told them about me. And they'd spent the last few days checking me out, maybe thought they'd try and frighten a confession out of me. The investigation was clearly going nowhere, and they were probably under pressure to tidy up the case. But why arrest me? Shouldn't they just have brought me in for questioning?

"Look…" I began, adopting a helpful tone, trying to find a way out of this nightmare.

"No, Mr. Mortimer, you look." It was DaSilva, putting down the half-eaten sandwich and leaning across the table, clasping his hands between us, large black hands with pink, calloused palms and swollen knuckles. "What you got to understand is that the two of us here, my colleague and me, we are here for one simple, single reason. To make your life just that little bit easier. Which I reckon deserves some kind of input from you, wouldn't you say?"

"Input? What input? I haven't done anything. Alright, so I didn't come forward when I should have done. That was wrong, I can see that now. But that's all. I didn't kill anyone."

"You left-handed, Mr. Mortimer?" This from Monroe, whistling out a plume of smoke.

I told him, yes, I was.

"Figures," said DaSilva.

There was silence for a moment. I looked from one face to the other. It was difficult to tell which of them was going to speak next.

"Mind telling us where you were that Monday night?" asked Monroe. "Say between seven and nine in the evening?"

I knew immediately what he was getting at. "I was at a restaurant called Toucan. Roo... Beatty and I had agreed to meet there. She wanted to talk, she was frightened about something."

"Toucan? The place off Washington, down by the tunnel?" asked Munroe.

"That's the one. West Village, kind of," I replied, trying to be helpful.

"You any idea what was frightening her?" This from DaSilva.

"Or who?" This from Munroe.

"I think it was a client. She was giving up the... the job, and she'd told me one of her clients didn't like it."

"You know this client?" asked DaSilva. He'd gone back to his sandwich, had taken another bite, and his cheek swelled out.

I told him I didn't. It was just a guess. Roo and I were going to talk it through when we met, I was sure of it. Put together a plan of action.

"Anyone see you there? A friend? Colleague?" He swallowed, licked his lips.

"Where?"

DaSilva gave me a look. Like a teacher, with a dim student; as though I hadn't been paying enough attention.

"Oh, you mean Toucan? Where we were supposed to meet? Well, no one I know." And then, like a bright beam of light: "But the cashier would remember me. Of course, of course. I left him a ten dollar tip, said if anyone turned up asking for me he should get them to call me at home. He'll vouch for me, he knows I was there."

I felt like a balloon released underwater, bursting to the surface. I'd established an alibi. An alibi. So easy. Of course. The cashier at Toucan. Now they'd have to let me go, count me out of their enquiries.

But DaSilva was shaking his head. He took the last corner of his sandwich, licked his fingers, then brushed off his hands. "Listen my friend. Places like Toucan wouldn't remember you if you left a hundred let alone a ten. And a couple of nights before New Years?

Give me a break."

"You mean you're not going to check?"

"We don't need to check." Munroe again, dropping his cigarette on the floor and stubbing it out; it was that kind of room. "You're it. The perp. You the boy. We got enough on you to send you away a very long time. Only it won't be some ditsy restaurant you're going to, with fancy French wines and six-course dinners."

"What could you possibly have on me?" I cried out, heart chilled by the coldness of the threat, everything spinning away from me. "I didn't do anything. How many times do I have to tell you that? I shouldn't be here. You've got it all wrong…"

"So," said DaSilva. "That's a 'not guilty', is it?"

"Of course I'm not guilty."

"Well, I gotta tell you, *Mr.* Mortimer, that's not how we're reading this here situation." This from Monroe, accompanied with a nasty, sharp little smile and a hitching tug of his trouser band.

"Like I was saying…" DaSilva continued. "You can carry on trying to convince us you got nothing to answer to all you like. But the longer you do that, the thinner our patience is gonna get. And the harder it's going to be for you." DaSilva spread his hands, as though, regrettably, there was nothing he'd be able to do to alter that course of events if that's how I chose to play it. Then his voice softened, a more reasonable tone. "Or, option two, you can help us out a little here, let us be of some assistance in your hour of need. Co-operating with the police and all. You know the kind of thing? You scratch ours, and you can bet on it we'll do our damnedest to scratch yours, yessiree."

Over by the window, Munroe grunted.

"Co-operate?"

"That's all. Co-operation. Nothing to it. Makes the world go round. So, let's see…" DaSilva pulled the file open, leafed through a couple of pages. "Now, we already know you killed Miss Carew that Monday evening, but what we'd really like to know is why? Why d'you go and stick her the way you did? She givin' you a hard time or something? Charging too much? Trying to stiff you? Threatening to spill the beans – what the great Cully Mortimer gets up to in his spare time? Or maybe you just get off on that kind of thing? Getting her naked, like we were talking about a while back; tying her to a chair, takin' a blade to her? Am I right here? Is that the kind of thing turns you on?

And what did you do with the knife? Where's that at? We'd really like to know. Go on, go ahead. Tell us. Think of it as therapy."

Another grunt from Monroe.

"I want to see a lawyer," I said, surprising myself, my voice icy, steady. I'd never been so cross in my whole life. I was so cross I'd gone and forgotten about being scared. How dare they suggest such things? How dare they treat me like this?

"Can if you want," said Munroe. "Just thought you'd like to help us out a tad first. Make things easier on yourself. 'Course, you think you gotta have a lawyer here before you say anything, then I do appreciate that sentiment. And it's your legal right, all said and done. Don't want you digging yourself deeper in the shit, do we? So, you want for us to appoint you one, or you got one of your own in mind?"

"I have my own." Which, of course, I hadn't. Never any need.

"So give the man a call," said DaSilva, nodding at the phone on the desk. "Switchboard'll put you through. Friday evening? Why, he's probably still in his office just waiting to hear from you."

At exactly that moment, the phone started ringing. DaSilva picked it up, said his name, and listened a few moments.

"Yeah…? You sure…? I owe you. Yeah… perfect."

DaSilva put down the phone and looked at his watch. Then, pushing back his chair, he got to his feet and gathered up his folder.

He gave me a sad look: "After what I just heard, Mr. Mortimer, he better be a damn good lawyer is all I can say."

≈

I didn't know it then, but I've learned since, that the lawyer waiting to see me that Saturday lunchtime in an interview room on the second floor of the 19th Precinct, some twenty hours after my arrest, was one of the Bar's more formidable criminal defense attorneys.

DaSilva would have approved. Or maybe not.

"Cerise Chase," she said, holding out a hand. "Of Chase McKay."

I closed the door behind me, walked to the table where she was sitting, leaned across and took her hand. For whatever reason, I hadn't been 'cuffed for the visit, like I had been for DaSilva and Monroe, but I wished I'd been able to shave, clean myself up a bit. I felt grubby and soiled. Not that she seemed to notice.

"Well, sit down, why don't you? Make yourself comfortable. I don't bite. Leastways not weekends."

I did as she said, and took her in. She wasn't at all what I'd
expected. A woman for starters. Late thirties, maybe. And colored.
If I'd had to guess I'd have said Caribbean – the Bahamas, Jamaica,
some quaint little calypso country in the sun. A very handsome
woman, too, no doubt about it. Her eyes were what I'd call wide and
wicked, her nose flattened at the bridge and darkly freckled, but her
lips more fine than full, jaw narrow and chin elegantly tapered. Her
hair, caught in a spray-like ponytail that burst from the back of her
head, was a rich, glinting copper in the neon and heavily crimped. She
was dressed informally, for the weekend, light blue jeans and thickly-
ribbed sweater, sleeves pushed up in folds to her elbows, with a wool
topcoat draped over the back of her chair. She wore no make-up that I
could detect and, beyond a delicate gold star brooch on her coat collar
and a man's watch on a loose crocodile strap, no jewelry. She was
maybe five-six, five-seven and, while not exactly fat, Miss Chase was
generously endowed.

"Read your column all the time," she continued, slipping on a
pair of owl-framed spectacles and pulling some papers from the slim
leather attaché case in front of her. And then, looking up at me. "'Bout
time you wrote something on soul food, Mr. Mortimer, you don't mind
my saying. Like MG Plates up in Harlem. Now there's somewhere.
Like they say – Mighty Grand."

"I'm not sure I'll be able to oblige right now."

"You mean, the paper sacking you?"

If words were a jet fighter, this one came right out of the sun, guns
blazing. And left me in a tailspin.

"They *sacked* me? The *Times* sacked me?"

"That's what it says in the *Post*."

"The *Post*? I'm in the *Post*?" More guns blazing. More tailspin.
The earth was spiralling up towards me. In less than a minute,
everything was going haywire. I'd been biting my nails for this visit
with a lawyer, so we could clear everything up and I could get myself
away to Maude and Jeff and Totnes Bay, and suddenly my world was
falling apart again. This was looking worse than the previous day's
encounter with DaSilva and Munroe. I'd expected a savior, but right
then there seemed none in sight.

Miss Chase nodded. "First edition. Front page. It'll make a fine
souvenir one of these days."

"Jesus H. So everyone knows? Everyone knows I've been arrested? And sacked?"

"Anyone who can read. According to the *Post*, the *Times* have you 'suspended pending enquiries'. But don't you worry, we'll get round to that one soon enough. Right now, though, it's the main article we need to address before we focus on anything else."

Right then, there was precious little I could focus on beyond what Miss Chase had just told me. Sacked from the *Times*? A story in the *Post*? Front page? It couldn't be. Just couldn't be.

"Are you okay?"

"I guess I... I just..."

...Just felt like crying was what I felt. But I didn't say that. I took a few deep breaths to steady myself. I'd started shaking again.

"I can't believe it... This can't be happening. This is just... just... ludicrous."

My companion smiled, a little thinly for my liking. "There's no use sugar-coating this, Mr. Mortimer. You are in one whole passel of trouble, I don't mind telling you."

"But I haven't *done* anything. I didn't kill Roo. Not in a thousand years. How could the police think for a second it's me?"

"They don't think, they know. Or rather, they like to think they know."

Which made me sit up. "Hold on a second, you're losing me here. I thought you just said I was in trouble?"

"Oh, you're in trouble, alright. Up to your neck, believe me. And getting deeper every minute. But being in trouble and being guilty, my friend, are not the same item. Not by a long ways. And certainly not in my book."

I thought about that for a moment. "So you don't think I'm guilty?"

"You ain't convinced me yet, Mister."

Which, quite unexpectedly, made me smile. I think I even chuckled. "I'm relieved to hear it." And then: "Who did you say you were with?"

"Chase McKay. A friend of yours brought us in when the story broke."

Sanchez. Thank God for Sanchez. I'd called him the night before, after DaSilva and Munroe were through with me, on a payphone down in the basement. He thought I was calling about my copy; had been trying to get a hold of me. I told him the story wouldn't be coming, and to run with something else. And then, swearing him to secrecy, I told him why. I'd been arrested, I was being held at the 19th Precinct on East 67th, and could he get someone there, a lawyer, someone to help me out?

"Told you to pay those parking tickets of yours," he'd said. It was a standing joke between us that I was the only man he knew in America who didn't drive a car, didn't even have a license. "As for lawyers," Sanchez continued, "got a whole department here, mostly sittin' on their butts and waitin' for pay day."

"No one from work, Sanchez. This is serious. I need a lawyer. A good one. And fast as you can."

There was a pause as he took this on board. Then: "Leave it with me. 19th you said? You need anything in the meantime?"

"Just the lawyer, please."

And the lady sitting opposite me, eyes twinkling, fingers spliced, was the lawyer he'd gotten hold of. Thank God for Sanchez.

"Sanchez Requol," I said.

"Pardon me?" Miss Chase frowned, looked puzzled.

"Sanchez Requol. At the *Times*. He was the one got in touch with your firm."

"Not our firm, he didn't." She turned and pulled a card from her topcoat pocket, looked at it, then tucked it away again. "Ben Harrison, at Lingfield Byers. That's who your friend got in touch with. Just met him down in reception. Put a flea in his ear, and sent him packing."

"I don't understand. You mean it wasn't Sanchez…? Then how did you…? Who…?"

"A mutual friend."

"Mutual friend?"

"Lydia Langhorn."

"Lydia? How on earth…?"

"The *Post*. She called me first thing. And I mean early."

"You know Lydia?"

"We were at law school together."

"Lydia. At law school? I never knew she went to law school."

I was given a wry, appraising look: "Harvard Law Review. Class of '85. From all I hear, I'd suggest there's a whole heap you don't know about Lydia Langhorn." And then: "How are they treating you, by the way?"

"How are they treating me? Well, it's not the Ritz Carlton, I'll tell you that. I'm sharing a cell with a recovering drunk who looks like he lives in a dumpster, a man with a scar on his face as long as 5th Avenue, and a couple of punks who are doing a real good job scaring the living daylights out of me. I've spent most of the last twenty hours behind bars, haven't slept a wink, and all I've had to eat is a dry bagel washed down with cold coffee."

"So no complaints then," she said, smiling kindly, then glanced at her watch. "But let's get down to business. In about forty-five minutes our friends out there are going to come knocking and this little meeting's at an end. Okay then..." She flicked through the papers she'd taken from her attaché. "Homicide. First degree..."

First degree? My insides concertinaed. Oh my God!

Cerise Chase looked up as though I'd just jumped out of my chair. Which probably wasn't so far off the mark. "You alright? You looked like you just got a shock."

"You could say." I blew out my breath. I was almost hyperventilating. "First degree. It's just so..."

"Classy. I know." She gave me a cheerful look. "What did you expect? DUI? But let's get on..." She turned back to her notes. "Victim: Belinda Carmichael. Buffy, to her friends."

"Roo. I knew her as Roo."

"Roo?"

"As in Carew. Beatty Carew. I didn't know her real name till this week."

Miss Chase looked back to her notes. "Age: Thirty-four..." she continued, almost to herself. "...Address blah blah blah... No previous. Ah, here it is... AKA Beatty Carew. And Millicent Weaver, and Lois Sabina, and Cara James, and Susan Tellinger, and..."

"Susan?"

Miss Chase shot me a look: "Name familiar? You know her?"

"Of course I know her. She's a colleague. Or rather was. She's editor on a magazine now. We're old friends. But how come Susan's name is an alias?"

My companion in that hot airless room flicked ahead through the pages until she found what she was looking for.

"October 26th. Miss Susan Tellinger reports theft of credit cards, social security card, driver's license, passport, and cash. Says she left her purse in a cab. Turned up in a drawer in the victim's apartment."

Miss Chase read on, then looked up from her notes. "Did you know she and the victim...?"

"Yes, I did."

"Who told you?"

"Susan."

"Not Roo?"

I shook my head.

She seemed to think about this for a moment, then took off on another tack. "You ever been to her apartment by the way? Roo's apartment, I mean?'

"A few times."

"And the last time was?"

"Christmas. A few days before the actual holiday. We'd had lunch..."

"And you went back to her place afterwards?"

"That's right," I said, and left it at that. I didn't elaborate – how Roo had told me my real present was back at her place, and why didn't I come fetch it? – and I hoped Miss Chase wouldn't ask, wondered what I'd say if she did.

But she didn't ask. Instead, she flipped to another page.

"So, let's see now. Yes. You ever see a brass dog in the victim's apartment?"

"A brass dog? I don't recall..."

"Old, brass, blacky-green color. Oriental maybe. About so high... kinda heavy." She tried to give it some scale with her cupped hands. "Kept it on the dining table?"

I remembered immediately. It had felt like a knuckleduster.

"I remember it."

"You ever touch it?"

"Yes. Yes, I did."

"You did? You mind telling me why and when?" Miss Chase leaned across the table, arms folded like DaSilva, her eyes latched onto mine.

"The first time I went there. Let's see... November. She told me to take a look around. I saw it, picked it up. Like you do. It was a fine piece."

"Uh-huh. And what about a computer?"

"I knew she had one. Saw it in her office."

"You know what she used it for?"

I shook my head. "Internet? E-mail? That sort of thing? Business. Keeping records, I guess."

"You could say." She picked up a sheet of paper and spoke as though she was reading from it. "Took the police computer boys a few days to find their way in apparently, but it paid off. A page bio on every single client – likes, dislikes, how often, how much. Some big names, too, by all accounts. And some equally big numbers." She put down the piece of paper and looked at me. "There was a letter too. A draft e-mail. The last she ever wrote. The day she died. To you."

For whatever reason, I felt a stir of unease. I couldn't for the life of me see what Miss Chase was getting at, what she was trying to establish, the direction this conversation was going in. Had I visited Roo's apartment? Had I touched the dog? And now an e-mail? She was like a softer version of DaSilva, but no less unsettling.

"You see her that day, by the way? The day she died?"

"We were supposed to meet up. But we never did. She didn't show. I waited a couple of hours at the restaurant where we'd agreed to meet, then went home."

"Which was? The restaurant?"

"Toucan. It's a diner. West…"

Miss Chase nodded. "So no witnesses then." It wasn't a question. DaSilva would have loved that.

For a moment I thought to say something about the cashier and the tip but I didn't. She'd probably say exactly what DaSilva had said. Instead, I just got riled up. "But that's where I was. That's where I was when she was murdered. You have to believe that."

"Trouble is, Mr. Mortimer, you can't prove it," she said gently.

"But it's the *truth*. That's where I was, for God's sake. Waiting for her to show. Why should I have to prove it?"

But as soon as I said it I knew how ridiculous it sounded. Of course I had to prove it. If I couldn't prove it, I didn't have an alibi. And if I didn't have an alibi…

"How did you set up the meet?"

"She called me. Left a message. I called her back."

"You still have the message?"

I shook my head. And then: "But what about phone records?"

"What about them?"

"Well, surely they'll prove she called me? And that I called her?"

"Yes, okay. But not what she or you might have said. Could have been an argument. You might have threatened her. She might have threatened you. Who's to say?"

I was trying to work that one out, when Miss Chase changed tack again. "So let's get back to the letter. The e-mail. You want to hear about it?"

"Sure. What did it say?"

"Well, according to the cops it appears Miss Carmichael, Roo, was not your biggest fan."

"Wasn't my biggest fan?" What on earth was she talking about now? This must be some kind of trick, I thought. Something to catch me out. "Well, that's just plain ridiculous. I mean, Roo and I were... we were lovers, for goodness sake. Since November. Thanksgiving. Believe me, we were in love."

Miss Chase held my eye. There was no expression on her face, but I knew she was taking in every word. And I knew what she was thinking. She didn't believe me. I slowed down, tried to gather myself.

"She was going to give it all up. The clients... you know? We talked about it."

"So she hadn't started charging you at this time?"

"Charging me? I've just told you..."

"Apparently, that was how she did it. The police've interviewed a number of her clients and their stories tally. Susan Tellinger included. Over and over again. The money came later. Not always, but mostly. And..." she looked back at her notes, "...your friend, Roo, met most of her clients the same way – through a legitimate property business."

"Relocate. And she called her clients 'accounts'." I wanted Miss Chase to see how much of Roo's business I knew about, that I was trusted, as though this would prove I was more than just another name, another 'account', and that whatever was written in the letter couldn't be true.

She threw me a look. "She tell you that?"

"Of course. She was always very open with me."

Miss Chase nodded. "So you want me to tell you what she said in that draft e-mail?"

"Whatever it said, it's not true. It simply isn't true. Not if it's like you say – that she wasn't my biggest fan."

My companion said nothing, but a smile started to curl across her lips.

I gave a little laugh, which was meant to sound dismissive but came out a little shaky, a tad nervous. "I know this is some kind of line, and I'm not falling for it. I know what I know."

"So you're not interested? You don't want to hear?"

I took a deep breath. She knew I wanted to know. "Go on then. What is it she wrote?"

"So far as I can establish – I've yet to see any transcript – Roo, Buffy, Milly, Susan, whatever her name was, wrote to you it was over. She'd had enough. Said she'd made a mistake. Said she was scared of you. Said you frightened her. Said she wanted to finish it. Didn't want ever to see you again. At least, that's how I heard it from the District Attorney when I finally got through to him at his place in the country."

I'd started shaking my head. This was ridiculous.

"And let's not forget the forensic stuff tying you in. Your prints on the brass dog that knocked her unconscious – they confirmed a match last night by the way. Then there's the stab wounds inflicted by a left-hander; using what appears to be a kitchen knife. And, last but not least, there's the fact that when she was left for dead by her assailant, whoever he or she may turn out to be, your lover managed to scrawl your name in blood on the floor with her toe. All that, and you've no alibi worth a cent."

I stopped shaking my head.

My eyes were wide, my mouth open.

"So like I said, Mr. Mortimer. Looks to me like you been delivered one whole heap of trouble."

Mince 'n' Grits

I remember once writing for the *Times*, when the arms dealer Adnan Khashoggi was imprisoned in Bern, Switzerland, how his meals were brought to him from the estimable Hotel Schweizerhof on Bahnhofplatz. I'm sorry to report there were no such comforts for me when, some three hours after my first meeting with Cerise Chase and following a brief appearance for arraignment at the Criminal Courts Building on Manhattan's Center Street, I was transferred, in manacles, to the State Correctional Facility in Brooklyn.

At State Correctional, unlike Bern's Genfergasse prison, food was delivered by means of the Roach Coach, a trolley-like contraption operated by an inmate called Fat Harry. He made the rounds four times a day. Breakfast at seven-thirty; lunch at eleven-forty-five; tea at three-thirty; and dinner at five-forty-five. A battery on the front axle powered the trolley and helped keep the hot food hot. The motor gave off a soft whining sound when the brake was released and the single gear engaged.

Fat Harry was an appropriate, if not altogether agreeable, choice for the Roach Coach. First, of course, he was fat. Very fat. Fatter even than the Receiving Sergeant at the 19th Precinct. Thyroid territory, surely; no one could eat that much. I was reminded of Napoleon's observation that God had created Frederick I of Württemberg as a means of demonstrating how far human skin could be stretched without bursting. The Almighty must have been trying a similar trick with Fat Harry. And he was tall, too, a giant, far taller than the Sergeant, well over six feet, which made him appear even more monumental. And menacing. He must have been in his sixties, but there was still a chilling sense of threat about him.

Before they made him a 'walk-alone', so Bantu in the next 'hole' told me, Fat Harry used to charge inmates a dollar a time to cup his breasts. When he leaned down to pull out your tray from the trolley slots, you could see them swing forward in the V of his orange prison shirt, and tremble against the cotton as he slid the food through the bars. Also, he had a way of looking at you, kind of sideways, out of the corner of sleepy, half-closed eyes; a slow, measuring look that was most unsettling and which, after my first encounter with him, I tried at all costs to avoid.

The other reason Fat Harry was an appropriate choice for driving the Roach Coach – depending on how you look at it – and the cause of his incarceration according to Bantu, was this. In 1977, on the evening the Dodgers faced off to the Cowboys for the 28th Super Bowl in Detroit, Fat Harry smothered his wife like a Rouen duck, cut her up, and casseroled her. He'd pretty much finished eating her six weeks later when police officers removed from his deep freeze the last remaining Tupperware containers filled, so Bantu told me, with what Fat Harry had sworn was nothing more than Hungarian Goulash.

Bantu just loved that part.

For a moment there, that first evening in State Correctional, I was tempted to tell my new friend how Hungarian *gulyás* had been a favorite of Madame de Staël's (she ate it for breakfast); that Goethe believed it contained health-giving properties; and that Casanova credited it with increasing his sex drive – for which reason, no doubt, the Carmelite order of monks were forbidden to eat it. But I thought better of it. It was unlikely Bantu was familiar with Madame de Staël or Goethe, and I didn't want to repeat the mistake I'd made in the holding cells of the 19th Precinct when I was rash enough to tell one of the two punks who I was, thus earning, when the connection was finally made – neither man what you might call a typical *Times'* reader – the names 'Cheeseburger' and 'Double'.

On his rounds, Fat Harry stopped five times before he got to Bantu and me. Each time he stopped, he served two cells. When it was my turn, cell 12, the number stenciled in white paint above steel bars, the twelfth 'hole' on what they called 'Hell's Hallway', last 'hole' on the top landing of a three-level wing in C Block Maximum Security, I waited for Fat Harry and the Roach Coach to move on before I collected my tray.

Of course, I shouldn't have been on C Block in the first place. Out of thirty-six prisoners accommodated on my wing, twenty were lifers-no-parole and most of the rest long-termers like my neighbor, Bantu, who was serving a fifteen-to-twenty – for 'getting caught' was all he would tell me. I, on the other hand, was a remand prisoner, and as such should have been accommodated in A Block.

Which is what Cerise explained the Monday afternoon she came to visit with me. There was just no room, she told me. She was sorry, but there was nothing she'd been able to do about it. Anyway, she added, having my own cell in C Block was probably a great deal safer than sharing one in A Block.

As always, I was to discover, Cerise had a way of looking on the bright side of things.

Which for someone in my predicament was vastly encouraging.

≈

Within fifteen minutes of meeting her in the interview room at the 19th Precinct, I'd felt right at home with Miss Chase. Or rather, Cerise, as she'd told me to call her by the end of our time together. And our second meeting that Monday afternoon out in Brooklyn confirmed my opinion of her. In another life she'd have made just a marvelous lunch companion. She was smart, she was sassy, she was bold and forthright. Intelligence just sparkled in her eyes, you could see it at once. Nor could I be anything but impressed at her efficiency. In the space of only a few hours, from the time Lydia got in touch with her Saturday morning to our first meeting, she'd certainly done her homework. Which gave me enormous confidence.

And she didn't pull any punches, which I appreciated. She was a woman who didn't intend wasting her own and her client's time not speaking her mind. Like she said at the Precinct House, I may have been in 'one whole passel of trouble', but in her book trouble and guilt were nowhere near the same item. Indeed, as she'd reeled off what sounded like a stack of damning evidence accumulated by the District Attorney's office – the draft e-mail, the matching prints, the left-handed wounds, my name written in blood on the floor, and no verifiable alibi – she did so in such a dismissive, derisory manner that I was left in no doubt that when the time came she would take the greatest pleasure blasting each spurious charge out of the sky. By the end of that first hour together at the 19th Precinct – despite the Prosecution's case against me and her dismaying disclosures with regard to the *Post* headlines and my sacking from the *Times* – she had quite restored my spirits, telling me she had no doubt, no doubt at all, that I was innocent of the crime I'd been charged with.

And even when she told me the likely outcome of my arraignment at the Criminal Courts and probable transfer thereafter to the State Correctional Facility in Brooklyn, that I would not be released that afternoon as I had hoped, but would be held in custody until a bail hearing could be scheduled, even then the prospect didn't bother me as much as it might have done a few hours earlier. Now, at last, I had someone on my side. I was in safe hands. And that made all the difference.

Indeed, if it hadn't been for Cerise, knowing she was in my corner, I'd never have survived the manacles.

A couple of hours after her departure, just as she'd said, mid-Saturday afternoon, three burly police officers strode into the caged basement and, while two of them watched with batons drawn, the remaining officer drew us out of the cell one by one and secured each of us with steel manacles, a wide leather belt and ankle restraints, the three components linked by a length of chain that looped through a hook in back of the belt to the next man.

The drunk had been the first to step out – he'd woken that morning, deep groans replacing snores – followed by Scarface, the two hoodlums and me, each of us stepping forward as instructed to be cuffed and linked. I remember noting how light the metal was, not as heavy as it looked. Across the hallway, in the facing pen, a half-dozen hookers who'd been brought in at various hours during the night, red glossy lipstick long faded, about as far away from Roo as you could imagine, looked on, laughing and shouting obscenities, until one of the guards rapped against the bars with his baton and sent them scuttling away, still bad-mouthing, back to their cots.

And through it all, I did what Cerise had counseled and just switched off to what was happening to me, just let it go, just let things happen.

"I know it'll be harder to do than it sounds," she told me, "but just try. There's nothing you can say or do that'll change anything right now, so don't sweat it. Just stay calm."

And somehow, don't ask me how, I managed it. When the time came I was ready.

With chains rattling, hobbled and shuffling, we were herded in file out of the holding area, stopping in line for every lock to be sprung and barred gate to be clanged open and slammed shut behind us, until we reached the reception area. Unlocking a door to the right of the Lost-Luggage counter, the same grey-haired, panting, overweight Receiving Sergeant who'd signed me in the previous afternoon, who'd taken my fingerprints and my photo, stood aside as his three colleagues steered us through into a dimly-lit tiled passageway which, a few yards in, the door slammed and bolted behind us, began to slope upwards.

After about twenty or thirty paces, my view restricted to the shoulders of the man in front of me – his shaved, pimpled and tattooed neck, the chain swinging between us, and our shoes scuffling over the tiles – we were told to stop. There was a rusty screech of metal up ahead, the sound of more locks being turned, and suddenly a light brighter than the neon above our heads flooded over us and a freezing gust of air rushed past as we filed out into the Precinct House's inner courtyard.

Backed up to what looked like the platform on a loading bay was a single-decker blue bus with its windows barred and painted out, its back doors swung open, with a guard at each one. While I waited for the men ahead of me to step forward, I looked over the roof of the bus to see fat flakes of snow tumbling down from a scrap of dirty grey sky, felt the cold air scorch my throat. Once in the van we were told to sit in the cubicles provided, and the same officer who'd manacled us now snapped our wrist chains into a clasp in the seats.

With a round of 'motherfuckers' from the two punks, the doors were slammed shut and locked, the engine gunned up, and we trundled slowly across the yard. Peering through a scratch in the blacked-out glass, I could see us turning towards a high wood gate set in the wall of the building. As the bus straightened I saw the gate swing open and, lurching down a ramp, we turned into the flow of traffic on Lexington and were off.

And in all that time, I'm proud to say, my heart didn't flicker, my stomach didn't turn.

Nothing.

Thanks to Cerise.

≈

That first meeting with my new attorney ended exactly when and how she said it would. At near enough the very moment the hands of the clock behind her head indicated the hour was up, there came a tap on the door and the Receiving Sergeant was there to collect me. We shook hands, and I thanked her for coming.

As she gathered up her things, she told me again not to worry, everything was fine, just be patient. And settling her coat over her shoulders, she said how she'd be sure to pass on my best wishes to

Lydia. She gave me an amused look as she said it, and I felt a sudden flush of guilt. I'd gotten so bound up in my own predicament I'd completely gone and forgotten that my new friend was there at Lydia's bidding. When she saw my look of dismay, she chuckled warmly and said she was only joking. She'd tell Lydia I was doing just fine, and had said to say a 'big thank-you'.

There was something else she said, too, that first meeting, something that helped keep my mind centered on other things as the shackles went on. After reviewing the Prosecution's case and listening to my side of the story, she finally spelled out what I surely should have worked out for myself.

"If it's not you killed your friend," she said, "then it's someone you know, Cully. Someone who knows you. Someone who knew the two of you. Someone who wrote your name on the floor. Simple as that. So start thinking names. Make a list."

She said it again when we parted in the corridor outside the interview room – her going one way, the Receiving Sergeant and I going the other: "Don't you forget what I said, Cully. Someone you know killed someone you know. And they've set you up for it."

Someone you know killed someone you know.

After she'd gone I couldn't get those words out of my head, repeating them under my breath like a mantra. A week earlier, I'd pretty much convinced myself the killer had to be a client, maybe the one who'd taken exception to Roo downsizing, the one Rudi had paid a return call on. But a week later, with me behind bars, that all looked a lot less likely. As far as Cerise was concerned, everything pointed to someone I knew, someone who knew me. And the more I thought about it, the more it looked like she might be right.

All the way through my arraignment (Cerise had warned me she would not be representing me officially until after this initial hearing – "take a court-appointed; he might make a mistake we can use later," she'd told me), and all the way to State Correctional out in Brooklyn, her words tumbled round in my head like a litter of playful puppies.

Someone you know... Someone you know... Someone you know...

Nothing she had told me so far – the story of my arrest in the papers, my sacking from the *Times*, the seeming weight of *prima facie* evidence stacked against me – nothing bothered me half as much as this. The fact that someone I knew had put me in this pickle, had set me up.

Of course, it didn't have to be a good friend, I quickly persuaded myself, just someone who knew about Roo and I.

Someone like Bruno, Roo's driver, with the gun under his armpit. He'd driven us round together, knew where I lived. And Roo had fired him, let him go. Thanksgiving Week. A month before Christmas. Maybe he harbored a grudge. Maybe he felt he had a score to settle, and thought to put me in the frame for it.

Or maybe it was Rudi. The other driver Roo used. Did he have a grudge too? Both men knew where she lived. Which apartment. Just knock at her door, and she'd open up for them. And all they had to do to cover their tracks was pin it on someone like me, make it look like it was me that had done it. Nothing simpler.

So, there was Bruno. And Rudi. And, by association, well, hey... I might as well include the people at Beartree: Jack, the captain, in his check sports coat and black trousers, and Bill with the Davy Crockett hat. They must have known the deal at Beartree, like as not known what Roo did for a living, and since our stay that Thanksgiving weekend they knew me too. If they were planning on killing Roo, for whatever reason, and looking to frame someone, then why not me? They all knew my name; any one of them could have written it on the floor in Roo's blood, and put together that e-mail.

These were the first names I conjured with as the blacked-out bus, gears grinding, trundled downtown to the courthouse and then over the river into Brooklyn. It was only later, after the gates of State Correctional swung shut behind us, after we'd been signed in, unchained, stripped, searched (the less said, the better), given prison overalls to clamber into, and finally led off to our cells, that I started looking closer to home, lured to it by its very impossibility.

Someone you know... Someone you know...

It suggested intimacy, friendship, history.

But how could that possibly be?

It implied that someone I held dear, someone I trusted and loved, someone I might have known for years, considered our friendship worthless. Someone prepared to sacrifice that friendship, and see me convicted for a crime I hadn't committed, to save their own skin. How could I possibly know someone like that, and not have seen through them? Just impossible. I valued all my friendships, and it was difficult to think those feelings were not reciprocated.

And anyway, I reasoned, who among my circle of friends knew about my relationship with Roo? At which point one name sprang immediately to mind. Well, there was Susan, of course. Susan. As if… But still. The link was there. She'd known Roo, been one of her clients and, by her own account at Spoonlickers, had been driven to near distraction by their relationship. What was it she'd said? '*Sooner or later I'm going to start hating it more than I love it. And then… well, then I don't know what I'm going to do.*'

And she knew that Roo and I were close, still saw each other. I might not credit it for an instant, but I was in no position to rule her out as a potential suspect simply because she and I were friends. After all, I was the one in prison. And I was the one who'd get to stay in prison if I couldn't sort all this out. Which sharpened the thought processes, I can tell you. Which was what Cerise had been getting at, I realized. Look closely at your friends, someone you always considered a friend.

I racked my brains. Was there anyone else I knew, apart from Susan and a handful of hardly-known, unlikely-sounding suspects like Bruno and Rudi and the guys at Beartree, who could have done this to me? No one I could think of. No one at all. But then, sitting quietly on my cot in cell 12, listening out with half an ear to the hums and echoes and shouts of prison life all around me, I began to extend the parameters, searching for any kind of link that might connect a friend of mine to this terrible deed. Just because I couldn't see any link, didn't mean to say that one didn't exist. It was speculation time again. And boy, did I speculate.

Take Daphne, for instance. There was no place surely for her on my list? We'd known each other an age, couldn't have been closer, nothing we wouldn't have done for each other. Surely it was just inconceivable that she could do such a thing. And anyway, how could she possibly know about Roo and I?

But wait up. I might imagine she knew nothing about us (I'd certainly never told her anything when we lunched at the Dharwar, or any of the other times we met through Fall and winter), but that didn't mean she couldn't have found out about us. Without my knowing.

For example, let's say her private eye catches Elliot out and passes on all the relevant information to Daphne, including Roo's address. Now, let's say Daphne comes up to the city to stake out her husband's mistress, to take a look at the competition first hand, which is the kind of thing I can imagine Daphne doing. Maybe she's even planning to catch them *in flagrante*, who knows? And who does she see as she trails Roo around? Why, her old friend, Cully Mortimer. And who's to say she's not prepared to sacrifice a friend to save a marriage, to secure a life, to deflect attention away from her?

Like Susan, the very idea that Daphne might try to frame me, why it just seemed so ridiculous. But who's to say? Just because something seems ridiculous, doesn't mean to say it's not possible. Just because you can't imagine yourself in jail, doesn't mean you won't end up there, right?

Just like it's possible my old friend, Felix, calls up Elliot one day and happens to mention, by mistake or as deliberate gossip, that their mutual friend, Cully, is dating a hooker called Roo. Maybe Roo even tells Elliot herself. I could just hear her having the same conversation with him that I'd had with her at Sutton Row. "It appears we have friends in common…"

But did they? And if they did, why? Out of mischief? Devilment? Who's to say? Who cares?

What matters is, Elliot finds out about Roo and me. From Roo, from Felix – it doesn't signify. He finds out. And then, maybe, Roo starts upping the ante, like she did with Susan, asking Elliot for more money. Which Elliot can't afford… Or maybe he wants out of the arrangement, and she won't let him go. Maybe she threatens to tell Daphne, and he panics. Panics enough to kill her and… why not, pin it on someone else? For the same reasons as Daphne. To save a marriage, to secure a lifestyle. And have the finger point somewhere else.

Then, of course, there's Avery. Who's to say Roo didn't tell Avery, after our stay at Beartree, that she and I were good friends? Just as she might have told Elliot. Showing off, perhaps; small-world kind of thing. So far as I knew, she and Avery hadn't seen each other since the Beartree negotiations. But what did I know? Roo and the truth, as I'd quickly learned, had often only a passing acquaintance. And since she knew from our drive back from Beartree to the city that I didn't much approve of her behaviour towards Avery in the sale of the Lodge, the chances are she'd never mention seeing Avery in case I drew the wrong conclusions, suspected her of being up to no good.

Which maybe she was. Because Avery was clearly vulnerable.

She'd fixed herself up good and tight with Player Leland, and the last thing she wanted was someone appearing out of her past. Which, let's face it, is how the sale of Beartree finally went through in Roo's favor. Maybe Roo, identifying Avery as an easy mark, had continued to apply pressure, threatening to share their little secret with Player. And Avery, now with a very great deal to lose, finally decided to do something about it. And arranged to have me implicated to save herself.

Once I started in on this line of thinking – which was exactly what Cerise had intended – it was difficult to draw the line. I became caught up in a tangle of 'what-ifs' and 'maybes', entranced and dismayed by the very possibilities, exploring the recent past with a surgical precision, sniffing out signs of infection.

Take Casey, for example. I hadn't spoken to her in months, hadn't seen her since before Europe, back in the summer when I worried that she might come running after me with a carving knife before I found myself a cab. Yet there, sitting on the cot in my cell, her name and her face swam into view, and I recalled with a chill something that had happened the day Roo and I went shopping with the new driver. We were coming out of Sulka's, and as I bent down to get in the car I could have sworn I saw Casey darting into a doorway across the street.

Maybe it was nothing, maybe it was something. I mean, who's to say Casey hadn't gotten obsessed with my leaving her like I did, started following me, seen me with Roo, and hatched a plan to have her revenge? To do to me what I had done to her, and have me pay the price. A double whammy. I wouldn't have put it past her. Right from the start, there'd always been something uncomfortably compulsive and committed about Casey. That steely, resourceful single-mindedness – the way she'd set off for Paris despite her parents' objections; the way she'd started her own business; the way she'd pursued me and led me on, taken the initiative.

Only to be cast aside, let down. Cruelly, callously.

Not something that Casey was used to.

She was even left-handed, for Chrissakes, and there were enough knives in her kitchen drawers to commit a hundred brutal slayings and never use the same one twice. Likely? Who's to say? Possible? Probable even? I guess. It's the kind of thing you read in the paper every day. And, I have to admit, there's no denying I treated her abominably.

Whatever else it did, all this hypothesizing, all this convoluted speculation kept my mind occupied, just like it had when I first found out about Roo's death, kept me from losing my way and feeling sorry for myself as I sat alone, but not alone, in my third-floor Brooklyn cell.

≈

Like she promised, Cerise visited Monday afternoon. Since C Block was maximum security and there were no remand facilities we met in a room divided by a counter and a ceiling-high screen of reinforced glass. There were four chairs her side of the divide, but only the one on mine. I pulled it out and sat down.

"Don't bother looking for a telephone, Cully. Just speak normally and I'll hear you fine," she told me, in an oddly dislocated tone. Her words matched the movement of her lips, but her voice seemed to come from somewhere behind me.

Being a weekday, she was dressed for the office – a severely cut grey two-piece over a white polo neck, and just a whisper of make-up. When I was settled, she glanced down at her papers. "You a Democrat by any chance?"

"Democrat...?" I wondered how my political inclinations could have any bearing on my case.

"What I'm getting at is," she said, looking across at me with a gentle smile, "it appears your man, Clinton, is taking the heat for you right now. Thanks to the Starr Report, the closest you come to any banner headline is the bottom of page three. That's in the *Post*. In the *Times*, there's been no mention since the Saturday edition."

"Well, that's something, I guess. Did you bring any newspapers with you?"

She shook her head. "Not while you're on C Block. So. How's the new apartment?"

"I'm okay. It's not as bad as I thought it'd be." And then, "Any idea how long I'm likely to be here? What'll happen next?"

Which is when she asked if I'd ever built a wall.

"You ever build a wall?" she said, in her lilting calypso voice.

"A wall? You've lost me," I said.

"You know. A wall. Brick or stone, doesn't signify."

No, I never had, I told her, wondering where this particular line of enquiry was leading, and what on earth it had to do with the questions I'd asked. Cerise, I soon discovered, had a way of coming at you from all angles, weighting her conversation with these disconcerting shifts and *non sequiturs.*

"Well, I'll tell you, Cully. We here in this legal profession of ours get to build walls every day of our working lives. It's what we get paid to do. And it's what the DA's office is doing right now. They're building a wall. Now bricks or stones, like I said, makes no never-mind. They both build a good high wall. But if you don't have the mortar to keep them where they oughta be, one on top of the other, you run the risk of seeing all your hard work come tumbling to the ground. Which is what's gonna happen to the Prosecution at the bail hearing. Or the trial – if this thing ever gets that far. I mean, it may all look good on paper, but in front of a jury? Up against me? Believe it, every one of those bricks or stones is goin' for a stroll."

She then went on to tell me that she hadn't been able to do anything over the weekend beyond go through the Prosecution's case in a little more detail, but first thing that morning, as my newly-appointed counsel, she'd applied for a bail hearing.

"And when do you think that might be?"

"Sooner than it ought to be, I'll tell you that for free," she said archly. "Seems Lydia's not the only friend you have in this here legal profession."

"I don't follow…"

"You know a Justice Cordell, by any chance?"

For a second the name meant nothing. Then I made the connection.

"As a matter of fact, I do."

Cordell was Maude MacAuley's maiden name. Justice Cordell was her father. It had been a while since the two of us had seen each other, but Maude was always passing on his best wishes. Which wasn't altogether surprising. The first time we met, Maude had brought him along for one of our lunches. I'd taken the two of them to Sutton Row which seemed to me an appropriate spot for a man of Justice Cordell's standing. I remember he'd recently had new dentures fitted and he looked stricken as, one by one, he felt compelled to discount the various treasures on the menu – the goose *confit* and *boeuf en croûte*, the 'English' cutlets, the crackling belly pork.

Suck and swallow food was what was needed, I told him, and though it wasn't on the menu I'd whispered to Gilbert, the Captain, to have the chef prepare a couple of soft boiled New England duck eggs to be served with a plate of Argenteuil asparagus which His Honor could use as 'fingers'.

Afterwards, the lunch was declared a great success and Justice Cordell, I recall, beamed with pleasure, as though somehow he'd cheated both the Fates and his orthodontist. Clearly Cordell remembered a favor. Thank God for Maude. She must have read about my arrest and gotten straight on to the old man. At least some good had come from the Press coverage.

"Well, he must owe you some, is all I can say," said Cerise. "His Honor called me up first thing this morning, friendly as you please, and said if there was anything he could do to expedite matters, I just had to ask. He might have retired, he told me, but that didn't necessarily mean his name didn't have some pull where it mattered.

"So I told him, friendly as you please, that I was looking to get you a bail hearing the earliest opportunity, and he agreed that seemed a most profitable route to pursue. That's all. Just that. 'A most profitable route to pursue'. And that was the end of the conversation. Two hours later, the Clerk of the Court calls to confirm Thursday afternoon. Last session of the day." Cerise gave me a look. "Now that's what I call influence or, what did he call it? 'Pull'. Anyone else you know in this profession I can lean on?"

"Do you need to lean on anyone?" I asked, suddenly a little unnerved. Hadn't she told me trouble was not the same as guilt?

"It always helps."

"Well, I can't think of anyone. If I do, I'll let you know."

"I hope you do."

"You sound uncertain. Do you think they'll grant bail?"

"With a fair wind. You have no previous record. The evidence against you is… well, flimsy."

Bantu, my neighbour on C Block, had said the same thing, but since I'd told him I was in for fraud, his assurances were not entirely comforting or convincing.

"And," Cerise paused, weighing her words. "We shouldn't forget the politics."

I must have looked bewildered at this. Because I was. Politics?

Was this another of Cerise's leaps?

"There's an election coming," explained Cerise. "Time to spring-clean. Get the place looking spry and shipshape. Tidy things up – satisfactorily. Clean slate, and all. And there's nothing like speeding up a high-profile case like yours if it looks like the Office of the District Attorney can get some mileage from it."

Mileage? I didn't like the sound of that.

And Cerise knew it, could see it in my eyes.

"I'll tell you straight, Cully. Whether you like it or not, you are in for a rough ride. This thing is not going to disappear, and the DA's office is not renowned for playing softball. You are a name. A face. And you work for a newspaper that has been openly hostile on certain issues. Political issues. You probably didn't know it, but that doesn't matter a hoot. They, the DA, City Hall, will be looking to get even, and this case promises to give them everything they could hope for. They know you're not going to run. They know you're not going to kill anyone else. And they're pretty sure they're going to win. So what have they got to lose? Playing fair and generous with you – by which I mean bail – is very much in their interests. It makes them look good before the trial's even started. And they can use you better out there than they can in here. Believe me, they'll try to manipulate everything you do, where you go, who you see. And the Press'll love it. One of their own? Forget it." She looked me right in the eye for this next bit: "Guilty or not guilty, Cully, you are going to suffer. If you thought you were well-known before this started, well, you are in for one serious surprise."

I remember, vividly, not wanting to hear any more right then. I'd deal with that later, when I was out of there. I changed the subject:

"Before we go any further, Cerise, I'd like to get some idea what kind of money we're talking about here? Your firm's fees, expenses, that kind of thing? I'm comfortable, sure, but I'm not rich…"

At which she waved her hand dismissively, as though to suggest she wouldn't be sitting there if I couldn't pay.

"You can afford us," she said. "But why don't we deal with the money when the time comes. Right now, there are things I need to know."

And for the next thirty minutes I answered a raft of questions – some obvious, some not so obvious – that she had drawn up.

How had Roo and I met? How often did we see each other? How much money did I earn? Did I have other assets? Had I ever traveled anywhere with her? Did I have any relevant travel documentation? Had she ever given me gifts? Had I ever given her any gift? Were there any cards or receipts that went with them? Any other letters or notes? How and where had our sexual relationship started? Who had initiated it? And was it genuine? Had I sensed any kind of subterfuge?

"You need to know all this stuff?" I asked half way through, trying to comprehend how any of this could possibly be pertinent.

Cerise gave me a hard, long look. "I need to know everything, Cully. Every tiny little thing. Even you're purer than the driven snow, I need to know it all. Just to be sure."

So I answered every question she put to me, told her everything that had happened, talking quietly, as though to myself, as though Cerise wasn't there, wasn't listening, trying hard not to think too much about the person I was talking about, a person I'd loved but would never see again.

When we were finished, Cerise filed away her papers in her attaché case as though she had enough to be going on with, and asked: "Did you do what I told you? The names? You given that some thought while you've been here? Like I said you should?"

I said I had, but they all seemed so unlikely.

"Which is what the killer will be banking on, whoever it is. But believe me, soon as you're out of here, Cully, you're gonna have to start chasing them up. One by one. If they're friends, they'll see you quick enough. And if they don't, well that says something, don't you think? But time for that later. Once you're out of here."

Which is how our meeting finished – with the promise that soon enough I'd likely be released, out on bail. In the firing line sure, but free. Which was a comforting thought as they led me back to my cell on Hell's Hallway.

≈

If the first night of my incarceration at the 19th Precinct had been a nightmare of fear, disbelief, and anxiety – sitting on the floor with my back to the tiled wall and the drunk bundled up beside me, while the two punks and Scarface taunted me from the cots they'd appropriated, wondering how long it would take the Receiving Sergeant to get in here and break it up if they decided to have a go at me – my second night, in a cell of my own at State Correctional, was a relative breeze.

The cell was the size of a small kitchen without the cupboards and work surfaces, maybe nine feet by twelve. There was a narrow cot with grey prison-issue blankets, roughly starched sheets and pillowcase (the starch, I discovered, made up for the cotton's thinness), a basin and seat-less lavatory bowl made from that thin brushed metal you get on airplanes, the kind of plastic chair you can stack one on top of another, and a hinged table where I ate my meals. The ceiling and walls were painted a light blue-grey, the floor was polished cement, and the opening on to the hallway set with thumb-thick steel bars.

The cells, or 'holes', on Hell's Hallway occupied only one side of the wing, set in a line, like I said, twelve to a landing. Through my bars the only thing I could see was a wall some thirty feet away with a line of opaque window tiles running from ceiling height to below my line of vision. Which, I told myself, was a whole lot better than looking into someone else's cell, and have someone else look into mine. The last thing I wanted to do was catch someone's eye, especially after my first encounter with Fat Harry, when he and the Roach Coach came to a halt outside my cell a couple of hours after my arrival.

"Thank you," I said, as he slipped my tray through the slot in the bars – a brown and white mush of mince and grits, it turned out.

For a moment or two, Fat Harry looked surprised that someone should have spoken to him.

"Why, it's my pleasure," he replied softly, refusing to let go of the tray, his eyes catching mine and then, with a leer, running down the length of my body as though judging a cut of meat.

Finally, with a hungry smile, he released the tray, paused the other side of the bars a moment longer, and then headed back the way he had come.

I was shaking when I sat down, at the sheer unspoken hostility of the encounter, though I had no clear idea right then what kind of threat someone like Fat Harry might pose. It was only later, long after he'd returned to pick up the dinner trays (I'd left mine jammed in the slot and had curled up on my cot pretending sleep when I heard the approaching whine of the Roach Coach), that I found out his name and what he'd done twenty-two years earlier on the evening the Cowboys played the Dodgers.

From Bantu, the man in the 'hole' next to mine.

I'd first seen Bantu as I stood on the landing waiting for the guards to unlock my cell and usher me in. He'd been sitting on the edge of his bed, hunched over a pocket chess board. A curtain of dreadlocks concealed his face, and he didn't look up the whole time I stood there. We'd already passed some dangerous-looking characters along that third-floor landing, the guards and I, but I remember feeling relieved that he didn't look too threatening, more contemplative than violent. About an hour after they locked me away, I heard a deep sigh from his cell, the sliding tumble of the chess pieces, and the snap of the clasps on the box. But that was all.

At around ten, the lights on the landing dimmed and the cell lights shut off. In the shadows I stripped down to my shorts and crawled into bed. I was lying there, looking at the ceiling and thinking about Casey, when I heard the squeak of bed springs in the next cell and a voice whisper through the bars.

"Bantu," he said. "Name's Bantu. An' you?"

I lay still a moment, wondering if I should pretend I was asleep. Were there rules here about talking after lights out? Would I get in trouble if I were caught? But there was something about the man's name and the gentle earnestness of the enquiry, not to mention the dreadlocks, the chess board, and the lack of interest in me when I'd stood outside his cell, that made me push back my bedding and move cautiously to the bars where, in a low voice, looking out into the darkened hallway, unable to see the man I was talking to, I told him my name.

"Just so's you know, Cully," Bantu continued, "ain't a good idea to go talking to Fat Harry. He ain't the kind of friend you need in here, you know what I'm sayin'?"

Which is when I discovered what Fat Harry was in for.

When Bantu had finished his story, with a chuckle and a "can-you-believe-that-shit?" I thanked him for the advice and information.

"Don' mention it," he said. "Catch you later."

The bed springs in the next cell squeaked again, and the conversation was over.

Which I found encouraging. I now knew I could have a conversation in jail that had a beginning and an end and didn't involve, even in a short exchange like this one, my life being threatened or my body abused. It seemed to me as good a start as I could hope for, and within minutes, curled back up in my cot, I was asleep.

Though I probably didn't realize it then, there's no doubt in my mind now that between them Cerise and Bantu helped make my short time in jail surprisingly acceptable. Though she only came that one visit, Monday afternoon, Cerise's brightness, her confidence, her gin-clear disdain for the charges leveled at me – and her straight-talking – all these sustained me, gave me hope in the days that followed her visit.

And in her absence, there was Bantu.

Bantu turned out to be a real savior, a quickly-made friend and fund of information. After breakfast Sunday morning he whistled me up ("Hey, there! Cully!") and by lunchtime, perched on the end of my bed, I'd pretty much learned all there was to know about day-to-day life on Hell's Hallway: Mondays, library trolley; Tuesdays, laundry; Wednesdays and Saturdays, showers; Thursdays, college studies; Fridays, film night; Sundays, chapel; and the obligatory and, in Bantu's case, longed-for exercise in the prison yard each day – he'd be pacing his cell an hour before call-up waiting for it.

He also briefed me on the guards and how to handle them. Lehmann, with the moustache: "An easy guy, plays chess – badly"; Roderick, the fat one: "Get you anythin' you needs from outside"; Diego, the dago: "Been doin' some college course long as I's been in here"; and Collins, the tall one with the wall eye, a bastard: "Watch out fo' him, just do whatever he say, quick as you can and no answer-back never, yo' hear?"

Cerise would have approved.

And soon enough, towards the end of that first morning, as I'd been expecting, Bantu asked what I'd done to get where I was.

So I told him I was a businessman, that I'd been arrested for fraud.

"What kind of business is that, you don' mind me askin'?"

"Selling space on the Internet." Don't ask me how I came up with that one.

"Yeah, I heard of th' Internet," he replied. "And what kind of fraud?"

I borrowed some money, I told him, hoping I wouldn't have to go into any greater detail.

There was a grim chuckle from the other side of the wall. "Oh, yeah, I like that. Borrow some money. Oh, yeah, man."

Sanchez would have just loved that chuckle, a deep groaning giggle that sounded like it was going to end up choking him.

"Oh, man," he managed, dragging in air at almost the very last moment. "Oh, man. Borrow some money. Oh, yeah. Oh, yeah."

To change the subject, not wishing to answer too many questions on Internet space selling, I asked why they called our landing Hell's Hallway?

He stopped laughing at that. "On account of all us no-hope niggers, just waitin' here for the next stop. An' all I got me is a remand in the next hole who won' be here no more 'an two minutes."

Which was comforting for me to hear, but not so comforting for him, I guessed. As it turned out, it was closer to a week.

We must have talked hours, Bantu and I, most of it during exercise hour (between four and five in the afternoon), taken in pairs in the scrubby yard between the looming grey walls of C and B blocks, separated from other prisoners by a ten-foot fence of coiled razor wire. Hands dug into pockets, hunched against the cold, muffled into our collars, we'd make our way up and down the sixty-yard stretch under a brooding scud of low cloud, faces stinging with the gritty sleet that accompanied us. Back and forth, back and forth, so many times you sometimes forgot you'd even turned at each end. Like one long walk.

"The only good thing in here's the food," Bantu told me during our first outing, artlessly, for I'd made sure he knew nothing of the real Cully Mortimer, the man who'd written 'Last Orders'. "Regular and lots of it," Bantu continued. "'Burgers, chops 'n' gravy, mince 'n' grits, all kindsa stew. The pasta's dry as dirt, but the meat sauce is okay; take my advice and have it with the mash. They do good mash here. And fried chicken, too. You like fried chicken? You oughta know it's my favorite. Iffen I can help you out with it, don' hesitate to let me know, you hear me?"

When I told him I hated it, I knew our friendship was assured.

"They say you got yo'sel' a lady lawyer," said Bantu, the afternoon Cerise came to visit.

I told him I did, wondering how he'd found out.

"Oh, man. She young or old?"

"Young, I guess. Late thirties."

"Oh, man. Oh, man. Me. I had a court-appointed. Got me a fifteen-to-twenty like it was the only thing he knew how to do."

"She's black, too," I added, just for devilment, wondering how he'd respond to that.

For a beat there was silence. And then: 'Oh, man, you'se blessed. You is surely blessed. Gal like that could get you life-no-parole, and still you'd think you was goin' to heaven."

'Blessed', I soon learned, was Bantu's favorite word. That, and 'annointed'.

"You know, you annointed, man. You not only got yo'sel' a hot black Mama lawyer, get yo' all out of here in no time quick, but while you'se in here you got yo'sel' the best hole on the landing. Bet you didn' know that. Been trying to get your place a hunnert years. And you just walk in, and you are there. Easy. You sure blessed. You annointed. Ain't no other way of figurin' it."

"The best hole? How come?" I asked. "You mean to say the cells are different?"

"Diff'ren'? Diff'ren'? Yo' bet yoh a-yass, they'se diff'ren'," replied Bantu. "You the end of the landing, right? Quiet as the grave, ain't it? I mean, anyone talking to you the other side of your hole? I mean, you bored yet with the level of conversation you getting from your neighbor? No, sir. 'Cos you ain't *got* no neighbor but me. So you gone cut down a half your neighborhood verbal. You'se twice as better off 'n me, I'm tellin' you. You'se annointed, man.

"See, Cully, I got a real sex case th'other side of me just never stops beatin' it, you know what I'm sayin'? All I hear is 'uh-uh-uh-uh' 'bout sixteen hunnert time a day. And when he ain't beatin' it, he sleepin', po' moth'fucker. He at it now, I'm bettin' you. Which is not the way you want to spend your day, right? Lis'nin' to all that. And 'foh you took over twelve, I had a mouth in there you wouldn' believe. Eighteen months, man, never stopped yakkin' one time. But now you there, my man, life is a whole lot easier. Tell you the truth, kinda hope you gets to stay a little longer than remand. Never know who gonna come along next, and I need a quality 'hood, a *quality* 'hood, you know what I'm sayin' here?"

Looking back now, I realize how fortunate I was having someone like Bantu in the next cell when, let's face it, it could as easily have been Fat Harry. Imagine taking a stroll with him. It was also fortunate how swiftly I adapted to my surroundings, how easily I fit the prison regime. Maybe, as Bantu and Cerise had said, it would have been different on A Block, but when the cell gate clanged shut behind me that first night in Brooklyn and I surveyed the small space allotted to me, where I would spend however long it was they decided to keep me there, I didn't feel panicked or anything. Sure, there was a churning knot in my stomach at the predicament I was in, at what was likely going to happen – the media, the attention, all that – but like Cerise had said there was nothing I could do or say that would change anything. And she was right.

Also, being in prison kind of insulated me from everything that was happening on the outside, everything that Cerise had told me about. The things people would be saying about me, the things they'd be writing about me, having to deal with everything that was surely circulating about me in the media right then. In a funny sort of way, it was almost a relief to be there. To be spared it all. Not to see it, or hear it, or read it. No need for explanations.

Another thing I think I responded to in jail was the comforting sense of order there and, save for my brush with Fat Harry, no real anxiety, no abiding feeling of threat. Especially with Bantu looking out for me, helping me through it. Despite the company – the neighborhood, as Bantu called our landing – I felt safe there. There were moments I even forget where I was, lying back on my cot, head to the bars, listening to him tell me about the time he did this thing or that thing. We had nothing in common, save our surroundings, but we got on just fine together. He filled the hours for me.

And so the days passed. Talking with Bantu, listening to his stories, occasionally having to think up something vague but convincing about selling space on the Internet (for a man who wouldn't be out of jail for at least another ten years he was for ever asking me questions about it), taking walks together ('amblin'' he called it), feeling the cold on our cheeks after the heat of the landing, and watching the sleet and snow scurry across the yard as though too scared to settle.

And then it was Thursday, and it was hard to think of anything but the bail hearing. The last session, Cerise had said. The day took forever to pass.

Bantu sensed it. "Don' fret yo'sel', Cully. You be outta here soon enough. Nothin' you can do but sit tight and wait it out."

Which is what I did, though suddenly the twelfth hole on Hell's

Hallway seemed a very small space indeed.

And at lights out, when I still hadn't heard anything, Bantu was the one who kept me calm, made me laugh, talked to me until I couldn't keep my eyes open another minute.

They came for me the following morning, about fifteen minutes before Fat Harry arrived with lunch. Before I knew what was happening, Lehmann was unlocking my cell and asking me to step out, while Collins stood a few feet away, thumbs tucked into his belt, one eye looking right through me, the other roaming around the ceiling.

I felt a great gust of relief. They didn't say anything, but I knew what was happening. I was out of there.

Out on the landing I stepped up to the bars of Bantu's cell to say goodbye and thanks.

He was playing chess like he'd been doing the first time I saw him, hunkered down over the board.

Well, I'm off now, I said, or something along those lines. It's been good knowing you kind of thing. Take care of yourself.

But he didn't move, didn't look up from the board.

Which surprised me. He'd clearly heard what I said, knew I was on my way, and that we wouldn't see each other again. But still he made no move to answer. Just kept his head over the board, dreadlocks trailing through his fingers.

Bantu? I said. Bantu?

No response.

Not really knowing what to do next, I turned away and followed Lehmann and Collins. It wasn't until we reached the end of the landing that I realized what all this was about, what it must be like to get to know someone, then see them released when you've still got to stay on. I began chiding myself for not being more sensitive.

But I was wrong. It was something else.

As Lehmann unlocked the landing gate and Collins ushered me through, Bantu's voice came floating down towards us.

"Good luck with the trial, Mr. First Degree."

I turned and looked back down the row of cells. At first I didn't understand what I'd heard. And then, the next instant, I did.

"You coulda told me is all I'm sayin'. You hear that? You coulda told me, you know."

Amsterdam Slow-Pot

For three, maybe four minutes I felt more alone than I'd ever felt in my life. I'll never forget it – the deep, icy emptiness of it. It was enough to take the breath away. It did mine.

I'd stepped from the shower, toweled myself dry, and pulling on a robe I walked through into my sitting room. And that's when it hit me, stopped me in my tracks. My lips tightened, my stomach churned, and a chill spiraled up my spine. Something terrible had happened here, and the echo of it remained. Even now, a week later, I could still feel the horror, the sense of outrage and disbelief at how DaSilva, Munroe and the two uniforms had pushed their way into my home and changed my life for ever.

Everything was how I'd left it, save a pair of knives from the kitchen, an old trilby hat I rarely wear, my overnight bag that I'd packed for Totnes Bay, my diary and appointments books, and the tape from my Ansaphone, all of which the two uniformed cops accompanying DaSilva and Monroe had bagged and taken away when they arrested me. But the apartment, the place I called home, was different.

I walked across the room, snapped down the open lid of the Ansaphone, and adjusted the four Arcimboldo prints I'd pushed out of line when they'd fixed on the hand restraints. Then looked back at the room. After a week's close confinement at State Correctional, it all seemed absurdly large, the lay-out of the furnishings oddly forced and false as though arranged for someone else. The life I'd once lived there suddenly seemed very far away, very distant. I wanted the phone to ring, the doorbell buzzer to sound, something beyond the dim drone of traffic nine floors below. But nothing happened. The room stayed as silent as the snow drifting and whirling past my windows.

Normally, whenever I came home, I'd sit at my desk, play back any messages, and call Roo. This time that wasn't possible. Instead, I called Sanchez who'd gone out to lunch and would I care to leave a message, asked the switchboard? I recognized the voice of the operator, and while she hadn't recognized mine she'd certainly recognize the name.

"Just say a friend from the 19th called. And he's at home," I replied cryptically, knowing Sanchez would understand.

It was the same with the other numbers I tried. No one at home.

Which was a disappointment. The sound of a friendly voice would have calmed me, brought me back in touch with everything, everyday life, the way it had been. But it wasn't to be. One after another, I dialed the numbers – Daphne at Netherlands, Maude in Totnes Bay, Marilyn Withnell in Copping County, Beejay Wilson, Junior Watson and, finally, Lydia (this last with trembling fingers) – leaving messages on their machines that I'd try them later. Determined to get a hold of someone, I called Susan at her office, giving my name to the switchboard girl and relieved it went unremarked. A minute later Haydn came on the line.

"Mr. Mortimer, how are you?" she said in a kind of awed way, as though she'd never spoken to an alleged murderer before and didn't quite know how to handle it.

I told her I was fine, thanks, and could I speak to Susan?

"I'm afraid Miss Tellinger's in New Mexico. She won't be back in the office till Monday."

A shoot, I asked?

"Well, I shouldn't say this, but seeing it's you. She's on retreat, a kind of spa-lifestyle thing out in the desert. Left at the start of the week. But I'll be sure to have her call you the moment she gets back."

I thanked her and hung up, wondering if Susan really was in New Mexico (on retreat?), or sitting at her desk, flapping her elbows like a chicken to say she'd flown off someplace, so as not to talk to me.

What was it Cerise had said? About friends wanting to see me. Or not. And what I should make of it.

Which is when I went back to my bedroom and looked out some clothes. I had a meeting with Cerise to get to.

It was all about to start.

≈

Cerise had dropped me at my apartment building a couple of hours earlier, recommending a shower and change of clothes, and had told me to be at her office at three that afternoon.

It was Cerise who'd been waiting for me outside State Correctional, and who'd driven me back from Brooklyn.

"You're surprisingly quiet for a man who just got out of jail?"

"I'm sorry. It's just… I think I let someone down, and it makes me feel kind of low."

"Someone in there?"

"The man in the cell next to me."

"Mmmmhh," was all she said. And then: "Don't you go getting soft on me now."

For a while we drove on in silence.

"You didn't ask how the bail proceedings went."

"Well, I assume they went okay."

"Oh, yeah. They went okay. Here." She pulled that morning's *Post* from between the seats and handed it to me. I unfolded it and scanned the front page. Nothing. I turned the page.

"Didn't you see it? Front page. Bottom left," said Cerise.

I turned back and looked again.

"Jesus H!"

The report was no more than a paragraph long with a two-line header: '*Million Bucks – Burger Man Bond*'.

"I expected the TV boys to be out here," she continued. "Probably didn't think we'd be able to raise the money that fast."

"Well, how in hell did you? I don't have that kind of money."

We were stopped at a red light, near the ramp to the Williamsburg Bridge. Across the river the towers of Manhattan smoked and steamed as tatters of low-flying snow cloud snagged their pinnacled heights and softened their outlines. Cerise looked across at me.

"Our mutual friend."

"Lydia? How on earth could she possibly raise a million dollars?"

"Actually, one point two million. Which is why we couldn't come get you yesterday. Lydia had to make some calls. The papers were signed this morning. She's coming to the office this afternoon. So be nice to her."

Cerise winked, the lights changed, and we drove up on to the bridge as an M train hammered by on the tracks above us.

≈

I'd expected Lydia to be waiting for me at Cerise's office which I got to right on time, showered, shampoo'ed, shaved, and snug in a black polo neck, tweed jacket, and thick green cords. But when I was shown through into Cerise's office there was only Cerise, coming round from her desk to greet me.

"I don't hardly recognize you," she said, letting go my hand and indicating one of the two chairs facing her desk.

"I thought Lydia was going to be here," I said, getting settled. "I called her from the apartment soon as I got in, but there was no reply."

"She'll be here, don't you worry," said Cerise, explaining how Lydia had been delayed. "You can say all your thank-yous then."

"I still don't understand about the money. I mean, I knew she had a trust, that she didn't have to work. But a million dollars?"

Cerise looked at me carefully. "Like I said, Cully, there's a lot you don't know about Lydia Langhorn. Maybe now's the time to find out. But let's get on," she said, returning to the chair behind her desk, reaching out and punching the intercom. "Willa, can you get Buzz up here?"

"I'm here already," came a voice from behind me, the words accompanied by a friendly double tap on the open door.

I turned to see a tall, rangey-looking man come into Cerise's office. He was long-limbed and broad shouldered, had pale blue eyes, short sandy hair sharply parted, and the tiniest ears I'd ever seen, like little wind-dried oysters. He must have been in his mid-forties but he still had the body of a college jock.

"Buzz, great timing. I'd just got to you. Cully, meet Basil Daverson. Buzz for short."

"Cully. A pleasure," he said, wringing my hand and then dropping down into the chair beside me. "You've sent me to some of the finest restaurants in this city I never knew existed. So, thanks for that. And for the laughs. You always make me laugh."

So unexpected. So gratifying. I liked him on the spot.

"Ah, I should explain," said Cerise. "Buzz works for us in situations like these."

"'Situations like these'?"

"I'm an investigator," Daverson explained. "I work full time for Chase McKay. Sometimes the firm needs a little inside information. Cerise likes to say I get around quicker than most." He glanced at Cerise for confirmation, and then turned back to me. "Apparently you have some names you'd like me to check out."

I looked across at Cerise.

"Buzz and I decided it's probably better you handle the people you know. The ones closest to you, people who are friends. If it's alright with you, Buzz'll deal with the rest?"

Of course, I said, and gave him the names and background of Rudi, Bruno ("he keeps a gun in a shoulder holster," I warned him), and the staff at Beartree. As I spoke, he pulled a notebook from his pocket and started jotting down the details.

"Bear as in grizzly, or bare as in buck-assed?"

"Grizzly, Buzz," said Cerise. "As in tear your arms off."

Daverson chuckled. "And just for reference, you don't mind my asking, who're the people you're going to be dealing with? In case there's any cross-over."

Feeling a little foolish, and not a little uncomfortable, I went through my roster of suspects: Daphne and Elliot Winterson, Susan Tellinger, Casey Webster, Avery Blanchard – calmly listing five friends I had no choice but to consider capable of betraying me. Which said a lot for my friends and, I guess, a lot about me.

Which is when Willa buzzed through to say Miss Langhorn had arrived, and my heart beat a double tattoo. Cerise said to send her on through, and the three of us turned expectantly to the door.

And there she was, breezing into Cerise's office, wide-eyed and smiling, blonde curls tumbling round her face. Before I'd even gotten to my feet, she'd dropped her old backpack on the floor, was across the room and hugging me to her as though, after many years of searching, she'd finally located a lost family member.

"Oh Cully, you can't imagine how happy I am to see you." She stepped back, holding me out at arm's length. "How are you? You look great. I thought you'd look ghastly, but you look great."

"Lydia, I…" I couldn't speak.

"Cully's feeling a little embarrassed about the bail money," said Cerise. "And surprised."

"Why, that's nothing. Goodness me, Cully, did you imagine for a single moment I'd see you locked away and not do absolutely everything possible to get you out of such a horrible place? Why, silly you. What are friends for?"

At which point, I'm ashamed to say, I did blub a little and clawed her back into my arms, feeling not a little emotional and foolish for it.

"You can't imagine…"

And so it had gone. The tears, the hugs, the looking at someone with new eyes – a real, true friend.

After we all sat down again – Daverson surrendering his chair to Lydia and perching on the corner of Cerise's desk – Lydia reached across for my hand and gave me a reassuring smile. "Believe me,

Cully, Cerise is the best goddamn lawyer in this kind of case, so you couldn't be in better hands. And I intend to be as much help to the both of you as I can." Still clasping my hand, she turned to Cerise: "How long do we have by the way?"

"I don't have dates yet," replied Cerise, "but we're looking around Easter is my guess. Bixon, at the DA's office, just can't wait to get moving." And then, turning to me. "But don't take it personally, Cully. It's the *Times* and Player Leland they're really after."

"How so?"

"Like I said, if you read your paper's editorials you wouldn't need to ask," replied Cerise with a wry smile. "Seems your Mr. Leland has something of a grudge against City Hall – licensing, building zone stuff, that sort of thing."

"Some major, major problems with a building extension application for a printing works in the Bronx that got turned down," Daverson chipped in.

"And for the last six months or so," continued Cerise, "the *Times* has gone out of its way to get its own back – rising crime figures, falling convictions, police corruption... you know the kind of thing. But now it seems the boot's on the other foot. The fact that you work for the *Times*, that you've been a guest of Mr. Leland's – 'personal friend' is how they'll tag you, by the way – and that you also happen to be charged with the gruesome homicide of a call-girl is almost too much for them to resist. Plus, like I told you, there's elections coming up and Bixon knows he needs to score some points for City Hall.

"Now we've got two options here, guys," explained Cerise, moving on. "Either we sit tight, wait for the trial, and have a jury decide on Cully's guilt or innocence. Or we do something about it. Try and get to the bottom of this." Cerise paused and looked at each of us in turn. "And if it's the latter, we're going to have to move fast."

≈

Which is why, the following Monday, only a few days out of State Correctional, after a weekend during which Lydia rarely left my side, I found myself in the back of a cab I'd flagged down outside Amsterdam Station, following a snow-banked road that, with Elliot at the wheel, we'd flown along more times than I can count.

Netherlands, appropriately, keeps itself to itself, and it's not till the last moment, when the country road leading to it has thinned to a ribbon, that the house flickers through the trees on your left and you know you've arrived. It also never loses its capacity to thrill, for it is a marvelous house, robust, red-faced, and ivy-mantled, its white detailing of shutter, gutter and window frame sparkling like sugared icing on the rim of a ginger snap. When we turned through the gates, I swear the cabbie whistled.

With a rich satisfying scrunch of gravel, we pulled to a stop in front of Netherlands' portico'ed front entrance. Telling the cabbie to wait, I got out and headed over to the door, trying to ignore the wave of anxiety that rolled through my mid-section. This was the first time I'd played detective, and I wasn't enjoying the role. It all seemed so school-boyish. Daphne? We were friends, for goodness sake. How could I possibly imagine…? But by the time I pulled the bell-chain, I'd managed to shut such thoughts away.

It had been Cerise's idea to arrive unannounced, and it had seemed a good one at the time. But the plan didn't appear to be working. After waiting a reasonable time, I pulled the bell-chain again but there was still no answer, no sign of life beyond the beveled glass panels of the front door.

Pulling my coat collar up, I went round the side of the house to the terrace where an age before Daphne had staged her firework display. The flagstones had been shovelled clear of snow, but their surface glistened icily in the pale sunlight and grated underfoot. Keeping close to the house, I looked through into the morning room, through the French windows down the length of the hall, and then into the dining room. But they were all dark and silent and empty.

"Mr. Mortimer, sir?"

It was about as bad a shock as the one I got when Roo came out and surprised me on her balcony. My body just seemed to disintegrate with one heart-wrenching shudder, snatching away any possibility of coherent thought or action. Standing right behind me was one of Daphne's two gardeners – Willings or Billings or something – a snow shovel angled over his shoulder.

"Thought it was you, sir," he continued, "and sorry if I surprised you some. But ain't no one home 'ceptin' Miss Dottie. You'll find her in the kitchen, sir. But no need to tell you that, I s'pose." And with a tip of the fingers to his old wool hat, he ambled off across the garden.

The kitchen was on the far side of the terrace, through an arched brick gateway that opened into a walled garden, and lights shone from its windows, even that early in the afternoon. Stepping up onto the terrace beneath a trellis strung with the thin winter branches of jasmine and honeysuckle that gave those distant summer evenings such scented delight, I peered through the windows. Dottie was standing with her back to me at the far end of the room. I tapped on the glass to let her know I was there, and pushed open the door.

After the sharp chill outside, the kitchen was blissfully, snugly warm, lights glowing off a range of copper-bottomed pans hung from the ceiling, and sparkling off blue and white china decked out along the shelves of a mighty kitchen dresser. There was a smell of bread baking, coffee perking, and a host of savory aromas. Aunt Jem would have been in her element.

But Dottie still had her back to me, hulling gooseberries by the look of it, swaying at the counter and humming lightly. She was wearing her latest Nike trainers (given her each Christmas by the boys), her usual striped cotton uniform, a thick jumper and white apron, its ties swaddled out of sight in her wide, woolen hips. And then I saw the headphones. She hadn't heard the doorbell, hadn't heard the tap on the window, or the kitchen door open, and wouldn't have known I was there had not Lutyens lumbered out of his basket with a grunting bark, brushing past her to snuffle around in my crotch, as he always insisted on doing with anyone who'd let him (I remember once accusing Daphne of actually training him to do it – for her entertainment – which had made her roar with laughter).

By the time I'd calmed Lutyens and wiped the slobber from my zip, Dottie had turned from the counter and was pulling off her headphones.

"Why, Mr. Cully, suh," she said, laying them beside a Discman on the scrubbed, scarred chopping table she was working at. "I do believe you done caught me day-dreamin'. There I wuz, listenin' to Ella, and it was like forty year ago, I do declare."

Which was the moment she gave me that look, the one I would come to recognize in the weeks ahead – even now, come to think of it. That certain look, that subtle re-focusing, usually followed by a minute change in the tone and pitch of a voice, as the connection was made. Cully Mortimer. Murder. Prostitute. That afternoon with Dottie, I remember, was the first time I saw it and recognized it for what it was.

I could also see she knew that I'd spotted it, and for a moment she looked a little flustered. But she quickly collected herself and, giving me a long appraising look that could have taught Fat Harry a thing or two, she said: "And just look at you, there, just thin as collards and white as icin'. When you last have yourself somethin' proper to eat, you don't mind my askin'?"

I told her I couldn't actually remember.

"Well, here," she said, coming round the table and pulling out a chair, "sit yourself down there while I fix you up some late lunch. I'm assumin' that'll be fine by you?"

"Well, if it's no trouble…"

"No trouble. No trouble, at all. No, suh-ree. Not at all. Nice to have the company."

I shrugged off my coat and she took it from me to hang behind the door, with a great deal of tut-tutting at 'the very state of you'. Tugging off my scarf, I settled myself gratefully at the table.

"So where is everyone?" I asked, thinking Daphne must have gone into Amsterdam for some shopping, or maybe lunch someplace with friends. "I was hoping Daphne might be around. Is she likely to be back any time soon?"

Which is when I discovered that Daphne wasn't even in the country.

"Why, Miss Daphne's gone off in Germany," replied Dottie, busying herself around the fridge. "Seein' Miss Shelley, she is, and doin' herself some shoppin' I'd guess."

Germany, I thought? It was the first I'd heard of it. The last time we'd met, Daphne hadn't said a word about any trip to Europe.

Dottie came back to the table with a tray, and set it down in front of me – a bowl of white-capped, scarlet-bellied winter radishes, a half-dozen slices of Dottie's own smoked venison *carpaccio*, and a tub of her country chutney. She drew out a chair across from me and sat herself down, watching me scoop up some chutney with a slice of the venison and chase it with a bite of radish. Flavors exploded in my mouth: the sharp, peppery radish; the warm, gamey smoothness of the meat; and the rich, spicy thickness of the chutney. I hadn't eaten anything like it for what seemed like months. And as I ate, I could feel her eyes on me.

When she spoke, her voice was sympathetic.

"Couldn't help but see you been havin' a time of it recently," she began. "Read about it all in the noose-peppers. Hard not to. And TV." She paused a moment, took a look to see how I was taking the directness of her approach.

I nodded, shrugged, my mouth full, tried to let her know it was okay for her to proceed.

Which she did. "And I'll tell you straight, Mr. Cully, I don't believe not a single, skewered word on it. Why, if you could do all them things they say you did, then you wouldn't have no darn trouble keepin' that hound-dog out of your privates or offen your leg, is all I can say."

Which, as well as being gratifying to hear, made me laugh, and put a tight little smile on her face.

"Maybe I should give you the District Attorney's telephone number and you can tell him that. Should make all the difference," I teased, taking up another slice of venison with a dollop of chutney.

And then, lightly, hoping Dottie wouldn't notice, I slipped into detective mode.

"So what about Daphne? What's she had to say about it?" It was the kind of question I could easily have been forgiven for asking. It was hardly prying.

"Tell the truth, Mr. Cully, I don't know whether Miss Daphne done heard about it. She left before you hit the headlines. Must've been… ooh, couple weeks ago now."

"Around New Year's?"

"There'bouts. The first or second maybe." Her brows gathered as she gave it some thought. "Now just hold on. I remember I'd got back from stayin' with my sister in Amsterdam the day before so, yes, she musta left the second. A weekend, it was. Here one minute, gone the next."

So Daphne had been in the country when the murder took place. And had left in a hurry a few days later. I didn't know what to make of that.

Which was disappointing. I'd hoped to establish an alibi for Daphne right off. I was certain she had no place on my list of suspects, and I was keen to see her eliminated from my enquiries. It was one of the reasons I'd decided to make Netherlands my first port of call. But given the dates, and the suspicious speed of Daphne's departure, well, there was nothing I could do but keep her on it. And, more frustrating still, I'd have to wait till she got back from her trip to take it any further, though I was sure, facts and alibis aside, that I'd just need to look her in the eye to know whether she was involved.

But in the meantime, sitting there with Dottie, I realized I could at least establish some frames of reference, what Daphne and Elliot had been up to, where they both were, around the time of Roo's death. And maybe, too, I thought, even settle this thing here and now, with no need to confront either of them. All it needed was Dottie saying that Daphne and Elliot had been there, at Netherlands, the night Roo died.

The important thing was not to alert Dottie. She was sharp as lemons, I knew well enough, and if she thought for a moment I was prying she'd have me up and out of that kitchen quicker than a mouse with a cat on its tail.

"Any idea when she's getting back?" I asked.

Dottie shook her head. "Didn't say when. Just went."

"And Elliot? Did he go, too?" I tried to make it sound disinterested, just chat.

"You ain't spoken to Mr. Elliot?" Dottie asked, with a squinty kind of look. As though she was surprised I hadn't. I could feel the skin on my neck start to pucker.

I shook my head, and told her 'no'. "Haven't seen Elliot, or Daphne for that matter, since... let's see now, early December, I guess."

We'd gone to the opera together and had dinner after. Knowing what I did about Elliot made it a difficult evening, and while he was getting us drinks at the Crush Bar during intermission, I'd asked whether Daphne had heard anything from her private eye? She'd smiled optimistically, crossed her fingers as though to say 'nothing yet', and I'd left it at that.

Which surprised me. I mean, nothing from an investigator after, what, four, five months? Either he was taking her for a ride, or Elliot had been very, very discreet. Which, after La Gave, I couldn't believe. Or perhaps Roo had been telling the truth? Perhaps she and Elliot had called it a day, and there was nothing for the investigator to dig up.

Dottie got up from her chair, reached across for the empty plates – the radishes, *carpaccio* and chutney quickly snapped up – and took them over to the dishwasher. "There's still some stew left from lunch," she said over her shoulder, loading the plates. "Won't take but a minute to warm up? Dumplin's could be a mite hard, but they'se still dumplin's."

That would be just dandy, I told her, and watched as she opened up the oven, took out two tins of glorious cornbread, and slid a big old Staub casserole dish back in their place.

While the stew warmed, she busied herself with the bread, knocking the loaves from their tins and laying them out on a wired cooling tray on the table. The scent was monstrously good, and I wondered whether a slice or two would find its way onto my plate with the stew. Without asking, she poured me a glass of wine and set it before me.

Sensing there'd been something left unsaid, thinking about her squinty look when I mentioned Elliot, I took a deep breath.

"So tell me. Elliot. Is he around?" Again an innocent enough question.

"Oh, he's around," replied Dottie, going back to the counter and returning with the bowl of gooseberries she'd been hulling when I arrived and which, settling in her chair, she took up again now. There was, I noticed, something dismissive in her tone of voice, and disapproving in the set of her shoulders, as she dipped into the bowl, both of which served to alert me.

"Here? At Netherlands? I didn't see his car."

Very easy, easy does it, I thought. Something's coming, something's coming. Don't frighten her off now.

"Not here, no suh. Mr. Elliot ain't been here since Christmas." And then, after further deliberation: "It's not my place to be sayin' anythin', you understand, Mr. Cully. But I been here long enough to have myself opinions, and speak them when I has a mind."

I nodded agreement, and sipped my wine, deciding that talking about Daphne and Elliot was probably a whole heap easier for Dottie than having to talk about me and the mess I was in. And, if I was lucky, I'd get her, sooner or later, to tell me all I needed to know to cross Daphne and Elliot off my list.

"I don't know what Daphne would do without you," I said. "Or Elliot, come to that."

Dottie didn't rise to the bait straightaway. Instead, she got up from the table with a "Stew should be 'bout ready", pulled on oven mitts, and a moment later brought the old Staub back to the table. The moment she lifted the lid and steam billowed upwards, I knew in an instant what the stew was – Dottie's famous Slow-Pot, somewhere between an Irish Stew and Norwegian *Lapskaus*, with salted beef in place of lamb.

"You want some cornbread with that?" she asked, as she ladled out a helping into one of Netherlands' blue and white bowls and passed it across the table. "Just done bakin' it. Should be cool by now."

"You're spoiling me, Dottie, you truly are."

She pulled a bread knife from the rack, carved off a wedge and laid it beside my bowl, its golden, spongey heart steaming.

"Seems to me you're in line for some spoilin', Mr. Cully. Reckon you deserve it after what you all been through… Not like some's I know," she said, settling the lid back on the casserole and returning it to the range.

"You mean Elliot?" I asked, with a lightness I didn't feel. "So what's he been up to now?"

I took my first mouthful of stew and closed my eyes appreciatively, as though to imply I was more interested in the taste of her stew than in any revelations she might have about Elliot. Frankly, it wasn't an easy balance to pull off but I must have managed it. The deception worked.

"I knowed Mr. Elliot since he first come here, when Miss Daphne's mother was still alive, and a fine gentleman he always been to me," she replied, coming back to the table and her bowl of gooseberries. "Couldn't take that away from him, no suh. But he always been a scallywag, you ask me. And seems old habits dies hard."

"Now, Dottie, you really are confusing me. What on earth is all this about?"

Dottie gave me a look across the table, stern and disapproving. "Seems Mr. Elliot's got hisself a lady friend. Miss Daphne done found out about it just afore Christmas, and there's no need me telling you all the fuss and hullabaloo that brought down upon us. No suh."

"I don't believe it," I said, but not too convincingly, not wishing to sound as though I really didn't believe her. So Daphne *had* found out. The private eye *had* tagged them. "Another woman? Is it serious?" I asked, realising that Roo must have lied to me about Elliot. Despite her assurances, they *had* gone on seeing each other.

"Serious 'nough for him to be stayin' in town, and serious 'nough for Miss Daphne to hightail it out of here. Lord knows how it's all gonna come out in the wash."

"So what happened, exactly?" I spooned up a dumpling, still light and springy despite the re-heating.

According to Dottie the confrontation between Daphne and Elliot had taken place the Christmas weekend, while I was out at Hyannis. It had been brewing, she said, since the holidays began. The boys had just left for a few days at the boathouse when Daphne confronted Elliot in the morning room. Dottie, who'd been cleaning silver in the dining room, had heard every word. She'd had no choice, she explained. If she'd tried to make for the kitchen to get out of earshot, they'd have seen her in an instant. So she'd stayed put, praying the argument wouldn't spill over into the dining room.

I nodded understandingly, swallowed the last of the dumpling, and set into the stew again.

"Miss Daphne said he should leave right way. Which he did. That Sunday night. He's stayin' in town for now."

"At the apartment?"

"Old one's sold. Got theirselves some new place down the East Side somewheres."

"And Miss Daphne? She stayed on?" I asked.

"I suppose she did. She sure didn't say nuthin' 'bout goin' anyplace. She was here when I left for my break the day after, and she was here when I got back."

"For your break…?" I felt my heart lurch. I knew she'd mentioned her break before, but I'd missed the importance of it.

"Like I said, with my sister in Amsterdam. For the holidays. That week after Christmas."

"So Miss Daphne was here alone? Till the first?"

It was becoming increasingly difficult to hold myself back. Every answer, every piece of information Dottie gave me made me think of another question, and made me desperate to ask it before I lost my train of thought and forgot it. And do it in a way that wouldn't arouse suspicion, or have Dottie clam up. Lord, it was all a mighty effort.

Dottie shook her head. "The kids came back New Year's Eve."

I finished the last of the stew with a dab of the cornbread, pushed away my plate, and wiped my mouth. Slowly, slowly.

"But alone here till then?"

"So far as I knows."

Which was when our conversation was interrupted by a tap on the kitchen window. It was Willings or Billings, the man who'd earlier scared me half to death on the terrace, reporting that my cabbie was getting impatient. Snow was on the way, and he was eager to be back in town.

It had gotten dark by the time I said goodbye to Dottie, thanking her for my late lunch, and for Elliot's new address which she'd written down for me while I pulled on my scarf and overcoat. When she handed me the fold of paper she did the most astonishing thing, she leaned up and gave me a kiss, patted my arm and wished me good luck, told me to come back just as soon as I could.

As we made our way down to Amsterdam, a thin dry snow dancing across the cab's windscreen, I wondered whether the new apartment that Elliot had moved into following his expulsion from Netherlands was one that Roo had found. I was still holding the piece of paper Dottie had scribbled the address on, a page of ruled paper torn from an exercise book. As I tilted it to the window to read the address, I noticed for the first time that there was writing on its reverse side. I flipped it over and, in the lights of downtown Amsterdam, tried to make sense of the words.

Two parallel columns set above a densely-packed paragraph.

Ingredients. Method. Laboriously hand-written in pencil.

It was a recipe. One of Dottie's.

My breath caught. I couldn't believe it.

Nothing less than her Amsterdam Slow-Pot.

As the cab pulled into the station forecourt, I could feel tears pricking in my eyes.

≈

"Look at it positively, Cully," said Lydia, scooping out the last of Mr. Wing's sweet and sour pork and dividing it equally between us. "You've achieved an enormous amount. Just fantastic."

We were sitting in her kitchen on West 14th, a top-floor apartment a couple of blocks back from Greenwich Avenue. It's a sweet little set of rooms in one of those old tenement blocks the City was going to tear down until a group of concerned conservationists, headed by Lydia, petitioned for a stay of execution. The plans had been put on hold and Lydia, who'd fallen in love with the building, bought the next apartment that became available. It was Lydia who'd driven me to the station that morning, and we'd agreed to meet up the moment I got back from Netherlands. Sensing my low spirits, she was going out of her way to encourage me.

"Listen, Cully. You've found out that Daphne and Elliot have split up because she discovered he was having an affair with Roo. Which you didn't know this morning. Which gives her a motive, whether you like it or not. You've also established that both Daphne and Elliot were not together when Roo was killed, and that Daphne had the opportunity to get to town and back again the night Roo was murdered without anyone knowing. Elliot, too, unless you can establish alibis. They sure had themselves good enough motives. And then, right after the murder, Daphne takes off to Germany without a word to anyone. So I'd say you've done pretty well on your first outing. What more do you want?"

What I wanted, I told her, was to cross both Daphne and Elliot off my list. What I wanted was to find out they'd both been at Netherlands the night Roo died, or with friends, or at a party, and were therefore innocent of any involvement.

But after a full day's work as amateur sleuth, I was still no closer to establishing that innocence. Sooner or later, I'd have to confront the two of them and play detective once again. The gentle enquiries, the sly questions, the traps and feints, the whole blessed underhandedness of it all, without at any time giving them any reason to imagine they were being interrogated, in short that I suspected them. If they saw what I was up to and they were innocent, they'd have every right never to speak to me again. And if they were guilty, they'd seal up tighter than a Kilner jar.

Which had put me in miserable spirits all the way back to the city.

Who was I kidding? How was I ever going to pull this off? Not even Dottie's recipe for Amsterdam Slow-Pot had quite made up for it.

"So when are you going to see Elliot?" asked Lydia, as she gathered up our plates. "Get his side of the story?"

"I'll call him tomorrow."

"Why not now?" she said, looking at her watch. "It's not too late. This time of night I could drive you round there…" she picked up the piece of paper Dottie had given me and checked the address, "… fifteen minutes at the outside. No time like the present, I'd say."

Normally, I'd have felt mighty put upon being chivvied along in this manner, especially by Lydia. But I guess that covering my bail gave her the kind of interest in my case which was hard to ignore. So far, Lydia and Cerise had done everything for me. Now it was my turn. Payback time. And even though I didn't much enjoy it I was grateful for their encouragement, their gentle prodding, their kicks in the butt. Without them behind me, I'd probably just have let it all go till the trial, hoping for the best.

Twenty minutes later, we pulled up across the street from a down-at-heel townhouse beyond Tompkins Square on East 6th. There were lights peeping through a gap in the curtains on the first floor. The snow that had chased me down from Amsterdam had gone, and the road glistened in the street lights.

Lydia switched off the engine, and peered across at the building.

"One bell," she said. "I thought you said apartment?"

"The last place they had was an apartment. I just assumed..."

Tsk, tsk, tsk, went Lydia. "Don't assume anything, Cully. You can't afford the luxury," she chided. "Facts. You need facts. This friend of yours, Elliot, may just have framed you for murder. And don't you forget that. You can't let down your guard, not for a minute. And if it means you lose him as a friend – so be it. Real friends would understand."

She rummaged around in her backpack. "Here, take this."

She held out a fist and dropped something in the palm of my hand. It was a small ball of dark, faceted glass – one of Lydia's crystals. She must have seen my expression. "I know, I know. You think it's all silly. But what harm can it do?"

"No harm," I replied, surprising myself and, smiling, I slipped it into my coat pocket. "Thanks."

"You're welcome," she smiled back. "I meant to give it to you this morning but I forgot. It's black tourmaline. Belonged to my mother. It'll protect you against negative energy. I'll wait for you."

There was no traffic at this time of night and within a minute I'd crossed the street and climbed the steps, narrowed by a heap of builders' refuse sacks stacked down one side. For the second time that day I found myself standing at someone's front door, wondering how on earth I was going to manage whatever it took to find out what I wanted to know. And wishing I were someplace else.

I looked back across the street, and I could see Lydia watching from the car. I waved, then turned back to the door, found the bell and pushed it, hoping it wouldn't work or that there'd be no one home to answer it.

But it did, and there was.

"Yes? Who is it?" Elliot's voice.

"Elliot, hello. It's Cully here," I replied, leaning towards the speaker. "Cully Mortimer."

"Cully. Good Lord, Cully." There was a moment's pause. "Well, hey, what a surprise. Er… Come on in, why don't you?" The lock buzzed. "And watch your step."

It was good advice. If Elliot hadn't said anything, I might easily have pushed open the door and missed the pair of wood planks that served as a bridge over a gaping hole in the floorboards.

The place was a mess, a building site. In the light that shone down from the first floor landing, I could just make out a long trestle table laden with tools and pots of paint in the center of an open-plan ground floor room, knotted lengths wires for future sconces curling out of the walls, and great scabs of fresh pink plasterwork that gave off a damp, dusty smell overlaid, I noticed, with a sinuous, inexplicable scent of citrus. A marble mantelpiece rested against one wall, the hearth where it was to be installed a sooty brick hole.

"I'm up here, first floor," Elliot called out.

I assumed he was on the phone, otherwise he'd certainly have come down to greet me. And then I reprimanded myself for making assumptions again. Lydia would have been furious with me. And, as it turned out, she'd have been right to be so. Elliot wasn't on the phone.

I made my way cautiously to the stairs and, testing the banister with every step, I climbed to the first-floor landing, turning to follow the spill of light down a narrow passageway. The citrus smell was stronger here.

"Welcome, welcome," said Elliot, as I stepped through a door-less door frame and stopped in my tracks.

Elliot was lying on a single bed in the center of the room, propped up on a bank of pillows and illuminated by a small bedside light. It looked like a stage set for something off-off-Broadway. Apart from the bed, the rug it stood on, the curtains behind it, a bedside table, an armchair covered in a dust-sheet, what looked like the ghetto blaster from Netherlands, a pile of cassettes and a portable TV balanced on a pile of manuscripts, the room was in much the same state as the one downstairs. A building site. On the floor by the table was the still-to-be-installed entryphone, a wire snaking away into the shadows. He didn't even have to get out of bed to answer the door.

"What on earth...?"

Elliot was wearing a paisley dressing gown over pyjamas, lapels neatly overlapping, grey hair sprung to attention. On one foot he wore a monogrammed slipper and on the other a bulky swathe of bandages. His left hand was similarly bandaged.

"Sorry I couldn't come down to open up for you. But, as you can see..." he gestured to the bandages.

"I can see, alright. Good Lord. What have you done to yourself?"

Pulling off my scarf, I walked across bare floorboards into the pool of light. With his good arm Elliot indicated the dust-sheeted armchair, and I dropped down into it.

"I did exactly what you might have done if I hadn't warned you. I missed that damned plank by the front door. Had a rusty nail open up the side of my leg and, this is the stupid part, as I fell I flung out my hand to try and break my fall," lifting the arm gingerly, "only to put it through a sheet of glass."

"Jesus H.," I said, feeling the faintest first prick of something out of place. For all his relaxed, dismissive insouciance, I detected a certain edge to him, a kind of discomfort it seemed, a pinch of guilt maybe, as though somehow I'd caught him unawares, turning up like I had, without warning.

"My sentiments exactly," he replied.

"I'm so sorry. It looks terrible. Are you in pain?"

"The drugs are pretty effective," said Elliot. "When the leg or arm start to throb, I just knock back a couple of those." He nodded to the bedside table, and a brown bottle of pills beside his cell phone. "Ten minutes later, the pain's gone."

"But how do you manage? Food? Getting about? I mean, you're an invalid."

"I guess that's where I come in."

The voice came from behind me. I spun round in my chair.

Standing in the doorway, arms folded across her chest, was a tall, slender-looking woman with long black hair, crew-neck sweater, pearls and slacks. She looked to be in her mid to late thirties, and her voice bore the traces of a French accent. Suddenly I knew where the scent of citrus had come from.

She smiled at me uncertainly, then looked across at Elliot.

"I'm sorry, darling," she continued. "There's no light in the bathroom, and I swear I hear something moving around in there – kind of a… scuttle-y noise."

That 'darling', soft and warm, was all it took. Slip or not, it skewered the both of us. I'm sure Elliot must've flinched, as though caught with his hand in the cookie jar. And if Elliot had been looking at me, he'd sure as hell have seen my jaw drop. I was so stunned it took me a moment or two to get to my feet.

It also took a few moments to order my thoughts. Could this be the woman Daphne had thrown him out for? The woman Dottie had referred to? The one I'd imagined was Roo?

I tried to look a little less astonished. First the state of him. And now the company. And hiding in the bathroom? No wonder he'd looked so uncomfortable. There was I thinking his uncertainty, his jitteriness, had something to do with Roo, when all the time…

The woman shivered, hugged herself tighter, then turned to me.

"So. Elliot? Should you make some introduction?"

"Of course, of course. I'm sorry, how rude," he replied, pulling himself together. "Cully," he continued, hurrying now to do the introductions, as though we were meeting at some publishers' party. "I don't believe you know Gaby. Gabrielle Deslandes. Gaby, this is an old friend, Cully Mortimer."

She stepped forward and we shook hands. I could see at once she recognized the name, maybe even my face.

Elliot saw it too. "You, er, you may have heard of Cully," he said with a certain embarrassed discomfort. "He's been in all the papers."

"And don't forget TV," I added with a polite little chuckle, as though to make light of what she clearly knew about me, as though what she'd heard and read could be so easily dismissed. With nothing more than a self-deprecating shrug, a laugh.

She smiled, said she was pleased to meet me, then went over and perched on the edge of Elliot's bed. As I sat back in my chair, I saw Elliot reach for her hand. The 'darling' had, indeed, done it. No point now, I suppose he thought, in trying to cover up. But I could see he was still not sure of his ground. His discomfort, I have to say, was just exquisite.

"I'm so sorry to barge in like this," I continued, not sorry at all, beginning now to feel a little more sure of myself. I could sense an advantage here, and knew it was mine. "You should have said something, Elliot. I didn't realize you had company... Maybe I should've called first. I'm so sorry. So thoughtless."

"No, no. Of course not. Great to see you, Cully. Can I get you a drink or something?"

Gaby made to rise from the bed.

I held up my hand. "No, no. Nothing. Nothing, thank you."

For a moment or two there was silence as Elliot tried to work out how best to proceed. I decided not to help him. This would be interesting. I looked from one to the other, smiling expectantly, as though waiting for one of them to start the ball rolling.

Finally, Elliot cleared his throat. "So, Cully," he began. "Well, what can I say? I guess, er, I guess all this must be something of a shock for you. All this..." He raised his bandaged hand, indicating the room and, by implication, the altered circumstances. And Gaby, of course.

"You could say."

Elliot took a deep breath. It was plain that at that very moment he wished the earth would open up and swallow him. "God, I really don't know quite how to say this."

He looked at Gaby, but she wasn't going to help him either. She had an amused look on her face as though, like me, she was interested to see what he would come up with. I was his friend after all. This was his call. He was on his own. He looked down at their clasped hands, then across at me.

"The fact is, Cully, I... well, I guess you'd say we've split up. Daphne and I. We're, we're... separated, getting separated." He began shaking his head. "To tell you the truth I'd rather hoped, you know, that Daphne might have said something?"

I shook my head and caught Gaby looking at me carefully, as though trying to gauge my feelings.

"Well, look," said Elliot contritely. "I'm really sorry. I mean, sorry you've had to find out like this. So... embarrassing." Elliot turned to Gaby, trying no doubt to order his thoughts as he explained the situation to her: "Cully and Daphne are great friends. Have been for years. It was Cully introduced us, as a matter of fact."

Gaby nodded, and Elliot turned back to me. He looked stricken. "I thought for sure she'd speak to you. One of your lunches. Tell you what had happened."

"Not a word. No. Haven't spoken to Daphne since our evening at the opera. But I knew something was up, which is why I came round."

Elliot gave me a questioning look.

"I was up at Netherlands today," I explained. "I was in the neighborhood and thought I'd drop by. But Daphne wasn't there."

"She's in Germany. Visiting with Shelley."

"So Dottie said. Told me she left in a great hurry, and that you were staying here."

"So it was Dottie told you?"

"Well, not in so many words," I replied. "You know Dottie. But it was clear something had happened. She looked very disapproving."

Elliot made a face – a kind of naughty schoolboy face. "I guess she would. I guess she would. It's all so…"

There was another uncomfortable silence.

"And it was Dottie told me where to find you. Hope you don't mind? Had to twist her arm, of course."

"I was going to ask you about that," said Elliot. "It's just we only got possession a month or so before Christmas… Haven't even had time to send out change of address cards. Not that I'm not delighted to see you," he tried a laugh. "I am. Of course."

"I didn't know you were buying somewhere new?"

"Didn't Daphne tell you?"

I shook my head.

"We started looking… oh, early last summer I guess. Took an age, but we finally found this place and fell in love with it. Early nineteenth-century. One of the first real townhouses."

I looked around the room. "I'd say you've got your work cut out."

"I doubt I'll be having much to do with it," said Elliot, quietly. "And it was always Daphne handled builders. Much more effective."

"So," I said, drawing the obvious conclusion, "it's final, is it? No going back?"

Elliot looked at Gaby, squeezed her hand, then turned to me and shook his head. "I'm sorry, Cully. I really am."

I sighed. "Well, don't be sorry. These things happen, I guess."

I could tell this went down well with Gaby. As though it confirmed their legitimacy. She lifted Elliot's hand to her lips and kissed it.

"But tell me," I continued, "why are you staying here anyway? I mean, it's a building site. Wouldn't you be more comfortable in a hotel? Or with friends. Or..." I looked at Gaby. "I mean... couldn't you... you know, the two of you... move in together or something?"

They looked at each other. Elliot smiled ruefully as he spoke.

"Problem is, ah, Cully, Gaby's husband hasn't yet been acquainted with the facts."

"I see, I see. Yes, I suppose that could make things a little difficult. So, ah, when did this all happen? The accident, I mean."

"Just after I moved in. The Christmas weekend. After the, er, the confrontation. Daphne told me she wanted me out of the house, but that I could stay here until I found somewhere else. So I got a few sticks out of storage," he gestured to the furnishings, "and had them delivered. The first evening here, Sunday wasn't it?" He looked to Gaby for confirmation, and she nodded. "Well, I let myself in, forgot about the hole and fell straight into it. If Gaby hadn't been with me, I'd have been stuck there till someone passed by on the street. I was in Bellevue best part of a week, thirty stitches in my leg, ten in my hand."

Sunday. Bellevue. A week.

It took a few moments to pin it all together, to understand the implications, before I realized what Elliot was saying. For a moment I didn't dare believe it. Elliot had an alibi. And it couldn't have been more cast-iron.

On the night Roo died, Elliot was in hospital.

"But enough about me," continued Elliot. "What the hell's been happening to you? My God. I couldn't believe it when I read about you in the papers. What on earth is this all about, Cully? Hardly your sort of territory, I'd have thought."

And hardly yours either, I thought back, but I didn't say anything. Certainly not with Gaby there. Instead, I got up from my chair, wound my scarf round my neck.

"It's a long story, Elliot. And now is maybe not the time." I said this with a certain tone I hoped he'd pick up on. "Anyway, it's getting late, far too late for visiting sick beds. Gaby, I'm very pleased to have met you."

She came over from the bed and shook my hand.

"Good luck," she said. "If it's any consolation you do not look to me like someone who could do the things they say you did."

"Don't leap to conclusions, darling," said Elliot, gripping my hand in farewell and squeezing it more tightly than he needed to. "The papers say he's a dangerous felon. No telling what he could get up to. It's always the quiet ones," he added, and gave me a grateful, private smile as he released my hand. Whether it was relief at the way I'd received the news of his and Daphne's separation, at the way I'd behaved towards Gaby, or for not mentioning Roo, it was impossible to say. Maybe all three.

And that was it. Five minutes later, having said my goodbyes, I was out of the house, down the front steps, and crossing the street. My feet hardly touched the ground.

Lydia was engrossed in a book on sun signs when I opened the passenger door and slid into my seat. Excitedly, I told her everything that had happened. Elliot was off the list. Even if Roo was blackmailing him, threatening to tell Daphne or Gaby or anyone else about their affair, there was simply no way he could have murdered her – not while he was in hospital, not with thirty stitches in his leg, and his left hand so heavily bandaged.

"Bet you're glad you took the crystal," said Lydia, as we drove uptown. "Two in one. Not bad going, Cully. Not bad at all."

I looked across at her, frowned.

"Two in one? I don't understand."

"Well," said Lydia, "it's hardly likely Daphne's going to kill Roo when the woman Elliot's having an affair with is Gaby. Why bother? If she's going to kill anyone, it's got to be Gaby. Don't you see? She probably doesn't even know about Roo."

And then, slowly, it dawned on me.

"Jesus H. I never..." My mind was racing, trying to fault Lydia's logic, to see if it held up. And it did. "Of course. You're right. How stupid of me. Of course."

It was past eleven when Lydia drew up at my apartment building. I felt suddenly exhausted, but elated too. Not only was Elliot off my list, but it looked like Daphne was, too. And in the same day. A few hours earlier I'd been just about ready to give it all up, but now I felt vigorous, confident, up for anything. I didn't realize we'd arrived at my block until Lydia spoke.

"Don't forget the meeting tomorrow. Eleven o'clock. At Cerise's office."

"I'll see you there?"

"If you want me there. I don't want to get in the way."

"You're not in the way," I said and, leaning across the seats, I kissed her goodnight. "And thanks. I don't know what I'd have done, what I'd do..."

Shush, she said, shush. "Get out of here, Cully, and go get yourself some sleep."

Which, with another grateful kiss on her cheek, is exactly what I did.

Pizza Rusticana

"What do you get for US$12.8 million? And counting."

Cerise Chase had her back to me. She was standing at the window behind her desk, looking west from her high corner office on 6th and 54th. It must have been just a fantastic view at sunset.

This was our second meeting at the offices of Chase McKay and I was the first to arrive, shown through by her assistant, Willa.

Cerise had scheduled the meeting the previous Friday afternoon, the day of my release, suggesting we get together at least once a week, starting Tuesday morning, to summarise and bring each other up to speed on developments: Daverson, on the minor characters in my list of suspects – Rudi, Bruno, the staff at Beartree – and any other matters he was brought in on; me, on my list of suspects, now minus two; Cerise, outlining the legal and political side of things – what the Prosecution was up to, what new evidence had come to light, the discovery of witnesses; with Lydia standing in as go-fer, advisor and, increasingly, comforter and general help-meet.

That first time we met together, Friday afternoon, I'd felt a little uncomfortable, exposed, vulnerable: just out of jail, still a little flushed from a too-hot shower, and scared that everyone I saw – on the street, waiting for a cab, coming up in the elevator to Cerise's office – would instantly recognize me, point fingers, give me a wide berth. I was relieved, and surprised, they didn't, though I have to admit there was a certain mischievous frisson being an alleged murderer walking so freely amongst them.

This time, in Cerise's office, I felt a great deal more comfortable, ridiculously pleased with what I'd managed to achieve – striking Elliot and Daphne from my list as easy as that – and just longing to pass on the news.

Instead, Cerise was talking money.

"Just so long as it's not your firm's standard fee," I replied.

"I wish, I wish," she said, turning away from the window with a "Hey, sit down, why don't you? Make yourself at home."

We got ourselves comfortable.

"No," she continued, "that's just about where we've got to on Miss Beatty Carew's current assets. And I say 'counting' because your friend left very carefully disguised tracks regarding her investments

– across the board, I might add. We've got a broker and financial forensics man downtown going through everything right now and, as of ten minutes ago, when we last spoke, there's still a way to go."

"Twelve million?" I was stunned.

"Could be more by now."

"Cerise, that's ridiculous. Roo was rich, I'll give you that. But not *that* rich. No way. No, no, no… Someone's made a mistake."

"No mistake, Cully." Cerise flipped open a file, lifted a couple of sheets and then, finding what she was looking for, she started paraphrasing the information, looking up every now and again to make sure I was taking it in, to see how I was responding: "Commercial holdings: 10,000 square-foot warehouse space a block back from the Brooklyn waterfront; a two-floor shop/office unit near Battery Park; and a street-front art gallery lease mid-Lexington. Residential properties: a couple of small, two-bed apartments out on the lower East Side; a one-bedroom loft in the Village; and, of course, her own apartment, bought 1996 for just under US$2m, valued for probate sale at US$3.1m."

"I simply can't…"

But Cerise wasn't finished. "Landholdings: 1,200 acres on the western slopes of the Big Horn Mountains on the Montana/Wyoming border; a sixty-per-cent share in a thousand acres around Redmond, Massachusetts…" she shot me a look – we both knew that meant Beartree, "…and a twenty-year renewable short-lease corporate holding in Jamaica, one acre, north shore. Holiday home by any other name."

"This surely can't be right," I protested. "Where… how did you get all this? How?"

Cerise read on: "Directorships of holding companies – the ones we've traced so far – include: Carib Properties; Clennon Mineral Engineering… they own the Big Horn spread," she explained. "Hi-Time Haulage and Limo Services; Phelps Brothers Financing; Relocate Property Services; Tiger Stripe Productions…"

I know I was shaking my head, but it wasn't because I didn't believe what I was hearing. I did. It's just it was all so… unfamiliar, a part of Roo I hadn't even guessed at, despite the clues.

"In addition to property and directorships she'd also been playing the markets. According to one of her brokers – she had three that we know of, by the way – the real action for your Miss Beatty Carew was IPOs."

"IPOs?"

Cerise gave me a look. "Where have you been, Mr. Cully Mortimer? Initial Public Offerings. Specifically, Internet start-ups. In the last sixteen months Miss Carew invested in a whole rash of them. And always very short term. Twenty-four hours. Thirty-six tops. Nothing longer. In and out. A 'flipper', her man at Brittain-Holford called her. A real dot-com dolly."

"You've lost me again."

Cerise shuffled the papers away, leaned back in her chair, and crossed her legs. I could see she was enjoying this.

"Listen up, Cully. Time was you needed to be in business at least three years and show four consecutive quarters of rising profits before going public. In other words you had to have a valid, established and profitable business before you went to the marketplace, with a whole raft of structured plans for development. But that was then and this is now, as they say. Now, it's a whole new ball-game. Especially in tech-related fields. Computers. The Internet. Now all you need is an idea, and you go public to get the funding to develop that idea. Before you even turn a dime. Which is what IPOs are all about. Basically, of course, it's hype. Whispers. Rumor. Stock can go crazy. 200-, 300-, 400 per cent rises in a day. Often far more. Get in at offering price, and there's a killing – no, a massacre – to be made for the savvy investor. But you got to be prepared for a downside. These are not established businesses. Which is why you don't hang around long. Like I said – in and out."

"And this is what Roo was doing?" I asked, recalling all the financial titles on her bookshelves, and suddenly remembering her client in the brokerage house off Wall Street.

"I'll tell you what her man at Brittain-Holford told me. Just the one example. Last Fall, your friend invested in a company called SoffNet. com. It was priced pre-trade by Goldman Sachs at 16 and opened at 22. Roo got 2000 at 24. By mid-afternoon, an hour before close, it had gone up to 63. When Roo bailed out it was 53. Can you do the math?"

I must have looked dazed.

"Near enough US$60,000 gross profit after fees and commissions. In a single day. No, less than a single day. Maybe eight hours."

"Jesus H…"

"Of course, you've got to have the money to play this game, and it appears she did take some pretty substantial losses in the beginning – which is maybe why she wasn't giving up the day job. But she clearly had sound information coming from somewhere, and my guess is it wouldn't have been long before she *really* hit the big time."

Cerise leaned forward to consult her notes again: "Since the last quarter of 1996 she's managed to see a year-on-year increase in her investment portfolio from an average 17 per cent per annum to nearer 30 per cent." She pulled off her glasses and tossed them onto the desk. "That's hedge-fund territory, Cully. The real deal. This was a very smart young lady. How old was she? Thirty-something? And working solo? Remarkable."

All I could think of was what Roo had told me at Beartree: '*Being a call-girl? For me, right now, it's just the gas that makes the motor run. You got cash-flow problems? You need a few thousand to keep things straight? Short on wages, tax, keeping the contacts happy, that kind of stuff? That's why. And there's nothing easier, Cully. A pair of scissors. Snip, snip. And you've covered yourself in a shortfall month. Others go down for less.*'

But back then I had no idea she'd been talking about a range of interests that Cerise was conservatively estimating in the millions.

"And then there's the jewelry," continued Cerise, reaching for another sheet of paper. "Citibank came forward the week the newspapers disclosed her various aliases, with four deposit boxes at two separate branches, each one filled with a stack of baubles – necklaces, bracelets, rings, brooches. You name it. Estimated value – a little under a million dollars."

Cerise looked to me for a reaction. I could only shake my head, thinking of the tiny emerald studs from G. H. Truscott on Fifth that I'd given her for Christmas. Two thousand bucks. Small beer. And she'd seemed so delighted with them. I wondered where they were right now.

"You ever look closely at the pictures in her apartment?" asked Cerise, shuffling through more pages, finding what she was looking for.

I remembered the nudes in Roo's bathroom, and a few of the paintings in the main room: the water-colors, the beachscapes, and others I hadn't recognized.

"Well, let's get the ball rolling with six original Aristide Maillol engravings. Christie's New York, who are valuing the contents of her apartment…" Cerise ran her finger down the page, "…suggest a minimum reserve for the set at $120,000. Which means they'll likely go much higher. Miss Carew also had a pair of small Stubbs, three Hewkins, a couple of Basquiats, and what their Russian expert calls a very fine collection of Imperial Tsarist snuff boxes." Cerise dropped the papers onto her desk. "The list goes on and on."

"Is there a will?" This from Lydia who, with Daverson, had snuck in half way through the report, with a "Hi, Lydia, Buzz. Take a seat," from Cerise, and a smile and a nod from me.

"As a matter of fact, there is. With four main beneficiaries: Her brothers and sisters. Dominic, Catherine, Jean and Quinn Carmichael. The problem is, it looks like the IRS will spend quite a while going through her portfolio for tax liabilities. Not to mention the SEC. Possible insider dealing, improper use of planning information, you name it – and on a wide scale. But all very cleverly done. Pillow talk, who knows? She plays the bimbo, and her clients show off. It happens. Whatever. The point is, any legacy could be a long time coming through."

For a while we sat in silence, absorbing this flood of information. Apart from the actual details of Roo's financial life – staggering though they were – what suprised me most was how on earth Cerise and Daverson had gotten hold of so much information in such a short space of time. They knew more about Roo in a couple of weeks than I'd even suspected in six months. Was there anything they didn't know? And what else was there? What else would they discover?

Suddenly my own successes the previous day seemed pitifully meager. At this rate Cerise and Daverson would have the whole thing wrapped by lunchtime. Thank God, I thought, they were on my side. But then, if this was how they were working at it, what were the Prosecution up to? That was a sobering thought.

"So, a very wealthy young lady," said Cerise in summation. "Very wealthy indeed. But what I can't get a handle on just yet is how she managed to balance it all? The property, the investments. How did she accumulate enough working capital? Even charging clients top dollar, which according to her records she did, there's a limit in all this. Like

I said, she took some pretty serious losses early on and her property holdings were highly leveraged until only a few months back. But she got through."

"Maybe she did a little blackmail," suggested Daverson. "High profile clients prepared to pay a higher rate to secure absolute discretion for her... services. Only it doesn't. She plays on their weaknesses, puts on the pressure. Gets greedy. Wants more."

"Could be," said Cerise. "Could be. What do you think, Cully?"

"It may sound strange," I said, "but I never knew anything about her financial doings; all this stuff you've told me this morning. The basics, sure. Clients, how she got Beartree, the apartment. Upping the rates, like I told you she did with Susan. But nothing on this scale. I never realized. Never suspected. Frankly, I can hardly credit it now."

"Which is good," said Cerise.

"How come?" I asked.

"Well, for starters it means you're out of that loop. We won't get the DA coming up with some fancy financial motive tying you in which we hadn't considered."

"Does this extend the list of suspects?" This from Daverson. "Clients maybe getting blackmailed? Partners, brokers, advisors... someone's skimming, and she finds out? Confronts them? And they need to cover their tracks?"

"Only if they knew Cully," said Lydia. "And that doesn't seem likely." She looked across at me, and I shook my head. "Of course," she continued, "if they were actively looking for a fall-guy, they could have settled on him by chance, just because he was around, you know. But it seems far more likely it's someone who knew Cully personally. As we agreed Friday."

Cerise glanced at her watch. "So, where do we go from here? How's the suspect list going?" She looked back at Daverson.

"I'll have the two drivers Cully mentioned in the next couple of days," he replied. "And I'm booked in for Beartree this weekend."

"Take someone with you," said Cerise. "You can charge it. Anything else?"

"Her passport. Or rather passports. Four of them, in different names. I got details. She traveled all over. In the last two years there's trips to the Bahamas, Columbia, Mexico, Brazil, and the Caribbean. She's also been to Europe – London, Paris, Rome, Munich..."

No wonder she always looked tanned, I thought.

"Vacations?" asked Lydia.

"If they were, she liked 'em short," replied Daverson, thumbing through his notes. "Never spends longer than four days anywhere. There and back."

"So probably work-related," said Cerise.

"I'd guess," said Daverson.

"My, my. Clients all over." Cerise turned to me: "So how about you, Cully? What have you been up to?"

Which is when I told them about Elliot and Daphne. How Elliot had been in Bellevue ("I'd better check that for you, Cully," said Daverson, noting down the dates); and Lydia's belief that if Daphne had found out about an affair with one woman, she was hardly likely to kill another. She'd concentrate on the serious contender. And that was Gaby Deslandes.

When I'd finished my brief resumé, Cerise sat back in her chair and smiled a *well-well-well-I'm-impressed* sort of smile, which made me feel rather good.

"So," she continued. "Who's next on your list?"

"Susan," I replied, without really thinking about it. "Susan Tellinger."

$\approx$

The last time Susan and I had spoken was the morning after Roo's funeral. She'd phoned while I was in the shower and left a message. I called right back. Her voice was still shaky, husky. I knew she'd been crying.

"Did you go? To the funeral?"

I told her I had, and asked how she knew about it.

"I called the City Morgue. Told them I was a copy checker at the *Post*."

I gave a short laugh. "Just like me. They must think the *Post* is pretty stupid."

"Isn't it, though? But look, hey, tell me. How was it? I just couldn't bring myself to go, but I thought about her all day. Just couldn't think of anything else. I still can't believe it. And Belinda Carmichael, for Lord's sake. What was all that about?" There was a brief silence at the end of the line, and then, her words sounding like they were dredged up from the depths of some terrible sorrow, "Oh Cully, doesn't it just all stink? I feel... I don't know... so lost, so... even though... you know... we weren't really going anywhere. And poor *you*. You must hurt real bad... You two were *so* close."

And so we chatted on, like we'd done since the news first broke, keeping our spirits up, and feeling sorry for each other as much as ourselves. As per usual we both cried a little, and finished up fixing a date to see each other for when I got back from my stay with Maude and Jeff MacAuley in Totnes Bay.

Back then, of course, Susan hadn't been a suspect. We were old friends, with a dead friend in common. And mourning. Just that. Now, of course, she was on my list. Had to be. She knew me. She knew Roo. That's all I needed to know. What I had to do now was establish an alibi for her. Or not.

Following our meeting that Tuesday morning at Chase McKay, it was Lydia made me pick up the phone. We'd got back to my apartment around two in the afternoon and were late-lunching on the last of my Milanos. Once again, if Lydia hadn't been there, I'm sure, despite my success the previous day and my increasing confidence, I'd have put the call off.

I was through to Haydn in seconds. I asked if Susan was about, and she told me her boss had arrived back the night before from her retreat in New Mexico, but was still out at lunch. She'd get her to call back soonest. I thanked her, told her I was at home, and put down the phone relieved at the let-off.

It didn't last long. Ten minutes later the phone bleated, and with a couple of clicks Susan was on the line.

"Oh my God. Cully. How *are* you? You're *out*."

"I got bail."

"I read it. The arrest, too. I tried to call, leave a message, but your answer machine wasn't operating."

I told her the police had taken my only tape. I still hadn't gotten it back, or bought a new one. And then: "I thought we might meet up?"

There was a moment's pause at the end of the line, as though Susan was trying to think up some excuse, but then I heard her bracelets clang against the mouthpiece as she put a hand over it. Through her ringed fingers, I could hear her storming at Haydn – one of her contributors trying to stretch a deadline by the sound of it: "Tell him, do it. Or he'll need dental work. I *mean* it. End of the month *latest*." She came back on line. "Sorry Cully, what was that?"

Two hours later I was sitting in the *Rituals'* reception area, thirty floors above Madison Avenue, flicking through the latest January issue. It was quite a shock to see a spread of Tubby in her Dalmation coat tumbling down the sand dune out on the island. And, I thought, closing the magazine quickly and putting it back on the table, just out of shot – Roo.

"Mr. Mortimer. It's a pleasure to see you again."

It was Haydn, just as fresh and preppy as I remembered. I got to my feet. She may have sounded uncertain when we spoke on the phone after my release from Brooklyn, but as we shook hands she held my eye with an admirable steadiness, smiling warmly as though genuinely pleased to see me. "Miss Tellinger said she'll be with you in just a few…"

It couldn't have been stage-managed better. I wondered whether Haydn knew her boss well enough to suspect she'd only been sent ahead to provide some kind of setting for Susan's appearance, now stalking out of the corridor leading to *Rituals'* editorial offices in a swirl of colors and fabrics, one hand clasped round a bundle of files and portfolios, the other pulling off her Chekhov glasses as she came up to kiss me. Since we'd last met she'd dyed her hair white, cut it as short as I'd ever seen it, and gotten herself a soft honey-colored tan, with a scatter of freckles across her nose and forehead. So she had been in New Mexico after all.

"Cully. Cully. It is just so *good* to see you. I can't believe it." Then, turning to Haydn. "Seven o'clock. Can you make it? Get some Krispy Kremes on your way in. We'll breakfast here."

No problem, said Haydn, and turned to me. "Like I say, it was good seeing you again, Mr. Mortimer. And… I guess, good luck. Hope everything works out. I'm sure it will."

It wasn't until we reached the basement parking level and slipped into the back seat of the company limo that Susan got to the point. In the elevator down, all she'd done was fill me in on all the usual horrors that beset her – looming deadlines, tardy writers, arm-twisting advertisers; the whole paraphernalia of publishing a magazine – while I restricted myself to complimenting her on the new haircut. ("A moment of madness, out in the desert," she said, raking her fingers across her shorn scalp). Dumping all her files and what-not on the seat between us, she pressed a button to raise the glass screen between us and the driver, dropped her voice a notch, and locked her eyes onto mine.

"Now, Cully. You and me are old friends. So tell me the truth. I can take it. I'll understand."

"Understand what?"

Susan took a deep breath as though about to submerge, and then let it all go: "Roo," she said. "I've got to know. I won't say a word, I swear. Is it true what they say? Was it you? Did you kill her?"

This, I hadn't been expecting. Our limo came up from the basement, bumped over a ramp and turned into Madison Avenue.

"Susan, you need to ask that? God's sake."

"I'm sorry, Cully. I had to. Right out. I had to know. And I knew I had to see your face when I asked it."

Just what I'd planned to do with Daphne.

"And I believe you." She reached out a hand and covered mine. "I believe you. I really do."

For a moment there, I didn't know what to think. Of all my suspects, Susan had been top of the list, the first name I'd come up with in Brooklyn. She'd bought property off of Roo, she'd had an affair with Roo, become an 'account', and knew only too well that Roo and I were friends, were close, maybe even that we were lovers. But now I wasn't so sure about her. What she had just asked me, what she had just said, was so unexpected, so much more direct than I'd anticipated. If Susan was lying, and she really was Roo's killer, she was putting on an Oscar-winning performance.

"So where should we go?" she asked, looking at her watch.

"Go?"

"Go. Get something to eat. A drink?"

"To be honest, Susan, I haven't been anywhere since they let me out. And frankly I don't think I could handle it. Not yet." Since leaving Brooklyn I hadn't had a single meal in a restaurant. I'd either eaten at Lydia's or at my place. Take-outs mostly. And Netherlands, of course. That was it.

"Then my place," said Susan. "Let's go there. I got some pizza left over in the freezer from the last shoot."

She pressed the intercom and told the driver to take us home, a loft apartment she'd had since her days at the *Times*, then turned back to me, eyes glittering with excitement. "So. Tell me. What was it like? Prison. Run me through it."

Which I did, telling her about my arrest and processing, my cell on C Block, Fat Harry, Bantu, and life on Hell's Hallway (she loved the name), quite content to keep off the serious stuff till we were alone, comfortably settled in her apartment.

Thirty minutes later we were there, spread out on a sofa, waiting for the pizza to heat, me with a glass of red wine, Susan nursing a vodka on the rocks. In a corner of the room, CNN was showing the latest footage of Kenneth Starr giving evidence before the House Judiciary Committee. Susan had the volume turned down in favor of Mozart. She'd kicked off her shoes, curled her feet under her, and was shaking her ear clips in her fist like a baby's rattle. For no better reason than not wanting to sound too keen for details, shooting off questions like I'd done with Dottie and Elliot, I'd decided to let her do the running. She didn't let me down.

"They said in the papers, after you were arrested, she wrote your name. In blood. With her toe."

"Not Roo. Whoever killed her wrote it. But it took a bit of time for the police to figure it out. The blood pooled on the floor and obliterated most of it, leaving them with what looked like 'ULLY'. I saw the photos."

Susan made a grunting sound. "Could as easily have been the 'ELLI' in 'Tellinger'."

Which took me aback. I hadn't thought of that.

"Whatever," she continued, "it was a stupid thing for the killer to do. Pointing the finger like that. Shouldna done it. Shoulda just left it anonymous."

"How so?"

"Because, Cully, writing your name out like they did maybe narrows down the field, makes it easier for the cops – like they don't get the whole city to chase after; it's you; done deal. Except in this case, of course, it isn't. You're not the one. And you and I both know it. Which means… it's gotta be someone you know. Or knows you," she added after a beat.

I shot her a look. "You said it."

Susan nodded, thought for a bit, then her eyes opened wide. "Well, I sure hope you don't think it was *me* killed her. No way, José. I mean, hold on there, Cully. There were maybe plenty of times I *felt* like killing her… I mean that, you know, metaphorically speaking… but I sure as hell didn't."

"Like you said, if it's not me – and it 'sure as hell' isn't – then it has to be someone I know. Why not you?"

"Why not me? Because. Because… it just wasn't." She took a swig of the vodka, and gave me an injured look, as though I couldn't possibly be serious. "I mean, you know heaps of people. It could have been any of them."

"It could only have been someone who knew me – and Roo. And, like you said, that narrows down the field."

"So how many names have you got on your list?"

"Three, four."

"And I'm one of them?"

I nodded. "You have to be."

"Well, don't you go looking at me, Cully Mortimer. I mean, heavens to Betsy! Whatever next?"

Fortunately, I guess, she seemed more amused now by the suggestion than hurt or outraged. Which gave me the nerve to continue. "It wasn't just the name that implicated me."

"There's more?"

"The killer was left-handed, like me…"

Susan started waving her right hand, rattling the ear clips. "Well, that's me off the hook…"

"They also have my prints on the weapon that knocked her unconscious – though that's just coincidence. I picked it up one time. A brass dog of all things." I paused for a moment, watching her carefully. "They also have a letter."

"A letter?" Susan frowned, looked intrigued.

"A letter from Roo to me. A draft, not sent. On her computer. In her e-mail file. And not very flattering by all accounts. With regard to me. Kind of bolsters the Prosecution's case. Ties everything in."

"What kind of letter? What did it say?"

"She wrote I frightened her. That she wanted out, but was too scared of me to say it to my face. Which sounds pretty bad, but couldn't have been true given the way we were."

There was silence for a moment, save the Mozart in the background.

"Were you and Roo… you know?"

I nodded.

"How long?"

"Just a couple of months." I knew what Susan had in mind. "And she wasn't charging, if that's what you're thinking. It wasn't like that."

Susan gave me a look. "You sure about that? You know the way she operated. I told you."

"I know what you told me, but this was different."

She looked at me doubtfully, a little sadly too. "If you say so…"

The timer on the oven started bleeping. Susan uncurled herself and loped through to the kitchen where she found plates, pulled out the pizza, tossed a salad, and brought everything back to the coffee table. Sitting on the edge of the sofa, she started sawing through what looked like a Collio's Rusticana. When she was done, she passed me a plate.

I thanked her, picked up the wedge of pizza and, without thinking, bit into it. A length of scalding onion slapped against my chin. "Jesus H., that's hot."

"Slow down, slow down, *muchacho*. Here," she said, reaching for some tissues and pulling one out for me.

I wiped away the onion. "So," I began. "You got an alibi?"

"You're beginning to sound like the cops."

"You got a visit?"

Susan nodded, tiny teeth chewing off a piece of pizza. "Didn't I tell you? A couple of guys. One was black, good-looking. The other, a weasel. A real charmer. They came to the office a few days after… you know, Roo's death." For a moment Susan's face looked like it might crumple, but she gathered herself quickly. "Of course, I'd been expecting it, knew the cops were gonna come knocking on my door sooner or later. Through Relocate, or my name in her address book."

"Or your purse."

Susan frowned. "My purse?"

"It was found in a drawer in her apartment."

"You're kidding me. Roo had it? I thought I left it in a cab."

"Sometime in October, right? And you were with Roo when it went missing?"

"That's right. We'd been out someplace. Took a cab back here."

"And she paid?"

"I guess… I don't remember…"

"When did you realize the purse was gone?"

"Here. Right here. Like immediately we got in."

"And she told you you must have left it in the cab?"

"Or the bar we were at… I remember she called them, but they couldn't find it, so we assumed it was the cab. So that was that, right?"

I remembered Roo leading the search for Kuto's watch out on the island, and smiled.

"Hey, it's not funny. There was my passport, driver's licence… And a stack of cash, too. For Roo. Had to pay her double the next date… and she had it all the time, goddamn her."

"And the cops didn't tell you? About the purse?"

She shook her head. "Not a word. All they wanted to know was about me and Roo. One question after the other. How long I'd known her. How we'd met. I didn't know what to think. Didn't know what to say. Didn't know what they knew. It was just horrible. I mean, they really made me feel guilty, you know, like I was the killer? So I told them everything. About the house on the island. And, you know, the other. The weasel, he loved that part. Couldn't barely hide that greasy little smile. Ugh." Susan shivered at the memory. "But all they really wanted to know was what I was doing the night… the night Roo was killed."

"Which was?"

Susan was taking another bite of the pizza. She stopped midway. "Hey, you really do think it could have been me, don't you? Not in a million years."

"Well?"

"You want me to give you an alibi?"

"Sure be a help. Either that, or a confession."

"Well, I can't. Either way. Like I said to the cops, I was here all evening. At home. Alone. Had a pile of work to get done. That's it."

Susan finished her pizza slice, bar the crust which she laid on the side of her plate, then leaned forward to pick at some salad leaves, and pour herself another hefty slug of vodka. This time she didn't bother putting the bottle cap back on.

"And what did they make of that?"

"The tall guy just nodded. The weasel smiled." Susan swilled the vodka round her glass, making the ice clink.

"And they left it at that?"

"Just told me not to leave town. They might want to see me again."

"And did they? See you again?"

Susan took a drink, shook her head. "The next thing I know, your picture's in the paper. The Testino one. I couldn't believe it. Nice shot, by the way. We use him, too. He's very good."

"So when did you last see her? Roo?"

For the first time Susan looked uncomfortable, as though this was a metre more trespass than she cared to tolerate. What I was asking was nothing to do with murder, it was personal. But after telling me so much about her and Roo at Spoonlickers, it was a little late in the day for her to start acting coy. And she knew it. She took a deep breath, and seemed to steady herself.

"The cops asked that, too," she said.

I didn't say anything. Her answer wasn't going to provide any alibi but, maybe, I thought, I might be able to identify some kind of motive. Or not.

"I called her, let's see, the day before Christmas Eve. What was that? A Wednesday?"

I nodded. The day after our Christmas lunch at Toucan. I was on my way to Hyannis and the Haddons. For some reason, I was surprised they'd seen each other so recently.

"And how was she?"

"Oh, she seemed great, you know. Really up," continued Susan, her eyes drifting across the room, coming to light on the silent TV screen. "Which is more than you could say for me. Christmas had kind of crept up on me, and I didn't have a thing arranged. *Nada*. A whole week by myself, and all of a sudden I didn't know if I liked the idea. Anyway, we close the office early and I decide right off, without thinking about it, that I want some company. And it just so happened I had the cash." She gave a dry little laugh, bitter as chicory. "So I thought, why not? Let's have some Christmas cheer. So I call her up and say come on over, and she says sure, give her an hour, she had things to do – what, don't ask me. Anyway, she arrives early evening and is real affectionate, which was nice. She seemed in no hurry to get things over with, and get out of here, like she had something else planned for later. So we sat and chatted, like some old friend had just dropped by, and had some wine. Which felt good. Also I had some coke – another Christmas treat – and we shared a few lines." Susan took another drink, rolling the liquor round in her mouth. "Which was when it all began. She started to get a little short with me, which is how things usually got going. It didn't surprise me. I guess it was the way she psyched herself up, you know?"

"How do you mean – 'short'?"

"Short, you know. Business-like. Did I have the money? Give it to me now, sort of thing. Which I did. She counted it, like always, and stuffed it in her bag, then started wandering around the place, picking up this, picking up that, wanting to know where I'd bought such and such, and how much I'd paid. You see that piece over there?" Susan pointed to a glazed terracotta vase holding a dried flower arrangement in the corner of the room. "A Moroccan honey jar. Quite old. Cost me an arm and a leg on a shoot in Marrakesh. One of a pair. That one there, the other in the bedroom."

"And? What happened?"

"Roo is what happened. Asked for it, first off. Said how nice it was, and how she'd like to have it. Call it a Christmas present, she said. I told her it was one of a pair, and no way was I going to split them up, or give her both. I remember I was laughing, as though she was joking. So she just went and tipped it up with her foot, took a great chip out of the rim. I was so mad, I can't tell you. Which is when she came for me, like she always did, when she'd gotten me angry. Just... you know..." Susan, unbelievably, looked embarrassed.

"Know what?"

"Sex, Cully. Sex. She came in on me and just... went for me, then and there. Jesus... that girl... And then, right after, cool as you like, as she's getting dressed, she tells me she doesn't want to see me again. It's over. For good, this time. That's it."

Susan began shaking her head, finished her drink in a single gulp and reached for the bottle. Her lips tightened and tears welled in her eyes.

"At first I think she's playing for more money, like she did the first time. Raise the ante again."

I watched another vodka slosh into her glass.

"But she's not. I ask her if it's that, if she wants more, and she just shakes her head. No, she says. It's just... over."

Which fitted with what Roo had told me she was going to do. She was quitting the game, just like she'd said.

Suddenly Susan looked broken, as though reliving the moment, speaking about Roo in this way, had finally caught up with her, overwhelmed her. That, and the vodka.

"I'm sorry… I'm so sorry, Cully. It's just…" And she leaned across the sofa for me to hug her, hold her as she wept, her new bristly hair scratchy under my chin, the vodka spilling on my sleeve.

When I left a half-hour later, Susan had recovered but the drink was starting to work on her. She was getting maudlin. Which was my fault, I guess. I'd done nothing to stop her refilling her glass, hoping the vodka might loosen her up, maybe make her trip over some detail. But it hadn't. All it did, finally, was make her roll her head, slur her words.

I told her to get to bed, said I'd see myself out, and left her curling up on the sofa, a little tearful, sad, lonely, with a brief kiss on the cheek and the promise that I'd call her. I knew how she must be feeling.

In the cab home, I tried to be a little more objective.

What to think about Susan?

Did I believe her, or not?

Had she killed Roo and framed me, or not?

It was as simple as that.

Well, for starters she had no alibi: I was having supper with friends; I was in bed with a lover; I was working late with Haydn. Any of those would have swung it. It could all have been so easy. But there was nothing. She had less of an alibi than me. So, she certainly had the opportunity.

Next. Motive. So far as I could see she had a pretty powerful one: Roo telling her their relationship was over. Nothing to do with money. Just over. Finished. And Christmas, too. Maybe Susan just got so mad that she just up and went round to Blaise Heights to have it out with Roo, one way or another.

And maybe there was jealousy, too. Maybe, despite what she'd intimated earlier, that she didn't know that Roo and I had been lovers, maybe Susan did know, had somehow found out about us. (Don't ask me how, I was just theorising here; maybe Roo had told her). And the fact we had something going that she didn't, just tipped her over the edge.

But then, if it had been Susan, how come she waited till after the Christmas weekend to go kill Roo? Why not that night when Roo called by, when she tells Susan it really is over? Why the delay? To plan it? To think it through? Put me in the frame?

And then it struck me, as the cab headed north, that if I'd been Susan, trying to deflect my suspicions, put me off the scent, I'd have made damn sure to lay an altogether different trail, paint a different picture. For instance, I'd never have admitted that the last time Roo and I had met it had ended in tears. If I'd been Susan, I'd have made it sound a great deal cheerier, friendlier. Something with a future. I mean, she could have told me they were planning on going to New Mexico together, something along those lines. And without Roo around to contradict her, who was to say they hadn't planned just such a thing? But Susan hadn't said that. She'd told me the truth, that that was how they'd last parted – badly. Like I said, if I'd been her I'd have definitely put a rosier spin on it. Played down the motive.

But she hadn't. She hadn't. She'd told me the truth, how it was, I was certain of it.

Bluff? Double bluff? There was just no telling.

Which meant, whether I liked it or not, believed it or not, Susan had to stay on my list. There was nothing else I could do but keep her there until, I hoped, some other development eliminated her from my enquiries.

≈

My phone was ringing when I got back to the apartment. I picked it up expecting to hear Lydia's voice, calling to find out how the meeting with Susan had gone. Or possibly Susan, good and drunk by now, alone, wanting to talk some more.

It was Elliot.

I knew he'd call sometime, after our brief but illuminating meeting the previous evening, but I was surprised to hear from him quite so soon. Curiosity, I guessed, must have been eating him up. Unlikely as it may sound, Elliot has a real appetite for gossip. Always passing on the latest scuttlebutt during our occasional lunches, or on our drives to Netherlands. And if Roo, as I now believed, had said nothing to Elliot about my having seen them together at La Gave, and if Felix had kept our confidence, it must have been some shock when Elliot opened the papers and saw my name and picture, arrested for the murder of a woman he'd been seeing for the past few months. He'd want to know everything – human nature. Couldn't resist it. So I wondered how he'd play it. As we exchanged greetings, I took the phone to my favorite Pierrepoint club chair and sat down. I had a feeling this would be a long conversation.

"I'm so sorry about last night," I began. "Barging in like that."

"No problem, Cully. It was good to see you again." I recognized a pause. "Even if the circumstances were a little... well, unusual."

"So," I began gently. "You and Daphne."

I could tell immediately that my mentioning Daphne caught him wrong-footed. What he'd called to talk about was Roo, that much was obvious. Everything we hadn't spoken about the night before. Out of devilment, I decided to string it out.

"Yes," he said. "I'm sorry. I know what you must think of it all and, like I said, I'm very sorry. I'm also grateful for your understanding. I wasn't looking forward to you finding out."

"It was a shock, I don't mind telling you. I really thought the two of you..."

"We were, we were. God, I mean it happened so quick. One minute there's Daphne and the kids and Netherlands, the next it's all change. I can hardly believe it myself."

"It was Daphne's private investigator, wasn't it? How she found out?"

There was a pause before Elliot replied: "That's right. How did you know?"

"She told me she'd hired someone. After that weekend at Netherlands. The fireworks? When you had to leave early?"

"Gaby..."

I nodded, switched the phone to my right hand. "I'm sorry. I'm sure you'll understand I couldn't say anything to you."

"Of course. Of course, you couldn't. It must have been awful for you. Very difficult. And I'm so sorry for that."

"She said she thought you were having an affair, and she was going to have you followed."

"I thought I was being discreet."

"Not discreet enough, I'd hazard. Fact is, I saw you once myself."

"You did? Gaby and me?"

"As a matter of fact," I said, getting myself comfortable, the moment approaching, "it wasn't Gaby."

"Not Gaby...? Cully, you've lost me. You really have."

"Someone else entirely." I didn't need to say anything more.

There was another telling silence on the other end of the line. At that moment I'd have given anything to see his face. You could almost hear him struggling to keep up. Cerise would have loved it, too.

"A Friday night," I continued. "Late June, wasn't it? A restaurant called La Gave. Your companion was wearing a red dress. Her name was…"

"Yes. Yes, yes. I know, I know. Shit. I don't believe it. So you've known all along?"

"Known about you and Roo? Yes. But not about Gaby. That rather came out of left field, you don't mind my saying. I thought you and Daphne had split up because she'd found out about Roo."

"Gaby," confirmed Elliot. "There were photos with the report. From the detective. So far as I can tell, Daphne never knew anything about Roo."

So Lydia had been right.

"But what about you, Cully? God, I couldn't believe it when I saw the papers. I never realized you two knew each other."

"Small world."

"You can say that again. But murder? Come on. I mean, who are they kidding? Anyone who knows you would know you couldn't do something like that."

"Remember what you said last night? It's always the quiet ones?"

Elliot laughed. "Cully. Please." And then he grew serious. "So what's it all about? What's going on?"

I told him what I'd told Susan. It was a frame. I had till the trial to find out who was behind it.

There was another pause at the end of the line. "Don't tell me. Which is why you just happened to drop by Netherlands? And then call in on me last night? Check it wasn't Daphne or me. Cross us off your list."

"You're right. That's exactly why. And I'm sorry." And I was.

"Don't be. I'd have done the same."

It was gratifying to hear him say it. A relief. It could so easily have gone the other way. I decided to redirect the conversation. "So how did you two meet? Roo, I mean? How did it all start?"

"A book launch. End of April. She came with the author." He said a name you just wouldn't believe. A real bestseller. Every book straight to number one. "Anyway, we were introduced, you know the kind of thing, got talking, and I happened to mention I was looking for an apartment, a house maybe. And she dug out her card and gave it me. Just like that. I'm assuming you know about Relocate?"

I told him I did. "So you call up…"

"And I get put right through. I tell her what I'm looking for, the kind of money, and she says she's got some things I might be interested in, and why don't we make an appointment to view? So we meet up, she shows me round a couple of places, and then suggests we stop off somewhere she knows for a drink. Well, that was it. I mean, who's going to say 'no' to a girl like Roo? Next thing I know, we're getting to be an item. Once, maybe twice a week."

"When did you find out she wasn't just a realtor?"

"About a month later. She asked for some money. I thought she'd forgotten her pocketbook and needed cab fare. I asked how much she needed, thinking, you know, a ten or a twenty, and she said a thousand dollars. Just like that. A grand." Elliot chuckled.

"And you gave it to her?"

"A grand? Come on, Cully, you know I don't keep that kind of money around. So, pretty stunned by this whole turn of events, I told her I'd have to pay her next time. Talk about walking right into it. I should have just called a halt right there."

"Where were you?"

"An apartment, not far from you actually. Viewing. That's where we did it. Empty apartments. She never took me back to her place, and I certainly never invited her back to ours. Just… places for sale. And only the nice ones. She'd call me, say she had something to show me, and was I interested?" Elliot paused, cleared his throat. "Ah, if I'm being insensitive here, Cully, just say the word…?"

"No. Go ahead," I prompted, and steeled myself. Right now I needed to know everything. Whether I wanted to or not. Like Cerise, the more I knew, the more chance I'd stumble on some clue, make a connection. Elliot might be off the hook as a suspect, but he might know something I didn't.

"Well," he continued, still clearing his throat. "I've got to tell you there's something very… erotic, I guess you'd say, about an empty apartment. No blinds or curtains. No furniture. Nothing. And there she is just slipping the deadbolt and taking off her clothes, you know, or hiking up her skirt. Real on the hoof stuff. I got more splinters and carpet burns I ever had my entire life. But it was, well, wild, you know? One time there's a roll of that bubble wrap left over from the movers? So she spreads it out, takes a tube of cream from her bag, and empties it all over. And that's where we do it, right there, on the wrap; all those little bubbles popping and snapping. I tell you…"

"It didn't bother you, the fact she was a hooker?"

"Did it bother you, Cully? I mean, I'm sorry and all, but we're not talking sequin hotpants on Times Square here. Beatty was something else. Even when I paid her, I never really thought of her as a hooker. She was… special. Wasn't she? I couldn't believe it when I saw it in the paper. That she'd been murdered. And then when they arrested you? Jesus, I didn't know what to think."

"I assume you got a visit from the police?"

"At work, would you believe? At work. Jesus!"

"They asked about Relocate?"

"To start with, so I told them what I knew. An edited version. Miss Carew had shown me some properties, but I hadn't taken up on any of them. Too pricey. Then, right out of the blue, they ask if I knew she was a hooker. Only when I read it in the papers, I told them. Which is when things started getting a little unpleasant. They just gave me this look as if to say, don't waste our time, sonny. They seemed to know everything. How often we met. How much I paid… the kind of things I liked doing. I couldn't believe it. They knew it all."

"She kept a log. Every detail."

For a moment there was silence on the other end of the line. And then, softly: "No wonder someone killed her."

"Why do you say that?"

"It figures, doesn't it? Maybe she was putting the screws on someone? Easy enough for her to do. The kind of clients she had."

"How do you mean? 'The kind of clients'?"

"Well, the money she charged for starters. They had to be up there. Well-heeled, I mean."

"Did you ever know any of them? Did she ever say anything?"

"No way. She was mighty discreet. And to tell the truth, I didn't want to know. That would have… well, spoiled it, I guess."

"Did she ever put the screws on you?"

"Did she tell you that?"

"All she ever said was she knew you. When I told her I'd seen the two of you together. Admitted that you were a client. Then, must have been a couple of months ago, she told me she'd ended it."

"Well, um, that's not strictly true, Cully."

"How so?" For a moment I felt a trickle of uncertainty. Was this another Roo lie? Was Elliot going to tell me something I didn't want to hear? Or needed to hear? I held my breath.

"One word. Gaby. She's a senior editor at Longuevilliers in Paris, and we, Florez Delisle, do a lot of work with them – foreign sales, translations, serialisations. She and I'd speak on the phone, see each other a couple of times a year – book fairs, that kind of thing; London, Frankfurt – and we'd always gotten along. She's a great girl. A real good editor, real smart. Then, start of the summer, her husband, some kind of banker, gets posted to New York, and Longuevilliers ask her to go with him and head up their operations over here. We started seeing each other. It got serious, and I didn't call Roo any more. That was it. It was over. Which was sad in a way, but by then it was two grand a pop. Too rich for my blood, Cully."

So Roo hadn't ended it. Elliot had. I wondered how many other men had ever called a halt. Not many, I'd guess. So, another lie. But one that came loaded with such… vulnerability. Despite myself, I was enchanted by her gentle deception. A man stops calling, and she says she's dumped him. So typical. So… Roo. For a moment there, I had to hold myself tight, grit my teeth. Roo was suddenly bubbling up to the surface.

"So tell me," asked Elliot, "how did you rustle up that bail? A million bucks?"

"I'm sorry…?" I said, pulling myself together.

"I said, how did you rustle up bail? If you don't mind my asking?"

"A friend."

"Would that be male or female?" asked Elliot. I could almost see his grin.

"Lydia Langhorn. I don't think you know each other."

Elliot chuckled. "You and your women, Cully. One day I wish you'd tell me how you do it."

≈

That night I slept badly, dreaming of Roo.

I was back in her apartment, standing by the refectory table, the brass dog clutched in my hand. One of her tall church candles was burning, throwing a gold glow around the room, stretching strange shapes across the floor, and playing against the skylight.

My legs and my arms were trembling, the weight of the dog tugging at my hand.

Bound in the chair, Roo moaned. A line of blood trickled down the side of her face from a lip-like gash in the side of her head where I'd hit her. She was wearing a blonde wig and nothing else. I saw her eyelashes flicker, and her tied hands flex.

Somewhere, maybe from the hi-fi behind the Chinese screen, came gentle Spanish chords plucked out of the shadows.

She moved her head, moaned again, and tried to sit upright.

But my bindings held her tight.

I felt the weight of the dog lighten in my hand, its shape change.

A smooth handle, a long blade catching the candlelight.

I stepped forward, drew back my arm.

And as her eyes opened, so did mine.

Humble Pie

"What I'd like to know," I said, "is how come you're so certain I'm innocent? That it wasn't me killed Roo."

It was a Saturday night, at Lydia's apartment. Cerise and I had come round for supper – a chicken and mushroom pie that Lydia told us was her absolute specialty, the exact same recipe she'd gotten from her mother who'd gotten it from her mother. Baked in a deep terracotta dish, she served it with mashed potatoes lava-flowed with butter, and tiny green peas that she'd simmered in stock and littered with flecks of dried basil. It was a delight. Hot, homely, and soothing on a chill, cowering, wind-whipped last weekend in February.

It wasn't the first time we three had sat there in Lydia's apartment, sharing some dish Lydia was always attributing to some or other member of her extended family and step-family, drinking wine late into the night and, the two of them at least, passing Lydia's small ebony pipe back and forth, tamping down the greeny-brown buds of Lydia's home-grown supply of marijuana, and filling the apartment with a sweet luxurious scent. Though I didn't smoke it myself, recalling my lost night with Roo out on the island, I swear it had a comforting effect on me all the same. Talk about secondary smoking!

Once or twice a week we'd meet up like this and spend the evening together, as though we had no other friends or family to spare time for, no other life beyond the puzzle that consumed us. Since my release from Brooklyn, the three of us had gotten close as tics. Us against the world.

It hadn't always been like that. During the first few weeks Cerise had tried to distance herself from me, as though to preserve a correct and proper client-attorney relationship, I guess. But her friendship with Lydia, she admitted over our first supper together, had made this distance increasingly difficult to maintain. So much so that Cerise had finally conceded that trying to keep her professional and private lives separate was, in this case, simply not worth the bean when her client was the very good friend of her very best friend.

Which explained Cerise's comfortable familiarity with Lydia's apartment – which drawer, which cupboard, which switch. Right away I'd spotted how well she knew the lay-out, how familiar the place was to her. She didn't need to be told where the bathroom was and, when Lydia asked her to fetch a ladle or the salt or the corkscrew, Cerise knew exactly where to look. As though the two of them actually roomed together. Which, of course, they didn't.

They were also deeply affectionate with one another, caring in the way old married couples make look so easy, so natural. Indeed, so close were they that at one time, early on, I even began to wonder – Cerise's absent husband notwithstanding –whether they might have been, or might still be, lovers. It was just the kind of arrangement I imagined Lydia might lean towards – something that suited her softly feminine character. She'd always looked too fragile and too delicate to handle or tolerate a man's ugly grappling, and in all the time I'd known her I'd never been aware of anyone significant in her life. But then, as Cerise had informed me the day we first met, there was a great deal I didn't know about this remarkable, tireless, and loyal friend. As it turned out, of course, they weren't lovers, past or current, just the very best of friends.

And my two staunchest allies.

Looking back I don't know how I'd have gotten through it all without them. I'd have been lost, cast adrift. Hardly a day passed without some kind of communication between us: phone calls, e-mails, the regular weekly meetings at Cerise's office, suppers at Lydia's, after-work drinks at a bar around the corner from Chase McKay's offices, with Lydia always on hand to drive me wherever I needed to go, goading me on, encouraging me – just always there, you know? My cause was their cause, and their enthusiasm for the chase, for its successful conclusion, sometimes made my own determination look pretty threadbare.

That Saturday supper we'd covered the usual ground, discussed how things were going: my meetings with Susan and Elliot, and the sudden and satisfying elimination of him and Daphne from my enquiries; my less than satisfying efforts in tracking down Casey and Avery; and my upcoming trial now slated for mid-May, according to one of Daverson's numerous contacts in the District Attorney's office. As Cerise had warned, with elections looming City Hall were desperate to pull off one last sure-fire, high-profile case. Mine.

That February evening, we'd also just chatted, table-side chat, about all kinds of other things. The Clinton-Lewinsky scandal, of course:

"He shouldna done it, simple as that," from Cerise. "And he should not have lied."

"He's in crisis; I feel for him, I really do," from Lydia.

"Was Monica always so… large?" from me. "Did you see that shoot Susan did of her in *Rituals*?"

I remembered, too, for an instant, a memory hastily bundled away, something Roo had told me about fellatio in our cabin bed at Beartree: "Forget the mouth, it's all in the fingers, Cully; thumb and forefinger. Work miracles, believe me. You wanna see?"

And then there was Lydia going on about one of her books. She went through books like a *patissier* goes through butter, always consumed by them. This one, the latest, was something about arctic exploration that made her want to "pull on snow-shoes and just go there, do it".

"Too cold," said Cerise, "for your warm blood. Don't you agree, Cully?"

And then me telling them how, a few days earlier, I'd been surprised by a *Post* photographer outside my building: "And then, immediately afterwards, this woman passing by on the sidewalk comes back to ask for my autograph. I ask her why she wants it and she says because I'm famous. And then, already suspecting the answer, I ask if she knows who I am. And she sort of giggles and says, 'Not rightly, no. But he sure does', meaning the photographer. And that was enough for her. In New York. I mean, really! Can you believe it?"

Which was about when, while Lydia cleared away our plates – not a scrap of pie remaining, not a crust of pastry left on the rim of the dish – I decided to ask Cerise how come she was so certain it wasn't me killed Roo?

It was something that had always bothered me. How could Cerise be so sure of my innocence? How could she just accept it so unequivocally? Unconditionally? Sure, she'd asked some tough questions, and she had a way of holding your eye so hard while she did it you almost got an ache from it. Or was she just putting on an act, so separated by the Law and its fine workings from my actual situation that she could only be what she had learned to be, and was paid to be? A defender. Someone who believed absolutely in the innocence of her clients because that was her job. Yet how could she be so certain?

"Who said I was?" Cerise replied with a sly grin, hooking her stockinged feet onto the stretchers of Lydia's chair. She was dressed like she had been the first time we met – a pair of blue Levis that somehow camouflaged her size, a t-shirt which didn't, and a beige cardigan that had the warm, worn look of a favorite. She had it draped over her shoulders and she hugged its empty sleeves around her.

"Well, *you* did actually," I said, going on to remind her of our first meeting at the 19ᵗʰ Precinct.

"So I did," she smiled, remembering. "Whiiiiiiiiich… ac-tu-ally… wasn't altogether honest of me. To tell the truth, Cully, I really didn't know for sure back then. You didn't look like any killer I'd ever met, but that didn't mean much."

"So what made you change your mind?"

Cerise paused, stretched back in her chair and gazed up at the ceiling as though deciding whether or not to explain herself. In the kitchen I could hear Lydia slotting plates into the dishwasher, and I remember thinking that in a past life – my professional life – I'd have marked her down for that, the sound of clearing up. But I couldn't deny it lent the evening a pleasantly domestic flavor which, over the last few weeks, I'd quite gotten to enjoy, something I hadn't really known for a long time.

"The hanger," Cerise replied finally, firmly, as though deciding to come clean. "Soon as I saw that clothes hanger I knew it couldn't be you. Not in a blue moon. You were clean. No other way to read it."

"The hanger?"

"You remember the scene-of-crime shots of Roo's apartment?"

I remembered them. A shiny spread of six-by-four black and white glossies. I'd seen them in Cerise's office at one of our first meetings, spilled out on top of her desk, and I'd shuffled through them while Cerise took a call from Daverson. I also remembered how Cerise had watched me as I sifted through them. I got the feeling they hadn't been left there by accident.

The apartment had looked the same as I'd last seen it, when Roo invited me up after Toucan for my second Christmas present: the bedroom, bathroom and dressing room, the sofas by the fire, the refectory table, the Chinese screen and Eames recliner, the gallery and stairs – everything photographed from at least a half-dozen angles.

There were also shots of Roo – slumped in the chair, arms and legs swollen where the cords bit into her, the pool of blood on the floor, black in the pictures, puncture wounds like tiny black lips – but these I hadn't lingered on.

"I'm thinking the bathroom, in particular," said Cerise.

I nodded. I recalled the photos: the mirrors above the vanity and the smooth marble catching the camera flash.

"On the vanity was a hanger," continued Cerise. "One of those really fine Aronson cherrywood hangars – ten bucks apiece. And in the dressing room, a wardrobe door was open."

"You have a better memory than me," I said, wondering where Cerise was headed for; how a hanger in Roo's bathroom and an open wardrobe door could possibly establish anything.

"Inside the closet that's open are Roo's dresses," said Cerise, warming to her explanation and doubtless savoring my frown. "Not jackets, not overcoats, not skirts, blouses, wigs, whatever. Just dresses."

"You've lost me."

Cerise smiled: "Well, Cully, it maybe wouldn't work in a court of law, but it does just fine for me."

"What'll do fine?" asked Lydia, coming in from the kitchen with another bottle of wine.

"I wanted to know how come Cerise is so certain I'm innocent."

"You mean my telling her didn't do the trick?" Lydia set down the bottle, and started work with the corkscrew.

"It's like this," Cerise continued. "The killer does the deed, right? But there's blood everywhere; a whole mess. And, we can only guess here, all over the killer, too. So what to do? Why, take a shower, of course; bundle up the bloodstained clothes in a bag; go to Roo's dressing room and select – a dress. Because the killer is a woman." Cerise gave me a look and started counting off on her fingers: "She takes the dress through to the bathroom, slips it off the hanger, puts the hanger on the vanity, and gets dressed in Roo's clothes. Which somehow, Cully, I can't see you doing."

"So why didn't the killer come prepared? Bring a change of clothes?"

"Maybe she didn't think it was going to get so messy."

"Who says the dress was for wearing?" asked Lydia, pulling the cork from the bottle and topping our glasses. "Maybe there wasn't as much blood as you suggest? Maybe the killer just wanted something to remember her by? Aren't they supposed to do that kind of thing? You know, take home a trophy?"

"I don't think so," said Cerise. "Not in this case."

"Or maybe," continued Lydia, playing devil's advocate with enthusiasm, "it was Roo left the hanger there."

Cerise shook her head. "So where's the missing outfit then?" she asked. "No trace of it, is where. And Roo was dressed in sweats when the killer called, like she'd just got back from a run. And another thing. You ever look closely at Roo's closets?" She turned to me. "I did. And you know something? Every hanger hook faces the same way – inwards. Easy to put away, easy to pull out. Every single one. Never seen anything like it. Not a one out of place. Your friend was a very, very tidy person. Almost obsessive. She would never leave a hanger lying around. No chance. But someone else did."

"So when did you reach this conclusion?" I asked, trying to get a grip on how persuasive this evidence was, and deciding it sounded pretty convincing.

"About the time we got you bail," replied Cerise.

"So… you knew all along it wasn't Elliot?"

"I guess."

"And you still let me suspect him? Go after him?"

"I reckoned you might benefit from the practice."

For a moment there I wasn't sure to be angry or not.

As it was, Lydia began to chuckle, then Cerise, and before long I joined in.

"There's another thing," continued Cerise, enjoying the attention now, swirling the wine around in her glass. "Something else that makes me think my little theory's a runner. Something else that ties in with the hanger."

"Which is?" asked Lydia, pulling out another kitchen chair so as not to disturb Cerise with her feet on the stretcher, break the flow.

"The security tapes for Blaise Heights. On the day Roo was killed, between 3pm and 9pm, the lobby video system recorded eight women and six men entering the building. All the women and all but one of the men have been identified, questioned and eliminated. During the same time frame eleven men and five women left the building. All have been identified save one woman. So one man, unaccounted for, enters Blaise Heights, and a few hours later a woman, unaccounted for, departs. The man wears a hat, a coat and scarf…"

"Not too surprising," said Lydia, sipping her wine. "It's cold out there."

"…And the woman also wears a hat, coat and scarf, very similar – if not identical – to the man's. And she's toting a Chanel carrier bag over her shoulder. One of Roo's? With bloody clothes inside? I mean, she's not going to leave any evidence at the scene now, is she?

"According to Buzz," Cerise continued, "the cops were fretting over what to make of that video footage when the computer boys found the e-mail on Roo's computer which tied Cully in with the name the killer scrawled on the floor. When they'd established you had no alibi, that you were left-handed, and then matched your prints on the dog that was used to knock her cold, they just never bothered with any other loose ends. I doubt they've even mentioned the video in their scene-of-crime report. They didn't think they had to. It was open and shut far as they were concerned. But not for me. Who was that man coming in, and who was that woman going out? I'll bet my partnership they're one and the same person. A woman." Cerise took a swig of wine. "Bricks and stones, Cully. Bricks and stones…"

"What about moustaches?" asked Lydia, leaning over to pull mine.

"Nothing visible. In or out of the building. Thanks to the scarf," Cerise replied.

"So this theory of yours with the hanger bears out a woman dressed as a man going in, and a woman in a dress coming out?" I said.

"Has to," said Cerise, her brandy brown eyes twinkling.

"But how could the killer be sure Cully would be… available?" asked Lydia. "I mean, without an alibi, say, at home alone, when she goes to Blaise Heights. It's all well and good writing his name in blood and putting that letter into Roo's computer and all, but what if, when Roo gets murdered, Cully's out with me, has a date? Someone who can vouch for him?"

"You've got to remember one thing, Lydia. Roo doesn't get murdered until the killer is *certain* Cully's *got* no alibi. I mean this wasn't some spur of the moment homicide. This whole thing was planned, and planned very carefully. The killer knew Cully'd be home that Monday. Just like she knew Roo would be at home."

"But how?" asked Lydia. "How could she know?"

Cerise shrugged. "Very easy. Since we've pretty much established the killer knows the pair of them, she probably knew about their movements. Or at least been able to find out about them. Like, Cully might have said something, let slip he's out of town until the Monday, without realising he's talking to the killer, setting himself up."

I tried to remember if I'd said anything to Susan, Avery, or Casey about the Haddon weekend, the remaining names on my suspect list. "Well, it certainly wouldn't have been Casey," I said. "I haven't spoken to her in months."

"Or maybe," continued Cerise, "the killer just calls up the *Times* the week before and asks to speak to Cully Mortimer. A PR company, a restaurant wanting to get a hold of him, that kind of thing. And the switchboard, or someone in his department, goes: 'So sorry, he's away. Won't be back till Monday.' So all she has to do is go round to Roo's place, say Monday afternoon, knowing she'll be there, and have Roo call him until he picks up the phone. Remember the other messages on his Ansaphone? And even he's got a date with someone, he'll cancel it when he gets that call from Roo. She's in trouble, she needs his help."

"And," Cerise went on, turning to me, "it was the killer told you where to go. Before that call, she'd have found out from Roo where the two of you go, your favorite places, and then she takes her pick. The most anonymous. Somewhere you'd never be able to establish an alibi. The kind of place you'd never be remembered in a month of Sundays. Toucan."

"The killer told me?"

"When you spoke to Roo that last time on the phone, I'd put my money on the killer standing right there beside her, telling her what to say. It had already begun. The whole thing maybe scripted. And that draft letter on the e-mail? That's when that would've gotten written."

There was a moment's silence as we took this in, broken finally by Lydia: "So how do the police think the killer got in?"

"You need a single swipe card for the entrance and all apartment doors. Or you can tap in a code, or call up and be buzzed in," replied Cerise, as though she was prepared for the cross-examination. "We have no way of knowing which happened. But what we do know is this: there was no doorman on duty that Monday. And the entrance lock is dodgy. Buzz used his Amex card, and on the fourth try the door opened."

"Never leave home without one," said Lydia, lightly.

"And then, of course, there's the brass dog," continued Cerise. "How come Cully leaves his fingerprints on that dog, but the forensic boys don't get so much as a smear on the tape he's supposed to have slapped across her mouth? Or the chair he tied her to? Or the hanger. Not a print anywhere 'ceptin' that dog." She shook her head. "There's other things, too, things that don't add up. Which is why, Cully, there's no doubt in my mind that you're innocent of the crime you stand accused of."

And with that Cerise eased her feet off Lydia's chair, stretched, covered a yawn, and looked at her watch. "Anyhow, time for this night owl to find her roost," she said, reaching down for her shoes, and pulling them on. I sensed a look pass between the two women, something unspoken, something negative. "Can I give you a lift, Cully? I'm going your way."

"That would be just fine," I replied, and went for my coat.

Lydia saw us to the door and kissed us goodnight, watching as we made our way down the hall to the elevator.

"You take care now, you hear?" she called after us, as the doors slid open and we stepped into the elevator.

"We will, we will," called back Cerise, and as the doors slid shut she pressed for the ground floor. "Fine ole pie, that Lydia cooks up. Make someone a fine wife one of these days," she said.

"Is there anyone on the scene?" I asked.

"Oh, yes," replied Cerise. "There surely is."

Which gave me an uncomfortable twist of surprise. I'd become so locked into my own situation that I'd not really given too much thought to Lydia's. I wondered when she and her admirer met up. In the last couple of months I hadn't given her much time free to pursue any romantic connection. And truth to tell I wasn't really sure that I liked the idea of it, sharing Lydia like that.

"You ever met him?" I asked, not wishing to sound too inquisitive.

"Oh sure," said Cerise.

"And?"

"He's a nice guy. Little on the straight side for me, if you know what I mean, but pretty much perfect for Lydia."

We reached the ground floor, crossed the hall, and stepped out into an icy night. "Car's just over there," she said, pointing her keys ahead.

A pair of tail-lights blinked as the locks opened, and we climbed in. I was curious to know more about Lydia's mystery man, but driving uptown Cerise changed the subject as though her friend's love life was no concern of mine: "How's it going by the way? You manage to get through to Casey yet?"

≈

Like I said, Casey had not been easy to corner.

The first time I called, a month or so out of Brooklyn, she'd hung up.

"Casey, it's…" and down went the phone.

The second time I called, about fifteen minutes later, she stayed on the line long enough to tell me I deserved whatever it was I had coming, and she hoped it hurt. When I suggested we meet up she said, simply, finally, "Why?" and hung up a second time.

A week later I nerved myself to visit Bonnebouche and confront her. I went around 4.30 on a Thursday afternoon thinking I could catch her between shifts. I can't say I was looking forward to the meeting. I knew I'd hurt her back in the summer when Roo had started to reel me in, treated her abominably even before Roo made an appearance, and wouldn't have blamed her for anything she might say, anything she might do. Frankly, I was relieved to be told by one of the waiters, when I pushed through the basement doors, that she was away skiing in Colorado, that she'd be back the following week.

I guess there's a certain irony that the day I did get a hold of Casey was a Monday. I knew I had to see her, however she might feel about it, and Monday afternoon seemed a good bet. I was right. I stepped through the doors into an empty restaurant, and, not wanting to surprise her, called out her name. A moment later she pushed through the kitchen doors with a chopping knife in her hand. Her hair was tousled and slick, her whites had lost their starch in the heat of the kitchen, and ski goggles had left a faint tan line round the eyes which gave her a rather owl-like, comical look.

"Hello, Casey…"

"Well, well," she said at last. "Will you look what the cat dragged in." Her voice was soft and unsurprised, as though she'd been expecting me, had even practiced the lines. "I didn't think you'd have the nerve coming back here again."

I stood just inside the doorway, waiting for some sense of invitation before I took another step forward. "Casey, I'm…"

"Don't even start, Cully," she continued, just as quietly. "Just turn around and get the fuck out of my restaurant."

I took a step forward.

"I mean it, Cully." Her voice was ice. She didn't need to raise the knife to be any more threatening.

"Listen Casey, I'm in trouble. I need your help."

Or rather, I thought, I need you to tell me where you were the night of Roo's murder. And can someone vouch for you? That's what I meant by 'help'. The subterfuge, the insincerity, made me feel even more uncomfortable.

"Oh, yeah? Like how? And why should I?"

"Because we're friends?"

"Oh, go on, Cully, get outta here. So you've got yourself in trouble, tough. Sort it out yourself."

Then she turned on her heel and disappeared into the kitchen, the swing doors flapping behind her.

Which I took to be a sign to follow her.

By the time I pushed through, she was back at her prep table slicing through a stack of peppers, not the round supermarket clones but warped, misshapen balloons of red and yellow and green that looked as if they'd come from some local country market. Maybe even France.

"*Poivrons?*" I asked, gently.

"I thought I told you to leave. There's nothing for you here." She didn't look in my direction but the frost in her voice reached clear across that snug, oven-warm kitchen. She finished a pepper, swept the strips to one side, and picked out another from the basket at her elbow.

"Casey, please…"

She slid the knife into the new pepper and cut downwards, opening up its hollow, seeded center. The two halves fell apart. She picked up the nearest, changed the knife from one hand to the other, and began slicing, clean and fast, the blade sliding past her bunched fingertips.

"Maybe it's you should be doing this," she said, and began to chuckle. "By all accounts you have a talent for it."

"That's a little mean," I said.

"Mean? Mean, Cully? Please." She began to shake her head.

"I didn't do it."

"You really think I give a shit either way?" Her venom surprised me.

"It wasn't me. It was someone who knows me, framed me."

"And you think I really care? Good riddance, I say…" And then, mid-slice, she paused, the blade resting against her fingertips. Then she laid the knife down and looked at me, astonishment dawning on her face. "I don't believe it," she said. "You gotta be kidding me?"

I shrugged, apologetically. If she'd let me I'd have continued to deceive her, taken the long way round. But she hadn't. She'd seen through me swift as a finger snap. Maybe I was going to get this over with quicker than I'd imagined. Maybe this was the way to do it. Out in the open. Straight.

"You think *I* did it, for God's sake? Killed your little bit of stuff? Why? Because I was jealous of her? To get back at you? To make you suffer like I did?" She turned back to the chopping board and picked up the knife, hefting it in her palm. "You're not worth the trouble, Cully. You never were. It's just I never realized it."

"Then tell me something."

"Tell you what?" she replied, belligerently, reaching for another pepper, though the one she'd been working on had not been finished.

"Tell me where you were, December 28th? The Monday after Christmas. What you were doing. Afternoon, evening time."

She started cutting again, the blade slicing through the pepper, snapping down on the board.

"Right where you see me now."

"So you have witnesses. Staff. Chefs." It was as I'd imagined. Casey may have had a motive but, as she had just confirmed, she hadn't had the opportunity. I felt a kind of release. I was glad, despite the chill welcome, that it wasn't her.

"Nope. We were closed."

"But it was a Monday. You're open Mondays. Leastways for dinner."

"Not that Monday. We were closed." Another pile of slicings was swept to one side, and another pepper dug from the basket and placed on the wood block.

"But surely…"

"Like I said, Cully. Not that one. Though why I'm bothering to tell you all this, after what you did, I can't rightly imagine."

"I appreciate it."

"Well, that makes me feel *real* warm inside." She'd started slicing again, chop-chop-chopping on the board. "I had two chefs down with the flu, a couple of waiters hadn't shown up after the holiday break, and I had a party of seventy for New Year. So I stayed *fermé*, Monday through Wednesday. Getting things organised."

It was not what I'd wanted to hear. No alibi.

"So you see what I'm getting at? You could have done it. You had the opportunity and... a motive."

She spun round on me. "Motive? Me? After what you did? Sure, I had a motive. And there's a lot of things I'd like to have done, believe me. But after a while, I thought about it and decided... You know what? You just weren't worth the trouble. Although I have to say I just love what you've gotten yourself into. Oh boy, oh boy. I couldn't have written it better even I was John Grisham. Time was I'd have loved every bit of it. But I'm all over that. After that first day when you were splashed over the newspapers, on TV, I couldn't get enough of it. I just couldn't believe it. Loved every word. 'Goddamn, *get* the bastard', I thought. 'Good riddance'. But after that, I didn't even bother reading about it. When I heard one of the chefs say something about you being released on bail, I just remember a sense of... oh, you know: 'Fuck. They could've kept him in a bit longer'."

I didn't know what to say. I'd guessed it was going to be hard, but not as hard – as hurtful – as all this. I really did feel bad about us. I really did regret what I'd done to her. But there was no way she was going to believe that now.

She turned back to the peppers, continued slicing. "You may think I'm stupid, Cully, but I'm not."

"I never ever said, or thought, you were stupid."

"Oh no? When you left here those afternoons? Always managing to sidestep any... talk? Where we were going? What it was all about? You *knew* the way I felt, and you just kept me hanging there, didn't you? Casey Webster – she'll do for the afternoon. A little something for the great bloody Cully Mortimer to amuse himself with. Just some silly girl you could take up and put aside whenever you felt like it."

I didn't reply. I knew the words would stick in my throat if I tried to deny it.

"At least you're not to trying to deny it." Casey finished the last of the peppers, and went over to the sinks to wash her hands. "Tell me," she said, tearing off a length of kitchen towel and drying her hands. "Was this Carew woman the one you told me about, back in the summer…?"

"Yes."

She gave me a look – hurt and incredulous.

"A *hooker*, Cully? A hooker, for Christ's sake? What got into you? What were you thinking?"

"I didn't know. Not then. I only found out later."

"Well, I hope you got your dollar's worth."

"I never paid. We were friends first, then lovers. When you and I were… together, we'd only just met. Nothing happened."

"But you wanted to be in the clear just in case a little luck came your way." She tossed the crumpled paper towel into a bin. "No baggage. No untidy loose ends."

"Something like that," I admitted.

I was surprised I could say it like that. Just honest. The truth. And strange to say, I found it didn't make me feel as exposed as I'd once imagined it would. In fact, it seemed to clear the air, as if a weight had been lifted.

She gave me a long, cool look, then returned to the chopping table and began clearing it, pepper slices into a china dish, left-over seeds and stalks into a stock pan.

"Believe me, I can understand someone wanting to shit on you, Mr. Mortimer. The way you operate, there's probably more than just me out there who reckon they've got a score to settle." She reached for a bottle of olive oil, uncorked it, and poured it over the peppers. "And some might even murder for it. But not me, Cully. That's just one step too far for me. And like I said, I just couldn't be bothered. As it is, turns out someone did me a favor."

"It's not enough," I said, quietly, regretfully.

"Not *enough*?" she snapped back, rounding on me. "Not enough for *what*? For you? For your defense? I've got to have an alibi suddenly? Me? Well, hey, that's just too bad. It's not going to happen. And you know something, Cully? I couldn't give a damn. I really couldn't."

Out in the restaurant the front door opened, and a murmur of voices, footsteps, carried through to us. "Now if you don't mind, I've got work to do."

≈

It was only later, as Lydia was helping me on with my coat after yet another debriefing supper ("You might think she wouldn't do it," Lydia had told me over a slice of cold meatloaf, "but there's no saying she didn't."), that we discovered a long, dark scar of grease staining the back of my coat, the coat Roo had pressed me to buy on our shopping spree.

Lydia spotted it first, tried to brush it off.

"What on earth have you gone and got on your coat, Cully? Why, it's ruined."

For a moment, I couldn't think what it was or how it had gotten there. Then I remembered Casey's kitchen, leaning against the side of a range while she sliced away at her peppers. She must have known. Must have seen the mark as she followed me out through the restaurant and locked the doors after me.

And she'd said nothing. Not a word.

Casey stayed on my list.

Caviar and Crackers

"*Professore!*" she said.

"*Principessa!*" I replied.

Avery Blanchard stood in the hallway of Suite 3004 on the thirtieth floor of The Carlyle Hotel. She'd opened the door within seconds of my knocking, and stood back as though to get a better look at me. Which, coincidentally, gave me the chance to get a better look at her.

I'd come to the Carlyle shortly after midday, again with no warning save the concierge calling up to announce my presence. For a moment, loitering around his elegantly lacquered desk while he made the call, I wondered what I would do if Avery said 'no', she didn't want to see me. What then? But she didn't. The concierge put down the phone, smiled warmly, and showed me to the elevator himself, even leaning in to press the right button for me. I knew then he knew who I was. Not just Mr. Mortimer, but Cully Mortimer. *The* Cully Mortimer.

Despite the hour, Avery was still wearing a dressing gown: thickly towelled and tightly cinched, the sleeves rolled up to her elbows, and the name of the hotel and its five stars stitched in scarlet copperplate on the breast pocket; it wasn't even her own. And there was no sign of jewelry either – no earrings, bracelets, rings – nothing. It was like she'd just finished her morning make-over and hadn't yet had time to reach for the jewelry box, or gotten round to deciding what outfit she'd start the day with. She was barefoot, too.

After our amused exchange of honorifics – I was rather touched she should remember, and already impressed by her stoicism – she stepped to one side and, with a Calvi-like sweep of her arm and a whimsical little smile, ushered me in to her new quarters.

A suite at The Carlyle is certainly no hardship posting and 3004, with its cozy, red-lacquered dining room, den-like study, sprawling drawing room, two bedrooms and twin tubs must be one of the finest in the city. In careless profusion are richly swagged curtains, deep wall-to-wall carpets overlaid with almost superfluous oriental rugs, fresh flowers in abundance, plump sofas and armchairs, and a no doubt well-insured collection of interesting gewgaws and second-division oils.

But grand as it is in terms of hotel suites, it was never so grand as a Player Leland lifestyle. And it clearly showed in Avery. Though her hair was glossy, sprung, and tidy, her make-up simply but expertly applied, and her nails shining as though the varnish was still drying, I decided, as I sank down into one of the sofas, that she looked somehow reduced. Diminished. But was putting on a brave face.

"So," she said, arranging herself on the sofa opposite. "How times change, Cully. You and me both."

≈

It had taken quite a time to find Avery, which I guess shouldn't really have surprised me. She'd eluded me twice before, following the deaths of two of her husbands, fading from view like a shadow when the sun slips behind a cloud. And she'd almost managed it a third time.

Avery's was the final name on my list of suspects and, appropriately, I'd left getting in touch with her until last. Also, of all my suspects, she was the one I knew the least, still furthest away from real, intimate friendship. Despite our many lunches and occasional *soirées*, the two of us had never really gotten further than a kind of guarded acquaintance. Maybe that would have changed, given time, but between Avery and I there was a certain reserve, an empty space that had yet to be filled, a sense of separation still to be breached.

I'd tried getting in touch with her a couple of weeks earlier, still smarting from my uncomfortable reunion with Casey. First I'd called Avery's private number at Player Leland's place in Adams Square, only to receive an automated answering message to the effect that: "Mrs. Blanchard is no longer available at this number. Please leave your name and number and a message will be forwarded."

A week later, when I'd still heard nothing, I tried again and received the same message. After calling the Leland country house in Fauquier County and getting a similar recorded message, I decided that Avery had crossed me off her Christmas list, and had issued instructions that any call from me should be sidelined. How easy it is for the rich to distance themselves from the unwanted. So cold, clinical, and final. If it had been anyone else, I'd have been suspicious, as Cerise had correctly suggested I should be, but with Avery Blanchard I kind of understood this freezing out. A lady in her position, Player Leland's official companion, could hardly afford to share a table at Cazzuola with an alleged murderer, or have him drop by for tea. I doubted even that Player Leland had needed to say anything; she'd have made the decision all by herself. Avery was like that.

It was only during a deli lunch with Sanchez at Dwight's Diner across the road from the *Times* that I found out the truth. After catching up on Larry, Lizzie, and McKintyre, and getting all the lowdown on the new 'Metro Life' section, the conversation turned to the tenth floor and Sanchez finally provided the lead I was looking for.

"'Course the boss is out of town, so no one knows what to do."

We'd been talking about the half-dozen writers the *Times* had tried out in my place as 'Metro Life' section lead. Only one, so far as I could see, had the requisite style, depth, and knowledge the column called for, but the tenth floor had still not committed. And it was the reason for their hesitation that interested me, rather than the relative merits of those contesting my column.

Player Leland. Out of town.

"Out of town?" I asked, antenna quivering.

"Paris. Europe. A couple of months now, must be." Sanchez smeared his ham sandwich with a near-fluorescent piccalilli and lined it up for attack, his brown fingers spreading across the soft white bread as though to seal off any edges that might give under the pressure of his bite. "Another domestic, so they say. Services dispensed with. You knew her, didn't you? Hefty tabs at that fancy Italian place that always got the tick?" He launched into the sandwich, managing to contain any spill.

I was astonished. "You're kidding? They've split up?" Doubly astonished, as a matter of fact, not just by the news, but that I'd neither heard nor read anything about it.

Sanchez shrugged, a cheek swollen with sandwich, his voice muffled.

"Maybe she did something the big man didn't approve of. Or there's someone else on the block. Who knows? All I can tell you is, she no longer resides in Adams Square. Where she is now, what she's doing, your guess is as good as mine."

In the event it was Daverson tracked her down. At one of our meetings at the offices of Chase McKay I'd said how I was having trouble getting through to Avery, had no idea where she was, and Cerise asked Daverson to chase it up.

"She's at The Carlyle," Cerise told me on the phone a few days later. "Has been for a couple months. Account settled personally by Mr. Player Leland. The suite's been pre-paid for four months. After that Avery Blanchard is on her own."

"Daverson?"

"Of course."

"Jesus H. How does he do it? There must be a million places she could have been. How on earth did he find her? And so quick?"

"That's why he works for me, Cully. He finds things out. How he does it, I don't ask and he don't tell me. Now, I'd suggest you get yourself over to The Carlyle, pronto."

"Why don't we just send Daverson?" I asked, half joking, half serious.

But Cerise was having none of it. "The Carlyle, Cully. Now."

Which is exactly what I did, five minutes after putting down the phone.

≈

"I'm so sorry," I began, looking at Avery, and then casting around the room. "Things don't seem to have worked out the way we might have hoped." It was as direct an allusion as I dared to the subject the two of us most often discussed at Cazzuola – the ensnaring of Player Leland, and the formal acknowledgement of her position.

"Like I said, you and me both."

I nodded, and Avery smiled, archly.

She was right, of course. Her and me both. What unexpected twists of fate had landed us here since that Thanksgiving presentation of Avery's portrait, and my elevation to 'Metro Life' lead. How the great had fallen.

I wondered, then, how to continue. Avery seemed to be giving no leeway here. Where was the start line? Who was going to kick things off? It was a strangely exhilarating moment as the two of us sniffed the air like animals on the shared border of each other's territory. And for the next few seconds there was what amounted to an uncomfortable silence, which, finally, thankfully, Avery broke.

"So, how did you find me?" she began.

"There was a story in the *Post*," I lied.

"In the *Post*?" She looked surprised, as though she wasn't sure whether to believe me. And then, much to my relief: "Damn papers. I knew they'd find out sooner or later." She leaned sideways along the sofa for a pack of cigarettes and lighter on a side table, showing a glimpse of hollowed, freckled collar bone beneath the bathrobe as she reached for them. She slid one out of the packet and lit it.

"I didn't know you smoked."

"All my life. But Player hated it. All his wives smoked. I decided not to." She gave me a look through the first whistling plume of blue.

"You did your homework."

I didn't mean it to come out the way it sounded. I held my breath.

After a pause, she replied: "In my line of business, Cully, it pays."

At first I thought I hadn't heard her right, but she followed it with a calculating look and I knew I had. I realized immediately that she was fishing, trying to establish whether I knew what she was talking about, what I might have heard from Roo. Sure, she knew about me and Roo – like everyone else who read the papers or watched the news on television. But did I know about her? Had I discovered from Roo what Avery had done in the years before we met? That was what she wanted to find out. I decided not to make it too easy for her.

"I don't know how much you know, Cully. Or if you know anything…"

I tried to look blank, mystified. "I guessed there was trouble when I read the story in the *Post*."

For the briefest moment, Avery looked uncertain. "You could say. Did the *Post* give any details?"

"Just a Diary sign-off piece. You know the kind of thing. 'Word has it…' The usual ten-liner and a question mark."

Avery nodded. "And when did you say you saw it?"

"I didn't say. But it must have been a week or so back. Didn't know what to make of it to tell the truth. You know the *Post*."

Avery nodded, still circling.

"Well, sounds like the *Post* got it right for once. I got my marching orders. Good and proper."

"He catch you smoking in the closet?"

"Something like that. But here am I forgetting my manners. What about *you*? It's not like I'm the only one in the fryer."

And so, as camouflage, I filled her in on everything that had happened to me, from the moment DaSilva and Munroe knocked on my door, through processing at the 19th Precinct, and my stay at State Correctional. We could have been huddled at our table at Cazzuola.

"So how was the food?" she asked when I'd finished my *resumé*.

"I won't be reviewing it, if that's what you mean. Though it'd make a great story."

She frowned, gave me a questioning look.

"I got my marching orders, too, remember? Doubt I'll be writing for the *Times* any time soon – however things pan out."

"I'm sorry to hear that," she said. She took a final drag of her cigarette, and tossed it into the fireplace. "I really did like your columns. You always made me laugh. Out loud, sometimes. The things you'd say – so... naughty, Cully. So mischievous. It's why I asked Player to have you come round that first time for dinner. Remember? I so wanted to meet you. I just knew we'd get along."

Which was sad, somehow, because, well, we never really had. Got along. Not the way it could have been.

"Speaking of which," she said, glancing at the clock on the mantelpiece. "What about some lunch?"

$\approx$

Fat Harry would have loved the Room Service trolley at The Carlyle Hotel. It arrived about ten minutes after Avery put down the phone, a wheeled table, crisply dressed with a white cloth, that rolled over the carpet with a rich tinkling of cutlery, glass and china. And the man pushing it was as unlike Fat Harry as it was possible to be – young, elegantly thin, with a mop of gloriously curled hair black as blood pudding. Italian? Spanish? Mediterranean, for sure. As though following a familiar routine, he snapped out a small cloth over the table between the two sofas, set out the various dishes and glasses and ice bucket, and, after Avery had signed the chit, he bowed and slid from view, the door clicking shut behind him.

"Hope you like caviar," said Avery, lifting a silver cloche to reveal what looked like a large molehill of Ossetra – in my opinion far finer, more subtle, and infinitely more enduring in terms of taste and flavor than the bigger-grained and more expensive Beluga – its small browny-black eggs glistening in a cut-glass bowl, nestled in a diamond pile peak of ice chips.

"I adore it," I said. "I like to eat it until my lips get all salted up."

"Till they stick together," she laughed, digging out a mother-of-pearl spoonful and ladling it onto a plate, wiping both sides of the spoon with a finger, I was delighted to see, before sliding the finger into her mouth. And then: "We have a lot in common, you and I."

"We have indeed," I replied, taking the plate from her, playing it as though we were still talking about the caviar, which I knew we weren't.

"But you know something?" she continued, serving herself, then slipping a napkin off a dish of thin dry melba toasts. "I just never ever got to like blinis. Great with maple syrup, sure. But caviar? Unh-uh. Blinis are just too... damp."

"If I was still writing for the *Times*, I'd have quoted you on that. 'Damp'. Got it in one. For me, it's always melbas. And they're just great with *foie gras*, too."

"You don't say. I should try it sometime."

"I think you should. You'd like it."

"Maybe while I still have the chance."

It's hard to tell how this conversation comes across on the page. It's about exactly as it went, as near as I can remember it, and I hope it comes out like I want it to, which is as some kind of delicious sparring. But it's almost impossible to figure how it must sound for someone who wasn't there. Me, I was there. I can hear her voice, the slant to it, the muffled pop as I levered the cork from the first of the two bottles of Krug, the dry rustle and snap of the melbas, the scrunch of the ice as the bowl of caviar shifted, the clink of glasses.

"A wonderful year," I said, sipping the champagne. "What a treat."

"Player's paying so we might as well take advantage, don't you think? Who knows how much longer the two of us will be able to."

"Who indeed?" I replied. And then, after a beat: "So what will you do now?"

"What I've always done."

I looked at her, waiting for the rest.

"Survive," she said. And then she seemed to decide something. "I hope you don't mind my saying this, Cully, but you never ever struck me as a hooker man. Or a killer come to that."

"Right on both counts."

"I didn't think so." Avery's eyes held me tight. "Did you know she was a hooker?"

"She told me. Said she was quitting."

"Uh-huh."

"I believed her."

"You love her?"

The question caught me napping. "I... don't know. Yes, I guess.

Maybe if we'd had longer… And you? Did you love Player?"

The silence that followed seemed frighteningly long. I didn't know whether I'd maybe overstepped the mark again. But then, she'd started it.

"Oooohhh. Now there's a question," she said, buttering a corner of toast with what looked like a full ounce of Ossetra and popping it in her mouth. As she crunched through it, she held my eye, then, behind sealed lips, she ran her tongue across her teeth so that not a single dot of black showed when, finally, she smiled and said: "Who knows? Maybe if we'd had longer together."

The ball was back in my court and, feeling more confident now, I lobbed it right back. The preliminaries had been dispensed with. The gloves were off. "So what happened?"

Avery looked round for her cigarettes, lit one, and leaned towards me, elbows on knees, two fingers clamped around her cigarette, smoke curling around her head, the caviar momentarily forgotten.

"A mutual friend decided to make trouble."

It was clear she meant Roo, not someone she and Player knew.

"Mutual friend?" I asked.

"Maybe, Cully…" she began. "Maybe we should stop all this tiptoeing around, and tell it how it is. It's what you want to hear, isn't it? Why you're here? I mean, you're not just stopping by, are you? Come to see how I'm… bearing up?"

"No, I'm not. Though in other circumstances I'm sure I certainly would have done."

"And I believe you would have, too. But for now you want something else, am I right?"

I nodded.

"You want to know if I killed your friend."

I nodded again.

"She tell you about me?"

"A little," I replied.

"Well, clearly enough or you wouldn't be here now, would you?"

"So what trouble did she cause?"

"Enough to put me back a decade. Enough to have me sitting here with my fine views…", she gestured to the windows, "…and bleak prospects."

"Tell me."

"I'll tell you everything you want to know, Cully, with pleasure.
What's to lose? Though I suspect you know more than you're
prepared to let on. Trying to trip me up maybe. But you won't. So I'll
be straight, tell it all." Once again she tossed the cigarette, unfinished
this time, into the grate, where it landed close to the first. "But I'll
also tell you right now, I did not kill her." She looked sadly round the
room. "Though I wish I damn well had."

"And why's that?"

Avery poured us more champagne, then sat back in the sofa, tucked
her legs under her, arranged the folds of her robe.

"Let's see. It was a couple months ago now. End of December.
We'd had Player's dreadful sister, Virginia from Virginia, staying for
the holiday. It had been a nightmare, you wouldn't believe. She'd
marked my card early on and she's never revised her opinion, though
give Player his due he never paid her the slightest heed. 'Course,
she'll be just delighted by all this.

"Anyways," Avery continued, taking a sip of the champagne, "the
morning dear Virginia left, the exact same moment as it happens,
a package arrived for Player. By then, of course, I'd read about the
murder. And I'm sorry, Cully, but I felt great about it, I can't tell you.
I was off the hook. Someone had just done me the biggest favor. Or
so I thought.

"Which is why I probably didn't pay too much attention to that
damn parcel coming up the steps, as Virginia was going down them. I
even signed for it, would you believe? And left it on the hall table for
Tally to pass on to Player. If I'd have known what was in it, I could
have just snatched it before he saw it. Right then. That would have
been that. But I didn't. Didn't connect. Just so pleased Player's sister
was gone. And so relieved our mutual friend was finally out of the
picture, you can't imagine."

She paused, reached for another melba, idly scooping up more
caviar, but this time just sucking it off the toast. "So it was Player got
the package and not me. It was only when I got back from lunch – with
Jim Jeffries, you know, Player's man at the Met? – that my lawyer
called, broke the news, that I realized the opportunity I'd missed, what
the package contained."

"Which was?" I was starting to get the dreadful feeling that I knew
what the package was. And, more to the point, who had sent it.

"It contained… information, Cully. Certain information regarding my past. Information Player had no knowledge of."

Avery fell silent, as though that was all she needed to say, as if that was all she wanted to say. She set down her glass and reached for the cigarettes, tapped one out and lit it.

"Information?" I pressed.

"Information… Information that I was not all he might imagine me to be… Information, I suspect, you may already be familiar with."

She gave me a long, narrow look, eyes crinkling against the cigarette smoke.

I didn't flinch.

"Anyhow, this information… According to my lawyer – who'd received a call from Player's lawyer, a senior partner at Scrimgeour Wedderburn – there was a raft of stuff. Clippings. Photos. You name it. And a short personal profile to accompany the illustrations: that I had seen off three husbands in suspicious circumstances, that I was a recreational drug-user, and that I was currently a shareholder in something called Beartree Enterprises – a name you may be familiar with – whose major asset just happened to be some high-tab whorehouse in the hills, much the same kind of operation, Player was informed, that I had run for a number of years in Los Angeles."

I nodded. I couldn't believe Avery was being so… upfront about it. And everything tallied. She'd even admitted to things I didn't know about, assuming I knew more than I did. I was increasingly certain she was telling the truth.

She gave me another pointed look. "I can see this isn't altogether news to you."

"No, it's not," I conceded. "She told me how you met. What you did."

"When was that?"

"November. On the way back from Beartree, as a matter of fact. She took me there for Thanksgiving. The weekend following your dinner."

"You don't say," she drawled, smiling mischievously. Then, perking up, she said: "What's it like? I never visited after the sale went through."

"Toney. A class act."

Avery nodded. "I can imagine. She had style, that girl. Right from the first time I met her. Knew how everything should be. We were two of a kind, Connie and me."

"Connie?"

"Beatty may have been the name you knew her by, Cully. Or Belinda. To me, she was Connie. Connie Taylor."

I thought about that. Another name, another life, another person. "So what did Player do?" I asked.

"I was out. Like that." She snapped her fingers. "I hardly had time to powder my nose. According to my lawyer, Player's man at Scrimgeour Wedderburn said his client had been called away on business, and would not be returning for at least a month. The house on Adams Square was to be closed up forthwith, and I was to move out. A suite," she gestured to the room with her cigarette fingers, "had been reserved for me here, and arrangements would be made to cover storage costs for my belongings. The Kalloway portrait included. Just like that. The following day my lawyer comes over with a contract he tells me he's been strongly advised to persuade me to accept. Under the terms of this agreement, I'm to receive a generous one-off settlement in return for my discretion and... my disappearance from Mr. Leland's life. 'Course, Player's no fool. The official line is I dumped him – as if! – which makes him look vulnerable, and therefore attractive, and me ballsy, my character and reputation intact. Which, I guess, could have been worse. It was also made clear I would be limited only to a discreet 'no comment. It's for the best', when the papers came calling."

"And you think it was Roo, Connie, who sent him that package?"

"I don't think she sent it, I know she sent it. Because she told me she would."

"She did? But why? Why would she want to do that to you?" But I knew.

Avery shook her head, slowly, sadly, leaned forward, and dropped her cigarette in the ice bucket. When she looked up her eyes were flinty.

"She was blackmailing me. Told me she'd send everything to Player if I refused to give her what she wanted."

"Which was?"

"A sizeable amount, Cully."

"Money?"

Avery gave me a look as though to say *what else?*

"And when was this?"

"December time. Soon after your trip to Beartree by the sound of it. She told me she was selling her share to some partner and quitting. Wanted out. Which squares with what she told you. Only she wanted something else. A safety net. Something to see her through."

"And you refused?"

"You betcha. This time I wasn't having any of it."

"This time?"

"She'd been putting pressure on me ever since she saw my picture in the paper. With Player. At the opera, if I remember right. After Bill died. One day she just pays a call, walks back into my life, breezy as you please, and wants to talk about Beartree which I'd just put on the market."

"She made you an offer."

"So you *do* know."

I shrugged.

"Apparently, she'd already put in a bid through the realtors which I'd turned down, not knowing it was Connie who'd made it. Now she wanted me to… reconsider." Avery gave a brittle little laugh, and tipped back the last of her champagne.

"Which you did."

"She knew and I knew that I didn't have a lot of choice. Like I said, I'd started seeing Player by then, once or twice a week kind of thing. But I knew it was going somewhere, and the last thing I wanted was Connie Taylor making his acquaintance. I had no choice but to go along with what she wanted. She gave me no option. At least I got something out of it."

"So you were involved in Beartree?"

"Not directly, no. I insisted on a small percentage of the take, and she agreed. Cash. Each month. No records to be kept. As a way of covering myself on the price she was paying. Which was extortionate, I can tell you. I could have gotten much, much more, and she and I knew it. But she had me."

Avery reached for the second bottle of Krug, tore off the foil and wire, and popped the cork. She poured a glass for herself, then handed me the bottle.

"Then, about six months after the sale goes through, she reappears.

At the Adams Square house, if you please? Miss Taylor to see Mrs. Blanchard, she tells the butler. So, of course, I see her. Can't do otherwise."

"And?"

"She wants to call a halt on the repayment scheme we agreed. As of right then. She hopes I don't mind." The brittle little laugh again. "I'd seen it coming, of course. Knew the payments would stop sometime soon after her name was on the deeds."

"So you agreed?"

"There wasn't much I could do, Cully. Just hoped that that would be the end of it. She had Beartree free and clear at a price you wouldn't believe. She'd told me she didn't intend giving me any more money. What else could I give her? I guessed that had to be enough."

"But it wasn't."

"She used to turn up the whole time. Every few months. A bit here, a bit there. Like she was asking Mommie-dearest for pocket money. I'd see her in the library and she'd just walk about, you know, kind of insolent, picking up this and that, looking at it, maybe putting it back down, sometimes slipping it in her bag with a sly grin like we were in cahoots, taking honey from the same pot."

"And you let her?"

"What was I going to do? And they were only small things – a photo frame, a snuff box, a letter opener. Small enough that Player never noticed. I could always get another frame, another letter opener, so I let her do it. Then, one time, she took a book down from the shelf, flicked through it like it was a comic, and slipped it in her bag. Tell the truth, I was glad it was only a book. Trouble was, it was the one thing Player noticed. Noticed it was missing. Some rare first edition. I mean thousands. He hit the roof. Had the staff in and questioned them. It was the day of the Thanksgiving party. Of all days. I was at my wits' end. He was so furious, I can't tell you. And Player angry is not a pretty sight."

My blood had run cold. I felt a shiver. There was no need to ask what the book was. I'd have put money on it. A lot of money. My Christmas present: Cristoforo da Messisbugo's *Banchetti*.

"She was a piece of work, I can tell you," continued Avery. "But that last time I saw her she wanted too much. There was just no way."

"Too much?"

"Way, way too much. So I called her bluff. Turned on her. Took her by surprise, too, which was nice to see. Said I wouldn't give her a damn dime more, and how she'd better go sell Beartree quick or I'd have the IRS and Police Department check her out. Which was when she threatened outright to tell Player. Maybe even leak it to the Press. Can you imagine?"

"So you paid?"

"Not a chance. I told you; I called her bluff. Refused to pay. I just didn't believe she'd dare go through with it." Avery sighed, and looked round the suite. "So here I am."

"She followed through?"

"For the next couple of weeks I was on tenterhooks. Couldn't think straight. Right up to Christmas. Then, when nothing happened, I began to relax. I'd frightened her off, I thought. I wouldn't hear from her again. I was in the clear. But of course… I wasn't, was I? She must have posted the package the day she died. And a few days later it lands on my doorstep."

Avery drained her glass.

"But that doesn't mean I killed her, Cully. Only wish whoever did it had done it a few days earlier. But it wasn't me, Cully. I'm not the one you're looking for…"

"Well, you've sure as hell got a cast-iron motive."

"I guess…" Avery smiled.

"So what about opportunity? Where were you the night she died?"

"Adams Square. Watching TV."

"With Player? Virginia?"

"They'd gone out after lunch. Drinks and supper with some friends of the family. Out on the island someplace. An overnight. Virginia had made it pretty plain I was not invited. Like she always does."

"What did you watch?"

"Really, Cully… I switched. This, that… nothing special."

As she answered my questions, Avery gave me a strangely amused look, as though she had the whole thing worked out, as though there was not a single question I could ask that she hadn't prepared for.

"Staff?"

"Sure. I had the kitchen make me a sandwich. Dolores brought it up."

"Any idea of the time?"

Avery wrinkled her nose, as though somehow it might help her remember. "Nine? Ten? Thereabouts."

"Any of the staff see you between Player and his sister leaving and Dolores bringing you that sandwich?"

"Not that I'm aware of, no. It's a big house. They come if you call. Otherwise…"

"So you had the opportunity?"

"You mean creeping out, going to her place, doing the deed, and coming back here without anyone noticing?"

"That kind of thing."

"Sure. Except there's just the teensiest little problem with that scenario."

"Which is?"

"Until I read it in the newspaper – Blaise Heights – I had not the slightest clue where Connie lived."

≈

"'Course she knew where the victim lived," said Daverson the following day.

The three of us were in Cerise's office. Lydia had a doctor's appointment and would drop by later. In the meantime, I'd told them about my visit with Avery. How she had both motive and opportunity, but couldn't have murdered Roo because she didn't know where Roo lived.

Which reasoning Daverson was now roundly knocking out of court.

"She sold Beartree to her, didn't she? Her lawyers would have had the address. Avery'd have seen it on contracts, exchange documents, everything. She may not have visited any time, but she'd sure know where Miss Carew lived. No question. Hell's bells, she could even have followed her there."

A lie. Avery had told me a lie.

Such a simple, easily punctured falsehood.

I was stunned. And felt stupid – and cross – that I'd fallen for it, been taken in. The previous afternoon we'd parted with promises to stay in touch, we'd kissed warmly. And as I stood on the sidewalk, waiting for The Carlyle doorman to find me a cab, I'd felt closer to her than I'd ever felt before.

And I'd crossed her off my list.

Now she was back on it. Right at the top.

"So what happens now?" I asked.

"She gets a visit from Buzz," replied Cerise. "Just like the others."

"The others?" I asked, looking across at Daverson.

"Miss Tellinger, Miss Webster," he said. "Just following things up."

"Following things up?"

"We bother them, Cully," said Cerise. "We trouble them. We really do. And then," she added, "we serve them with subpoenas. Witnesses for the Defense."

Chili Beef

I have no clear memory, or, to be more accurate, no real understanding of what it was that Cerise, Daverson, and Lydia with her Harvard Law Review cooked up, on my behalf, in the weeks leading to my trial. Precisely what they were trying to achieve, how they planned to conduct my defense, the kinds of tricks they might or might not have up their sleeves, remained as airy, elusive and intricate as the tax advice I get each year from my accountant, an insider's game of second and third guessing that often left me spinning.

At first, at our meetings in Cerise's office or at Lydia's apartment, I tried to follow their discussions, the points of law, the arguments for and against whatever course of action they were proposing – sometimes quite heated – and made a point of asking questions when something, usually plainly obvious to them, eluded me. Lots of questions. I liked to think that these enquiries, and sometimes my suggestions, contributed something to the team effort, that the more I understood what was happening in this time of preparation, the better my chances of survival. And maybe I might just come up with something that the others had overlooked. But I never did, while the answers my companions gave me often served only to increase my confusion. And the way they delivered those answers, with a kind of gentle patience – as though I were somehow holding them back – soon persuaded me to leave off asking them anything at all. There was always Lydia, later, when we were alone together, to try and explain, in a language I stood a chance of following, what she, Cerise, and Daverson were trying to do.

So far as I can remember everything seemed to hang on the word 'circumstantial': that I had no sustainable alibi worth its salt; that I had not come forward when Roo's murder was reported; that I was left-handed; that Roo had written my name in blood on the floor with her toe – or something approximating my name; that my fingerprints showed up on the brass dog used to club her unconscious; and that I featured so threateningly in a draft e-mail letter. Those were just bricks, Cerise was always telling me, but where was the mortar? In her opinion there was none. It was all... circumstantial, she kept repeating, and told me how she could put a dozen people in the stand who could, as easily, as circumstantially, have committed the murder.

The Prosecution's wall didn't deserve to stand, and under her probing, she assured me, it wouldn't.

"But people still go to jail on circumstantial evidence," I remember saying. "Don't they?"

"Not when I'm representing them, they don't," replied Cerise. "Just you wait and see."

Which was all I could do, once I'd played my part in the drama and gone through my list of suspects, narrowing them down to Susan, Casey, and Avery.

Wait and see.

But despite my slowness in following their legal shenanigans, and despite the occasional bout of anxiety – usually soothed away by Lydia – what I did know was that I couldn't have been in better hands. There seemed no way the DA's office, no matter how determined they were to score a high-profile victory and have me back behind bars, could be as committed to my prosecution as these three people were to my defense. It was like having Perry Mason fight my corner. Despite the odds, we just couldn't lose.

This maybe naive notion was aided and abetted by the incontrovertible fact that I knew I was innocent, that I'd been framed, most likely by one of my three suspects, one of whom, in the end, would surely somehow be revealed. At no time, even in my worse moments, did I truly believe that I'd return to jail. It was simply not conceivable.

Cerise, of course, was the driving force – a veritable *chef de cuisine* mustering her brigade and arranging her arguments like so many exotic ingredients. She was a remarkable woman. You could see the brilliance bubbling away clear and scalding as blanching water. Whatever the DA's office came up with – some new witness, some new development, a crucial piece of evidence – she always had a bead on it, just shot it right down before it got a hold of us in any negative way. Because of this, just being in the same room with her made me feel I'd already won and, with a mix of dread and exhilaration, I always looked forward to our weekly get-togethers in her office.

These meetings varied in length – mostly an hour, but often less, sometimes more. It was her way of keeping abreast of things, reviewing whatever developments had taken place during the preceding week. According to Lydia, my case was one of three major actions Cerise was preparing for trial, all slated for commencement in the weeks leading up to Labor Day. But Cerise Chase never looked like she lost a wink of sleep over any of them. Never snapped, never got irritable, impatient, or tetchy, was never anything but piercing, imaginative, bold. And always, without fail, supremely confident in her ability to send the Prosecution packing.

Which was a marvelous thing, believe me, though God alone knew what she charged for all this energy on her clients' behalf. Just a look at the offices of Chase McKay was enough to tell you the bottom line here would hurt something dreadful – the view from its windows, the soft plush of its furnishings, the busy-ness of its team of paralegals and support staff, the muted trill of phones, and the scent of hot-house blooms as extravagant as anything Leland's gardeners in Fauquier County could produce.

On the single occasion I brought up the matter of money with Lydia, after I'd discovered that as well as putting up the bail money she'd been paying Chase McKay's retainers, she told me to put it out of mind, that on my acquittal all costs would be restored, and that if I wanted to pay her back why I could treat her to a ruinously extravagant night on the town when the secondary action that Cerise was running against *Times*, in the manner of my dismissal and for subsequent inaccurate and libelous reporting, was settled in my favor. Which, with Cerise at the helm, was a sure-fire certainty, she told me.

According to Lydia-speak, Cerise was the most centered, the most focused person I would ever meet. When Cerise set her mind on something, she did it. Without doubt or hesitation. Not even astronomic offers from other law firms had swayed her resolve when she announced her decision to turn down a partnership at Delaney Agincort in order to start her own practice, a practice that six years on had yet to suffer a single, significant courtroom defeat.

"I've never known her rattled," said Lydia. "She simply rises above any problem you'd care to put her way. Just a wonderful, wonderful person."

And then there was Daverson, Cerise's right-hand man, with his crepe-soled lace-ups and tight little ears, his wide-pleated, belted trousers and extravagantly colorful ties, usually to be found sprawled in one of Cerise's chairs as though listening to the team coach outline the play for the next quarter, or sliding in at the last minute with something new to prolong the meeting. If you were picking teams, he'd be the man you'd want on your side – dogged, determined, nothing he couldn't find out, get a hold of.

Which, of course, was Daverson's specialty. In no time at all he'd traced Bruno and Rudi, Mr. Polo-Neck and the Finger-Breaker, Roo's drivers, and established watertight alibis for the both of them. Bruno Stratta, a retired police officer with a wife and three kids, had been at a testimonial dinner for a colleague the night of Roo's murder, and had a table full of cops to vouch for him if Daverson wanted to check it out (which, of course, he did). He'd even found out why Roo had let him go – topping up his chargeable hours, and running the cars for his own gain. As for Rudi Seligman, well he'd gone and gotten married that day in Las Vegas; had the marriage certificate right there to prove it.

Daverson also got the lowdown on Beartree, as per Cerise's directions, and had, without trying, he promised, notched up close to five figures for a three-night stay with his wife. Either over a drink with Jack in the salon, or with Bill in the saddle, he'd found out all there was to know about Beartree, most important of which, he told us, was that every staff member, without exception, was a second-time offender. One more strike etc... So no one, but no one, talked about who visited or what went on in the cabins in the woods. Also, they were paid exceptionally well – better than they could normally expect for ex-cons – and they even had the free use of that north shore holiday home in Jamaica for a fortnight each year as a perk. Or fishing in Montana. They could take their pick.

"By the way," said Daverson when he'd finished his report. "You know why they call it Beartree?"

We all shook our heads.

He turned to me. "You ever take a close look at the timber used to build the Lodge? Those massive logs?"

"I'm not sure I..."

"The scratches on them? Seems a long time ago this was some special spot bears went to. Some kind of gathering place. When the first settlers arrived they found this glade of trees, and on every darned one of them the bark and wood were shredded by the claws of these animals. One after another. All of them bore some terrible mark. And it was these trees that were cut down to build the Lodge."

He paused, look at us one after another, and seemed so satisfied and entertained by this nugget of information that it was hard not to share his innocent delight.

Daverson also followed up my visits to Susan, Casey, and Avery.

I remember Susan calling me after he visited. She said he scared her. "He said he was a friend of yours, Cully. Just checking things out. Did you know that? Is that legal?" To which I responded by saying he was employed by my lawyer so it must be legal and that he was only doing his job, which seemed to calm her.

Avery also called after his visit, said how charming he was. "Just going over a few details on your behalf, and would I mind? Just the sweetest kid. Told him anything I could do to help out, just to let me know." For which I thanked her.

As for Casey, there was just a message on my machine. "Don't you ever, *ever* send some… *fucking* gorilla round here, *ever* again."

It was also Daverson who managed to get his hands on a list of Prosecution witnesses long before the DA's office decided to provide full disclosure. Obvious ones like the arresting officers, DaSilva and Munroe, the police pathologist who examined the body, a couple of the forensic team who worked the scene of crime, and a lot of names that came from way out on left field. Totally unexpected – and all the more shocking for it.

I remember Cerise scanning the names, trying them out on me, looking for some slant. It was a sobering experience:

"Carlo Mascotte?" she asked.

I shook my head. "Never heard of him."

"Your doorman, as was," said Daverson.

"A Prosecution witness?" I was stunned.

"Clearly doesn't like you," said Cerise.

"Told me it was Mr. Mortimer petitioned for security cameras in the block," explained Daverson. "Which, when they were fitted, is when he got let go by the building's trustees."

"That's true, I did. But I never thought the board would fire him the moment the cameras were in. He was on that door for years."

"All the more reason, Cully," said Cerise. "And consequently easy enough to question his credibility under cross."

"He lives in the Bronx," continued Daverson. "Has an invalid mother to support."

I could have done without that last piece of information. I felt stricken.

Cerise turned back to the list.

"You ever hear of someone called Alitzia Pryzwynski?"

Once again I told her the name meant nothing.

"Well, she sure knows who you are," said Daverson.

I shook my head. Nothing.

"Polish. Third generation. Ran some restaurant on the Lower East Side. Zdenka's Kitchen?"

For a moment I didn't make the connection and then: Babush. Of course. The woman who'd clasped Roo's face in her hands. But how on earth could she have anything to do with this?

"Yes," I said. "I do know her. But I only met her the once." And then I paused: "You said 'ran' – past tense."

"Closed down by Health and Safety after inspectors paid a call. No license, no zoning, no permissions. Every kind of health code violation and City ordinance infraction you care to imagine. Apparently the regulars raised a petition, but it didn't do any good. The lady says she knew Miss Carew years, from the time she used to live in that neighborhood. Just the most caring girl. Then one day she comes in with Mr. Mortimer here, and this Alitzia Pryzwynski just knows right away you're trouble, can see the girl's frightened of you. Apparently there was an argument…"

"An argument? How could there have been an argument? About what? We'd only just met. It was our first date."

"And, something that really riled her," Daverson continued. "Apparently you promised not to write about the restaurant, but went right ahead and did just that. Which is how the Health and Safety boys picked up on it."

"And when she sees your picture in the paper, she just lifts the phone and offers her services, looking to get her own back," added Cerise. "Like I said, bricks and stones, Cully. But no mortar."

It may have been just bricks and stones to Cerise, but it was a whole lot more to me. Indeed it was times like these, when I learned how people actually felt about me, that I was at my lowest. It was just so… shocking to learn how people I thought liked me actually despised me, were happy to see me in this predicament. I couldn't believe it. And I'll tell you, it hurt.

Which was when Lydia really came into her own.

Lydia. Sweet, caring Lydia, with her glass crystals and incense (she even had a joss-stick holder on the dashboard of her Oldsmobile estate, and a silver tube of L'Occitane sticks in her glove); Lydia, with her Santana, Dr John, and Van Morrison (albums, would you believe?); and, around that time, Lydia and her tapestry work (the latest of her frequent enthusiasms, though altogether less messy than her pottery and painting) – the delicate, comforting application of needle through stiffened mesh, half-glasses on the end of her nose, as often as not talking me through the importance of court protocols and defendant behavior while she stitched ("Not a flicker of response to anything you hear, Cully. Just keep your eyes on the table top, the court seal behind the judge's chair, the stenographer, or Cerise. But nowhere, repeat, nowhere else").

Like Cerise, though on a much more intimate, approachable level, Lydia was just a Godsend. Her faith, her generosity, her endless patience – she didn't even say anything when I chewed my nails, just looked on kindly and poured me another glass of organic wine, or heaped another spoonful of her grandmother's Cottage Pie on my plate.

Through it all, Lydia gave me the backbone I lacked, made everything that was happening seem somehow positive and important and – would you believe it? – 'growthful'. I'm not sure about her choice of word, but there was no denying I'd done some growing in the last few weeks. I felt… different, changed, but still steady, as though one sort of order had gone, been snatched away, only to have another take its place. Now, instead of weekly deadlines to meet, I had Cerise's weekly briefings to attend; instead of half-a-dozen fancy restaurants a week, I ate mostly at kitchen tables – both Lydia's and my own; and for the first time since Roo I was seeing someone, Lydia, on a very regular basis. Which was a very strange, yet comforting, experience.

The real surprise, however, and another thing I was grateful for, was the generous forbearance of Lydia's mystery man – the one Cerise had hinted at, of whom there was never any sign or reference – who allowed us so much time together: early mornings, late evenings, suppers, lunches, weekends. Once or twice I was tempted to ask Lydia about him, but somehow the moment never seemed right. When she wanted to talk about him, that would be the time. It was her call.

Which is probably why she never asked about Roo, thinking she should leave it to me.

What duffers we were.

≈

As the date for the trial drew near, one of the most frequently discussed subjects was the man we were up against: Bixon. Arthur Arnold Bixon. Senior prosecuting counsel at the District Attorney's Office who'd been assigned the case on the strength of his hit rate, which was formidable. For all her talk of bricks and stones, and mortar – or the lack of it – I believe I detected in Cerise a grudging respect for her adversary.

The first time I saw him, quite by chance, was on TV, smiling thinly on the steps of the courthouse where I was due to appear. I was skimming channels at the time, and though I didn't recognize him I saw his name at the bottom of the screen. Even on my small portable television Bixon looked big, well-set in the shoulders, with a thick wedge of auburn hair he kept pushing back off of his brow, a dash of freckles that bunched up around icy blue eyes as he squinted in the camera lights, and a thin and inadvisable moustache. His voice was sharp and abrupt, the words spoken through freckled, chapped lips and punctuated with a range of 'uhs' and 'ahs' that reminded me of JFK.

The newscast I saw him on, he'd just won three consecutive life terms for that guy who held up a mid-town pharmacy, gunning down the proprietor and two customers. He called it, "A good result, uh, one we in the, ah, District Attorney's Office, ah, have... every reason to feel, uh, satisfied with, very satisfied with." And the whole entire time he spoke, he didn't take his eyes off the camera, a steady, unwavering look, as though sending out a personal warning to all the bad guys watching, looking into the camera like he was searching them out back there behind the lens, me included. And I can tell you, I felt a chill. I didn't like the look of him at all. Not one little bit. He looked... hungry, malicious, ruthless, which I guess is how a prosecutor should look.

Cerise had already warned me that Bixon liked to eyeball his victims whenever he could, usually walking back from the witness box to the Prosecution's table, or in the corridors of the courthouse. The prospect of those cold, loveless eyes latching on to mine was not a prospect I savored. This was the man who was after my hide, and within the month he wouldn't need to look to camera to see me. We'd be twenty feet apart, even closer if Cerise decided to put me on the stand.

Our first, formal appearance in court, to select a jury, was scheduled for a Wednesday morning, the first full week of May, with the trial proper slated to commence the Monday following. It was Lydia who picked me up for the ride downtown.

"Looking good," she said. I was wearing the suit she'd suggested, with a white shirt and dark blue tie. "You got your crystal?"

I patted my pockets and frowned.

"Oh, *Cully!*"

She was actually pulling in to turn round and go back for it when I slipped the faceted glass ball from my inside pocket and held it up for her to see, swinging from its chain, blue and gold light glancing through it.

"Cully, you…" and, despite our destination, we began to laugh.

New York's County Court House stands on the southern flank of Foley Square in downtown Manhattan, a grey, pillared, and pedimented monstrosity that appears to cast a shadow even when the sun isn't shining. Contrary to popular belief, there are no little side doors you can slip through to avoid the unwelcome attention of the Press, and positively no parking around its perimeter. Because of this last restriction, Lydia had scouted out a basement parking lot a couple blocks back from the courthouse, and that Wednesday morning we walked the rest of the way, a breeze off the river lifting the pashmina she'd shawled round her shoulders as we started to climb the courthouse steps.

Which is where we were ambushed by a gang of photographers who appeared from nowhere, catching us, arm in arm, in a series of bright, white, strobe-like flashes that seemed to carry us all the way to the doors of the courthouse.

Cerise was waiting inside, and fell in beside us.

I guess I must have looked shocked.

"You better get used to it, Cully. It'll be a lot worse next week."

As things turned out, I didn't have to wait that long. It was about to get a whole lot worse right then.

We'd taken the elevator to the second floor and we were following the 'Jury Selection' signs down a wide marbled corridor when I saw someone up ahead I seemed to recognize. He was standing in a doorway talking to a young woman, and looked increasingly familiar the closer we came. As it turned out, he was standing in the very doorway we planned using. Which is when I realized who it was. Bixon. As he stepped aside to let us through, he gave a polite nod to Cerise who returned it with a small smile, then turned his ice-blue eyes onto me, letting them wander over me as I passed through the door, as though inspecting a cut of beef he intended for his lunch. It was as bad as getting the once-over from Fat Harry. Worse, come to think of it. At least Fat Harry and I had bars between us.

And it didn't stop there. For the two days of jury selection, just as Cerise had warned, Bixon used every opportunity to catch my eye and nod knowingly, or smile with a kind of hungry anticipation. It was, I told Cerise and Lydia during our first lunchtime recess, a most unnerving experience.

"So don't look," said Cerise, as though it was the simplest thing in the world to resist Bixon's cold blue eyes searching you out.

"Just do what I told you," said Lydia. "Court seal, table top, stenographer, or Cerise. Nothing else. Just blank him out."

Which, from then on, as we worked our way through the list of potential jurors, I tried to do with varying levels of success. Sometimes I managed to keep my eyes averted whenever Bixon looked like turning in my direction, other times I couldn't resist a quick glance. And always paid the penalty. Those cold, calculating eyes locking on to mine, squinting, freckles bunching, and that thin little smile twitching his moustache.

Gotcha.

At the end of the second morning, earlier than expected, Bixon and Cerise finally agreed a jury and the selection process was terminated. The members of this jury – four middle-aged black men who didn't look the sort to read the *Times*, a snappily-dressed Latino Cerise had been desperate to get, a couple of housewives, two elderly ladies who looked like retired librarians, and three white middle-management types in collars and ties – were advised by the selection judge to return at eight-thirty prompt Monday morning to assemble in Courtroom Two where Justice Wheating would hear opening statements from Defense and Prosecution.

And that was that. For now we were free to go.

"Lunch?" suggested Lydia, as the three of us reached the bottom of the courthouse steps, thankfully free of photographers.

"Why not," said Cerise, checking her watch. "But a quick one. I've got a two o'clock deposition and I can't be late."

They turned to me. I hadn't been expecting this.

"I... I'm really sorry," I began, "I didn't think... You see, I'm already having lunch. With Daphne Winterson. She called last week. She's back in town. I guess I should have mentioned it." And I felt an immediate flush of guilt. After all the work these two women were doing on my behalf, here was I leaving them high and dry. And with Daphne off my list of suspects I could hardly claim my date was case-related.

"Well, that's just fine, Cully," said Lydia, a little disappointedly, taking Cerise's arm. "Then it's just the two of us," she said, brightening, as though that was exactly the outcome she'd intended and hoped for.

Cerise gave me a look I couldn't read, Lydia smiled and turned away, and I felt wretched. Pretty much all the jurors they'd wanted had been selected, and they were in celebratory mood. I should have thought. I could so easily have seen Daphne another time.

≈

I was still feeling wretched when I pitched up at Sri, a new Thai diner on the edge of Chinatown, only a short cab ride from the courthouse. Daphne had raved about it on the phone, given me the address, and told me she'd book us a table. Her treat.

In the last few weeks I'd started returning to restaurants in quite a big way. After a couple of lunches at Dwight's Diner with Sanchez and the odd meal out with Lydia and Cerise, I'd found that the experience wasn't as daunting as I'd first imagined. And, in a perverse sort of way, I'd come to rather enjoy the celebrity – or should I say notoriety? Not to mention the occasional discomfort my presence caused a number of people. Some of the *maître d*'s who knew me from the old days shook my hand, and showed me to the big table. Others took one look and thought not of the esteemed food writer from the *Times* who'd given them a good word in his columns but '*I'm shaking hands with the man who hacked some high-class hooker to death*', before hurrying me to hidden-away tables in corners and shadows.

Since my meeting with Avery at The Carlyle, I'd survived a long

lunch at the recently opened and hyper-popular Cooling & Co with
Larry Daley and Liz Kovacks, who kept reaching across the table to
hold my hand (the both of them, would you believe?); at a packed
Danny's one Saturday night for pitchers of beer and feather steak
sandwiches with McKintyre who didn't, thank God, want to hold my
hand; and, only a few days earlier, at Mornay's, about as high profile
as you can get in this town, where I'd followed at a funeral pace as
Gaby maneuvered Elliot's wheelchair between the tables. No one had
asked for an autograph, but I could see that most of our fellow diners
recognized me as the procession passed by, saw them start whispering
when they made me. It was odd, too, to eat out and not take notes.

As for Sri, it was the kind of place that, a few months earlier, would
have made my heart beat faster, the kind of place that simply wrote its
own fifteen hundred words. Just a fabulous little hideaway, mid-block,
its entrance almost completely concealed behind a shoulder-height,
stepped display of exotic fruit and vegetables put out on the sidewalk
by the owners of the Asian supermart that occupied the ground-floor
premises.

I walked by twice before I spotted the name, daubed in child-
like strokes of canary-bright yellow on a blood red door, squeezing
between collared sacks of rice and pulses, boxed bunches of pak choi,
and trays of taro, yam, and other assorted tubers, to reach it. Inside
was a lantern-strung hallway and rickety flight of stairs thick with the
heady scents of crushed coriander and garlic, lime, mint, sweet basil
and, as I climbed higher, that pungent galangal.

At the top of the stairs, a slip of a girl with a bonnet of shiny
black hair parted a set of silk drapes and bowed me through into a
high-ceilinged dining room far, far distant from the toot of horns and
rush and bustle of the street below. Here were twenty or so tables
separated one from the other by a dozen silk flags hanging from the
ceiling. Each was printed with a tail-chasing dragon, and stirred by a
half-dozen rattan fans driven by some ancient string and pulley device
that disappeared into the darker reaches of the room where, doubtless,
woks clattered on hobs and hot oils spattered and hissed.

So far as I could tell Daphne, sitting at a table between the third
and fourth flags in the middle of the room, was the only westerner,
save me, in the whole place. But I still wouldn't have recognized her.
She was burrowed into a menu and, if it hadn't been for the alice band

and the young girl bowing me to her table, I swear I'd have walked right past. Since our night at the opera in December, the last time we'd seen each other, she looked to have lost a ton of weight.

"Daphne, you look... great," I said, after the kisses and hugs, dropping into the seat opposite. "I can't believe it."

"Nor can I. Isn't it fabulous?" Delightedly, she smoothed her hands over her waist and hips to outline the loss. "A sixteen to just about a twelve, at a squeeze. Just fabulous. And now I'm gonna put it all back on."

She turned to the girl who'd shown me to the table and reeled off her selection from the menu, just as she always did:

"*Khai Suan*...

"*Yam Pla*...

"*Kaeng Masaman*...

"...and, of course, *Nua Pad Prik* – that's chili beef to you and me, Cully, but I'll bet you the bird it's the best you've ever eaten. Like Japanese *tataki* only better."

The girl took no notes, bowed once, took the menu from Daphne, and made to move away.

"Oh, and two Singhas, iced glasses, please," Daphne called out, sliding her spectacles into a thin leather wallet. There were cigarettes beside her chopsticks, and she pulled one out and lit it. "So, my darling," she began, drawing in the smoke. "It's been so *long*. An age..."

"I was sorry to hear about you and Elliot..." I started, but Daphne cut me short.

"Enough, Cully. We can talk about all of that later. After you've told me every *word* about what's been happening to *you*." She reached across the table for my hand. "How have you *been*?" she asked.

I shrugged. "Bearing up. Wanting it to be over with, you know? And missing you. And Netherlands."

"And we've been missing you, my dear. So tell me. What's been going on? I just can't believe it."

And so I told her – everything. About Roo and our time together, about my arrest, jail, and how everything pointed to someone I knew putting me in the frame for a murder I didn't commit, relieved that I didn't need to check Daphne for motive or opportunity. It was a tale punctuated by the arrival and removal of banana leaf platters laden with bite-sized packets of crispy chicken skin and shrimp paste, bamboo steamers filled with fluffy lemon rice, and fired clay pots bubbling with coconut curry. And the chili beef, of course – credit card slices of choice fillet, rubbed with salt, pepper and crushed garlic, vibrantly spiced with green and red chilies, and flash-fried in a splash of sesame oil. Daphne was right. It was the best, even if she did remove the slivers of chili and tap them on to my plate. Packed in a wallet of crispy lettuce and sprinkled with a lush green confetti of coriander, it was one of those dishes you remember twenty years after you taste it. And mourn for.

"A few months ago, I'd have rushed back to my apartment to write about this place," I told her, as the last of our dishes was cleared and a fresh paper cloth slipped across the table.

"And now?"

"Just sit and enjoy, I guess."

"Sounds good to me," smiled Daphne. "So will you go back to the *Times* when this is all over?"

"You mean, when the jury says 'not guilty'?"

"Well, they will, won't they?" Daphne looked horrified there could be any other result. "I mean this lawyer, Chase, you said on the phone she seems pretty certain."

"I just don't know, Daphne. Like I told you, sometimes I think to myself for sure I'll be acquitted. And then sometimes I... well, sometimes I can really panic – late at night. If I can't get to sleep right off. Or, when I'm not expecting it, there's some piece in the papers – where I've been seen, what I've been doing, rehashing the charges against me; always accompanied by some menacing comment from the DA's office. That can really get to you. As for the *Times*, who knows?"

"Did I tell you the *Frankfurter Allgemeine Zeitung* called you the '*Claus von Bülow of the Kitchens*'? I rather liked that," she said with a grin. "So why don't you use the Press yourself? You know how. You're a newspaperman, for God's sake. Play them at their own game. Give 'em hell, Cully."

"According to Cerise, that's not a way to go. Get about, sure, and live your life, but keep it low profile. Don't get drawn."

And all things considered, I continued, Cerise had been right. Since my release from Brooklyn, she'd fielded no end of requests for interviews and turned down flat every single one of them. She'd even said 'no' to Connie Chung and Larry King. No point having someone steal our thunder before your day in court, she'd explained.

Even Susan, who'd wanted to squeeze in a back-page questionnaire piece for May *Rituals*, which would hit the newsstands around the time of my trial, got the thumbs down. Even when I said Susan was offering copy approval, Cerise still shook her head.

At first, of course, I'd been astonished by the interest in my case, the coverage. I was hot property. Far bigger than the restaurant critic who'd written the piece about Billy 'Butcher Boy' Bradford's last meal, and caused cattle futures to tumble back in the Fall. Indeed, I wasn't even a food critic any more, just Cully Mortimer, friend and confidant of Player Leland, and alleged killer of a high-society call-girl. There was even talk of books and film deals. But Cerise blocked it all.

"And what it's done – all this low profile stuff – is take the story off the front page," I explained. "Let's face it, there are other things happening – that school shooting, the Clinton thing, Bosnia. And you can't just keep telling the same old story. Newspapers need an angle. And that's what we haven't given them."

"So, who do you think did it?" she asked finally.

"One of three people," I replied; no need now for her to know that she and Elliot had also featured.

"Do I know them?"

"I think you met Susan one time, editor of *Rituals*. At some restaurant launch?"

"Oh, I remember, she was real nice. Strange looking, but nice. I thought she was a date."

"Gay. She dated Roo."

"You're kidding me. Dated Roo?"

"Well, 'dated' is maybe not quite the word. She was a client."

"Which is why you think she may have done it?"

"Something like that."

"And?"

"The two others you won't know. Casey Webster, runs a restaurant down on West 50th. We had a thing last year. And Avery Blanchard."

Daphne shook her head. The names weren't familiar. And then, "You know I met her one time?"

"Roo? You met Roo? Now you're kidding me."

"I promise. Recognized her picture straight off. Didn't know she was a hooker though. She was a real estate agent when I met her. With Elliot. Last summer, I guess. We'd decided to sell the apartment and get somewhere new, something a little bigger. I told him to start looking, narrow a few places down, and then I'd come visit and take a look.

"Which is what I did. I remember quite clearly, you and me had been having one of our lunches and afterwards I went round to the address he'd given me. And there he was with this really gorgeous woman. And classy. Not realtor classy, if you know what I mean… But *real* classy. Like she owned what she was showing us, some duplex on Lexington and another place just along aways from you. Beautiful looking creature, much nicer than the Press pix.

"Tell the truth," continued Daphne, sipping jasmine tea, "I thought, maybe, Elliot was doing more than viewing properties with her, so I called my investigator right after and had him check her out. But she was clean. Nothing suspicious. He said they saw twenty or so properties together, maybe more, but then Elliot was seeing a lot of others, too, with other realtors, and the two of them always shook hands and went their separate ways when they came out of the buildings. It was kosher. Even if it does turn out she was this high-fallutin' call-girl on the side."

I wondered what Daphne would have said if I'd told her what really went on in those empty apartments. But that was just too cruel to contemplate. So I said nothing, just let her carry on without any comment.

"Anyway, I was about to call off the hunt when finally we got something. Some French woman. A publisher. Just got in to town, and here I have pictures of them together and I know it's over. They're at some restaurant. They're kissing. They're holding hands. And you know me, Cully. I don't stand for any messing. So I confront him round Christmas and… well, that was it. Told him to move his things out. Said he could stay at the townhouse we'd finally gotten until he sorted himself out, and then – lawyers at dawn."

"He told me. I saw him. And Gaby."

Daphne shook her head, like she couldn't believe the way it had worked out. "What's she like? I haven't seen her… you know – in the flesh. Just the photos."

"Young, pretty. What can I say?"

"Figures," said Daphne.

Later, out on the sidewalk, we looked for cabs.

"Now, I just want you to know, Cully Mortimer, that every weekend this dreadful trial drags on I expect you up at Netherlands, you hear? And when it's all over, I want you to think of it as your home and come stay with us just as long as you want."

"Us?"

Daphne eyes twinkled as I flagged down a cab for her.

"Oh. Didn't I tell you? His name's Lionel. Lionel Teuffel. I brought him back from Germany with me. He's an architect. He's going to do up the townhouse. You'll like him, I promise."

I opened the cab door for her, and she slid in.

Winding down the window, she continued: "And you know what? The one time in my life I go get thin, I meet a man who likes the fuller-figured woman."

And then, as her cab pulled away, she leaned out the window and shouted: "See you in court."

≈

Monday, May 10th.

Not a date I'm ever likely to forget.

The place: New York County Court House, Foley Square, Lower Manhattan.

The occasion: The People and the State of New York versus Culver Mortimer Sykes.

I got up early, well before six. No need for any alarm.

I remember my legs shaking as I walked to the bathroom. A couple of times, brushing my teeth, bent over the basin, I felt like heaving. Had to force myself to eat something. A bowl of muesli, some toast, a cup of tea. Then I dressed – a light blue linen suit, white cotton shirt, dark blue tie, my Berluti loafers for luck. I felt like I was getting dressed for the last time in my life. So I didn't rush it. Must have re-knotted the tie a half-dozen ways. And my moustache. Couldn't decide whether to brush it to the sides for a parting. Or leave it down and full. I can do either; the bristles are the texture of my eyebrows – easily manipulated. Whatever, it was a useful distraction.

Afterwards, as content with my appearance as I was likely to get,

I stood at my desk, looking through my window to the Park, a low yellow sun streaming through a thin haze of white cloud. It maybe sounds silly now, facing a sealed window like I was, but as I stood there I took a series of deep breaths as though inhaling all the oxygen that all those trees in the Park were pumping out.

Which was when the buzzer sounded. Six-thirty on the button. No need to use the entryphone to know who it was.

The Oldsmobile was double-parked. Lydia had leaned across to open the passenger side and was back behind the wheel, gripping it with tight little fists. A joss stick smoldered in its holder on the dash.

"Sandalwood," I said, ducking into my seat.

"It's cleansing," she replied, pulling out into the early morning traffic without checking her mirror. For Lydia this was par for the course; she drove as if hers were the only car on the road, oblivious to the flashing headlights, angry horns, and a screech of brakes somewhere behind us. "I had to make this choice," she continued, peering over the wheel. "The sandalwood for the cleansing, or the stephanotis for calm."

"Both might have been good."

She glanced at me, to see if I was teasing her. I hadn't been. It was simply an observation.

"That's the point, Cully. You can't do both. You have to choose. Otherwise they work against each other."

"So. Cleansing, calming, or confusion."

"Exactly," replied Lydia.

Now that I *was* teasing, she didn't appear to notice. I looked across at her and suddenly realized she was scared, and only barely managing to keep herself together. I reached over and patted her arm, and from her fleeting, anxious smile drew an odd sort of strength. Maybe this was how people felt when they stood in front of a firing squad. Do it well, or do it badly. Right then and there, I decided I'd try to do it well. For her. For this strange little woman who'd stood by me so steadfastly those last few months.

It took us a little over an hour to get downtown, park the car in our basement slot, walk the two blocks to the courthouse, and jostle our way through a pack of reporters and photographers, following the signs to Courtroom Two on the third floor.

Cerise was waiting for us at its doors, dressed in an understated grey two-piece pinstripe pantsuit. For some inexplicable reason I shook her hand, as though meeting her for the first time. She held it a beat longer than she should have done. Which was all she needed to do. I felt charged.

"So," she said, bending down to pick up her briefcase, straightening, looking at us. "We all set? Good. Then let's go take that itty-bitty little wall of theirs apart."

≈

Of course, I'd always hoped it would never get this far. A court house, a courtroom. Lawyers and clerks. A judge, and jury of my peers. The stalls crowded with onlookers. Members of the Press. Friends and enemies...

All there for me.

I'd hoped, from the moment I caught that train to Amsterdam to play detective with Daphne, that I would discover who had killed the woman I loved. That I would catch a friend in a lie, that I would clear my name.

But I hadn't.

All I had were three friends, one of whom was prepared to let me undergo the ultimate ordeal. To be tried for my life and my freedom, for a crime I had not committed. A friend who would let me suffer in their place...

Casey, Susan, or Avery...

And now here I was, left to the whim and weight of argument and counter-argument. The full and binding process of the Law. All its mysteries, its maneuverings, its dull and dread formality. And its finality. Guilty or innocent. One or the other. Nothing between. Everything dependent on the evidence and the testimony of witnesses, and the interpretation and credibility of that evidence and testimony. Time had run out for me. There was nothing more I could do, save sit in my chair and watch and listen as a drama unfolded. My drama.

Mostly, in the days and the weeks that had now reached their end, I'd been sure that my innocence would be enough, that if it came to a trial I'd be acquitted. That sense and reason and truth would prevail. That Cerise would break down that wall of bricks and stones, just as she'd always promised. But sometimes, at dead of night, alone in my bed, awake or in my dreams, I would hear the clang of steel, the turning of locks, the shrieks and cries and moans of Hell's Hallway.

And all I would see was a life behind bars. After everything I'd known and done and loved, just that tiny cell, its foldaway table and plastic chair, starched sheets and thin grey blanket, mince and grits on a molded tray, and a seat-less brushed metal lavatory. Just that. Nothing more.

And now the moment had come. My trial. The trial of Cully Mortimer.

A week, or two. Maybe three. But no more, Cerise had promised.

And then I would know what the future held for me.

It was like setting out on a high wire over fathomless depths.

Putting one foot in front of the other, and trusting that I would reach the other side.

≈

After the coziness of the juror selection room, Courtroom Two was a big, brooding beast of an affair – all lofty cornicing and polished wood. It reminded me a little of a Methodist Chapel – spare and somber, with dark paneled walls and two lines of empty boxed pews either side of a long aisle of shiny lino tiles.

Ahead, like some kind of raised altar, flanked by state and national flags, was the judge's bench, a witness stand on the right and, close by, the jurors' choir stall. Below the judge's podium stood a pair of desks, the smaller of the two occupied by a young woman preparing her stenography machine, and the other, judging by his black gown, by the Clerk of the Court, a big bluff man bald save a horseshoe of grey hair, busily shuffling through a stack of papers. Leaning against the witness stand, three court bailiffs, all of them uniformed and armed, thumbs tucked into belts, chatted amongst themselves without bothering to look up.

Since she was not an official member of the Defense team, Lydia took a seat in the front row, directly behind us. And for the next thirty minutes, as paralegals from Chase McKay brought in armfuls of boxed files or conferred with Cerise, I either sat and looked straight ahead, or turned to speak with Lydia. Which, I discovered, was an excellent way of seeing who was coming in to find a seat: Daphne, of course, just like she'd promised, mouthing a conspiratorial 'Hi, how are you?' from four rows back behind the Prosecution table; Maude MacAuley from Totnes Bay, coming over to give me a hug and wish me well; Sanchez and Doug McKintyre, lumbering in together;

BeeJay Wilson, in his sleek Wall Street strip; Luke Withnell, who'd called the day before to say his wife, Marilyn, couldn't make it but hoped it would be okay if he dropped by; and a whole heap of other friends – the Tillotsons down from Boston, Adam and Nat Edwards from Poughkeepsie, even Bill and Junior Watson all the way up from Charleston – which made me feel kind of warm and supported.

But no Casey, no Avery, and no Susan. I hadn't heard a word from any of them since the subpoenas were served, and I wondered how they would be feeling. Or rather, how one of them would be feeling.

There were other faces I recognized, too, but they all looked away when they caught my eye: Carlo, my old doorman; Alitzia Pryzwynski, in a pinned hat and elaborate fox-fur stole; and a grey-faced Don Draper from the *Post* who'd written some real nasty pieces about me.

But Mr. Carmichael, Roo's father, sitting stiff-backed a couple of rows behind Daphne, did not look away. When I caught his eye, he held it until it was me turned away. No expression on his face. Beside him, at the end of the row, Dom looked to his lap, probably fingering Kuto's Breitling Chronoliner.

Now and again, I chanced a look across at the Prosecution table. Bixon was already there when we arrived, and most of the time he had his back to us as he conferred with colleagues. The one time our eyes did meet, he didn't give any kind of acknowledgement, not a glimmer of recognition – nothing at all. As though I didn't exist. It was almost as unsettling as one of his hungry smiles. I just didn't count. Far as he was concerned, I was dead meat.

By nine o'clock the place was pretty much full to bursting, a hubbub of low voices and squeaking footsteps, the punch and swing of the courtroom doors as late arrivals bustled through, Lizzie Kovacks and Larry Daley among them, waving brightly as they squeezed through to a pair of free seats at the back.

And then, about ten feet to the left of the judge's bench, a door in the panelling opened and, with a swirl of black robes and a stirring in the folds of the state and national flags, all conversation died away.

The Clerk of the Court got to his feet.

"All rise. Justice Claude William Wheating presiding. The People and the State of New York versus Culver Mortimer Sykes…"

And so it began.

Uptown

"You heard, of course?" said the first woman, stirring her coffee.

"Cully?" said the second.

"He won his suit. Against the *Times*."

"So I heard…"

"And big damages."

"Big?"

"Well, maybe not big, you know, not in the scale of things," said the first woman, putting down her spoon. "But very handsome all the same. For someone like Cully."

Lunch was over. The restaurant, someplace on the Upper East Side, was emptying. In the kitchen the ranges cooled. Out back in the alley, a *sous-chef* maybe sat on the kitchen steps and smoked a cigarette.

"I heard he left the city?" prompted the second woman, whom I've known an absolute age and who told me this story the last time we spoke.

"Completely. Never been back," said her companion. "Carolina someplace. On the beach." She lifted the cup and sipped at her coffee. "Pity, really."

"How so?" asked my friend.

"Well, he could be a bit of a bore sometimes, all that food stuff, but, well, he did give very good lunch."

They'd both laughed.

When the first woman finished her coffee, she nodded to the waiter.

My friend reached for her bag. "You or me?" she asked.

"Why don't I do it the next time?" her companion replied, and took up her napkin, dabbed at the corners of her mouth. "'Course, if Cully were still around we wouldn't have to bother…"

Murphy's Landing

I sold the Manhattan apartment right after the trial. Had everything professionally packed and brought down here. Never set a foot in the place myself. Never wanted to. Gave the movers my old key and new address. Simple as that.

It was after the Clerk of the Court swore in Alitzia Pryzwynski towards the end of the third afternoon session that everything fell apart. As Bixon approached the stand to question his witness, I heard the courtroom doors push open behind us and footsteps come squeaking down the aisle. Crepe-soled shoes on lino. The next thing I know, Daverson's hunkering down beside us, whispering to Cerise. He takes an envelope from inside his jacket, and passes it to her.

The envelope was unsealed. Cerise flipped it open and scanned the contents; three, maybe four sheets of paper. Then she stood, leaned forward on pool-player fingertips and, sweet as you please, interrupted the proceedings at almost exactly the moment that Bixon asked Alitzia Pryzwynski to state her full name and occupation.

Which, like I said, was when the bricks and the stones came tumbling down.

Counsels for Defense and Prosecution summoned to Justice Wheating's chambers.

A tense, ten-minute whispering wait in the courtroom till they reappeared.

A soft, sly smile on Cerise's face.

A scowl on Bixon's. Almost a snarl.

Proceedings adjourned, brought to a close with an abrupt double tap of the gavel.

Case dismissed, charges dropped, all over bar the formalities.

And pandemonium.

Hand-shakes, hugs and tears in the courtroom and, outside on the courthouse steps, flashlights and microphones and tape recorders thrust in my direction, every shouldered TV camera wrapped in a crumpled plastic jacket to keep off a squall of spring rain, hurrying us all along in a tangle of umbrellas to a waiting cab.

Over.

It was over.

≈

According to Daverson, who'd been tipped off by a contact at the 19th Precinct, a woman had called the real estate firm handling the sale of Roo's apartment and made an appointment to view. At right about the time we took our seats at the start of that third day of the trial proper, she and the realtor had met in the foyer of Blaise Heights, and ridden up together to the forty-seventh floor.

The realtor had shown her round the apartment, and told police she felt pretty optimistic the woman was going to make an offer. They'd been through the main room, the kitchen, Roo's bedroom, dressing room and bathroom, and were up on the gallery when the woman dug around in her bag, took out a letter, and handed it to the realtor.

"Tell them all I'm so, so sorry," she'd said, and before the realtor could do a thing about it the woman had taken the key from the terrace door, stepped through, and locked it from the outside.

The realtor later testified how the woman dragged a chair to the balustrade, slipped off her shoes, and climbed up onto the parapet.

There was no hesitation, the realtor said, no second thoughts.

In the blink of an eye she was gone – just the chair, the shoes, and an empty terrace.

As quick, as final as that.

She'd also taken off her ear clips, though the realtor hadn't noticed that. According to the medical examiner at the County Coroner's hearing I attended, he'd found them later, clenched in her hand.

The woman who jumped was Susan Tellinger, and it was a copy of the letter she'd given to the realtor that Daverson had gotten a hold of, and handed to Cerise in the courtroom.

Apparently the police had already followed up Susan's instructions.

In her apartment, laid out on her bed, they'd found a six-inch Kusshi boning knife, a pile of bloodstained clothes, a towel, and a neatly folded Calvin Klein dress.

Tests were being carried out, but...

≈

Like I said, I live out on the shore now, close to the Delaware Maryland border, in an old wood-clad boathouse that Daphne heard about. She insisted on driving me down to take a look. It's a nice place, quiet, there's a few houses a mile or so down the beach, and that's about it. Nothing closer. Apparently the boathouse once belonged to... but then that's another story.

Talking of stories, there's a small local newspaper we all get hereabouts. A weekly. Out of Winton, the nearest town. Recently I started thinking I might try my hand at some kind of beachcomber piece, stories washed in with the tide, that sort of thing. Once a month, maybe. Of course, I don't have to work for a living out here. Thanks to the Times *I can get by very comfortably.*

Or rather, we can get by.

You see, I have company now.

She moved in maybe three months after I got here. Just arrived one afternoon, a bandanna tied round her head, baggy shorts, hiking boots, thick woolen socks rolled down over her ankles, and that old back-pack of hers slung across her shoulder, as though she'd trekked cross country to get here.

I was out front, sawing driftwood at the trestle, when I heard the screen door screech open and the rapid tapping of knuckles on the loose glass pane. When I came round the side of the house I had a shock, I can tell you, when I saw who it was standing there. Hadn't seen or spoken to anyone in days.

She didn't say hello, didn't wait for me to say anything, just came to the rail at the end of the porch, looked down at me standing there with the saw in my hand, and launched into this whole thing.

Finished up by saying she'd thought about it long and hard, and made up her mind. Whether I liked it or not.

And so, of course, she stayed.

And I found I could handle the company, even came to like it.

Lydia. Whoever would have guessed?

≈

We walk the beach together, Lydia and I. She likes a low tide, I like it high. When it's high we walk side by side, arm in arm. When it's low, I might as well be walking by myself; she's all over the place, picking up shells and stones and bleached splinters of wood and those green sea-dusty pebbles of glass. She carries this linen bag over her shoulder, and puts whatever she likes in there. By the end of our walks, the bag sort of rustles as she moves, crunching against her hip.

When she first started fashioning these bits and bobs into jewelry, they didn't look like much to tell you the truth. But she stuck at it, in a Lydia sort of way, and though I can't imagine any woman wanting to wear any of it, it wasn't long before all the big stores and chi-chi boutiques were clamoring for the stuff. Evelyn, who came down to visit one time but will not return (she was thinking Hamptons and had a rude awakening), is probably most put out. Though knowing her, she hasn't wasted a minute telling everyone that, yes, of course, didn't you know? Lydia Langhorn is family. I can hear her say it from here, the way she does.

Lydia has her own studio out back, a small four-room wood-clad shack where she lives and works. It came with the boathouse rental, and didn't take more than a week to knock into some kind of shape and make habitable. She's only got the one floor, but we've made it real neat and cozy. Furniture from a local sale-room, some of her paintings, her pottery and, outside the front door, running the length of the porch, about a hundred different wind chimes she only takes down when there's a storm forecast.

Like I said, it's out back behind the boathouse. There's no view of the sea, but she doesn't seem to mind. From her big window, she looks inland over the small creek that passes the property, out across the flats where the waders step.

I get the dawns, and she gets the sunsets.

Just about evens, she says.

Which is the way we like it.

Sometimes she cooks and invites me over, one of her mother's pies or a stew. Sometimes I cook (I've learned to do a real good carbonara*) and invite her over.*

It's a fine arrangement, and we wouldn't have it any other way.

Not too much, not too little. Perfect ingredients.

By the way, there's maybe one last thing I should tell you.

Lydia Langhorn is going to have a baby.

Come the New Year, Cully Mortimer is set to be a Dad.

Cully Mortimer
Murphy's Landing
Assateague Shoreline
Marlyand
December 1999

About The Author

After graduating from Hertford College, Oxford, Martin O'Brien joined Condé Nast and was travel editor at British *Vogue* for a number of years. As well as writing for *Vogue* he has contributed to a wide range of international publications, and his books have been translated into Russian, Turkish, French, Dutch, Spanish, Portuguese, German, and Hebrew. He lives in the Cotswolds with his wife and two daughters.

Printed in Great Britain
by Amazon